The Hanging Club

ALSO BY TONY PARSONS
FROM CLIPPER LARGE PRINT

The Murder Bag
The Slaughter Man

The Hanging Club

Tony Parsons

W F HOWES LTD

This large print edition published in 2017 by
W F Howes Ltd
Unit 5, St George's House, Rearsby Business Park,
Gaddesby Lane, Rearsby, Leicester LE7 4YH

1 3 5 7 9 10 8 6 4 2

First published in the United Kingdom in 2016
by Century

A CIP catalogue record for this book is available
from the British Library

ISBN 978 1 51007 767 6

Typeset by Palimpsest Book Production Limited,
Falkirk, Stirlingshire

Printed and bound by
T J International in the UK
Printforce Nederland b.v. in the Netherlands
Ligare in Australia

MIX
Paper from
responsible sources
FSC
www.fsc.org   FSC® C013056

For Fred Kindall of Kentish Town

A great multitude had already assembled; the windows were filled with people smoking and playing cards to beguile the time; the crowd were pushing, quarrelling, and joking. Every thing told of life and animation, but one dark cluster of objects in the very centre of all – the black stage, the cross-beam, the rope, and all the hideous apparatus of death.

Charles Dickens, *Oliver Twist*

Sir, executions are *intended* to draw spectators. If they do not draw spectators they don't answer their purpose.

Dr Samuel Johnson

PROLOGUE

After Prayers

After Friday prayers Mahmud Irani walked back to where he had parked his taxi and within a few minutes he had picked up the man who was going to kill him.

The man was standing opposite the entrance to London Zoo, dressed in a suit and tie, the jacket buttoned up despite the steaming midday heat. His eyes were hidden behind dark glasses and he had one arm already raised in the air to hail a cab, as if he was fully expecting Mahmud to be driving round Regent's Park's Outer Circle immediately after prayers, as if he knew he was coming.

As if he had been waiting.

Mahmud pulled up beside him, smelling the animal stink of the zoo in summer.

'Cash only, boss,' Mahmud said.

The man nodded, glancing at his phone before showing it to Mahmud. On the iPhone's screen there was a map of the City with a red marker pinpointing their destination.

Newgate Street, EC1.

1

Less than four miles away but it meant crossing the middle of the city in the stagnant traffic of lunch hour. Mahmud grunted his reluctant assent and watched the man slide into the back seat.

In silence they drove east through the sweltering city.

Mahmud was turning his taxi onto Newgate Street when he glanced in his rear-view mirror and saw the man removing a small leather credit-card holder. Mahmud sighed. How many times did you have to tell these stupid people?

'*It's cash only,*' he repeated, harder this time, tugging at his polo shirt, the sweat sticking.

But the man was not getting out a credit card.

He leaned forward between the gap in the front seats and placed an old-fashioned razor blade firmly against Mahmud Irani's left eyelid.

Mahmud drew in his breath and did not let it go.

He felt the thin cold steel of the blade's cutting edge settle into the folds of soft flesh beneath his eyebrow. The fine layer of skin covering his eye fluttered wildly against the razor blade. Pure naked terror rose up inside him.

'Please,' Mahmud said. 'Please. Just take the money. It's under my seat.'

The man laughed.

'I don't want your money. Keep driving. Nice and easy now.'

Mahmud drove as if in a dream, driving with one eye squeezed closed, trying to concentrate on

2

the road ahead with a razor blade pressed against his eyelid.

Following the man's directions, he drove to the end of the street and then turned left onto a huge building site. It was deserted, one of those little pockets of total silence and emptiness that suddenly surprise you in the city. Another tower of glass and steel was being erected here, but there was nobody working this afternoon. They were all alone. Ahead of them was a yawning hole in the uneven ground.

'Down there,' the man said.

'I have a wife and children.'

'Too late for all that now, pal.'

The razor blade pressed more firmly into Mahmud's flesh and he felt his eyeball move, a sick rolling feeling as the eye recoiled from the cutting edge. Mahmud drove into the hole and down, bumping over a speed bump and then over some random rubble before entering a vast basement twilight.

What was this place?

Mahmud could not tell if it had once been an underground car park or if that's what it would be in the future. Right now it was simply a massive expanse of empty space with a very low ceiling; a subterranean basement with no lights apart from the shafts of summer sun coming in from somewhere.

'Where are we going?' Mahmud said, unable to stop himself talking, and this time the man slid the razor blade very gently across his eyelid, just one inch, but enough to cut into flesh and make Mahmud cry out from the shock of sudden pain.

A warm trickle of blood oozed slowly around the curve of Mahmud's left eyelid.

And he did not speak after that.

They got out of the car and that was a moment when Mahmud thought he could run away if he was not so stricken with terror, so paralysed with disbelief that this was happening, so appalled by the warm blood that ran now on either side of his left eye, so scared witless that he did not fully register the chance to escape until the moment had passed.

Then the man stood behind Mahmud, the razor blade returned to the soft fold of flesh above the left eye and the man's other hand gently taking the taxi driver's wrist.

They walked across the wide-open space to a door.

They went down some steps.

The air got colder.

They descended into total darkness and walked along a narrow passage until suddenly a thin shaft of natural light was coming from somewhere high above their heads. Mahmud could see ancient white brickwork that was stained green by time and weather. It was very cold now. The summer was on another planet. The air was fetid with what smelled like stagnant water. It was like stepping into another world.

And then there were the others.

Three of them.

Their faces hidden by black masks that revealed only their eyes.

One of them had a red light shining in their hands.

It was some kind of camera, and it was pointing at Mahmud Irani.

There was a stool. A kitchen step stool. Mahmud could not understand what was happening as hands helped him onto the stool and something was placed around his neck. The blood was in his eyes as he watched the man from the car consulting with the one who held the camera. Mahmud wiped away the blood with the palm of his hands and he tried to balance himself, afraid he would fall from the stool.

His fingers nervously felt his neck.

It was a rope.

They had put a rope around his neck.

He looked up and saw that it was attached to a rusted tangle of ancient pipes in the ceiling.

Hands were touching his arms. He heard a metallic click. He found that his arms were secured behind his back.

And now the words came in a torrent. Now he had no difficulty at all in speaking. Now even the razor blade pressed against his eyeball could not have shut his mouth.

'I have a wife and children!' he screamed, and his voice echoed back at him in this secret basement.

Wife and children!
Wife and children!

'I'm just a taxi driver! Please! You have the wrong person!'

The man from the car was covering his face with a black mask. Like an executioner. He turned to Mahmud Irani.

'*Do you know why you have been brought to this place of execution?*' he asked.

Mahmud stuttered, 'What? This – what? I don't understand. What? I'm a taxi driver—'

But then the words choked in his throat because, beyond the red light of the camera, one of them was sticking A4 sheets of paper to the worn white bricks of this underground place.

The A4 sheets of paper were portraits that had been downloaded from the Internet.

They were all the faces of girls. Young girls. Smiling girls.

And, yes, they were all smiling, every one of them – although some of them had smiles that were stiff and shy, and some had smiles that were natural and full of confidence.

They all smiled in their own way. The school photographers had insisted upon a smile, encouraged them to smile, tried to make them laugh.

They were formal portraits, the kind that a school takes every year to record and honour a student's growth, and they caught the girls at the fleeting moment in their lives when they were poised between the children they had so recently been and the women they would one day become.

The smiling faces watched Mahmud Irani.

And he knew these faces. All of them.

He had known them in rooms full of laughing men. He had heard the girls scream for help when no help was coming. He had seen them blurry and on the edge of unconsciousness, foggy with cheap booze and strong drugs as their clothes were removed.

He had laughed at those girls with all the other men.

And now his words were edged with bitterness and contempt and anger.

'Whores,' he said. 'Cheap whores who like drink and drugs. Sluts who show themselves. Girls who like men. Many men. Typical girls of this country. Oh, listen to me! These are not decent girls! Will you listen to me?'

Someone was kicking the stool he stood on.

'Whores,' spat Mahmud Irani, and then he said no more, not another word, because the stool was gone and all at once the rope around his neck cut deep, deep, *deep* into his throat and his feet were kicking wildly at nothing but the air.

He soiled himself immediately.

The red light watched him squirm and writhe and twist, wild with panic and pain, so much pain, his body thrashing desperately at the rope that cut into his flesh, deeper and deeper every second.

The rope first compressed his jugular vein and

7

then the much deeper carotid arteries, stopping the flow of blood to his brain, abruptly turning it off, his brain instantly swelling, making Mahmud's eyes roll back into his head and his tongue loll out of his flapping mouth and a choked gurgling sound come from somewhere deep inside his throttled neck.

The red light watched Mahmud as he was strangled by the rope around his neck.

And the pain!

Mahmud did not know that there was so much pain in the world. The minutes passed as slowly as centuries. But after what seemed to him a thousand years but was less than five minutes he finally stopped kicking and his arms went limp by his side.

Mahmud Irani choked out his very last strangled breath in that secret white-brick basement that hides deep below the city.

The red light went out.

And on the wall, the faces of the girls were still smiling.

PART I

THE BLACK STAGE

CHAPTER 1

We sat in Court One at the Old Bailey and we waited for justice.

'All rise,' the bailiff said.

I stood up, never letting go of the hand of the woman next to me. It had been a long day. But finally it was coming to the end.

We were there for the man she had been married to for nearly twenty years, a man I had never known in life, although I had watched him die perhaps a hundred times.

I had watched him come out of their modest house in his pyjamas on a soft spring evening, a middle-aged man wearing carpet slippers, wanting to do only what was right, wanting to do nothing more than what was decent and good, wanting – above all – to protect his family, and I had watched the three young men who now stood in the dock knock him to the ground and kick him to death.

I had watched him die a hundred times because one of the young men in the dock had filmed it on his phone, the small screen shaking with mirth, rocking with laughter, the picture sharp in the clear light of a March evening. I had watched him die again and again and again, until my head was full of a silent scream that stayed with me in my dreams.

'He was a good man,' his widow, Alice, whispered, gripping my hand tight, shaking it for emphasis, and I nodded, feeling her fingers dig deep into my palm. On her far side were her two teenage children, a girl of around sixteen and a boy a year younger, and beyond them a young woman in her late twenties, the FLO – Family Liaison Officer.

I believed the Central Criminal Court – the proper name of the Old Bailey – was no place for children, especially children who had watched their father being murdered from the window of their home.

The FLO – a decent, caring, university-educated young woman who still believed that this world is essentially a benign place – said that they were here for *closure*. But closure was the wrong word for what they wanted in court number one.

They wanted justice.

And they needed it if their world would ever again make any kind of sense.

When I had first gone to their home with my colleagues DCI Pat Whitestone and DC Edie Wren on that March evening, the last chill of winter had still been clinging on. Now it was July and the city was wilting in the hottest summer since records began. Only a few months had gone by but the woman and her children were all visibly older, and it was more than just passing time. The three of them had been worn down by the brain-numbing shock of violent crime.

For our Murder Investigation Team at Homicide and Serious Crime Command, West End Central, 27 Savile Row, the case had been straightforward. You could not call it routine, because a man having his life brutally taken can never be considered routine. But there was incriminating evidence all over the smartphones of these three blank-faced morons in the dock, and the blood of the dead man was all over their hands and their clothes. It was an easy day at the office for our CSIs.

We were not hunting criminal masterminds. When we arrested them, they still had fresh blood on their trainers. They were just three thick yobs who took it all much too far.

But the case felt personal for me.

Because I knew him. The dead man. That lost husband, that stolen father. Steve Goddard. Forty years old.

I had never met him in life but I knew what made him leave his house when the three yobs were urinating on his wife's car. I understood him. I got it. He could have let it go – ignored the noise, the laughter, the obscene insult to his family and the street where he lived, the mocking of all that he loved.

And I could even understand that it made no rational sense at all to go out there in his carpet slippers to confront them. I could see why it was not worth it, why he should have turned up the television and drawn the curtains, and watched his children grow up and get married and have

13

their own children, and why he should have stayed indoors so that he could grow old with his wife. I got all that.

But above all I understood why this decent man did not have it in him to do nothing.

'Members of the jury, have you reached a verdict?' said the judge.

The jury spokesman cleared his throat. I felt Alice's fingernails digging into my palm once more, deeper now. The faces of the three defendants – immobile with a kind of surly stupidity through most of the trial – now registered the first stirrings of fear.

'Yes, Your Honour, we have,' said the jury spokesman.

Juries don't give reasons. Juries don't have to give reasons. Juries just give verdicts.

'*Guilty.*'

'*Guilty.*'

'*Guilty.*'

And juries have no say in sentencing. We all looked at the judge, a papery-faced old man who peered at us from under his wig and over his reading glasses as if he knew the secrets of our souls.

'Involuntary manslaughter is a serious offence,' intoned the judge, glowering at the court, his voice like thunder. 'It carries a maximum penalty of life imprisonment.'

A cry of, '*No!*' from the public gallery. It was a woman with a barbed-wire tattoo on her bare arms. She must be one of the boy's mothers, I thought, because none of their fathers had been spotted for nearly twenty years.

The judge rapped his gavel and demanded order or he would clear the court.

'Public concern and the need for deterrence must be reflected in the sentence passed by the court,' he continued. 'But the Criminal Justice Act requires a court addressing seriousness to consider the offender's *culpability* in committing the offence. And I accept the probability that the deceased was dead before he hit the ground due to a subarachnoid haemorrhage, making this a *single punch* manslaughter case.'

'But what does that *mean*?' the youngest child, the boy – called Steve, like his dad – murmured to his mother, and she shushed him, clinging on to good manners even in this place, even now.

It meant they would be home by Christmas, I thought, my stomach falling away.

It meant the bastards would get away with it.

It meant that it didn't matter that they had kicked Steve Goddard's head when he lay on the ground. It did not matter that they had urinated on his body and posted it on YouTube.

None of that mattered because the judge had swallowed the defence's evidence that the man who attacked three unarmed boys was dead before he hit the ground due to a pre-existing medical condition.

Get the right brief and you can worm your way out of anything.

'I am also obliged to accept the mitigating factor of self-defence, as the deceased was attempting to assault the defendants,' said the judge. 'I note you are all of good character. And I therefore sentence you to twelve months' imprisonment.'

It was over.

I looked at Alice Goddard's face. She didn't understand any of it. She didn't understand why her husband was dead thirty years before his time. She did not understand what the judge had said or why the defendants were laughing while her two children were quietly weeping. I wanted to say something to them but there was nothing to say. I had no words to offer and no comfort to give.

Alice Goddard let go of my hand. It was over for everybody apart from her and her two children. It would never be over for them.

Alice was smiling, and it tore at my heart. A tight, terrible smile.

'It's all right, Max,' she said. 'Really. Nothing was going to bring my Steve back, was it?'

She was anxious to make it clear that she did not blame me.

I looked at the defendants. They knew me. I knew them. I had seen one of them weeping for his mother in the interview room. I saw another one of them wet his pants at the prospect of imprisonment. And I saw the other one empty-eyed and indifferent through the entire process, beyond recall, beyond hope.

When they had been arrested, and when they

were questioned, and when they were charged, the three young men had seemed very different.

A coward. A weakling. And a bully.

Now they were one again. Now they were a gang again. Yes, they were going down, but they would be home in six months. Taking a life would have no real impact on their own lives. It would no doubt give them a certain status in the cruel little world they lived in.

The anger unfurled inside me and suddenly I was out of my seat and walking towards them. But the court bailiff blocked my path, his hands slightly raised to show me his meaty palms, but saying nothing and offering no threat if I dropped it right here.

'Leave it, sir,' he said.

So I did the smart thing. I did nothing.

He was a typical Old Bailey bailiff with a demeanour somewhere between a diplomat and a bouncer, and he looked at me sympathetically with the faintest hint of a smile – sad, not mocking – and I let the moment pass, choking down the sickness that came with the rage.

And my face was hot with shame.

The three youths in the dock smirked at me before they were taken down.

I had seen that look before.

Too many times.

It was the look of someone who knows they just got away with murder.

CHAPTER 2

ater that day we watched the man hang.

We saw the film of his death on the big HDTV screen that's on the wall of Major Incident Room One in West End Central, at first not sure what we were seeing, not even convinced it was real, still stunned by the fact that you can watch a man being executed online.

It was early evening and we were standing at our workstations, ignoring the phones that were ringing all over MIR-1, as the man was helped onto the kitchen step stool and a noose was slipped round his neck.

And the terrible exchange between the two men.

'*Do you know why you have been brought to this place of execution?*'

'*What? This – what? I don't understand. What? I'm a taxi driver—*'

The voice of the first man muffled by some sort of mask. The voice of the second man choked with terror.

'Who is he?' DCI Pat Whitestone said.

'IC4,' said DC Edie Wren, running a hand

through her red hair, her eyes not leaving the giant screen. IC4 meant the man – the one we could see, the one with the noose around his neck – was of South Asian descent. 'Maybe forty years old. Unshaven. Jeans. Polo shirt. Lacoste.'

'A Lacoste knock-off,' I said. 'The little crocodile's looking in the wrong direction.'

'Where is that place, Max?' said Whitestone.

I took a few steps closer to the screen. The film was sharp but the room was dark. In the shadows I could glimpse white tiles or bricks, stained green and yellow by time and the weather.

I felt I had seen it before. It was some part of London that was just round the corner, and yet a hundred years away, and beyond the reach of memory. I took a step back.

'I don't know,' I said.

'What are they doing to him?' said Trainee Detective Constable Billy Greene.

Then the stool was kicked away and we did not speak as we watched the man hang, his body twisting and squirming in the air, and there was no sound but the strangled gurgling coming from his throat. When the hanging man began to soil himself the cameraman turned away and I caught glimpses – nothing more – of two or three figures in dark clothes, their faces covered in black masks, only their eyes showing, their backs pressed against those yellowing walls.

'There's three or four of them,' I said. 'Maybe more. Wearing ski masks. No, not ski masks –

19

they're tactical Nomex face masks, or something similar.' A pause. 'They know what they're doing.'

The man's face began to change colour as the life was strangled out of him. Then he was still and it ended. A film lasting ten minutes and twenty-one seconds that was suddenly trending all over the world.

'You seen this hashtag?' Edie said, hunched over her laptop. 'It's everywhere: *#bringitback*.'

'Bring *what* back?' said TDC Greene.

'Play it again,' said Whitestone. 'Answer the phones, Billy. Find out where the hashtag comes from, Edie.'

Edie began tapping on her keyboard.

'Does that look like a hate crime to you, Max?' Whitestone said.

'It looks like a lynching,' I said. 'So – yes, maybe.'

'Here,' Edie said, and then a panel appeared in a corner of the big screen.

There was a black-and-white picture of a smiling rabbit-faced man from the middle of the last century. The account was called @AlbertPierrepointUK. No message. Just the hashtag – *#bringitback* – and a link to the film.

'It's got just under twenty-five thousand followers,' Edie said. 'No – over seventy-eight thousand followers. Wait—' She leaned back in her chair and sighed. 'Wow, popular guy, this Albert Pierrepoint. Why is the name so familiar?'

'Albert Pierrepoint was the most famous hangman this country ever had,' I said. 'He carried out more

20

than four hundred executions, including a lot of the Nazis in Nuremberg.'

'Metcall have had a 999,' Billy said, putting down the phone. 'From a woman who recognises the victim.' He looked up at the screen and winced at the man once more locked in the final throes of agony. 'The woman's a Fatima Irani from Bethnal Green. The man is Mahmud Irani. Her husband.'

'How do you spell his name?' Whitestone said. 'Got a DOB? Got a description of what he was wearing?'

Greene read from his notes. Then he looked up at the screen.

'She said her husband was wearing jeans and one of those shirts with the little crocodile,' he said, and stooped to retch into a wastepaper basket. It took him a moment to recover. 'Sorry,' he said.

'Play it again,' Whitestone said. 'Have a drink of water, Billy. Are you looking on the PNC, Edie?'

Edie Wren was running the name of *Mahmud Irani* through the Police National Computer.

'He's been away,' she said, meaning the man had done time. 'Did six years of a twelve-year sentence. He was part of the Hackney grooming gang. They targeted girls as young as eleven. A lot of the girls – but not all of them – were in care. Some of the gang got life. This Mahmud Irani was found guilty of trafficking – he's a taxi driver. He *was* a taxi driver. He got off relatively lightly.'

We watched him hang for the third time.

'Maybe not that lightly,' I said. 'If this is connected.'

A young Chinese man appeared in the doorway of MIR-1. He was Colin Cho of PCeU – the Police Central e-crime Unit, jointly funded by the Home Office to provide a national response to the most serious crimes on the Internet.

'We're looking for Albert Pierrepoint,' he told Whitestone, nodding at the big screen. 'He – they – seem to be using exactly the same tech as terrorists, pornographers and whistle blowers. The account is running through an anonymiser designed to hide all digital footprints. But it's not Tor or 12P. It's something we have never seen before. The site's under a lot of pressure – political, media, users, concerned parents – to take the film down in the name of decency, but we've persuaded them to leave it up there while we try to trace the sender's IP address. Off the record, of course.'

'Thanks, Colin,' Whitestone said, glancing at her phone. 'Metcall tell us we've got a body. In the middle of Hyde Park. No positive ID yet.' She looked at the screen and then at me. 'But the responding officer says the deceased is wearing one of those shirts with the little crocodile.'

'Hyde Park?' I said. 'The body was found in the actual park?' I looked up at the screen, at the subterranean space with the stained white tiles. 'They didn't do this in Hyde Park.'

I thought of the underground car parks of the big hotels on Park Lane, running down the east side of Hyde Park. But none of them looked anything like the room where they strung up Mahmud Irani. That place was from some other century.

In the panel of the TV screen we could see that @AlbertPierrepointUK had gone viral.

TRENDS
#bringitback
#bringitback
#bringitback
#bringitback
#bringitback

'I think somebody just brought back the death penalty,' I said.

Edie pressed play and on the screen Mahmud Irani was about to hang again.

'But who'd want to do that to him?' said the new boy, TDC Greene, and I remembered that Hackney grooming gang and the thought came unbidden as I headed for the door.

Who the hell wouldn't?

CHAPTER 3

There was something strangely peaceful about standing in the middle of Hyde Park on a warm summer night, nothing moving out here but the Specialist Search Team doing their fingertip search off in the darkness, and the CSIs quietly getting kitted up as DCI Whitestone and I contemplated the corpse.

You could tell it was him.

There was enough moonlight to show the crocodile on his polo shirt was still facing in the wrong direction and what looked like severe burn marks around his neck.

So even before the divisional surgeon had arrived to officially pronounce death, and long before his next of kin had the chance to formally identify the body in the morgue, we knew the identity of the body lying under the trees of Hyde Park.

'Mahmud Irani,' Whitestone said quietly.

'So it's not a hate crime,' I said. 'He wasn't killed because of his race or religion.'

'All murder is a hate crime. Do you know what that gang did to those girls? They branded them, Max. Can you believe that grown men would do that to children?' She shook her head. 'Some people deserve to be hated.'

I looked away from the dead man and inhaled clean air. Hyde Park stretched on forever. Londoners always complain about how cramped and crowded their city is, but Henry VIII used to hunt wild boar right here. Even today, London was still a city with fields. The white lights of the West End burned bright from far away, an orange glow rising high above them, like the sun coming up on another planet.

Whitestone stared silently at the corpse.

She was a small, fair-haired woman in glasses, neither young nor old, and if you saw her on the train you would not think that she was one of the most experienced homicide detectives in London. I would not speak again until she spoke to me first, for these were the crucial minutes when the Senior Investigating Officer takes a look at the pristine scene, the body exactly where it had been found, letting it all sink in, learning what she can before we start filming, photographing and bagging evidence. Those last moments when the scene is untouched.

Even the blue lights of our response vehicles seemed very distant, as though they were waiting for a sign from the SIO; a large circle of blue lights in the darkness of the massive park, sealing us off from the outside world. I could see DC Edie Wren and TDC Billy Greene interviewing the Romanian men who had discovered the body while preparing for an illegal barbecue.

'OK,' Whitestone said. 'I've seen enough.'

I raised a hand to the Crime Scene Manager and on her word the CSIs moved. I saw that our POLICE DO NOT CROSS tape now ran down the length of Park Lane and was patrolled every twenty metres or so by uniformed officers.

'You've locked down all of Hyde Park?' I said.

'Because I can always bring the perimeter in later,' Whitestone said quietly, her eyes not leaving the body. 'But I can't *extend* it later. Better to make the crime scene too big than too small. Let's take a closer look.'

We wore blue nitrile gloves and white face masks and under the plastic baggies over our shoes we stood on forensic stepping plates that were invisible to the naked eye.

Whitestone and I both carried a small stack of the stepping plates – transparent, lightweight – and we carefully placed them on the grass before us as we created an uncontaminated pathway to the body. We crouched down either side of Mahmud Irani.

'First hanging?' Whitestone said.

I nodded.

She pointed with a gloved index finger at the livid, lopsided markings around his neck.

'You only get that mark from hanging,' she said. 'Any other ligature strangulation will leave horizontal marks.'

'But this is diagonal,' I said. 'It runs from low on the neck on one side to just below the ear on the other.'

26

Whitestone nodded.

'Because the rope – or belt, or bed sheet, or wire, or whatever it is – angles towards the knot. See how deep it is? He was strangled by his own body weight. The rope compresses the carotid arteries, turns off the supply of blood to the brain. In judicial hangings, they used to snap the second cervical vertebra – the hangman's fracture, they call it. More humane. These guys didn't bother with any of that. They just strung him up. But hangings always look like this – the angled strangulation mark. What's unusual about this one is that it's not a suicide.' She stood up. 'Every hanging I ever saw until tonight – and I've had my share – was either deliberate or accidental suicide.'

'Accidental suicide?'

'Autoerotic asphyxia. You know. Sex games that kill you.'

'Oh.'

'It tends to be a male pastime, like doing DIY or watching cricket. Women seem less keen on autoerotic asphyxia. But strangulation apparently heightens the intensity of orgasm. And what could possibly go wrong?' She nodded at the body. 'What's unique about Mahmud Irani is that his hanging was not for the purposes of masturbation or ending his life. It was murder. Who uses hanging to murder someone?'

I thought about it.

'Somebody who wants revenge?'

'No – somebody who wants justice.' Her eyes

27

scanned the park. 'This is not the killing ground, is it? He didn't die here.'

I thought of the white-tiled room where no light seemed to shine. And I thought of the underground car parks that were in this area, not just by Hyde Park but also under the grand hotels and the fancy car dealerships of Park Lane. None of them, as far as I knew, looked even remotely like the room in the film, which looked like somewhere that should have been torn down a hundred years ago.

'So they chose to move him from the kill site to the dumping ground,' I said. 'Why would they do that?'

'Makes it harder for us,' Whitestone said. 'Now we can't run forensics on the kill site.'

'Yes, but it makes it more dangerous for them. Why risk someone seeing them dump the body? Why not leave him where they'd strung him up?'

Whitestone thought about it.

'Because they wanted us to find him,' she said.

We watched the Specialist Search Team inching their way across Hyde Park on their hands and knees. In the distance, a German Shepherd from the Dog Support Unit began to bark.

'What I could really use is the rope they did it with,' Whitestone said, more to herself than me. 'Ropes can speak volumes. The kind of rope. The kind of knot.'

Fierce white arc lights clicked on and lit up the scene like a film set. The body of Mahmud Irani looked horribly broken in the glare, the agony of his death imprinted on his lifeless face. The crocodile on his shirt stared off in the wrong direction, as if averting its gaze from the large stain on his jeans.

The Area Forensic Manager and his CSIs were already sweating inside their Tyvek suits, blue gloves and forensic face masks. A van with blacked-out windows came trundling across the parched grass. The mortuary van. And behind it I saw the great white marble arch that marks the junction of Oxford Street, Edgware Road and Park Lane. And something whispered through the trees, like the sigh of the uneasy dead.

'This was Tyburn,' I said. 'Maybe that's why they took the chance of dumping him here. The dump site could be part of a ritual killing. Maybe the most important part. Because this was Tyburn.'

'Tyburn?' Whitestone said. 'The public gallows?'

I nodded. 'The Tyburn tree – the three-legged gallows pole – was at Marble Arch. This spot was where London had its public execution site for almost a thousand years.' The great triumphal arch glowed with the lights of the night. 'Fifty thousand people were hanged right where we're standing,' I said. 'And they weren't just killing him, were they?' I looked down at the body of Mahmud Irani and the lopsided wound on his neck. 'They were punishing him.'

CHAPTER 4

Just before three o'clock on a sun-soaked Monday afternoon, Stan and I waited for Scout outside the school gates, both of us struggling to contain our emotions.

Our small red Cavalier King Charles Spaniel was always excited at the school gates – all those kids, all that attention, all those compliments – but for me today was special because it was the last day of the school year.

And we had made it.

The children began to appear and the waiting crowd of parents surged forward.

I saw the long blonde hair of Miss Davies – my daughter Scout's beloved teacher – and then there were little girls whose faces I recognised and finally Scout herself, carting a huge folder and wearing a school dress that was the smallest they had in stock but still came down well below her knees.

Miss Davies saw me and smiled, waved, and gave me a big thumb's up.

I wanted to thank her – for everything – but too many parents were milling around her, giving her gifts, wanting a word before the long summer break, so Stan and I stood and waited at the school gates, his tail wagging wildly and his round black eyes bulging with excitement.

'We watched a film because it was the last day,' Scout said, by way of greeting. 'It was about a Japanese fish called Ponyo.' She spotted the face of a friend who she hadn't seen for at least five minutes.

'*MIA! MIA! MIA-MIA-MIA-MIA-MIA!*'

'Bye, Scout!'

'Bye, Mia!'

Scout gave me her folder stuffed full of the year's work. Her name and class printed neatly on the front.

S c o u t   W o l f e, 1 D.

On top was one of her early works, a picture called 'My Family' that I remembered from last September. In the picture Scout's family was just a little stick-figure man who didn't even have a briefcase to call his own and a little girl with brown hair and a red dog. That picture had torn at my heart last year because the man and the girl and the dog had seemed lost among all that white space. But now it made me smile.

We made it!

We drifted away from the school gates, and all around us there were best wishes for the holidays, and plans being made to stay in touch, and I felt a sense of relief that was almost overwhelming.

All parents want the same things for their children.

But the single parent wants something extra. The single parent wants to survive.

If Scout and I could get through the first year of school, then I knew we could get through anything.

She took Stan's lead, wrapped it twice around her thin wrist, but the dog was still skittish, as if the thrills of the school gates had yet to wear off. He was sniffing a lamppost, wild-eyed and lost in his own world, that world of scent that dogs live in, when he suddenly looked up and spotted a well-groomed poodle on the far side of the road. Without warning, he tried to dive into the traffic and Scout had to hold him back with both hands.

I took the lead from her and we both stared at Stan, who only had eyes for the poodle on the far side of the road.

'He's reached sexual maturity,' Scout said. 'You're going to have to face it, Daddy.'

The homeless man sat on the pavement in the shade of the great arched entrance to Smithfield meat market.

He wore an old green T-shirt, the sleeves far too long, threadbare camouflage trousers and combat boots with no laces. There was a baseball cap in front of him containing a few coins. Everything about him said ex-serviceman.

Without looking up, he spoke to us as we walked past.

'Spare fifty grand?'

The line made me smile. It was a good line. Unexpected.

And then my smile froze because I knew that voice from years ago. Not the voice of this man but the boy he had once been. A time when I knew that voice as well as I knew my own.

I slowly turned and walked back to him, Scout and Stan following me. And he looked up – a light-skinned black man who had not shaved for a while, who had not slept in a bed last night, and who had not eaten properly for a long time.

But it was still him.

'Jackson Rose,' I said, and it wasn't a question, because there was no doubt in my mind, and I saw the shock of recognition dawn on that familiar face.

'*Max?*'

How long had it been? Thirteen years. Another last day of term in what was for us the last school year of them all. But for the five years before that, we had been closer than brothers.

One of those childhood friendships that you never find again.

I held out my hand and helped him to his feet and he grinned and I saw the gap-toothed smile I remembered, although one of his front teeth was chipped now, and we hugged, both laughing at the improbability of it all. Then we stood apart, shaking our heads. Time overwhelmed us.

I looked at his filthy army fatigues.

He looked at my daughter. And our dog.

And then we laughed again.

'You're a father?' he said.

I nodded. 'Yes.'

That gap-toothed grin. 'Congratulations.'

'Thanks.'

He held out his hand to Scout and she solemnly shook it.

'Jackson Rose,' he said.

'Scout Wolfe,' she said, and she watched him as he crouched down to make a fuss of Stan. 'Are you my daddy's friend?'

'That's right, Scout. And do you know what they say?'

Scout shook her head.

'I don't know what they say,' she confessed.

'You can make new friends,' Jackson Rose said, looking at me. 'But you can't make old friends.' He gave me that gap-toothed grin. 'Isn't that right, Max?'

'You're coming home with us,' I said.

Something passed across his face.

'I can't come home with you and Scout,' he said, looking away, and I saw that he was ashamed.

'Why not?'

He hesitated for a moment then gave a short, embarrassed laugh.

'Because I really need a shower,' he said.

'We've got a shower,' I said.

Then I looked at Scout, wondering if she would be worried by the presence of a stranger under our roof. But she reached out and took Jackson's hand.

'My friend's called Mia,' she told him.

We took him home.

My plan was to order a Thai takeaway, or pizza, or whatever he wanted, but as soon as I mentioned food he was at the fridge door, looking at what we had.

'I was a cook in the army,' he said. 'You like curry, Scout? Everybody likes curry, right?'

Scout looked doubtful. She had never tried curry.

'This is a special curry,' Jackson said, pulling out onions, carrots, chicken. Mrs Murphy, our house-keeper, kept stuff in there. I was more of a scrambled omelette man. 'A Japanese curry,' Jackson said, and I saw the boy he had been, and how nothing could stop him once he had decided on a course of action. 'Not too spicy,' he said, with a reassuring wink to Scout. 'Don't worry about a thing.'

And it was delicious. The three of us ate Jackson's Japanese curry with the heat of the day wearing off outside, and Stan sleeping in his basket. When Scout had finished her first curry and gone off to her room, Jackson and I smiled at each other.

'You're sleeping rough, Jackson?'

He laughed.

'Purely temporary. And what about you? Anybody else coming home?'

I shook my head.

'It's just us,' I said. 'Me and Scout. This is it.'

His big wide smile. Then it slowly faded. 'What happened, Max?'

I wasn't sure if I could explain it to him, or even to myself.

'I met a girl, and we fell in love, and then we had a baby, and it was the most beautiful baby in the world. And then things were harder than we ever thought they would be. No money. Her career stalled. My job was all hours and maybe sometimes I was too wrapped up in it. And this girl, Jackson – she was a beauty.'

'What's her name?'

'Anne,' I said, and I wondered if I would ever be able to say that one little name without a stab of pain. 'And she met someone else. A good-looking guy with plenty of money.'

'Nothing like you then?'

'Nothing like me. She fell in love.' I paused. This next bit was tough to talk about. 'And got pregnant with his kid. Walked out on us. Now she's got a new life, got a new family – and me and Scout, we had to get on with it, too. And we did.'

'This Anne – she still see the kid?'

'On and off. It's patchy, to be honest. She's busy with this new life. Happens all the time.'

'Yes, it does. But it's still hard.'

'It's actually not *that* hard because Scout is the best thing that ever happened to me, Jackson. And because it feels like everybody we know is rooting for us.' I thought of Mrs Murphy. I thought of Miss Davies. And I thought of Edie Wren, who could talk to Scout more naturally than anyone in the world.

'Lot of support,' Jackson said.

'We're doing all right,' I said.

The cardboard folder that Scout had brought home was on the dinner table. Jackson leafed through it.

'What about you?' I said. 'Wife? Kids?' I remembered how much girls had liked him. For his looks, and for his wildness, and for his lack of fear.

He shook his head.

'Not me,' he smiled, as if the thought had never even crossed his mind, and when he rubbed his eyes and stifled a yawn, I saw how exhausted he was. 'I've been too busy feeding the British Army.'

'You're worn out,' I said. 'Come on.'

I showed him the little spare room at the far end of the loft and he said that he might have a nap for a bit and I told him that was a good idea.

'I'm glad to see you, Max,' he said, and I knew that I would never have a friend like him again.

'Me too,' I said. 'Do you need anything?'

He smiled shyly and I cursed my stupidity.

Jackson needed everything.

When I came back with clean clothes, towels and toothbrush, he was standing by the window, staring down at the meat market. He had pulled off his boots, socks and T-shirt, and I saw that his entire torso – his back, his chest, and his shoulders – was one mass of scar tissue. The skin looked as though it had been torn off and then carelessly pulled back together. It was livid, corrugated, discoloured, and it made my throat constrict with shock.

'What happened?' I said, echoing his question to me.

'I served my country,' smiled Jackson Rose.

CHAPTER 5

'So that's the plan?' said Edie Wren early the next morning. 'We work our way through the list of everyone who hated Mahmud Irani because of his conviction for grooming? That's our MLOE?'

Major Line of Enquiry.

I nodded. She whistled.

'Long list,' she said.

'Then we better get started,' I said.

I had parked the BMW X5 in a courtyard of a low-rise block of flats on the hill that slowly rises from King's Cross all the way to the Angel. We were in Islington, but this was not the Islington of cool cafés and million-pound studio flats. This was the other Islington, where the council houses stretched as far as the eye could see. Even this early in the day, the heat was building.

'We run the TIE process on everyone who had good cause to hate the victim,' I said.

Trace, Interview and Eliminate.

'We're doing this in the absence of the kill site,' I said. 'And in the absence of any other suspects, clues or leads.' I looked up at the bleak block of flats. 'Sofi Wilder was eleven years old when she met Mahmud Irani.'

'Jesus,' Edie murmured.

'Now she's eighteen. Sofi was one of the gang's first victims, and has had a lot of physical and mental problems. Apparently she doesn't leave her home.'

'Why are we looking at this poor kid? Max, this is a total waste of time.'

'Not Sofi,' I said. 'We're looking at her father – Barry Wilder. Threats were made in the courtroom on the day of sentencing.' I read from my notes: *'I'm going to kill you. I'm going to hunt you down and fucking kill you.* And there's something else. The dad – this Barry Wilder – he's been away.'

'What for?'

'Assault. Football violence. Twenty years ago.'

Edie looked doubtful.

'Lynching a man is a bit different from giving the away supporters a good hiding,' she said.

I shrugged.

'Look what they did to his daughter,' I said. 'Come on.'

We got out of the car and found the flat.

Barry Wilder opened the door. He had a shaved head and a short-sleeved Ben Sherman shirt with fading tattoos on arms that had been built up by manual work rather than a gym. THE JAM, said one tattoo. MADNESS said another. He was a forty-something skinhead but he looked as though life had kicked all the aggression out of him. He glanced at our warrant cards but seemed too shy to make eye contact.

'Mr Wilder? I'm DC Wolfe and this is DC Wren. We would like to ask you some questions about Mahmud Irani.'

He nodded. 'All right. You don't need to talk to our Sofi, do you?'

'It's you we're interested in,' Edie said, and he seemed relieved.

He let us into the flat.

A large, heavy-set blonde was sitting by the window, furiously smoking a cigarette and blowing the smoke out into the warm summer day. Unfiltered Camels. Her mouth flexed with loathing at the sight of us.

Jean Wilder. Sofi's mother.

'Ma'am,' I said, and my greeting was ignored, and she continued to smoke her cigarette as though she hated it.

Edie and I sat on the sofa, Barry Wilder in the armchair opposite us. I got a closer look at the body art on those thick arms. There were some ancient football tattoos, as faded as Egyptian runes. You couldn't even tell if he was Tottenham or Arsenal.

'You're aware that Mahmud Irani has been murdered?' I said.

I heard a door open, glimpsed the face of a young woman, frightened and pale, and watched the door silently close.

Sofi.

'Mr Wilder, I hope you understand that we have

41

to talk to you because of the relationship between Mahmud Irani and your daughter.'

The woman at the window exhaled.

'They didn't have a *relationship*,' Mrs Wilder said quietly. She took a deep drag on her cigarette. 'What do you think? They were boyfriend and girlfriend? Relationship! Why don't you ever do your job? It's not much to expect, is it?'

'Ma'am,' Edie said. 'Please.'

'You're in my home,' Mrs Wilder said, totally calm. 'And you're talking about my daughter.'

Edie looked at me and let it go.

'I need to ask you about threats that you made on Mahmud Irani's life,' I said to the father.

Mrs Wilder stubbed out her cigarette with something like fury. But the big man in front of us nodded mildly, his hands rubbing together as if he was washing them.

I tried to make my voice as neutral as possible.

'This is what you were heard to say in court, OK?'

'OK.'

I read from my notes. '*I'm going to kill you. I'm going to hunt you down and fucking kill you.*' I looked at the man. 'Did you make those threats?'

'Yes.'

Mrs Wilder came across the room. She had tried to cover the smell of cigarettes with smells that I knew – Jimmy Choo and Juicy Fruit chewing gum.

'Do you have children?' she asked me.

'This is not about me, ma'am.'

42

'Why are you scared to tell me the truth?'

'I have a daughter,' I said.

'How old?'

'She's five.'

'She'll grow up,' Jean Wilder said. 'They always do. You can't imagine it now but she'll grow up so fast that it will make your head spin. And you should get down on your knees and pray to God that she – your daughter, who I am sure you love like you love nothing else in this world – never has a man like Mahmud Irani and his friends catch her scent. Because what we have been through in this family is worse than hell and it is worse than death and it could happen to anyone with a daughter in this country today. And the people who are meant to protect children? The policemen and the social workers and all the professional do-gooders? They look the other way when children are tortured and raped.' A breath escaped her mouth, and she shook her head in wonder. 'They look the other way.'

'I do appreciate how much you've suffered,' I said. 'But this is a murder investigation and we are obliged to make enquiries.'

I turned to her husband.

'Did you have any contact with Mahmud Irani after he was sentenced?' I said.

But Jean Wilder spoke for him.

'Barry didn't do it,' she said. 'When was it? He was here. He's here every night. We all are. The three of us. Where would we go? Why would we want the neighbours and people we don't even know staring at us – pointing at us – looking at Sofi as if she was less than human. Yes, my husband said those things. Screamed those things at the top of his voice. No doubt he meant it at the time. Because when they were in the dock, they were *laughing* at us. Those stinking Paki bastards who wrecked our lives.'

'Please,' I said.

But she would not let it go.

'You say you have a daughter,' she said, as if there was the possibility that I might be lying. 'What would you say if they treated your daughter like a sex toy and then they laughed at you?'

She was very close to me now. I could smell the unfiltered Camels and the Jimmy Choo and the Juicy Fruit.

'I've had no contact with the man,' Barry Wilder said quietly. No doubt he had been a violent youth when he was running riot at the football, but I could see no violence in the man now, only a bottomless sadness, and a grief that was never-ending.

He looked at the floor and washed his hands with each other.

'I said those things, yes, I did say them, I don't deny it, but I didn't see the man since the trial, not until they showed that film on the Internet.' At last he looked me in the eyes. 'The film of him being hung,' he said.

We stared at each other in silence.

And then I thanked him and stood up.

Jean Wilder followed us to the door.

'You useless bastards!' she said. 'You tiptoe around these gangs because you're terrified of looking racist.'

I turned to look at her.

'Mrs Wilder, I don't tiptoe around anyone,' I said quietly. 'I was not a part of the investigation into Mahmud Irani and the Hackney grooming gang that abused your daughter and neither was DC Wren here. Those men were criminals and they got what they deserved.'

She pushed her face close to mine. Too many cigarettes, I thought. And too much Jimmy Choo.

'She could have *loved* someone,' she said. 'My Sofi. And she could have gone to college and she could have had a normal life, but that's all gone now.'

I opened the door. Jean Wilder reached across me and closed it. She had not finished with us yet.

'Do you know what they did to her?' she said 'To all those girls? You think you know – because you skimmed some report or you caught it on the news. *But you don't know.* They flattered these children, and gave them attention, then filled them with booze and drugs and took them to rooms where men were waiting. Dozens of the leering, stinking bastards. They gang-raped these children. They filmed them. They invited their friends round. All their stinking Paki cousins and Paki brothers. They *branded* them.' A rage and grief swelled up inside her and it was no different from vomit. She choked it back down. 'They put

45

cigarettes out on their bodies and laughed about it. *They fucking laughed.* My daughter – my little girl – my baby – has cigarette burns on her breasts and buttocks—'

Barry Wilder roared.

'ENOUGH!'

Jean Wilder's eyes were shining as she watched her husband lumber towards us. She placed a hand on her husband's arm, and patted it once.

'He had nothing to do with it,' she said, suddenly very tired. 'But you know what? I wish he did!'

I gently opened the door.

And this time she let me.

'And what would *you* do, Detective?' she said, laughing at my eagerness to get out of that broken-hearted home. 'If it was your daughter – in those rooms – with those men – what would *you* do about it?'

I said nothing.

I couldn't look at her.

She followed us to the door.

'You catch them?' she said. 'The men that hanged Mahmud Irani? Give them a medal.'

We were walking to the car when I looked up and saw the face of the girl at the window. Sofi. The curtain closed and she was gone. Edie and I didn't speak until we were back in the car.

'You didn't answer her question,' Edie said. 'What would you do if it was Scout, Max?'

'Oh, give me a break, Edie.'

We both knew what I would do.

CHAPTER 6

There is a hanging tree in the Black Museum.

It is a horizontal wooden triangle supported by three legs and it rests in a quiet corner of what is officially known as the Crime Museum. It is draped with perhaps two dozen hangman's nooses, all individually labelled with the name of the man or woman they executed.

'It's a replica of the triple-tree at Tyburn,' said Sergeant John Caine, the keeper of the Black Museum. 'The gallows was portable, and that's one of the reasons that nobody can ever agree about where Tyburn actually stood, although they were hanging people there for centuries.' He sipped from a mug that said BEST DAD IN THE WORLD. 'They moved it about, see.'

I touched one of the nooses.

It was just four thin strands of rope running through a metal eyelet to form the noose. Other ropes were much thicker, twice the size, strands of heavy rope woven together and running through a big brass thimble to form the noose.

'The thin ones date from the eighteenth century,'

Sergeant Caine said. 'The thicker ones are more modern. They go all the way to 1969, when the death penalty was abolished in this country.'

'You've got a lot of ropes in here, John. I never noticed before.'

'We've hanged a lot of people in this country. You could fill a stadium with the people they hanged at Tyburn alone. Some of these nooses date back to 1810 when there were 222 offences that were punishable by hanging, including robbing a rabbit warren and shoplifting.'

'But why would anyone use hanging to murder someone?' I said, touching one of the nooses as if it would reveal the answer. 'Why not just shoot them or stab them?'

'Because they want revenge,' said Sergeant John Caine. 'Let me show you something.'

It was a battered black leather suitcase. Inside was a length of rope, a leg strap and a hood that had once been white but was now yellow with age, folded as neatly as a handkerchief.

'This is Albert Pierrepoint's suitcase,' John Caine said. 'People misunderstand Pierrepoint. They forget how important he was to this country. He didn't simply represent punishment. He represented justice – right up until capital punishment started being seen as wicked and cruel and not very nice. But before that, Pierrepoint was a national hero. Who do you think hanged all those Nazi war criminals after the Second World War? Old Albert went to Germany twenty-five times in four years and strung up over two hundred Nazis. Not that he enjoyed it much, because they were making him do job lots – a dozen or so at a time. Old Albert was a bit of a perfectionist, with a lot of professional pride in his work.' He had a sip of his tea. 'The people who killed this child abuser – they use a picture of Pierrepoint online, don't they?'

I nodded.

'So they want justice,' I said. 'They want revenge.'

John gently closed Albert Pierrepoint's suitcase. 'And what's wrong with a bit of revenge?' he said.

My phone began to vibrate. *EDIE WREN CALLING*, said the display. Her voice was tight with adrenaline.

'We've got another hanging,' she said. 'Go online and watch it.'

'I'll be back in the office in fifteen minutes,' I said. 'I'll watch it then.'

'Max,' she said. 'Go online and watch it *now*.' Edie Wren took a breath. 'This one is live.'

We watched the second man hang on John Caine's computer.

At first it looked like exactly the same set-up with the camera aimed up at a terrified man standing on some kind of stool as the same voice asked the same question.

'Do you know why you've been brought to this place of execution?'

But the picture was far sharper, and there was

a date and time stamp running in the bottom right-hand corner, as if they wanted the world to know that this public execution was going out live.

It was the same room. You could see the walls more clearly this time, and they seemed to be rotting with age, brickwork that was once white crumbling to yellow and green and brown.

'Where's that look like, John?'

We leaned in closer. I heard John Caine quietly curse.

'I feel like I know,' he said. 'But I don't remember.'

The condemned man on the stool was babbling with terror. There was a rope being placed around his neck and it snaked off out of shot to the ceiling. He was a much younger man than Mahmud Irani, and dressed in a suit and tie. And white.

'Do you know—'

And then suddenly it all went wrong. The man in the suit was half jumping, half falling from the stool, and the noose could not have been secured to the ceiling because although it was around his neck it didn't stop him falling from the stool and then the camera was dropped and there was nothing to see and only the sounds of a furious struggle and the soft thud of punches thrown into flesh and bone and the weeping of a man who was suddenly aware that there was no escape.

As the camera was picked up, I saw some dark figures taking their places against a wall, standing like masked sentries under a single 8 x 10 inch photograph that had been attached to the wall of a smiling boy, perhaps eleven years old, wearing school uniform as he posed happily for the photographer.

I looked at the boy's smile and I knew with total certainty that the man being forced onto the back of the stool had somehow killed him.

'*Do you know why you've been brought to this place of execution?*'

Someone was kicking at the stool. The man flapped his arms and I saw that his hands were not tied. But the noose was still around his neck and now it was secured to the ceiling.

'There's four of them,' John Caine said. 'At least. Four that I can see. Black tracksuits – I think I saw a Nike logo. They're all wearing tactical Nomex face masks – that's what those masks are. The one who held the camera is the one who did the heavy lifting when the victim tried to do a bunk. A very big geezer. Can't see much of the others.'

The man on the hanging stool screamed once. '*No!*'

'But who is he?' John Caine said. 'And who's the kid?'

The man in the suit hung.

With his hands unbound, he fought against the rope tightening around his neck more fiercely than Mahmud Irani had fought it, he clawed at his neck, he ripped and tore at it, he lashed wildly with his legs and he tried to scream in protest, although no sound was possible other than the terrible noise that a man makes when he is being

51

strangled to death. But he fought more fiercely and so it was over more quickly.

The man stopped kicking. The screen froze, one spot of fresh blood on the eye of the lens.

'Why don't they just stab him in the eye?' I said, getting out my mobile phone.

'Because that would look like murder,' John Caine said. 'And – I'm just guessing here – they think that murder is too good for him.'

I watched the digital world react.

    #bring it back
    #bring it back
    #bring it back
    #bring it back
    #bring it back

'You want me to drive you to West End Central?' John Caine said.

'Thanks,' I said. 'But it's faster to run.'

He was still staring at the screen.

'Where *is* that place?' he said, as if he should know.

CHAPTER 7

I ran all the way to 27 Savile Row.

It was early in the evening but the heat was sticking to the city and I was soaked in sweat by the time I climbed the stairs to the top floor of West End Central. Major Incident Room One was already crowded.

DCI Whitestone was deep in conversation with our boss, DCS Swire, the Chief Super, as the two women stood before the giant TV screen, watching the man in the suit and tie hang one more time.

I realised with a jolt that they seemed relieved.

'But are we *sure*?' DCS Swire was saying in her hushed Margaret Thatcher voice. 'Are we absolutely *sure*, Pat?

'Yes, ma'am,' DCI Whitestone said. 'The victim is definitely an IC1.'

IC stands for identity codes and it is the system our people use to describe ethnicity. IC1 meant the man who had just been hanged was a white man of North European stock.

Mahmud Irani had been an IC4.

'Good,' said the Chief Super. 'Then whatever the motive – it's not race. Thank God for that!'

Edie Wren was furiously pounding her laptop as she conducted a conversation with Colin Cho of the Police Central e-crime Unit. TDC Billy Greene was on the phone fending off a reporter who had somehow been put through from the switchboard. And there was a shockingly attractive young woman I had never seen before who had her laptop plugged into one of the MIR-1 workstations. She was watching the same segment of the new film over and over again.

'Do you know why you have been brought to this place of execution? Do you know why you have been brought to this place of execution? Do you know . . .'

She had a long pale face, very serious, and the kind of hair that doesn't move so much as swing. When she leaned forward to stare at the screen her hair swung forward, like a long black veil falling over her serious face, and she pushed it back, biting at her lip with concentration.

'DC Wolfe,' I introduced myself to her. 'Are you running some kind of voice analysis on that dialogue?

But she just glanced at me for a second and then turned back to the screens, pushing back the long black veil of hair, a glint of gold on the third finger of her left hand. So that was the end of that conversation.

Edie Wren looked up from her workstation. On the screen before her I could see the online traffic reacting to the second hanging.

United Kingdom Trends
#bringitback
#bringitback
#bringitback

'It feels like it never went away,' Edie said.

'Who is she?' I said, nodding towards the woman with the swinging hair.

'Tara Jones. Speech analyst. Voice biometrics, they call it.'

'Is she any good?'

Edie shrugged. 'Tara's meant to be the best. But she hasn't given us anything yet.'

Then a mid-Atlantic voice called me.

'Max? Come and have a look at this.'

Dr Joe Stephen, a forensic psychologist from King's College London, was at a workstation with someone else I didn't recognise, a bald but bearded middle-aged man with a sweat patch in the shape of Australia on the back of his corduroy jacket. They were also watching the hanging. And I saw that the man with Dr Joe was not middle-aged at all. Beyond the bald head and the beard he was perhaps only thirty but there was something prematurely aged about him. His head was remarkable – so oval that it looked like a rugby ball impersonating a hard-boiled egg.

'Murder by hanging is almost unknown, isn't it?' the strange young man said.

Dr Joe nodded. 'But the unsubs – sorry, the unidentified subjects – don't think of it as murder.'

55

He had an American accent softened and smoothed by half a lifetime in London. 'They clearly believe they are carrying out the death penalty for what they consider a capital crime.'

The young man nodded thoughtfully.

'Capital from the Latin *capitalis*, of course,' he said. 'Literally *regarding the head* – a reference to execution by beheading.'

'Max,' Dr Joe said. 'This is Professor Adrian Hitchens. He lectures in history at King's College.'

I held out my hand but Professor Hitchens ignored it. He was looking at the frozen image on the screen before him, the last frame of this latest online execution – a glimpse of the worn, ruined brickwork of the kill site.

I took my hand away.

Perhaps he was thinking very deeply about where the kill site could be. Or perhaps he thought I was the janitor.

But my feelings were not too hurt. The Met are always wheeling in these experts for a bit of specialist advice. Some of them – like our resident psychologist Dr Joe – stick around for years. But most of them are wheeled straight out again when they prove to be no help with our enquiries. There was a very good chance that I would never see Professor Hitchens again.

Or the woman with the swinging hair.

The history man jabbed a fat finger at the screen. It was stained yellow with nicotine.

'The building looks late Victorian,' he said, more

to himself than Dr Joe or me. 'I'm guessing some kind of public works.' He nodded at the dank white walls, stained green and yellow with the rot of a hundred years. 'A madhouse? A prison? Yes, almost certainly late Victorian.'

DCS Swire and DCI Whitestone joined us.

'Hitch,' the Chief Super said to the history man, as if they were old buddies. 'I understand DC Wolfe here has a theory about where the first body was dumped.'

Whitestone nodded encouragement at me. 'You thought it could be significant that the body was left in Hyde Park, right, Max?'

I nodded. Professor Hitchens still wasn't looking at me.

'Tyburn,' I said. 'We found the first victim on the Park Lane side of Hyde Park. Not far from the site of Tyburn.'

He looked at me at last.

'Where this country hanged people for a thousand years,' I said.

Professor Hitchens grinned at me, though there was no warmth in his smile. His chipped teeth also looked old beyond their years. I wasn't crazy about him, to tell you the truth.

'I know what Tyburn was, Detective Wood.'

'Wolfe.'

'Detective Wolfe,' he said, and he turned in his swivel chair to address the room at large. Fat yellow fingers tapped the armrests of his chair. 'But Tyburn was most emphatically *not* in Hyde Park.'

'No, I know that, but—'

'The location was further north – according to the Rocque map of London in 1746. Are you familiar with Rocque's map of 1746?'

I briefly shook my head to confirm I was not familiar with Rocque's map of eighteenth-century London.

'The actual location of the Tyburn Tree was on the traffic island where the Edgware Road, Oxford Street and Bayswater Road all meet,' Hitchens said.

'But they're not going to dump a body in the middle of a traffic island, are they?' I said, and watched him bristle, unused to being contradicted. I suppose these big-shot academics get used to students hanging on their every word. 'What about that kitchen step stool, Professor?' I said. 'That look late Victorian to you?'

Whitestone shouted across the room to Wren. 'Still no ID of the vic, Edie?'

Wren shook her head. 'Colin's monitoring the online traffic and Billy's got an open line to Metcall, but nothing yet.'

Metcall, also known as Central Communications Command, is responsible for public contact. If someone hit 999 because they knew the man who had just been hanged online, it would come through to them first.

'Play it one more time,' the Chief Super said.

TDC Greene hit the button and we watched in silence as the scene unfolded again. Somehow

58

repeated viewing had not drained the hanging of its power to shock.

The man in the suit and tie fighting for his life. The desperate struggle before he was dragged onto the stool they used for a makeshift scaffold. The last words he would ever hear: '*Do you know why you've been brought to this place of execution?*' His strangulation on the end of a rope. His hands unbound, tearing at his throat.

And the boy. The picture on the wall of the smiling young boy, who smiled just as sweetly and innocently as the girls had smiled when Mahmud Irani died. Smiling from beyond the grave, smiling for all eternity.

'What the hell are they doing, Dr Joe?' Whitestone said quietly to our psychologist.

'The ceremony is everything,' Joe said. 'The ritual seems to be at least as important as the punishment. Both of these killings have been as choreographed as anything you would see at the Old Bailey. But instead of wigs they wear black masks. Instead of a judge and jury it's the unsubs. And in the dock, you have the accused.'

'With no chance of getting a suspended sentence,' Whitestone said.

'But the ritual – the ceremony – whatever you want to call it – is a statement and a warning. And, above all, it's an expression of power,' Dr Joe said. 'That's the crucial thing. It's an expression – and a reaffirmation – of power. In a normal court of law it is a reaffirmation of the power of the state. The unsubs no doubt see what they're doing as a reaffirmation of – I'm guessing here – some higher form of justice, some higher and more noble and less fallible law. A reaffirmation of the power of the people.'

'Got it!' Wren shouted. 'The name of the victim!' She listened to her phone and I saw her face register something that I could not read. 'And the name of the kid on the wall,' she said, all the euphoria suddenly leaving her. She ran her hands through her red hair and slowly hung up the phone.

'OK,' she said. 'The victim of the hanging is – was – Hector Welles. Thirty-five years old. Single. A trust fund manager in the City. Sent down for causing an accidental death while driving.'

'The boy on the wall,' I said.

Edie nodded. 'Welles was driving his Porsche 911 when the kid rode his bike into the street.' She hit her keyboard and the same photograph of the smiling boy filled the giant TV screen.

'The child was killed outright?' Whitestone said.

'He was in a coma for six months. In the end the parents switched off the life-support machine. The boy's name was . . .' She glanced down at her notes. 'Daniel Warboys,' she said.

I took a breath.

'Daniel Warboys? What part of the world was he from?'

'West London. Hammersmith.'

'Do you know this child, Max?' Whitestone said.

'I think I've met his grandfather,' I said. 'Paul Warboys.'

There was silence in MIR-1.

'*The* Paul Warboys?' the Chief Super said.

I nodded.

Paul and Danny Warboys ran West London back in the day when Reggie and Ronnie Kray were running the East End while Charlie and Eddie Richardson ruled the roost in South London.

I could easily believe that Paul Warboys had a grandson named after his beloved brother Danny.

'How long did Hector Welles go down for?' Whitestone asked.

'He was sentenced to five years for dangerous driving,' Edie said. 'Also fined ten grand and banned from driving for three years. Let off with a slap on the wrist because there was not a trace of drugs or booze in his bloodstream. And also because he had the best brief that his employers could buy and apparently he wept a lot in the dock. In the end, he served just under two years. And they even gave him his old job back.'

We were silent. The phones had stopped ringing. The only sound was the low drone of the cars down on Savile Row and the laptop of the voice analyst with the swinging hair.

'*Do you know why you have been brought to this place of execution? Do you know why you have been brought to this place of execution? Do you know . . .*'

'Two years for knocking down a little kid,' I said. 'It's not enough, is it?'

CHAPTER 8

Paul Warboys was the last of the line.

The last of those old gangsters whose names were known to the general public. The last of the career villains who wore suits and ties and had a short back and sides even when everyone else in the Sixties was growing their hair, wearing flares and dropping acid.

The very last of the true crime celebrities.

Back in the Sixties and Seventies, Paul Warboys and his brother Danny held court in West London, from their Hammersmith home to the massage parlours, knocking shops and drinking dens of old Soho. While Ronnie and Reggie Kray nursed their grievances in dingy East End boozers and Charlie and Eddie Richardson rattled around their South London scrapyards dreaming of striking gold in Africa, the Warboys brothers sucked the juice from the West End.

Paul and Danny Warboys had made more money than all of them.

'Nice gaff,' said Edie Wren as I steered the BMW X5 down the great sweeping driveway of the Essex mansion where Paul Warboys and his wife lived when they were not in Spain.

I could see staff dotted all around the grounds. A man trying to capture a solitary leaf that glided on the pristine swimming pool. A team of gardeners fussing around the flower beds and mowing the lawn. A maid in traditional black-and-white uniform giving strict instructions to a supermarket delivery driver.

But Paul Warboys opened his front door himself.

'I've been expecting you, Max,' he told me, almost smiling. 'Come in.'

Paul Warboys was dressed for the beach and had a deep tan that did not come from a spray can. Polo shirt, khaki shorts, flip-flops. Chunky gold jewellery clinked on his thick muscled arms. No tattoos. His thinning patch of hair was dyed an unbelievable shade of blond but he looked like what he was: an extremely fit old man who had not had to worry about money for a long time.

'I thought you might come alone,' he said, squinting over my shoulder at Edie Wren.

'I can't do that, Paul,' I said. 'You know that.'

'Trace, Interview and Eliminate,' he said. 'Right, Max?'

'DC Wren, Homicide and Serious Crime Command,' Edie said, holding out her warrant card.

Paul Warboys' smile grew bigger. His teeth were the dazzling white of a game-show presenter. Then he nodded.

'Put it away, sweetheart,' he told Edie. 'I believe you.'

We followed him into the living room. An English Bull Terrier padded across the carpet towards me, wagging his stumpy tail. I held out the back of my hand and the dog bent his magnificent sloping head towards me, confirming we had met before.

'Bullseye remembers you,' Paul Warboys laughed, scratching the dog behind his ears.

Bullseye had once belonged to an old face called Vic Masters, who I had found dead in a ditch on Hampstead Heath. Bullseye had stayed with me, Scout and Stan until Paul Warboys had come to claim his dead friend's dog.

'I never knew about your grandson,' I said. 'I'm sorry.'

He nodded briefly, folding up something within himself. He wasn't from the generation that needed to share every emotion with the rest of the world.

'Yeah. Well. Thanks. No reason why you should have known, is there? A little boy getting knocked down by a car. It's not news, is it? The story got a paragraph here and there. But nobody was holding the front page.'

'But I would have thought it was news,' I said, as gently as I could make it. 'The grandson of Paul Warboys . . .'

He laughed. 'It's news now!' he said. 'Now that bastard got hanged by the neck until dead.' Another laugh, harder this time, and it was laughter in the dark, full of something bitter and raw. '*Now* it's news!'

A woman came into the room.

A tiny blonde woman, maybe fifteen years younger than her husband, and she also seemed dressed for some beach far away, with the blue-and-gold batik wrap she was wearing and a tan the colour of teak.

'Doll,' Paul Warboys said. 'This is DC Wolfe.'

'The young man who looked after our Bullseye?' she said. 'Of course. Thank you.'

Doll Warboys shook my hand, and the chains on her tanned arms made the same sound as her husband made when he moved, a soft clinking sound, the sound of money in a life that had not been born into money.

'Hello, love,' she said to Edie, and I was reminded of the London I knew when I was growing up, where *love* was almost a punctuation mark, an endearment casually bestowed on total strangers. But when Doll Warboys smiled she seemed very tired, as if she had been awake all night tormented by old wounds.

Her grandson had been killed many years ago, but the execution of the man who did it was still trending online. All the old pain had been awakened. She smiled and left us. Edie and I took the chairs across from the sofa where Paul Warboys sat with Bullseye's monstrous head in his lap.

'Someone killed Hector Welles,' I said.

He shot me a ferocious look. Paul Warboys had

65

always been friendly to me, thanks to our connection to Bullseye, but I was under no illusion that we were anything resembling friends. And even now, even after all these years since the Warboys brothers had been almost as famous as the Krays, I could still see the serious violence in the man.

He got his rage under control.

'We don't say that name in this house,' he said very quietly, his fingers deep in Bullseye's fur. The dog whimpered with something between pleasure and pain. 'We *never* say that name, Max.'

It was a threat as much as a statement.

'But I have to talk to you about him,' I said.

'I understand that you have to run your fucking Trace, Interview and Eliminate,' he said. 'But this is my house and we never say the name of the man who killed my grandson in this house.' He waited for me to contradict him. 'OK?'

Edie had her notebook out. 'Where were you when Hector Welles was being hanged?'

Under the deep tan, his face flushed with fury, the kind of fury that once enabled him to order the amputation of an informer's tongue. But then he laughed.

'I was home with Doll,' he said, and I was reminded that he had been answering police questions since before Edie Wren and I were born.

'How did you hear about it?' Edie said.

'How do you think?' he said. 'The phones started ringing. Ringing and ringing and ringing they were. Friends. Family. Former colleagues. Some of them were laughing. Some of them were crying. And they all said the same thing. *Go online,* they said. *Go online, Paul, because someone is stringing up the bastard that killed your Danny.'*

'And you can corroborate your alibi?' Edie said.

'Darling, I can give you all the corroboration you need. But let me ask you a question.'

She held up her notebook as if to protect herself. 'Mr Warboys—'

'Do you know how long ago it was that I last hurt someone for profit or pleasure?' he said. 'A *lifetime.* When people talk about the Krays and the Richardsons and the Warboys, they forget that it was all over before most people in this country had colour television. They came after us, love. Your lot. Your mob. And we all went down hard. Charlie Richardson got twenty-five years in 1966 – when England won the World Cup! A couple of years later, Reggie and Ronnie went down for thirty years – the longest sentence ever passed at the Old Bailey.'

'And you and your brother both served life sentences for murder,' Edie said. 'For removing your lawyer's tongue.'

'The evidence was circumstantial,' he said. 'But my point is that our generation – those days when family firms ran London – ended fifty years ago. We all went away for a long time, and we either died inside or we came out into a changed world. You know – lovely modern multicultural Britain,

67

where the blackies, the Pakis and the Iraqis all deserve their slice of the pie or it violates their human rights.'

'Yes,' said Edie. 'If only we could go back to the good old days when Reggie and Ronnie Kray were helping little old ladies across the street.'

He waved a dismissive hand.

'Now you're just taking the piss,' he said, sounding almost bored. 'But if you honestly think that the world is a safer place these days than when Reggie and Ronnie and Charlie and Eddie and Danny and myself were young men, then you are kidding yourself, young lady.'

He leaned forward and looked from Edie to me.

There was no warmth in him now.

'Do you actually know what happened to little Daniel? My grandson? He was riding his little bike over a zebra crossing when *that bastard* came along in his fucking Porsche and mowed him down. Daniel was in a coma for six months before they turned off the life support. Do you know why we've got the dog? Why the dog's with us? Because Daniel's mother – my youngest – can't look after a dog any more because she has never been right since her boy died. She has the lot. Depression. Pills. Panic attacks. Self-harming. Falling to bits. Can't even walk a dog twice a day. Can't get out of bed to feed old Bullseye. Can't get out of bed to wash herself or take her daughter to school. She can't see the point to any of it – you know. Fucking living. *That bastard* wrecked lives, Max. Served two years for what he did to a child. I served twenty years for what I did to grown men.'

'But nobody has the right to kill him,' I said. I found that I would not say the name of Hector Welles in this house. I did not understand if it was out of respect to young Daniel Warboys, or his grandfather, or if it was because I hated him too.

Paul Warboys shook his head.

'That's your law, Max. It's not mine.'

He leaned back. Edie Wren closed her notebook. She looked at me and I nodded. Time to go.

Paul Warboys walked us to the front door in silence. There he placed one large hand on my arm. I looked at his face and his pale blue eyes were shining with tears.

'You ever hear of a man called John Favara, Max?'

I shook my head. 'Who was he?'

'John Favara was a man who lived in New Jersey many years ago. One day in 1980 this John Favara ran down and killed a twelve-year-old boy. This child's name was Frank Gotti – that ring any bells, Max?'

I nodded. Now it was coming back to me.

'Frank was the son of John Gotti,' I said.

Paul Warboys chuckled. 'John Gotti – the Dapper Don. The boss of the Gambino family. The last of the old school Mafia bosses. And then this John Favara knocks down and kills young Frank Gotti. You know what happened next?'

'Yes,' I said. 'The guy – John Favara – was

69

abducted and never seen again. And the assumption is that he was murdered for killing the boy.'

'But Gotti and his wife were on holiday in Florida when Favara disappeared,' Paul Warboys smiled. 'So they were in the clear, weren't they? Long way from Florida to New Jersey.'

'Didn't they also call Gotti the Teflon Don?' Edie said. 'Because nothing ever stuck? And didn't Mrs Gotti attack John Favara with a baseball bat prior to his disappearance?'

'Feels like the least she could do,' Paul Warboys said.

He placed a scarred hand on our arms so that we could not take our leave. His knuckles were stark white against his suntan where the skin had been torn off and grown back. I had seen hands like that before but only on professional boxers.

He leaned close to our faces.

This was very important to him.

'My point is this,' Paul Warboys said quietly. 'If I had killed the bastard that murdered my grandson with his car, I would have a much better alibi than the one I've got.'

Then he laughed.

'And I wouldn't have done it online,' he said.

CHAPTER 9

Jackson went for his run at first light.

As the sun came up around five the door to his room quietly opened and I stirred from the last stage of sleep, that shallow sleep that is full of dreams, as he padded across the loft to get Stan. By the time I got up an hour later the dog was curled up on his favourite chair, happily exhausted, and Jackson was in the kitchen, making porridge for us, his hair still wet from the shower. He already looked stronger than when we had found him.

He smiled his gap-toothed grin and nodded at the sleeping Cavalier.

'Stan likes the ladies,' Jackson said. 'You're going to have to watch that.'

'He's still a puppy,' I said. 'He's just friendly.' Stan was snoring. 'You wore that dog out.'

'I think it was the cute Labradoodle he met down by the river who wore him out,' Jackson laughed, tipping blueberries into the porridge.

Then his face became serious.

'Thanks for all this, Max. You know – putting me up. I appreciate it.

'No problem.'

'I'll sort myself out soon,' he said. 'Find my own place.' He tugged at the wrists of his long-sleeved T-shirt. He preferred to keep his scarred arms covered, even here in the loft. Even with us. He flashed that gap-toothed smile. 'You know what they say about house guests and fish,' he said. 'They start to smell after a while.'

I shook my head. 'Stay as long as you like.'

'I might have a look across the road for work.'

'At the meat market? Good idea. They always need grafters.'

He grinned, pleased that I liked his plan, and placed a bowl of porridge in front of me.

And the truth was I liked having Jackson around. He had been with us for two days now, and he did everything he could to make himself useful – walking the dog, making breakfast. And I realised that I had missed having someone that close in my life. It was true what he said – you can make new friends but you can't make old friends.

Scout emerged from her bedroom, wild hair and bleary-eyed. 'You kept Stan on lead, right, Jackson?'

'I promised you, didn't I?'

My phone vibrated. DCI Whitestone.

'We've got the body of Hector Welles,' she said. 'They must have dumped it during the night.'

'Where did they leave him?'

'About one hundred metres from where we found Mahmud Irani.'

'In Hyde Park?'

'No. This one – if you can believe it – was found at the junction of Oxford Street, Bayswater Road and Edgware Road – on that massive traffic island right opposite Marble Arch. You know where I mean, Max?

'Yes,' I said. 'Tyburn.'

DCI Whitestone and I came out of the white CSI tent, both of us sweating from the heat and the sight of the dead body of Hector Welles. She wiped her brow with the back of her hand.

'He's a bigger mess than the first one,' she said.

'They secured Mahmud Irani's hands behind his back,' I said. 'They didn't get the chance to do that with Hector Welles.'

'It looks like he tried to tear his own throat out.'

'Yes – and he still couldn't shift the rope around his neck. Irani never quite believed what was happening to him, but Welles knew exactly what they were going to do – he had probably seen Irani hang on YouTube – so he fought like hell. Before they had his neck in a noose, and then when he was hanging. This one fought for his life, Pat. And that's what made all the mess in there.'

We had thrown up our perimeter around the traffic island where the body of Hector Welles had been found and it had effectively shut down central London. The POLICE: DO NOT CROSS tape stretched from Park Lane in the south to Oxford Street in the east to Edgware Road in the north to Bayswater Road in the west. The blue lights of more than twenty Rapid Response Vehicles pulsed and shone in the summer morning, brighter than the sun, and beyond them you could see four of London's great roads, empty of traffic.

Dozens of uniformed officers patrolled the perimeter. Specialist Search Teams fanned out in every direction, fingertip-searching the area around the traffic island and beyond. Somewhere out in the endless city streets, the blare of all that paralysed traffic filled the air.

'You sure you want to maintain this perimeter?' I said. 'We've shut down West London and the rush hour hasn't started yet.'

'I told you before – I can always bring the perimeter in later,' she said. 'But I can't take it out later. Who found the body?'

'Owner of one of the Lebanese supermarkets on the Edgware Road. Edie's taking his statement now. He was coming in to work about five.'

'But they didn't dump him at dawn, did they?' she said. 'And nobody noticed a dead body in one of the busiest corners of London during the night?'

'Maybe they thought he was drunk or stoned or another Romanian gypsy getting his beauty sleep. Probably nobody even clocked him. This traffic island's not lit up at night. They knew what they were doing.'

We stared out across the great green expanse of Hyde Park. Just beyond the perimeter tape at Speaker's Corner, I could see Professor Adrian Hitchens in conversation with a young uniformed police officer. The professor had a motorcycle helmet under one arm and sat astride what looked like an old 500cc Royal Enfield, its faded blue paint worn down to shiny silver and freckled with rust.

Edie Wren walked up to us.

'You told that freak the first body was dumped where Tyburn used to be,' she said. 'You told him and he wouldn't listen, would he? Some expert he is.'

'I wasn't sure myself. Not until the second body. But now they're rubbing our noses in it. They want the world to know they've brought back capital punishment.'

Edie looked around at the pristine white monolith of Marble Arch, at the start of the West End proper on Oxford Street, at the grand hotels running all the way down Park Lane, and at Hyde Park, an endless sea of green in the very heart of the city.

'And remind me – what's so special about this place?' she said. 'Why does it mean so much to them?'

'There's probably more history where we are standing than any place in the country,' I said. 'For a thousand years, Tyburn was the country's most celebrated place of execution. More than fifty thousand men, women and children were hanged here. London was always a city of execution – in the eighteenth century you couldn't enter the city without seeing a line of gibbets – but Tyburn was always special.'

'Dr Joe says that ritual and ceremony was important to the perps – as important as the punishment.'

I nodded. 'It *matters* to them that this was where Tyburn stood. It's *important* to them that their victims are hanged, and then dumped here. I'm sure they wish they could do it on the pavement outside the Odeon Marble Arch. But I'm hoping they care too much, that it's *too* important to them. I'm guessing that they are so obsessed with all that symbolism that we will have our chance to nail them.' I turned to look at our SIO. 'You want to get Marble Arch staked out?'

'I should have done it sooner,' Whitestone said. 'After the first one. It's not a difficult place for a team of undercover officers to watch, especially in summer when there are more bodies sleeping out around Hyde Park and Marble Arch. But if they do it again, they have to come back here. And next time we'll be waiting.'

'And they're going to do it again, aren't they?' I said.

'I don't see how they can stop now,' she said.

Edie consulted her phone. 'The Divisional Surgeon has arrived to check that Welles is really dead,' she said. 'I'll escort him in.'

I looked at Whitestone.

'And the history man is here,' I said.

'Let's give him one last try,' Whitestone said.

I walked across to the perimeter and the old-looking young man who was waiting there. He had got off his bike and placed the helmet on the pillion and was sucking on a soggy roll-up cigarette. It did not seem to be giving him much joy. Despite the motorbike, and despite the fact that it was going to be another brutally hot day, Professor Adrian Hitchens wore a two-piece corduroy suit, a shirt and tie and a V-neck jumper that had been munched by moths long gone. His head still looked remarkable to me – so egg-shaped that it was almost pointed. It glistened with heavy beads of sweat.

'Professor Hitchens,' I said.

'I feel that we got off to a bad start,' he said. 'You and I. Your theory about Tyburn – I dismissed it out of hand. That was wrong. You were correct. And I apologise.'

I shrugged. 'It was just a hunch. I also told you that they would never dump a body on a traffic island in the middle of the West End.' I nodded to the white tent. 'And that's exactly what they did. So I was wrong, too,' I said.

I held out my hand to him and he went to shake it until he saw the blue latex gloves I was offering him.

'Put these on and keep them on until you sign out at the perimeter. Don't touch anything. Follow my instructions at all times.'

He signed in with the uniformed officer and put on the gloves and baggies. The officer and I held up the DO NOT CROSS tape as Professor Hitchens eased his great bulk under the tape. I had never seen a man so young who was so fabulously unfit.

'Take your time, sir,' the young uniform said, without irony.

Safely under the tape, Hitchens smoothed his corduroy suit and cleared his throat. We began walking towards the white tent and I found I had to slow my pace so that he could keep up.

'We need to find the kill site,' I said. 'If the dump site has a ritualistic value for them, then possibly the kill site will have some significance too. The place where both the victims were hanged feels like it should ring some bells. There can't be many late Victorian basements left in this town. If we find the kill site, it leads us to them. Any thoughts on where it could be?'

'Where we are right now is London's primary place of execution, as you so correctly observed.'

'But they didn't do it here, did they? They dump the bodies at Tyburn but they can't hang them here. So where's the next best thing?'

'If ritual is that important to them, they're spoilt for choice. It could be any one of a number of places of execution. Kennington Common, Shepherd's Bush, Tower Hill, Charing Cross. Pirates were hanged at the execution dock at East Wapping. There were executions at Smithfield – although burning and boiling were preferred to hanging, especially during the sixteenth-century heresy trials. Charles I was executed in Whitehall. But Charles was beheaded – if we are talking specifically about *hanging* . . .'

78

'What about Newgate?' I said. 'Didn't they have hangings at Newgate after they stopped public executions at Tyburn?'

Professor Hitchens nodded his great oval head.

'In many ways, Newgate would be their obvious choice. There was a gaol on that site for eight hundred years and after Tyburn's gallows were abolished in 1783. public hangings continued at Newgate for almost another hundred years. Hangings were as popular as FA Cup Finals. Huge crowds would turn up to watch. The crush was apparently phenomenal. Often there would be a few dozen dead when the crowds went home for their supper. But Newgate Gaol was closed in 1902 and torn down in 1904.'

'And nothing remains?

'The prison was completely demolished so they could build the Old Bailey on top of it. There's a plaque on the wall of the Old Bailey. But Newgate was essentially wiped off the face of the earth. The theory was that they were replacing one kind of brutal British justice with another more enlightened kind of justice. There were no executions at the Old Bailey.'

We stopped at the white tent.

Inside, the Tyvek-suited CSIs in their blue gloves, baggies and face masks photographed and filmed and dusted, moving with a kind of insatiable curiosity, determined to record absolutely everything, like tourists on some hostile planet.

I looked at Hitchens.

'And are you really going to help me, Professor? Don't waste my time, Hitch – may I call you Hitch?'

'Please do, Detective.'

'If you're just looking for a few juicy anecdotes to share with your colleagues over sherry evenings back on campus, then you can bail out now. You don't have to like me. But if you stick around, you do have to help me.'

'I want to help you. I truly do.'

I looked at him for a while.

Then I nodded and took him inside to see the body.

Hector Welles.

What remained of his neck was a pulp of raw and bloody meat. As we watched, a CSI armed with long surgical tweezers carefully plucked something from the shredded meat of his neck and expertly slipped it inside a plastic evidence bag.

The history man's mouth dropped open with a kind of sickened wonder.

Professor Hitchens stared at the body in disbelief. I have no idea what he had been expecting. But it was not this – a man who, in his last desperate minutes, had tried to remove the rope strangling him by attempting to rip open his own throat.

Hector Welles looked as though he had been flayed alive from his chin to his chest. There was not a piece of skin left intact, just a sickening mass of minced meat where his neck used to be.

Professor Hitchens said, 'Dear God . . . what does he have stuck in his neck? They're not . . .'

The CSI gently removed something else with the tweezers. There were ten of them in total.

I nodded.

'Fingernails,' I said. 'Hector Welles' fingernails. When he was hanging, he tore at the rope around his neck so hard he ripped out all of his fingernails.'

Professor Hitchens quietly emptied his stomach over the blue baggies on his shoes.

A summer breeze stirred the tent.

I shuddered, my skin crawling at the proximity of all that ancient horror, and the wind in the trees of Hyde Park sounded as if all the ghosts of Tyburn were moaning.

CHAPTER 10

I was packing my kit bag for the gym. Scout was off for a sleepover with her friend Mia, and down on the street the meat market's night was just beginning. After the day I had spent at Marble Arch, I knew that sleep would be a struggle for me if I did not exhaust myself at Fred's.

Then Edie called with what felt like our first breakthrough.

'The good news is we've got prints,' she said. 'All our forensics are back for Mahmud Irani and Hector Welles and the same print is on both of the victims' clothes.' I could hear the excitement in her voice. 'It's a glove print, Max, but really sharp. A thumb. A left thumbprint on both of the dead men.'

Most criminals believe that gloves hide fingerprints. But it is not true, especially with more modern gloves made of latex or something similar. The thinner the glove, the more likely the telltale ridges, whorls, arches and loops are to be left behind.

'And what's the bad news?' I said.

'None of it rings any bells on IDENT1.'

IDENT1 is the country's major database for storing fingerprints and contains the fingerprints of knocking on for ten million people. That only leaves about fifty million people who are not on there – the part of the population who have never come into contact with the police.

'And both of our potential suspects are on IDENT1,' I said. 'Because both Paul Warboys and Barry Wilder have criminal records.'

'Wilder for his youthful indiscretions at the football, and Warboys because crime was what he did for a living,' Edie said.

'Are we sure it's not them?'

Fingerprint analysis is not the exact science that it is always cracked up to be in the movies. Fingerprint officers have been known to get it wrong. Until 2001, a sixteen-point standard existed for fingerprint matches – meaning there were sixteen identical points required on a latent print to legally match it to a suspect. The system was scrapped because it didn't work.

'It's not even close, Max.'

'But we still don't have the kill site, so we don't have prints on surfaces, do we?' I argued. 'Paul Warboys or Barry Wilder could have glove prints, fingerprints, footprints and DNA all over the kill site. This one print found doesn't mean either Barry Wilder and Paul Warboys – or both of them – weren't there. It doesn't mean they had nothing to do with it.'

'It makes it a lot less likely though, doesn't it?'

I had to give her that. 'Yes.'

Jackson came into the loft, soaked in sweat from his evening run. Stan got off the sofa and padded across to greet him. The pair of them stared at me talking on the phone.

'You know what this means, don't you?' Edie said.

'There's a very strong possibility that these guys don't have criminal records.'

'Clean skins,' Edie said. 'I bloody hate clean skins. I'll see you in the morning, Max.'

'This is the thing on the news,' Jackson said, his fingers scratching the back of Stan's neck. 'The Hanging Club.'

I nodded.

'So what are they?' Jackson said. 'Some kind of vigilante group?'

'We have a psychologist who works with us,' I said. 'Dr Joe. American. His theory is that they think of what they're doing as capital punishment. They don't think they're committing murder. They don't see it like that. They believe they are carrying out a death sentence.'

'But they're only killing scumbags, right? A child groomer and a hit-and-run driver.'

I smiled. 'They're not allowed to kill anyone, Jackson. It's against the law.'

He looked thoughtful.

'Still – it can't feel good having to go after them. For you, I mean, Max. Like you're a lawyer or something.'

I shouldered my kit bag.

'Did they give you any choice about going to Afghanistan, Jackson? Did they ask you if there was somewhere you would prefer to go?'

He shook his head.

'You went where you were sent,' I said. 'Same here. We just do our job. That's all we do. The law's not just there for nice people. I'm off to the gym.'

'Bit late to be training,' Jackson said.

'I need to work off the day,' I said. 'Or I'll never get any sleep.'

'I'll come with you.'

'You just had a run.'

He laughed. 'Another hour of cardio won't kill me.' He looked thoughtful. 'I'm just saying – what they're doing is illegal. But does that make it wrong?'

'You talk like you admire them.'

'And you talk like you don't. A child groomer, Max. A hit-and-run driver. No great loss.'

'That's not the point.'

'What is the point?'

'The point is – who made them God? Who elected them judge, jury and executioner? They're not the law.'

'I forgot,' he smiled. 'You are.'

'I was at the Old Bailey,' I said. 'Some boys kicked a man to death. His name was Steve Goddard and he was forty years old. They got off too lightly and it made me mad. I was going to go for them. I wanted to wipe the smiles off their faces. I wanted to hurt them, to punish them in a way that the court had not punished them. I wanted to give them what they deserved. Stupid, right? I've got Scout to raise. I'm no good for her sitting in a jail cell. But it was a moment. Then one of the court ushers got in my face and the moment passed.'

'That's you, Max. For some people, the moment doesn't pass.' He paused. 'But the hanging's weird. A funny way to do it, I mean. You ever see anything like this before?'

I shook my head. 'Never.'

'Even if you hate these bastards, why would you go to all the trouble of stringing them up?'

I smiled at him. 'What would you do? Beat them to death with your spatula?'

He didn't smile back. His dark eyes slid away from me.

'If I wanted to kill someone that deserved to die, I wouldn't hang them.'

'What would you do, Jackson?'

He shook his head. 'I wouldn't put a rope around his neck.'

'But what *would* you do? Put a bullet in their brains from half a mile away?'

'I'm no sniper, Max. I'm a chef. But I'd get close enough to smell what they had for breakfast.' He stared at the open palms of his hands as though noticing them for the first time. 'Then one in the head,' he said. 'And one in the heart.'

We were silent. Then he gave me his gap-toothed

grin and the moment was broken. He gestured at my bag.

Fourteen-ounce gloves. Shirt. Shorts. Trainers. Gum shield.

'Can you lend me some kit?' said my friend.

We banged the bags at Smithfield ABC.

One of Fred's famous circuits – ten three-minute rounds on the bags, alternating the heavy bag and the speedball, with one minute between rounds for ten burpies and ten press-ups. No rest for your heart. Recover while you work.

'You're so lucky to be training!' Fred shouted at us. 'If it was easy, everybody would do it! Pain is just weakness leaving the body!'

Halfway through I stood back from the speed-ball, trying to catch my breath, reaching for that second wind while Jackson whaled away at the heavy bag, the dull thud of leather against leather. He had on one of my long-sleeved T-shirts that was a size too big for him.

He laughed at my exhaustion.

'I was always tougher than you!' he shouted.

It wasn't true. I was always tougher.

But he was wilder.

There was a crowd of drunks in Charterhouse Street.

More than anywhere in the city, Smithfield was the neighbourhood that never slept. The meat market worked all night. The clubs on Charterhouse

Street had them dancing till dawn. Pubs had licensing laws that saw the clubbers and meat porters having a pint at first light. Drunks were no big deal in this part of town.

But the men in front of us now were the ugly kind of drunks. They were standing outside one of the clubs, being refused entry. Politely but firmly. Jackson and I stepped into the road to walk around them as they argued with the men on the door.

'I smell pig,' one of them said. The smallest one. The runt. They are often the mouthiest. Napoleons in polo shirts.

We kept walking.

I saw Jackson glance over his shoulder and then look at me.

'Keep walking,' I said.

'That might not be an option,' he said.

They were following us. I looked over my shoulder. Five of them. Polo shirts in the warm summer night. Kebab stains down the front. Three of them were holding bottles. One of the bottles exploded between my feet.

Glass and beer everywhere. Then they were in front of us.

'Where you off to, pig?' one of them said, stepping forward, right in my face. I could smell cigarettes and beer and junk food. Working himself up into a frenzy, the way they always do before the violence starts. 'I think you know my mate, pig. I think you helped to send him down.'

I took a long step back, giving myself enough room, and I aimed a big right hand at his heart. That always slows them down and shuts them up. A hard punch in the heart. Nobody is expecting a big punch in the heart.

And I missed.

He swivelled to address his friends just as I threw the punch and I caught him high on his shoulder, a skimming shot that spun him around and kicked it all off.

Suddenly there were punches in my face, wild punches that scuffed against my ear, my forehead and high on my cheekbone. Nothing punches. Then one caught me flush on the jaw and the next thing I knew I was on my hands and knees. A foot slammed into my ribs. And another, the other side this time. I could not get up.

And then, through their legs as they continued to kick me, I saw Jackson.

The runt who had screamed in my face went down first. Jackson aimed one low, hard kick at his knee, the side of his foot connecting with bone and ligament, ripping them apart, sending him down with a scream that turned them all around.

Jackson wasted nothing.

These were not the same as the kicks that were pounding into me. These were expert, economical movements, shocking in their violence, his foot raising and turning and aimed at knees. And connecting. Another one hit the deck, his face twisted with agony. Two of them went for Jackson at once. He stepped forward, lifted his hands and inserted both his thumbs into their eye sockets. As they whirled away, howling, their hands clutching their faces, he kicked their knees. It wasn't the kind of fighting you learn in a boxing gym. There was nothing fair about it. There was no respect for his opponent. He destroyed them. I wondered if they would ever walk again.

One man was left standing. Jackson moved swiftly towards him and swung his body, his right elbow connecting with the man's mouth, showering front teeth across the pavement. He kicked both of the man's knees before he hit the pavement.

Then he was helping me to my feet and we were running.

We did not speak when we were running. And we did not speak as we cleaned ourselves up and I dressed the wound that he had on his elbow, his flesh torn away by the front teeth of the last man.

And then we looked at each other.

'What kind of chef were you?' I said.

CHAPTER 11

A Media Liaison Officer was meant to be briefing DCI Pat Whitestone before the press conference at West End Central. But it was the Chief Super, DCS Swire, who was doing most of the briefing.

'The message we need to send, Pat, is that nobody takes the law into their own hands. Because that doesn't improve the law. It destroys it. Just keep hammering that point home.'

'Phone call, ma'am,' TDC Billy Greene said.

Behind her glasses, DCI Whitestone's eyes flashed with anger.

'I said no calls, Billy.'

'You'll want to take this, ma'am.' He hesitated. 'I'm afraid it's your son.'

Whitestone took the call and I went to the window where Edie Wren was staring down at the street. The circus was arriving. Camera crews, satellite vans, and dozens of reporters.

'And they're not even serial killers yet,' Edie said.

'Give them time,' I said. 'They've done two. They only need one more to make the grade.'

'Are you all right, Pat?' the Chief Super said behind us.

Whitestone was white-faced with shock.

'It's Just. My son. My Just. I thought he was staying with a friend last night. But he's at the hospital. They tell me he's been there all night. There's been . . . an incident. Someone – a gang – put a bottle across his eyes.' She fought to control herself. She took her glasses off and polished them. 'Ma'am,' she said to the Chief Super. 'They say – they think – the doctors think there's a chance he could lose his sight.'

To me Whitestone's son was a shadow that I had glimpsed on a computer screen late at night when his mother Skyped him from our office. They talked of the domestic minutiae that fill a family's life – homework, meals, triumphs and disappoint- ments, the plans for tomorrow. It suddenly felt as if he would never be the same boy again.

'Go to him,' the Chief Super said. 'Just go.'

'But the press conference—'

'Just go to your son,' Swire said, and she physically escorted Whitestone to the door of MIR-1. 'Go to him now. Nothing is more important.'

When Whitestone was gone, the MLO stood before the Chief Super, shaking her head.

'But who's going to take the press conference?' the MLO said.

'The investigation's senior officer,' the Chief Super said, and she looked at me without enthusiasm.

★ ★ ★

I stared out at the massed ranks of media who had crammed into the briefing room at West End Central. My mouth was dry and my palms were wet. My shirt stuck to my back and my mind was totally blank.

'Good morning, everyone,' I said. Nobody looked up.

'Wait a minute,' the MLO said. 'Your microphone's not on.'

'Bloody hell,' I said, one second after she had turned it on. Now they were all looking at me. Some of them were smiling. Someone shook his head.

'Ah,' I said. 'My name's DC Wolfe and I'm going to give you a briefing on the two murders we are currently investigating.'

I looked at my notes. But they were already shouting questions at me.

I tried to remember the message. The message I had to hammer home. The message about the law not existing when someone takes it into their own hands. Feedback howled out of the microphone.

'DC Wolfe?' a tall, hard-looking redhead said. 'Scarlet Bush.'

'Scarlet,' I said.

'How do you feel that the online community sees these men as heroes?'

'They're not heroes,' I said.

My mouth twisted to show the absurdity of the very idea. It was bone dry although curiously my back was warm and wet with sweat.

'What we have seen in these two films,' I said. 'That's not the law – that is what happens when the law breaks down.'

Scarlet Bush shook her head.

'But the two men who died had both done unspeakable things. One was part of a grooming gang. The other crippled and killed a young boy. How can you stand there and say—'

'It doesn't matter what they've done,' I said, and the room went wild.

'*It doesn't matter what they've done?*'

'*It doesn't matter what they've done?*'

'*It doesn't matter what they've done?*'

I reached for my water just as I caught DCS Swire staring at me from the back of the room. Somehow I knocked the water over.

'Oh, fuck my giddy aunt,' said the Media Liaison Officer as water spread across the front of her dress.

Scarlet Bush laughed.

'The victims of both these evil men were *children*,' she said. 'Blameless, innocent children who had their lives destroyed by wicked men. And you say it doesn't *matter* what they've done?'

'What I meant—'

The MLO leaned across me.

'No more questions!' she shouted into the microphone.

'One last question,' said Scarlet Bush. 'How do you sleep at night, Detective?'

★   ★   ★

It was online news by the time I got to the hospital.

'IT DOESN'T MATTER WHAT THEY'VE DONE!'
Callous cop insults the innocent
By Scarlet Bush, Crime Correspondent

Bad day at the office, I thought.

Pat Whitestone was sleeping in the hospital waiting room.

She was curled up on a row of plastic chairs that were fixed to the sticky carpet as if somebody might decide they were worth stealing. Without her glasses her face had an unguarded look that was so different to the woman I knew from work, she almost looked like someone else.

I went to get myself a cup of coffee from a vending machine that I had passed on the way in. It came out black and boiling hot. I stood in the corridor, sipping it as it cooled down, watching the cancer patients in their dressing gowns smoking their last cigarette of the day beyond the big glass doors of the main entrance. When I came back to the waiting room, she was awake and sitting up.

'Max,' she said, and I knew that there had been no real rest for her in this place. She slowly put her glasses on and I had never seen her face look more vulnerable.

'How's your son?' I said. 'How's Just?'

She nodded, as if struggling to understand their new reality.

'He – uh – lost his sight in one eye.' She shook her head. 'Somebody hit him in the face with a bottle, Max.' She put on her child-sized trainers, ran her fingers through her messy blonde hair. 'In a club. A fight. Over some girl. He was meant to be looking at some girl. And his right eye – his right eye took the full force of the blow and the left eye got a shower of glass fragments. He's lost that right eye, Max. That's gone. That's mush. Forget about that right eye, Max. The left eye has a detached retina and all the bits of glass in it and – uh – they are trying to save that other eye. Dr Patel is doing his best, Max. But there's glass . . . bits of glass . . . in his eye . . . his left eye.'

'Pat,' I said. 'My God, Pat.'

She scratched her head. She sighed. She exhaled.

'So that's where we are,' she said. 'Waiting for news about his other eye.' She shook her head and then she looked at me and her face stirred with the start of a smile. 'What about you?'

'Me?'

'I left you in the lurch. Up at West End Central. The press conference. How did it go?'

'You didn't see it?'

'No.'

'Of course not. Of course you didn't see it. It went well.'

'That's good, Max.'

I felt like putting my arm around her. But she

looked me straight in the eye and I saw that she was still the woman I knew, she was still my boss, she was still the most experienced homicide detective in 27 Savile Row, and the moment passed, even though her eyes were wet with tears, even though I had never felt closer to her.

I sat down next to her.

'What happened, Pat?'

She shook her head. She told me the story in broken fragments. Because it made no sense and yet at the same time it was all horribly easy to imagine.

'Just the usual teenage rubbish,' she said. 'It started with a lie – Just told me he was going to play video games at his friend's house. I believed him. And his friend told his mother the same lie. And instead they sneaked off to this place. To have a few drinks. To pretend that they're not children any more. It's what teenagers do, Max. Some boys out – Just and a couple of his friends from school – nice kids – they were in some little pub off the Holloway Road – then suddenly these other boys were shouting at Just – that he had looked at a girl – but his friend – I spoke to his friend – his friend sat in the hospital all night long, too scared to go home – he said that Just didn't do anything – he didn't even see this girl – but they – one of them – this gang – the Dog Town Boys, they call themselves – they put a bottle across his face – and it broke – the glass – and his eyes . . .'

I took her hands in mine.

She needed to say no more. It was the kind of ordinary madness that happened every night of the year. But it usually happened to someone else.

'We're such a small family, Max. Me and Just. You don't realise it until a time like this. I feel like I should call someone. But who can I call? My parents are dead. I don't have brothers or sisters. There's no one to call, is there?'

'What about his father?' I said, and when I saw her face twist with anger I knew immediately it was the wrong thing to say.

'He's dead to us,' she said. 'He left us to get on with it. And we will get on with it. Even this.'

Then we were silent until a doctor appeared in the doorway. A thirty-something Asian in blue scrubs, in a rush. He looked around the waiting room.

'Miss . . . Whitehead?'

'Whitestone,' she said, standing up. 'Where's the other doctor? Dr Patel?'

'Dr Patel's shift ended. I'm Dr Khan. I've just come out of surgery with your son, Jason.'

'His name is Justin.'

'Exactly.' He looked at her, his face a mask, and my stomach fell away. 'It's not good news, I'm afraid,' he said, consulting his notes. 'We managed to remove the fragments of glass from your son's left iris and its supporting tissue but unfortunately the optic nerve has been detached from the back of the eye . . .'

He looked at her, nervously licked his lips, waiting for her to fill in the terrible blank.

But she said nothing.

'What does that mean, Doctor?' I said.

'The eye is a sphere with a transparent bulge at the front – the cornea – and a stalk – the optic nerve – at the back. The glass was in the cornea but the optic nerve – which carries visual impulses to the brain – has been severed . . .'

'What does it *mean*?'

'Vision is not possible without the optic nerve.'

'So he's . . .' she said, swallowing hard. Swallowing it all down. The rage. The grief. The fear. The disbelief. Emotions that I could not begin to imagine because it was not my child in that operating room. She could not say the word. It seemed as if she would never say it, as if she would live and die without ever saying the word. And then finally she said it.

'Blind?' she said. 'He's blind?'

The doctor was saying something about the benefits of counselling but Pat Whitestone wasn't listening. She was gone, calling her son's name, out of the waiting room and into the corridor.

'Just! Just! Just!'

'You can't—' a nurse said at their station.

'He's resting after the operation,' said another nurse outside her son's room. 'You mustn't—'

But she must and she did.

I followed her.

The room was in darkness and so was her boy, still unconscious from the general anaesthetic.

99

There were white bandages over his eyes that covered half his face.

'My beautiful son,' Pat Whitestone said, sinking to her knees beside the bed, and then the tears came, hopeless tears that seemed as if they would never stop.

'I'm here now,' she said.

I stood by her side but I did not touch her and I did not speak.

And I wished there was a father and grandparents and siblings in this room to help her carry a weight that she should never have to carry alone. But there was only me.

'Those bastards,' she said. 'Those fucking bastards.'

She closed her eyes and began to rock back and forth and her mouth tightened with a rage and a violence that I had never seen in her before. And as I watched her she gasped, as if she suddenly couldn't breathe, and lifted her face, her eyes still screwed tight, as if she could actually see the bastards who had done this to her son, as if she could see their faces, as if she could see them getting what they deserved.

As if – and the thought came unbidden – she could see them screaming for mercy as they swung from the end of a rope.

CHAPTER 12

When I got to 27 Savile Row in the morning I was hoping to see Pat's familiar figure running the show up in MIR-1, but she was clearly still at the hospital with her son.

TDC Billy Greene was putting a photograph of Hector Welles on the whitewall that he must have downloaded from Welles' company's website – one of those official portraits that big corporations take of their staff, Welles smiling with shrewd, bright-eyed confidence, as though your money would be safe with him.

It sat next to the police mugshot of Mahmud Irani.

Colin Cho and a couple of his people from the Police Central e-crime Unit were hunkered down around a laptop. Dr Joe was eating a frozen yogurt as he contemplated the giant map of London that covered one wall. And the voice analyst – Tara Jones – was at a workstation, replaying the one line of dialogue from the hanging of Hector Welles, repeatedly stopping and starting the film as her black hair swung across her face and she pushed it away.

But no DCI Whitestone.

'No word from the boss?' I said.

Billy shook his head. 'Should I try to contact her?'

I thought of the blinded boy in his hospital bed.

'Leave her,' I said.

I was acting SIO now.

'*Do you know why you have been brought to this place of execution? Do you know – do you know – do you know?*'

The graph on her laptop jumped and fell in time to the words.

'How's it going?' I said, but Tara Jones ignored me, and continued to pore over that solitary line of dialogue.

'*Do you know – do you know – do you know?*'

Still looking sickened from his viewing of Hector Welles, our history man, Professor Hitchens, stood before the giant map of the city.

'So the spot where Hector Welles' body was discovered,' Dr Joe asked him. 'That was Tyburn?'

'As far as we can ascertain,' said Hitchens. 'But it's not quite so simple. DC Wolfe was correct – this was Tyburn. But the reason Tyburn's *exact* location is disputed is because Tyburn's Triple Tree was portable.' Hitchens glanced at me. 'Tyburn was certainly here – though the gallows was probably in twenty different places over the course of the centuries. But the area seems to have deep significance for the – what's the word? – the perps.'

'And what did they do?' Edie said. 'Back in the

day. They just assembled their moveable gallows like an IKEA flat-pack and then strung them up?'

'The condemned stood on the back of a horse-drawn cart,' Hitchens said. 'The rope was attached around their neck to the cross-beam of the Tyburn tree. The cart drove off and death was by strangulation rather than broken neck. The condemned were mostly drawn from the ranks of the poor, but Samuel Pepys saw one of his closest friends – a gentleman – hanged at Tyburn. It wasn't quick and it wasn't pretty. And it wasn't meant to be.'

'So if we want to stake out the area,' I said, 'what counts as Tyburn?'

Hitchens traced a large area on the map that seemed to cover Hyde Park and a hefty chunk of the West End.

'The area just north of Marble Arch probably saw most of the fifty thousand executions. But all roads in this area lead to Tyburn. Until the eighteenth century, Park Lane was called Tyburn Lane and Oxford Street was called Tyburn Road.'

'So they could dump a body anywhere from Hyde Park Corner to Oxford Street and still call it Tyburn?' I said.

Professor Hitchens shrugged. 'Theoretically,' he said.

'You *really* think they'd come back here with every plain clothes copper in the Met looking for them?' Edie asked me.

I looked at Dr Joe for the answer.

'I think they'll find the temptation to stick to

their ritual almost impossible to resist,' he said.
'If they kill again.'

'And you think they will, Dr Joe?'

'I don't think they can stop themselves. I think
they have set themselves the task of punishing
all the wicked in the world.'

'And who are they, Dr Joe? What kind of men
are we after?'

'They are men who clearly believe that justice
has been thwarted. They're obsessive about the
judicial process – or at least their version of
the judicial process. The Albert Pierrepoint obses-
sion, the kangaroo court, the reading of charges. I
would guess they have some experience of the law
and they didn't much like it.'

I waited for him to say what we were both
thinking. But he just finished his frozen yogurt,
because it would have sounded like blasphemy in
here. So I said it for him.

'They could be cops,' I said.

'Possible,' said Dr Joe.

I turned to the woman with the swinging hair.
She had her back to me.

'How we doing on the voice recognition,
Tara?'

She ignored me, and stood up to pitch an empty
coffee cup into a wastepaper bin. She was a tall
woman in flat shoes. One of those tall women who
are never really comfortable with their height.
Leggy. Slim. At first I had thought she was shy or
self-contained. Now she just seemed indifferent to

the people in this office. Especially me. She sat down and played the same piece of tape.

'*Do you know why you have been brought to this place of execution?*'

I felt a surge of irritation.

'Max?' Edie said. 'I don't think that you were ever properly introduced. Tara is—'

And Tara Jones turned and looked up at me, as if seeing me for the first time as she pushed back her swinging black hair that fell across her pale and serious fabulous face.

And I finally realised that Tara Jones was deaf.

'This is what I've found,' she said. 'It is the same voice on both the Mahmud Irani and the Hector Welles tape. The voice has the glottal stops of a London or southeast England accent, but there are distinct signs of modification – think of it as an Estuary accent that has learned Received Pronunciation. In other words, the subject is not speaking with the voice that he grew up with. Either he has had elocution lessons or, more likely, moved to a social strata beyond the environment of his parents. It happens a lot. For most people, a university education will do it.'

And I thought about her own voice.

There was nothing wrong with it. But now I knew of her deafness it was as if she was saying the words but not hearing them.

'And there's something else,' she said. 'There is an unusual cadence to some of his sentences, as if there was a foreign language spoken in his home. And he can speak it too.'

I was impressed.

'And you know all that from one sentence?' I said.

I smiled at her.

She didn't smile back.

'Voice biometrics – the digital analysis of speech patterns – is all done by software,' Tara Jones said. She gave me a cool look. 'So I think you'll find that my deafness is no impediment to my job.'

'Of course not,' I said, my face flushing with shame.

The door to MIR-1 opened and DCI Whitestone walked in. She seemed ten years older and ten pounds thinner than when I had seen her last night. She looked shattered. She stared at us and we stared back.

The silence was broken by Billy Greene.

'Jesus Christ,' he said. 'We've got another one!'

Then it was on the big screen.

A young man with tightly cropped hair was being led into that room where the sun did not reach, as the dark figures hovered in the background pinning something to the white brickwork stained green with the ages.

'There's no time-and-date stamp,' Edie said.

I turned to Colin Cho.

'Is this live?' I said.

He shook his head. 'I don't know, Max.'

'*Is it live?*' I shouted.

'I don't fucking know, Max!' Colin shouted back. 'Give us a chance!'

The PCeU team desperately huddled around a single laptop. The phones all began to ring at once because they were about to reach the magic number. Three is the magic number.

The Hanging Club were about to become serial killers.

I looked at DCI Whitestone for guidance. But she had slumped down into a workstation as if she was tired beyond belief, as if she had not slept for days.

And her eyes never left the big screen.

'Marble Arch, Edie,' I said. 'Go with her, Billy. I'll call CTC and get some bodies down there in case they're dumb enough to dump the body in the same place.'

CTC – also known as SO15 – is Counter Terrorism Command, a special operations branch in the Met. They have over a thousand surveillance officers at their call. Before I came to 27 Savile Row, I had been one of them.

I looked at Whitestone to see that I had made the right move. But she was still staring at the screen.

Edie Wren and Billy Greene went out of the door just as up on the big screen the noose was placed around the young man's head.

'Do you know why you have been brought to this place of execution?'

He did not reply.

He blinked back tears and I saw the track marks of the long-term heroin addict on his arms.

'I wonder who he killed?' Whitestone said, her voice small and far away, as if she was talking to herself.

'It appears to be live,' Colin Cho said. 'Thank you all for your patience.'

There were photographs on the white-brick walls that had been stained green by time.

Two photographs.

A smiling soldier, in black and white, a British soldier of the war against Nazi Germany.

And a colour photograph of the same man, some sixty years later, an old man now, leaning back in an armchair and grinning with a modest Christmas tree behind him.

'According to the online community,' Colin Cho said, 'the old gentleman is Bert Page, a Normandy veteran and a retired Fleet Street printer, who is still in a coma after being mugged by Darren Donovan, a heroin addict.' A pause. 'And Metcall has received numerous confirmations that the young man in these images is Darren Donovan . . .'

'So – if that's true – they're not just hanging murderers now,' Dr Joe said.

'And it was never only murderers that were hanged at Tyburn,' Professor Hitchens said. 'In the eighteenth century there were two hundred offences punishable with death in this country. Vagrancy. Theft. Sacrilege. Being in the company of gypsies for one month . . . They hanged seven-year-old children who stole a letter, and they hanged highwaymen, and they hanged the men who executed Charles I.'

'I want these identities confirmed,' I said. 'The old man in the photos and the young man they're hanging. I'm not taking the word of the online mob.' But, deep in my bones, I already believed it. Darren Donovan, a drug addict, had attacked and robbed an elderly man for a few coins. And now he was going to pay for his crime. With his life.

'Do you know why you have been brought to this place of execution?'

This was the most leisurely hanging.

Darren Donovan did not plead for mercy as Mahmud Irani had pleaded for mercy.

Darren Donovan did not fight for his life as Hector Welles had fought for his life.

He was pathetically passive as he was helped up onto the kitchen stool. He meekly inclined his head as the noose was placed around his neck. The only sign of his abject terror was the way he could not stop shaking.

And then there was a noise.

A single sound just before they kicked the stool away.

I looked at Tara Jones. And I saw the screen before her, with the sudden spike at that single sound.

'What was that, Pat?' I said. 'A name? Did somebody say a name?'

109

Whitestone gave no sign she had heard me.

I looked at Tara Jones.

'I don't know,' the voice analyst said. 'But I can work with it.'

And then they hanged him.

'Dear God,' Dr Joe said, and he turned his face away.

But the rest of us in MIR-1 watched as the stool flew away and Darren Donovan's legs kicked out at eternity, his tongue lolling, his eyes bulging in his head and the dark stain spreading on the crotch of his ragged jeans.

And when the life had been strangled out of him, the camera cut away to the smiling face of a young soldier who was off to storm the beaches of Normandy.

I looked at Whitestone as she stared at the screen, her face a mask of indifference, watching it all with a terrible calm, as if some people deserve to die.

CHAPTER 13

Mrs Murphy was dozing on the sofa with Stan on her lap when I got home.

Our loft was silent because Mrs Murphy always watched TV with the sound turned down when Scout was sleeping. As I kicked off my shoes and padded to Scout's room, Stan half-opened his eyes, yawned widely and snuggled back down.

It was another night when the heat would not quit and Scout had kicked off the single sheet that covered her. She stirred as I pulled it back up.

'Daddy?'

'Sleep now, angel, it's late.'

'But Jackson went to work.'

'They have to work at night in the market.'

'Mmm.'

She buried her sleepy face in the pillow and it made me smile.

'You enjoying your summer holiday?'

'It lasts forever.'

I laughed.

'It feels that way when you're little. The bigger you get, the faster the time goes. Sleep now, angel.'

'And you too.'

'I will.'

But after Mrs Murphy had gone home, I sat in the window, looking at the blaze of Smithfield meat market. Dozens of white-coated porters were unloading vans and trucks, but I couldn't see Jackson.

At midnight the five-ton clock bell of St Paul's Cathedral – Great Tom, they call it – struck the hour and I called Edie. SO15 had sent a dozen surveillance officers to Marble Arch.

'I can't see the others,' Edie said. 'But then I guess that's the point.' I could feel her frustration. 'Do you really think they're going to leave a third body here, Max?'

'It feels like a long shot because I don't see how they can do it without getting collared. They must know we'll be waiting for them. But at the same time, I don't see how the crazy bastards can resist it.'

I told Edie to go home.

My old colleagues at SO15 would be out there all night. They would be the homeless man sleeping in Hyde Park, and they would be the courting couple snogging in the doorway of a closed department store, and they would be the late-night dog walker and they would be the dark figures sitting unnoticed in parked cars.

And they would be waiting.

I turned off the lights and was about to go to bed when I saw my MacBook Air on the kitchen table, exactly where I had left it. But the laptop was closed now and I was sure I had left it open. Stan stirred in his basket as I powered up.

I went on Safari and hit *Show History*.

And it wasn't my history.

Last visited today
The Hanging Club – Google search
@AlbertPierrepointUK – Twitter
Mahmud Irani – YouTube
Hector Welles – YouTube
Tyburn – Wikipedia, the free encyclopedia
The Hanging Club – Wikipedia, the free encyclopedia
Albert Pierrepoint – Wikipedia, the free encyclopedia
Bringing Back the Death Penalty – *Daily Mail* Online
'Let 'em dangle!' – *Sun* Online
Public executions are back – *Guardian*
@albertpierrepoint – Twitter
Darren Donovan – YouTube
Darren Donovan – YouTube
Darren Donovan – YouTube
Darren Donovan – YouTube
Darren Donovan – YouTube
Vigilantes Hang Third Man – *Daily Telegraph* – *Sunday Telegraph* – *Telegraph* Online

There was more. Much more. Reams of the stuff. I glanced towards the big windows where the lights of Smithfield shone. I had told my old friend that he could use my laptop whenever he needed it. It looked as though he had spent all day on it, reading about just one thing.

I closed the laptop and went to bed. But when sleep came it seemed to abruptly jerk just out of reach, jolting me awake, and I spent hours trying to get comfortable, trying to empty my mind, trying too hard to fall asleep. I must have dropped off at some point because in the light period of sleep, the last part of sleep, when dreams come in the shallows, I found myself waking from a dream of Marble Arch in the darkness and slipping from my bed and walking to the window.

It was still early, before five, but the rising sun was turning the great dome of St Paul's as white as bone. And at the meat market, the night shift was over and Jackson was coming home.

I watched him cross Charterhouse Street, grinning at something one of his workmates had said, and the light of the new sun was so dazzling on the front of his white porter's coat that at first you could not tell that it was smeared with fresh blood.

A few hours later I stood alone in MIR-1 looking at the floor-to-ceiling map of London and sipping a triple espresso from Bar Italia.

Professor Hitchens came in with his motorbike helmet under his arm, already sweating inside his corduroy.

'Tyburn,' he said. 'It's a river, isn't it? That's where

everything else comes from. Tyburn Road, Tyburn gallows – it's all named after the River Tyburn. The Tyburn is one of the great underground rivers of London.'

'The gallows is named after the river?' I said.

He nodded his egg-shaped head. 'Look at this,' he said.

He produced a battered book from his saddlebag. *Thames: Sacred River* by Peter Ackroyd. Professor Hitchens found the page he wanted and pointed a fat finger at a passage. He began to read:

'*There is some intimate association between the river and what we call "paganism". Something has settled there. The river in some sense becomes the sacred witness of punishment . . .*'

He looked at me with his eyes shining.

'Don't you see? *The river in some sense becomes the sacred witness of punishment!*'

Tara Jones walked in and stared at us. Hitchens continued reading.

'*It is perhaps not coincidental that the two major sites of execution on land, Tyburn and Smithfield, were adjacent to the Thames tributaries of the Tyburn and the Fleet.*' He shook his head with wonder. 'Can't you see what it means?'

'Wait a minute,' I said. 'Let me get this straight. London's underground rivers – the Tyburn and the rest – they once flowed over ground?'

'Yes!'

'So what happened to them?'

'We built this city on top of them.' He waved at

the giant map on the wall. 'As the city has grown over the centuries, the rivers became deeper. The London sewer system is built on the template of the city's underground rivers. But they're still there.'

I looked at the map, and back at him.

'So the Tyburn – the River Tyburn – still exists?' I said.

'Of course!'

'Where does it flow?' I said. 'Show me.'

He pointed at a great swathe of green towards the top of the map.

'The source of the Tyburn is Hampstead. It runs south – parallel to the Finchley Road, down to Swiss Cottage, through Regent's Park. In the West End it follows the path of Marylebone Lane before passing through Mayfair and into the Thames.'

'We're probably standing on it,' Tara said.

Hitchens' prematurely aged face split into a wide grin.

'Savile Row? I would say that it's extremely likely the Tyburn is directly below us.'

I thought about it, let it settle.

'They're not going to go back to the site of the gallows because they know we'll be waiting. But – if they are so obsessed with the ritual of punishment – they could still leave the body in the Tyburn – the River Tyburn.'

'It has to be a possibility,' Hitchens said.

'How many miles of river are we looking at?' I asked.

He shook his head. 'The Tyburn winds and turns . . .'

'Ballpark figure, Professor.'

'It could be as many as ten miles.'

I shook my head.

'Only someone much more important than me can authorise a search of that scale.'

I called the Chief Super's office. They put me straight through and I told her what I wanted.

'Where's Pat Whitestone?' DCS Swire said.

The truth is I didn't know where DCI Whitestone was or if she was ever coming to work again.

'Ma'am, I believe she must be with her son at the hospital.'

A pause.

'Do it,' she said. 'Send everyone you can down there. But I want them all out at the end of the shift.'

'Ma'am?'

'London sewers have the highest concentration of cocaine of any waters in Europe.'

For a moment I had the image of London's paranoid coke users all flushing away their drug of choice.

But that wasn't quite it.

'The city has the highest number of cocaine users in the northern hemisphere and their urine all ends up in the sewers,' DCS Swire told me. 'The trace cocaine in London's waste waters is 500 per cent higher than anywhere else in Europe. If anyone stays down there too long, we're going to start

117

getting cardiac arrests. And then we're going to start getting lawsuits. So one full shift and they're all out, understood, DC Wolfe?'

'Yes, ma'am.'

I'll tell them not to inhale, I thought, heading for the door as I speed-dialled Edie Wren.

Tara Jones called me back.

'I got the voiceprint of that sound we heard on the latest film,' she said. 'It's not a name. And it's not a word.'

'What is it?'

'It's laughter.' She shook her head as if she could not understand such a thing, and a veil of glossy black hair swung in front of her lovely face. I watched her push it away. 'The noise is a short bark of someone . . . laughing. What does it mean?'

'They're starting to enjoy it,' I said.

We had been looking in the wrong place. They were never coming back to the site of Tyburn gallows. So almost one hundred officers – Specialist Search Teams from West End Central and New Scotland Yard, surveillance officers from SO15's Counter Terrorism Command – spent eight hours of a long summer day wading through the miles of sewers that trace the flow of the Tyburn.

And at the end of a long shift we knew this was the wrong place too.

I showered and changed my clothes at West End Central but I felt that I could still smell the ancient stink of subterranean London on my skin. MIR-1 was deserted apart from Hitchens, who was sitting at a workstation reading his Peter Ackroyd book. I stared up at the great map of London that covers one wall of MIR-1.

'Where does it come out?' I said.

'What?' He didn't look up from his book.

'This river. The River Tyburn.' I took a step towards the map. 'The Tyburn is a tributary of the Thames, right?'

Now he was looking up.

'Yes.'

'So it doesn't flow into the sea,' I said. 'And it doesn't disappear underground. At some point the River Tyburn flows into the River Thames.'

'That's correct.'

'Where?'

He quickly pulled his iPad from his saddlebag and found an ancient map of London.

'The Rocque map of London in 1746,' he said. And then, 'Vauxhall Bridge.'

'So the Tyburn flows into the Thames at Vauxhall Bridge?'

'Yes.'

'It will be quicker if we take your bike,' I said.

Vauxhall Bridge rose up before us as Hitchens tore down Millbank on his old 500cc Royal Enfield with me riding pillion.

Downriver the sun was sinking behind Battersea Power Station. On the far side of the Thames

I could see the great tiered building housing MI6, the Secret Intelligence Service, at Vauxhall Cross. Hitchens steered his bike in the empty forecourt outside Tate Britain and we left it there.

We found some stone steps that led down to the Thames Path, the walkway that runs along the riverbank. I started towards the bridge, Hitchens struggling to keep up with me.

'Down there,' he panted. 'A culvert.'

I was directly opposite the MI6 building when I saw it. A large round hole punched into reinforced concrete, big enough for a man to stand up in, pouring a shallow but steady stream of water into the Thames. The culvert was one level lower than the Thames Path, and I realised that it was invisible from the road.

'Is that it?' I said. 'That's the Tyburn?'

I don't know what I had been expecting.

His breathless voice was behind me. 'According to Rocque—'

But I was already going down the steps that led right on to the riverbank and so I missed what Rocque had noted in the eighteenth century. I stepped into the culvert and the water covered my shoes. I took another step and peered into blackness. But the concrete culvert looked too modern to mark the end of a river that had flowed here for thousands of years.

Hitchens hesitated at the mouth of the culvert, keeping his feet dry.

'This can't be it,' I shouted, and my voice echoed back to me.

'What's that?'

'I said—'

And then I saw the body.

One arm reaching from the deeper darkness of the culvert. The limb bare, white and – as I edged through the water towards it – I saw the ghastly scars of heroin addiction, the track marks on the limb looking like a child's join-the-dots game.

Hitchens called out to me. 'Detective?'

'This is it!' I shouted.

I went further into the black hole and the water was deeper here, over my shoes, and much colder. And there he was – Darren Donovan, perhaps ten metres back from the Thames, his cropped head face down in the black waters of the Tyburn.

Then the darkness suddenly rose up and slammed into me, knocking the wind out of me and throwing me backwards against the curved wall of the concrete culvert.

I banged my head hard against the wall and sat down in the water with a thump, the base of my spine smacking against the reinforced concrete.

And then I felt the hands around my throat.

I was thrown onto my back as if I was weightless, the hands never letting go, digging deep into my flesh, their grip tighter now.

Large hands. Strong hands. Trying to kill me, trying to choke the life out of me.

I stared up at the large figure in the darkness,

and I kicked out wildly, clawing at the hands around my neck and then raking the thick muscled arms, reaching for where I knew his eyes would be but unable to find them, unable to get even close, all the strength ebbing out of me with every passing second.

Already my breath had stopped. Already the blood had stopped.

'Detective?' Hitchens said at the entrance to the culvert. 'Max?'

The hands let me go.

I was aware of the dark bulky figure splashing towards the light. I tried to call out to Hitchens but found I could not speak. I tried to get up but found I could not move. Sickness overwhelmed me. Far away someone was calling my name.

But I was bone-tired, suddenly far too exhausted to respond, and so I lay back and closed my eyes for just a little while, needing a moment before I got up and went on, my head resting in the ancient waters of the Tyburn.

PART II

THE CROSS-BEAM AND THE ROPE

CHAPTER 14

I sat on a bench by the Thames watching the sun go down in a blaze of red over Chelsea while a couple of detective inspectors from New Scotland Yard did the hot debrief, the interview that takes place in the golden hour after a major incident. There wasn't much to tell them but we went over it again and again and again as the sun sunk lower over West London.

'He was big,' I said. 'Freakishly big. Abnormally strong. Tossed me about as if I weighed nothing.'

One of the detective inspectors stifled a yawn. The other one closed his notebook.

'Funny thing is,' he said, 'that when you get dumped on your arse, they tend to get bigger and stronger every time you tell the story. You want us to drive you to an A&E?'

I shook my head.

'Nothing broken,' I said, and they both gave me their cocky Scotland Yard grins.

The press were waiting for me when I arrived at West End Central in the morning.

They were milling around and sucking down

caffeine under the big blue lamp that hangs above the entrance to 27 Savile Row, young journalists and older photographers, maybe twenty of them, sent out to collect whatever scraps they could on the story that was dominating the rolling news. They stirred at the sight of me. I recognised Scarlet Bush but I did not stop walking. They all crowded in with their little digital microphones and their cameras and their questions.

'DC Wolfe? Scarlet Bush, *Daily Post*. Is it true that you were assaulted when you found the body of Darren Donovan? What's that mark around your throat, Max? Did the Hanging Club do that to you?'

They followed me inside. A uniformed sergeant, red-faced with irritation, stepped out from behind his desk and began shooing them back. The questions became nastier when they knew I wasn't going to answer them.

'Is the Hanging Club doing a better job than the police at cleaning the streets, Max?'

'How does it feel to be hunting heroes?'

'What about the victims? Do you ever think about them?'

'Did you see one of them, Max? Did you see one of the Hanging Club?'

No, I thought. But I know a man who did.

In a quiet corner of MIR-1, Professor Adrian Hitchens sat working with a police sketch artist.

'No, no . . . those eyes are wrong . . . can you erase that and try again? Could we possibly have another go at the mouth?'

126

It's never easy. Anyone who sits down with a police sketch artist has been a witness to a serious crime. They are attempting to recall a face that they saw for only moments, usually during a criminal act that was accompanied by extreme violence. In the case of our history man, he was attempting to remember the face of someone who had come barrelling out of a culvert without warning and knocked him flat on his ample backside.

I nodded to the police sketch artist, a woman around thirty who looked as though she had the patience of a Zen monk. She had probably grown up wanting to be the next Picasso or Edward Hopper.

'How's it going?'

She showed me her sketchpad with a half-smile. She had drawn the outline of a large oval-shaped head with a sizeable nose in the middle and a pair of ears stuck to the side. And that was it. I looked at Hitchens.

'So we're looking for Mr Potato Head?' I said.

'I can only draw what he saw, Max,' said the sketch artist. 'And Professor Hitchens doesn't know what he saw.'

He wrung his hands. 'I'm sorry, I'm sorry.'

'How long have you been working on this?' I said.

The sketch artist glanced at her watch. 'Couple of hours?'

I shook my head and stared at Hitchens with disbelief.

'Tell me one more time what happened,' I said.

He brushed his nicotine-stained fingers across the great sweaty dome of his head.

'You entered the culvert. When you didn't come back out, I called out to you because I was worried. I can't recall exactly what I said . . .'

'You said, *Detective* and then you said *Max* – and that was when my assailant let me go and did a runner . . . Then what?'

'I was trying to text you,' Hitchens said. 'I was looking at my phone when I heard footsteps in the water – moving very fast. I thought it was you – and I looked up and . . . I stared straight into his face just before he sent me flying. And that's where you found me. Sitting on my backside.'

Tara Jones came in and began clearing her desk. She saw me looking at her and nodded, sending a torrent of black hair forward. She pushed it off her face and began packing away the hardware that was scattered all over the workstation she had used for the last month.

I patted Hitchens on the arm. 'You saw him. You did, Adrian. Briefly – very briefly – but you saw him. But it's just out of reach.'

'I don't understand why I can't recall . . .'

'It's the shock of violence. Even if you were used to it, this would be hard. And you're not used to it. You just had one of the worst experiences of your life. Don't feel too bad. I looked at him too and I didn't see a thing.'

'But you were in darkness and I was in blazing sunshine . . .'

'You want me to try some software?' the sketch artist asked.

In recent years there has been a move to improve facial composites with what we call a feature recognition system – the witness is shown complete faces until a final image emerges. But I shook my head.

'Pencil and pad still works best,' I said. 'Just keep trying,' I told Hitchens.

'I am . . .'

'Try harder.'

I walked over to Tara Jones. I had worked out by now that I needed to be directly facing her before I started talking. She looked up at me and smiled politely.

'You're leaving,' I said.

'My contract with the Met was for a month. And the month's over. So . . .'

'Thanks for your help with the tapes.'

She laughed. Good teeth. So white and even that there must have been an orthodontist in her childhood. Middle-class teeth. I wondered what her parents had been like and how they had dealt with her disability. As far as I could tell, it had not stopped her doing anything she wanted.

'I didn't do much,' she said. She slipped a thin MacBook Air into a messenger bag. 'But then – in my defence – they didn't say very much, did they? I've run full voice biometrics of everything we have.'

I suddenly realised that it was unlikely I would ever see her again.

'May I ask you something, Tara?'

She nodded, shoving back her hair, the wedding ring a glint of gold among the black.

I hesitated. 'You don't do the thing with the hands,' I said.

She wasn't offended. If anything, she just seemed a little weary, as if she had explained this one so many times that it was becoming a chore.

'Signing? No, I don't sign. Why – can you read sign language?'

I felt stupid.

'No – I just . . .'

'Not all members of the deaf community sign,' she said, very patiently. 'It's a misconception that all deaf people sign. It's very much a personal choice. I can speak and I can read lips. I don't consider myself to be culturally deaf. That is, I don't define myself by my lack of hearing.' She zipped her messenger bag shut. Her desk was clear now. She smiled brightly. 'OK?'

I nodded. 'Thank you. For everything.'

I wanted to know more but there was no time.

Edie Wren was standing in the door of MIR-1 and beyond her I could see Dr Joe Stephen, checking his messages.

Tara Jones was ready to leave 27 Savile Row.

And the dead were waiting for me.

CHAPTER 15

The three dead men lay naked on their stainless steel beds in the Iain West Forensic Suite at the Westminster Public Mortuary, untroubled by the temperature that is forever kept just a degree or two above freezing point.

The first thing you noticed about them were the large Y-shaped incisions on their torsos where Elsa Olsen, our forensic pathologist of choice, had chopped open their ribcages with exactly the kind of green-handled pruning shears you can buy in any gardening centre to trim your roses. And the next thing you noticed were the burn marks around their necks.

'Cause of death was strangulation,' Elsa said. 'All three of them. Method of death was almost certainly some kind of wire noose.'

'Not rope?' I said.

'Rope would probably leave trace evidence in their wounds,' Elsa said. 'And I couldn't find any rope fibres. I suggest they used some other kind of material.'

'And they know what they're doing,' I said.

I stared at the cadavers. Mahmud Irani. Hector

Welles. And Darren Donovan. Three men of wildly disparate ages, income and background. Irani had the soft spreading gut of a man who had spent a lifetime sitting down. Welles had been a confirmed fitness fanatic, spending hours pushing himself in parodies of manual labour. And Donovan had abused his body with Class A drugs since his early teens but still had the unearned slimness of youth.

Even their crimes were very different.

Irani had been one of a gang that abused vulnerable young girls for years. Welles, the heartless hit-and-run driver who was found wanting in a mad moment. And Donovan was a career junkie who regularly mugged elderly pensioners for his next shot of poison.

They did not look so different now.

Elsa considered the three of us shivering inside our blue scrubs and hairnets. On one side of me Edie Wren was impassive, her pale young face a mask of professional curiosity, but on the other side I could feel Dr Joe shaking with tension. It is never an easy thing to step inside the Iain West Forensic Suite for the first time.

'So are you SIO on this investigation, Max?' Elsa said.

'Acting SIO,' I said. 'Until DCI Whitestone returns. Dr Joe's with us looking for signatures, if that's all right with you.'

The tall Norwegian pathologist nodded, anxious that she should only have to say all this once. She slowly circled the dead men on their stainless steel tables.

'Life flows through the neck,' she said. 'The fragile, essential neck. Blood is pumped from the heart to the brain. Oxygen flows to the lungs. Compress the neck hard enough, and all that abruptly stops. You see the marks on their necks?'

On all three of them, the hanging mark angled diagonally across the neck, the highest point almost touching the left ear, where the noose's knot had been. On all three men, the furrow of the hanging mark was far more shallow here. But it was pale yellow on Darren Donovan's neck, a darker yellow on the raw skin of Hector Welles' neck and a dark brown on Mahmud Irani, the earliest victim.

I felt the thick bile of revulsion rise up inside me and I swallowed it down. Deep breath, Max, I told myself. It's about to get worse.

With a long thin stainless steel implement, Elsa gently prised open the mouth of Mahmud Irani. Then she did the same with Hector Welles, and finally Darren Donovan.

'See that?' Elsa said, her blue eyes bright. 'When a man has been hanged, his tongue turns purple.'

Dr Joe had begun to pant like a dog on a summer's day.

'I'm OK,' he said, not looking at me. 'I'm fine. Really.'

'This is how strangulation by hanging works,' Elsa continued. 'Once the noose is around your neck and there is nothing to support you, you are

133

killed by your own body weight. Strangulation compresses the carotid arteries in the neck, shutting off the supply of blood to the brain and causing the brain to swell so much that it plugs the top of the spinal column. This causes a reaction known as the vagal reflex, which stops the heart. The compression of the neck closes the trachea and aborts the supply of oxygen to the lungs. So – no blood to the brain and no air to the lungs. Bad news. The victim passes out due to suffocation. And then he dies.'

'How long does it take, Elsa?' I asked.

'It depends. But it is not a quick way to die. Strangulation by hanging takes at least five minutes, but no more than twenty.'

'Do we have any defensive wounds?'

'There are no defensive wounds on Mahmud Irani or Darren Donovan, although there *are* signs of advanced intravenous drug use on Mr Donovan.'

'What does advanced mean?' Dr Joe asked.

'The veins of his arms had collapsed and he was shooting up between his toes,' Elsa said. 'But Hector Welles is the only one of them with extensive defensive wounds.'

I remembered Welles fighting for his life as the dark figures struggled to control him.

He knew what they had done to Mahmud Irani.

'There are contusions and welts on Mr Welles' arms where he was restrained,' Elsa said. 'Some facial bruising where he was punched or kicked.' She smiled sadly at me. 'But unfortunately no skin tissue under his fingernails, Max. Apart from his own.'

In the glare of the Iain West, the flayed neck of Hector Welles looked like the self-inflicted scars of some bizarre tribal ritual.

'Hanging is of course a popular method of suicide. But Mr Irani and Mr Donovan both have burn marks on their wrists where their hands were secured behind their backs, precluding suicide. Mr Welles did not have his hands secured behind his back, making suicide a theoretical possibility – in fact, most suicide hangings look exactly like Mr Welles, as they change their mind when it is far too late and attempt to claw the noose from their neck. But the extent of his defensive wounds eliminates that.'

'And three million hits on YouTube of the guy being hanged,' Edie said.

Elsa Olsen looked at her sharply.

'I'm looking at the medical evidence and *not* what's trending on YouTube, Detective.'

'Of course,' Edie said.

Elsa nodded curtly. 'And a suicide victim is unlikely to be cut down and dumped in the middle of Marble Arch. The dead don't move themselves,' she said. 'In all three cases, the manner of death was murder.'

'Anything you can give us about the knot?' I said.

The way a knot is tied and the type of knot used might have been a priceless lead, I thought, remembering Pat Whitestone's words when we had found Mahmud Irani. But Elsa shook her head.

'Sorry,' she said. 'For that I would need to see the rope or the wire or whatever it was. The neck markings are not enough to go on.'

'We still don't have a kill site, Elsa,' I said. 'How long had they been dead when we found them?'

'They're all different. As you know, rigor mortis sets in after approximately two hours and then the body gets progressively stiffer. And then we follow the twelve-twelve-twelve equation. Twelve hours to get stiff. Twelve hours to remain stiff. And twelve hours for the body to lose that stiffness as it begins to decay. Rigor mortis had just begun to set in on Mr Irani, suggesting he had been dead for around twelve hours when he was discovered. The second victim, Mr Welles, had advanced rigor mortis. He had been dead for approximately twenty-four hours. And the body of the latest victim, young Mr Donovan, was losing the stiffness of rigor mortis. And you can see that his skin has a greenish hue around his head, shoulders and abdomen. There's also a degree of bloating because of gases accumulating in the cavities. His internal organs had longer to break down.'

'Because the bodies are becoming harder for us to find,' I said.

'And there's lividity on the back of Mr Irani,' Elsa said, nodding at Edie. 'Would you be so kind, DC Wren?'

Together the two women turned the cadaver of

Mahmud Irani onto his front. The skin around his shoulder blades, back, buttocks and calf muscles was pale and surrounded by ugly purple blotches that looked like bruises. Dr Joe looked at me.

'That's the lividity,' I said. 'Those marks that look like bruises. Think of lividity as stagnant blood. When you die, your heart stops beating and your blood stops moving. Gravity does the rest. The blood settles. But you don't get it where the body touches the ground. Lividity can help us determine how long someone has been dead and if the body has been moved.'

'The technical name is *livor mortis*,' Elsa said.

'From the Latin,' Dr Joe said. '*Livor* meaning *bluish* and *mortis* meaning *of death*.'

Elsa and Edie heaved the dead man onto his back.

'The lividity on Mr Irani strongly suggests that he lay undisturbed for most of the time between death and discovery,' Elsa said.

'What does that mean?' asked Dr Joe.

'It means they didn't move him very far,' I said. 'So the kill site has to be within – what? – one hour's distance of Marble Arch and Vauxhall Bridge.'

'That narrows it down to all of Greater London,' Edie said.

'I can also tell you they were all taken down minutes after death,' Elsa said. 'If they had been left hanging, the furrow of the neck wounds would be much deeper.'

We stared in silence at the bodies. I felt myself shudder.

It's just the cold, I told myself. Just the bitter cold in here.

'And there's something else,' Elsa said. 'A professional hangman works on a system of variable drops. It was the method used by this country's most famous executioner – Albert Pierrepoint. Saddam Hussein's goons used the same method. How heavy the body is, how far it needs to fall to separate the second and third vertebrae in the neck and cause instant death. It's called the hangman's fracture. If the drop is too long, the victim is decapitated. These people – the Hanging Club – clearly don't bother with variable drops. Despite the charade of hanging, they essentially strangle their victims.'

She gave Edie Wren a severe look.

'And I watch YouTube, too,' Elsa said. 'But what's interesting is that the most recent victim appears to have died in less than half the time of the first two. Examining the damage to the carotid arteries and the spinal column, I estimate that Mr Irani took thirteen minutes to die, Mr Welles took ten and Mr Donovan took just five.'

'What does that mean?' asked Dr Joe.

'It means they're getting good at it,' I said.

We were back in the changing room, taking off our scrubs, when Dr Joe began talking about signatures.

'The three murders are more than ritualistic killings,' he said, pulling off his hairnet. 'Among the unknown subs there's a clear hierarchical structure at work.'

'Yes, it's always the same one who asks the question,' I said. *'Do you know why you've been brought to this place of execution?* He's the leader.'

'Everyone has their role to play and yet they are capable of acting in the interests of the group,' Dr Joe said.

Edie pulled off her hairnet and shook her hair out. 'When Hector Welles tried to do a runner, they all jumped on him at once. Or at least, three of them did. And then they went back to their roles. And they all have a strict role to play, don't they? Somebody to speak. Somebody to film. Somebody to watch. And somebody to be executioner.'

'Judge, jury, witness and hangman,' I said. 'But what are the signatures, Dr Joe?'

'A strong facility for organisation. An ability to be totally ruthless. A strict hierarchy that has room for individual endeavour before the hierarchy reasserts itself.'

'You really think they're cops?' Edie said.

'Not necessarily, although it's a possibility. I think that at least one of them has some kind of specialist training in upholding social control. And I believe that probably more than one of them has experience of some kind of public service. Someone with experience of an institution that sanctions those who violate laws or harm the state. Someone who has been disappointed in the limits and failures and compromises of that institution. So a serving or ex-police officer is one possibility. But equally we could be looking at one or more unsubs who has experience in the prison service or some other branch of criminal justice.'

As I watched Dr Joe thinking I knew what he was going to say next, and I had to stop myself from saying it out loud, from blurting it out, as into my mind leapt the image of my oldest friend and his gap-toothed grin.

'Or even the military,' Dr Joe said.

My phone began to vibrate.

The woman on the other end of the phone was crying and apologising all at once. It took me a moment to realise that it was Alice Goddard, the widow of Steve Goddard, kicked to death outside his own home.

'I'm sorry to call you, Max, I didn't know who else I could call . . .'

'Slow down. Take a breath. What's wrong?' I said.

But all she could do was to keep apologising and crying.

In my line of work, we move on. There's always the next case, there is always some fresh human misery coming down the line. But the victims of crime, they don't move on. They can't move on. They remain forever stuck in the moment that their life changed, the shock and the pain never diminishing with time. And beyond all the grief that never dies, there can be practical problems. When justice is done, there is usually someone out there raving about the injustice of it all.

The three pieces of pond life who killed Steve Goddard all had friends and families. And sometimes, after pond life has been locked up, these friends and families feel they have a point to prove and a debt to settle.

It can take the form of low-level harassment. It can be petrol poured through a letterbox. It can be anything in between. That's why I had given Alice Goddard my card and told her that she could call me any time. If the friends and loved ones of the pond life came calling, then I wanted to know about it.

But this was something else.

'It's my son,' she said, her voice breaking.

I parked outside the Goddard house and took a moment to adjust. The first time I had seen this quiet suburban street, the uniforms were putting up a tent and tape, the CSIs in their white Tyvek suits were dusting, filming and photographing. And Steve Goddard was lying dead, his body half on the pavement and half in the road.

I remembered that there wasn't much blood. And I remembered the devastated family who were inside: Steve Goddard's wife and son and daughter, Alice and Steve Junior and Kitty, the three of them holding on to each other as this brutal new reality kicked in and they started to unravel.

I blinked my eyes and the memory faded and it was just another suburban street on a summer evening. I took a few deep breaths and walked up the short garden path to the door of the Goddard family.

Alice greeted me with a warm, embarrassed smile. Her eyes were red raw, but she had made a real effort to regain control.

'It's Steve Junior,' she said. 'He's got a knife.'

I found the kid in the local park.

He was in the deserted playground, sitting on the swings, puffing on a cigarette.

The last time I had seen Steve Junior was at the Old Bailey. What was he? Fifteen? Sixteen? He had looked like a young boy that day, overawed and baffled by his surroundings, his shirt too big and wearing a tie that his mum had done up for him. Now, just weeks later, he looked like a bitter young man.

'Steve? Remember me? DC Wolfe.'

His eyes met mine and then slid away. There was some shouting in the distance and we both looked over to where it had come from. A group of boys and one girl were sprawled over a distant park bench.

I sat down on the swing next to Steve Goddard Junior.

'Is anyone bothering you?' I said.

He looked at me with disbelief. Then he laughed and shook his head.

'Is anybody *bothering* me? Is that your question?

My dad gets kicked to death and you ask me if anyone is *bothering* me?'

'Since then, I mean. Is anyone getting on your case since the trial?'

I watched his eyes fill with tears. 'I'm going to be bothering them,' he said. 'Don't you worry about that.'

'Is that what the knife is for?'

Silence.

'I understand why you want to get even,' I said. 'It's natural. What happened to your dad – to your family – it's not fair, is it?'

'No. It's not fucking fair. You got that right.'

'So what you going to do? What's the plan? Stick a knife in one of them when they get out? Stick your knife in all of them?'

Two teenage girls went past arm in arm. They looked at me and Steve sitting on the swings and walked away consumed by mocking laughter.

'Why are you even here?' he said.

'I don't want anything worse to happen to your family.'

His mouth twisted.

'What could possibly be any worse than my dad going outside to ask for a bit of peace and quiet, and then getting his head kicked in? What could be worse than that?'

'You getting locked up in Feltham.'

He frowned. I wondered if he had the knife on

him. Then I saw the bulge in the pocket of his hoodie and I didn't have to wonder any more.

'What's Feltham?' he said.

'Feltham Young Offenders Institution,' I said. 'It's a prison for male juveniles near Hounslow. If you stick your blade in one of those creeps who killed your dad, that's where they will send you. Because you're under eighteen.'

He looked at me and for the first time I thought that I might be getting through to him.

'I understand how you feel, Steve. I understand why you want to do it. And I can even understand why they deserve it. I saw your dad the night he died.'

The boy flinched as if he had been slapped.

'And I saw you that night,' I said. 'And your sister Kitty. And your mum. And I was there in the Old Bailey when those three bastards got off with a slap on the wrist. But that doesn't mean you should take the law into your own hands. Because if you do, then the law is going to come down on you. And I promise you, Steve, you are not the kind of lad who thrives in Feltham.'

I stood up.

'Get rid of the knife,' I said. 'On your way home – drop it down a drain. The first drain you see. Then go home and take care of your mum and your sister. They need you more than you can imagine.'

I began to walk away.

His voice called me back.

'Is that it?' he said. 'Is that the only reason I can't get even with the bastards? Is that the only reason I can't stick a blade in those bastards who killed my dad? Because of what will happen to me if I do?'

'Yes,' I said. 'It's the only reason. But it's the only reason you need.'

CHAPTER 16

In New Scotland Yard's Room 101, Sergeant John Caine put the kettle on while I walked into the Black Museum and stared at the hanging tree. More than twenty ropes were draped over the three-legged gallows' pole, arranged with the loving care of decorations on a Christmas tree. Next to the hanging tree there was a framed photograph of Albert Pierrepoint and a quote from 1974.

'The fruit of my experience has this bitter aftertaste. Capital punishment, in my view, achieved nothing but revenge.'

'Sorry, no triple espresso in here,' John Caine told me, holding out a mug of steaming tea. He took a sip from his BEST DAD IN THE WORLD mug.

'You're having a bit of a quiet week, aren't you?' he said. 'Nobody's been hanged on YouTube.'

I nodded. 'Three murders in July and now nothing for the first seven days in August. Why would they stop, John?'

'Lots of reasons why they might jack it in. One of them might have died. They could have fallen

146

out with each other. Somebody's wife found out what her old man has been doing and begged him to stop for the sake of the kiddies. Or – most likely reason a crew stops – they might think that they've been rumbled and you're going to kick down their front doors at five o'clock tomorrow morning.'

I laughed bitterly.

'Not much chance of that happening.'

DCI Whitestone had not turned up for work this morning because her son was having another operation on his eyes. This meant I was still the acting SIO. In the absence of any leads, I had done what I always do when I need guidance – come for a cup of tea at the Black Museum.

'Or one of them lost their nerve,' John said. 'Or all of them lost their nerve. Or they've ticked off everyone on their kill list. That's possible. Or they're quitting while they're ahead because they're intelligent enough to know that if they keep doing it, they'll get caught.' He took a thoughtful sip of his tea. 'Maybe they're cashing out while they're ahead.'

'You ever meet a villain that smart?'

'Not yet.'

'Me neither.'

I inspected the ropes on the hanging tree. The oldest – four thin strands now black with age – was two hundred years old. The newest – in pride of place at the front, like the star on top of a Christmas tree – dated back to 1969, the year that capital punishment was officially abolished. It was

147

made of eight thick strands of hemp that were gathered in a large brass thimble. They looked slick and sticky.

'Vaseline,' John said. 'Stops the rope from burning off skin. That's the Sixties for you – when they hanged you with a bit of compassion.'

'What am I doing wrong? I'm no nearer to them than I was a month ago.'

He adjusted the ropes on the hanging tree. If anything was touched in here, then he wanted it to be exactly as it was before.

'You're not following the leads you've got,' he said.

'But I don't have any leads. No kill site. No witnesses. No prints that are worth a damn – nothing that shows up on IDENT1.'

He looked at me as if I was missing the obvious.

'You've got two men with criminal records who both had serious beefs with two of the dead,' he said. 'Back in the day, Paul Warboys and his brother Danny gave Reggie and Ronnie Kray and Eddie and Charlie Richardson a run for their money. Paul Warboys didn't get a life sentence just because he took out a lawyer's tongue with a bolt cutter. He got life because the lawyer bled to death. Now – if Paul Warboys would kill a man for talking to the police, what's he going to do to a man who runs over and kills his grandson?'

I shook my head.

'But I don't buy it. Warboys is retired. He's been retired for twenty years.'

'You don't think he'd come out of retirement for the man who knocked down and killed his grandson?'

'But we ran a Trace, Interview and Eliminate on Warboys. Of course we did. And he made the point – and I thought it was a good point – that if he had wanted Hector Welles dead, he would not have bothered with putting a post on YouTube.'

'And does he have a cast-iron alibi for when Welles was hanged? Because he had a very good one the time that lawyer had his tongue taken out – Warboys and his brother were miles away, doing the Lambada on the Costa del Sol. But that didn't stop a judge finding him guilty and sending him down for life.'

I thought about it.

'The funny thing is, Warboys *doesn't* have a cast-iron alibi for when Welles was killed,' I said. 'He was at home with his wife and we have no other witnesses to confirm it. But that makes me believe him. As he said to me himself – if you were going to invent an alibi, you would come up with something much better than that.'

I drank my tea. It was strong enough to stand up your spoon in. Real builder's tea.

'It's the cast-iron alibis that I never quite believe,' I said. 'Good tea.'

'Thank you. And then there's Sofi Wilder's dad,' John said. 'Barry Wilder. He did time, didn't he?'

'Yes, but that was kid's stuff. Years ago. And he was in a different league from Paul Warboys.'

'But look what they did to his daughter, Max. Look what they did! This grooming gang, they got away with it for so long because everyone was afraid of seeming racist. The police, the social services – we practically held their coats while they were raping and torturing children.'

'I'm not denying he's got motive. But Wilder is another one with an alibi that's not good enough to be made up, another one that says he was home with the wife watching television. And what about Bert Page? How does he fit into this?'

'Who's Bert Page?'

'The Normandy veteran that Darren Donovan put in a coma for fifty pence. As far as we can see, Bert Page doesn't have any violent criminals to avenge him. In fact, despite all the hand wringing in the press, Bert doesn't have anyone to give a toss about him. He was living in care until Donovan put him into the hospital. There's a middle-aged daughter in Australia and that's it. Why would someone want to hang the nasty little creep who hurt him?'

Sergeant John Caine shrugged.

'I don't know, Max,' he said, making a minute adjustment to one of the ropes on his hanging tree. 'Maybe just because it's the right thing to do.'

At the end of the working day Edie Wren and I stood outside a big house in Canonbury Square. We were close enough to Highbury Corner to hear the unbroken rumble of the traffic on the Holloway Road and Essex Road, but Canonbury Square itself was green and leafy, like a millionaire's fantasy of the English countryside.

Edie consulted her phone as I rang the doorbell. 'Tara Jones lives in the whole house?' she said. 'The *whole* house?'

A child in his pyjamas opened the door. Maybe three years old. That age when they stop being babies and start being the person they will be for the rest of their life. And I could see Tara in the child. The pale face, the huge green eyes and especially that almost Asian hair.

I crouched down so that our eyes were at the same level.

'Is your mummy in?' I said.

'Yes,' he said, but a Filipina nanny came to collect him and a man appeared, still wearing the suit and tie he had worn to his office in Cheapside or Canary Wharf.

'Can I help you?' He had an accent that was full of privilege and a nose that had been broken more than once, the telltale signs of someone who had played a bit of rugby at his private school.

'I'm DC Wolfe and this is my colleague DC Wren from West End Central,' I said, standing up. 'I believe your wife is expecting us?'

He nodded and went to get her, leaving Edie and I alone on the doorstep. Down the corridor we could see large mirrors, tasteful prints on the walls, a home of money and taste.

Edie chuckled softly. 'And to think I felt sorry for her when she arrived in Savile Row,' Edie murmured. 'You know – the brave young deaf woman making her way in the world. To think *I* felt sorry for *her!* She's got everything, hasn't she?'

'Yes,' I said. 'I guess so.'

Then Tara Jones was in front of us in a white T-shirt with those tight trousers with the hoops around her bare feet. She pushed back her hair and she didn't smile and she didn't ask us to come inside.

'Tomorrow we're bringing in Paul Warboys and Barry Wilder for further interviews,' I said.

'On the weekend?' she said.

'The law doesn't stop for the weekend,' I said.

'And you want to know if they're lying,' said Tara Jones.

CHAPTER 17

The summer had a different rhythm to the rest of the year and I did not drive home after we said goodnight to Tara. I didn't need to go home.

Now Scout was at school, our lives revolved totally around term dates, pick-up times and all the everyday details of school life. But it was different in the long summer holiday.

Many of Scout's friends had gone off on holiday, but there were always plenty more still in town, and my daughter was a popular child –and not just with her classmates. Parents loved her too because she was polite, sweet-natured and – just shy of her sixth birthday – already a veteran of the sleepover. Scout wasn't one of these children who had been pushed into the sleepover too soon and then wakes up in tears at 3 a.m., demanding an Addison Lee cab to take her home. Parents, kids – everyone loved her.

Tonight Scout was away at her number one sleepover destination – with her best friend Mia in Pimlico – and as I watched Edie walk off to join the revellers on Upper Street where she was meeting her married boyfriend in some funky new bar, I realised I had no reason to hurry home.

So instead of heading south to Smithfield, I turned the BMW X5 north and drove to the far end of the Holloway Road, to the Whittington Hospital, where Darren Donovan's elderly victim slept in the darkness that is somewhere between life and death.

Bert Page lay in a room full of flowers.

There were flowers on every available surface of his small room at the Whittington, flowers in every state from brown decay to full bloom, many still wrapped in their cellophane. I checked a few of them for the cards of well-wishers, but there was nothing.

I sat down beside the old man, my eyes stinging with helpless fury at the state of him.

Bert Page was a tiny man, almost child-size, and his frame did not seem strong enough to cope with the vast array of machines attached to his frail body.

He had tubes snaking up his nose and mouth and down into his windpipe from the ventilator giving him his next breath. An intravenous drip pumped two soft bags of fluids into one of his stick-like arms. Monitors traced lines of green, yellow and red for his heart rate and blood pressure.

I leaned closer to see some sign of life. Beyond the tubes that covered much of his face, he did not appear to be sleeping. He was not in anything recognisable as sleep. It was in a state far deeper than sleep. I had never seen anyone look so far from life with their heart still beating.

Frayed striped pyjamas hung loosely on the tiny old man's emaciated frame and I could see the white hair on the papery skin, and the rough tattoo just above his heart, smudged with the passing of the years.

6 - 6 - 44

The sixth of June 1944. D-Day. I tried to imagine Bert as the teenage soldier he had been, landing on that Normandy beach, but it felt like it was another lifetime. I took his hand, the one that didn't have the tubes keeping him alive, and it was like holding a small bird, just delicate bones held by a thin layer of skin.

'Oh, Bert,' I said out loud. 'What did that bastard do to you?'

The door opened and a nurse let in a young doctor. The nurse disappeared and the doctor came in, consulting his notes. He looked Greek or Turkish. Very young, very tired.

'I'm Dr Safik.'

Turkish then, I thought. I stood up and shook hands, telling him my name as I showed him my warrant card. He really looked at it and I realised that he had already seen a few warrant cards in his short career.

'Detective Constable Wolfe?' He gave me back

my warrant card. 'By your rank, I'm assuming you're not the Senior Investigating Officer?'

'Acting.'

'How can I help you? Presumably you're not investigating the assault on Mr Page?'

'I'm investigating the murder of Darren Donovan, the man who assaulted Mr Page.' I looked at the old man in the hospital bed. I did not like saying Donovan's name in this room. 'What can you tell me about his visitors?'

Dr Safik's mouth twitched with distaste.

'He doesn't have any, as far as I am aware. That's not unusual these days. But it's unusual for a man that attracted so much widespread sympathy as Mr Page.' The young doctor almost smiled. 'It didn't appear to do him much good, did it? All that attention from the media.'

'Does Mr Page have any chance of recovery?'

'He's in what we call a state of unrousable unconsciousness. Do you know what the Glasgow scoring system is, Detective?'

I shook my head.

'It's a numerical system used to assess the extent of a head injury. It's based on motor response, eye opening and so on. A score of seven indicates a full coma.' He glanced at the old man. 'And Mr Page is a seven. Recovery at his age? It's unlikely.'

'And he has no visitors at all?'

'Not as far as I am aware. You should talk to the nurses' station. I know there were some members of the press sneaked in when the attack first happened.' I suddenly remembered a horrific photograph of Bert Page in an Intensive Care Unit shortly after he was robbed by Darren Donovan, the old man's face so swollen and discoloured that it barely looked human. 'There's a daughter in Australia who can't quite manage to get over to see her father before he dies. But, no – Mr Page does not get visitors.'

I inhaled the sweetness of Bert Page's hospital room.

'Then who sends him flowers?' I said.

Saturday night was slipping into Sunday morning when I finally arrived home. Stan roused himself and padded across the loft to meet me, his strawberry blonde tail wagging with welcome.

Jackson was sitting at my laptop, wearing some of my old clothes – a black T-shirt that said LONSDALE LONDON in white letters, faded Levi 501s – that I did not recognise at first because he had washed and ironed them so well.

'You should have seen Scout when Mrs Murphy packed her off with little Mia and her mum,' he said. 'She was so excited.'

I felt the pang of the parent who is absent too often.

'Is it OK to use the laptop?' he said. 'I was just checking the news.'

'Anytime.'

He closed the laptop.

'You should try to get away with her yourself,'

Jackson said. 'They give you holidays in the Met, don't they?'

I nodded. 'We get twenty-five to thirty days, depending on length of service.'

I tended to use my days off walking Stan on the Heath. Were Scout and I really going to go on holidays like normal families? Two weeks in the sun? I couldn't quite imagine it. And what would we do with Stan? He didn't have a passport. And he was part of our little family, too.

'Remember that holiday home my folks had when we were kids?'

The family that adopted Jackson had a cottage on the coast of Kent. I remembered a pebble beach, bunk beds and the salt tang of the English Channel. The sea was freezing even in the height of summer. When I was eleven years old, it had seemed like heaven.

'Sand Pebbles,' I said.

'Sand Pebbles!' Jackson laughed.

'It's still there?' I said. 'Sand Pebbles is still there?'

'They never sold it,' he said. 'They rented it out before they died, but now it doesn't even get rented out. I spent a couple nights there before I came up to London. It's not in great nick, but you and Scout can use it anytime.'

He pulled on one of my old red Realm and Empire hoodies and started for the door. For a moment I thought he was going to the little holiday home on the coast.

'Work,' he said.

'OK.'

Stan followed him to the door and then came padding back into the loft when Jackson had left. I stared at the laptop but resisted the urge to open it, and I resisted the urge to look at his browsing history. There seemed to be no point. I felt like I already knew what it contained.

Instead I walked to the window and I stared down at the great meat market of Smithfield. It was in total darkness because London Central Markets, to give Smithfield its official name, is not open at the weekend or Bank Holidays.

So wherever my oldest friend was going, he certainly wasn't going to work.

CHAPTER 18

I looked across the table at Paul Warboys. He held my gaze but his expression was pleasant. I had never seen anyone so calm in an interview room. But then he had done this many times before.

'OK, are we ready?' I said. 'Is everybody ready?' I glanced at Edie Wren, sitting by my side, and Warboys and his lawyer on the other side of the small table. 'When I press this button, we will start recording . . .'

Warboys smiled gently at the beep, his deeply tanned face as creased as old leather. He crossed his arms and his heavy gold jewellery clinked in the box-like room. His lawyer hovered at his side, staring at me over his reading glasses, ready to pounce.

'All right,' I said, 'this interview is being recorded and may be given in evidence if any case is brought to trial. My name is DC Max Wolfe and I am currently serving with Homicide and Serious Crime Command here at West End Central, 27 Savile Row, London. The other officer present is DC Edie Wren. The time is – look at that – exactly noon.' I nodded at the elderly gangster on the other side of the table. 'Please state your name and profession.'

'Paul Warboys. Businessman. Retired.'

'Further to our previous interview at your home, Mr Warboys, I'd like to ask – what were your movements on the day that Hector Welles was abducted and murdered?'

The lawyer leaned forward. 'I'd like to remind you that my client is not under arrest.'

Warboys held up a hand. His lawyer sat back in his chair.

'I was at home. All day. All night.'

Most people become impatient or irritated when they are asked the same questions more than once. But not Paul Warboys.

'How did you learn about Welles' death?'

'I told you before and now I'll tell you again.' It was said with a wry smile. 'And I'll keep on telling you the same thing as many times as you like. The phone started ringing. And then it didn't stop.'

'Who called you?'

'Everybody called me, Detective. And they all said exactly the same thing: "*Somebody just hanged the bastard who killed your grandson.*" I'm paraphrasing.' His pale blue eyes glistened with tears and he laughed, amused at himself, the old gangster who was still capable of crying. 'That's what they all told me. Somebody lynched the bastard who knocked down little Danny when he was crossing the road.'

Paul Warboys smiled at me again. His teeth were white and even. Most of those old London faces

161

didn't care too much about their dental work. I couldn't imagine Ronnie and Reggie Kray worrying about their flossing. But Paul Warboys had spent a lot of money and time getting his teeth to look that good.

'Did you ever meet Barry Wilder?' I asked.

He shook his head. 'Who? Sorry, Max. You're going to have to give me a clue.'

'Barry Wilder's young daughter was a victim of Mahmud Irani's grooming gang.'

'Ah. Mahmud Irani. The first one they hanged.'

'Yes, the first one. I'll ask you again – did you ever meet Barry Wilder?'

'No.' He laughed. 'You want me to take a lie detector, Detective? I'm willing.'

His lawyer shot forward. 'Paul, I strongly advise—'

Warboys again silenced him with a raised hand.

'It's not necessary,' I said. 'But I appreciate the offer. I'm concluding this interview.'

I looked at the one-way mirror of the interview room.

And I smiled back at Paul Warboys.

Because I had someone much better than a lie detector.

I walked Warboys to the main entrance of West End Central.

Doll, his wife, was waiting for him under the big blue lamp that hangs outside 27 Savile Row. She came to his side and gave him a quick, fierce hug, gold chains sliding down her thin brown arms. She peered into her husband's face.

'You done?'

He nodded. 'For now.'

A chauffeured Mercedes was idling by the kerb.

'Are you going back to Essex?' I said.

'Spain,' he said. 'Just for a few days. My brief can give you our schedule.'

I nodded. 'OK.'

He held out his hand to me and I shook it. But then he wouldn't let go. He kept my hand in his grip, and he held my gaze with his cold blue eyes.

'I'd like to wish you luck in your investigation,' he said. 'But my grandson was the best thing that ever happened to me, Max. An innocent little boy who never did anyone in this world any harm. And I really hope these chaps – the Hanging Club – get away with it.'

Up in MIR-1 Tara Jones was running voice biometrics on a recording of the Paul Warboys interview. His laconic old London accent filled the room.

'*Paul Warboys. Businessman. Retired.*'

It was a voice from an old London that no longer existed. It made the graph on the screens in front of Tara jump like lightning. When she looked up at us, Edie said, 'So, Tara – what's the difference between a lie detector and voice biometrics?'

'Approximately the difference between a horse and a Ferrari,' Tara said. 'A polygraph – or lie detector – is hundred-year-old technology. It records physiological changes during questioning – blood pressure, breathing, heart rate, sweating and so on. And it's fine if you are screening new employees. You'll know if they're lying about their CV, their qualifications and their smoking habits. But for someone like Paul Warboys? It just doesn't work as well as it does in the movies. Someone like Warboys will be aware of what we call countermeasures. Confidence, controlled breathing, establishing a friendly – or at least a workable – rapport with the questioner. Confidence, above all. Not being scared by the process or his environment. That's why a polygraph is not considered reliable evidence in a court of law. It is Jurassic technology. But voice biometrics does what we want a lie detector to do.'

We let her work. I stared down at the street, sipping a triple espresso from the Bar Italia until Tara Jones leaned back in her chair and ran her hands through her hair.

'He's telling the truth,' she said.

In the afternoon Barry Wilder came in. There was no lawyer with him. But his wife Jean was there. She was waiting in the corridor outside the interview room with him, furiously stubbing out one unfiltered Camel on the floor and immediately lighting another one. Barry Wilder got to his feet at the sight of us, moving in weary slow motion, as if every movement took enormous effort.

'There's no smoking in this building, ma'am,' Edie told his wife.

Jean Wilder glared at her and muttered under her breath as we went into the interview room.

'Little ginger cow.'

Edie shook her head and let it go.

Barry Wilder eased himself into the chair opposite us.

'OK,' I said, 'this interview is being recorded and may be given in evidence if any case is brought to trial. My name is DC Max Wolfe and I am currently serving with Homicide and Serious Crime Command here at West End Central, 27 Savile Row, London. The other officer present is DC Edie Wren. The time is 3 p.m.' I nodded at Barry Wilder. If he had once been a man of violence then he looked as if all the violence had been knocked out of him.

'Please state your name and profession.'

'Barry Wilder. Builder.'

'Thank you. Did you ever meet a man called Bert Page, Mr Wilder?'

He looked startled. 'Who's Bert Page?'

'Bert Page was a war hero. Landed on Juno Beach on D-Day. Won the Distinguished Service Medal. Then, a lifetime later, Darren Donovan put him in a coma.'

'Ah, Bert Page – the old gentleman who got mugged by the junkie they just strung up. No, I never met Mr Page. But he sounds like a fine old man.'

'Did you have contact with Mahmud Irani after he was released from prison?'

Wilder hesitated.

165

I felt Edie tense beside me.

'Yes,' he said.

We waited. I stared at the faded football tattoos on his arms. I saw now they were two crossed irons. West Ham.

'I got a knife,' Barry Wilder said quietly. 'I was planning to stick it in his heart.'

I heard Edie exhale by my side.

I leaned forward.

'Mr Wilder, I want you to understand that you are not under arrest but you do have the right to have a legal representative present,' I said. 'And I have to remind you this interview is being recorded and may be given in evidence if any case is brought to trial.'

He ignored me.

'I wanted to kill him,' he said.

Then he waited.

'Go on,' I said. 'You wanted to kill him . . .'

'I thought I could kill him. I thought God would forgive me because of what he did to our Sofi. The way he ruined her. The way he took her life away from her and nobody did anything to stop him. Not you and your lot. And not me, the one man she should have been able to trust. The one man who should have protected her. And I didn't, did I? Her own father didn't protect her. Mahmud Irani and those men took her to those rooms and then they filled her with drink and drugs and then they did whatever they wanted to.' He shook his head. 'Whatever they wanted, they did to her. And then they phoned their friends and their fucking brothers, and they came round to do what they wanted to my daughter. They made their own pornography. That's what they were doing with her. And when we got her back, she was pregnant. Did you know that? *Did you?*'

'No,' I said.

'She lost the baby and I thanked God. And how can I live with myself, thanking God for the death of a baby?'

'Tell me about the knife,' I said.

'I said I was going to kill him in the courtroom. You knew that. You quoted the exact words! When they all went down for whatever pitiful little stretch they got. When the judge gave them their slap on their wrists. When all those evil bastards were laughing at us. I said I was going to kill him, didn't I? So then I got the knife and I waited for him at the mosque where he prays every Friday.'

'What happened?'

'I couldn't do it.' His voice choking now. 'I didn't have it in me. I wanted him to die – and I wanted to be the one who did it – but I was not enough of a man to do it.'

'Did you ever meet Paul Warboys, Mr Wilder?'

'Paul Warboys – the gangster?' He shook his head. 'No,' he said.

I reached across and turned off the machine quietly, anxious not to intrude on a grief that would never end.

★　★　★

Outside the interview room, Jean Wilder had a cigarette in her mouth. She brandished it at Edie, to show that it wasn't lit, but when she got to her feet and got in my face, I could still smell the scent of tobacco that she always carried with her, and I could still smell the Jimmy Choo perfume and Juicy Fruit chewing gum that she used to cover it.

'Will you ever leave us alone?' she said. 'You useless flat-footed fools. *He didn't do it.* We have been through hell in this family. Mahmud Irani destroyed this family and my husband didn't do a thing. Why don't you arrest the stinking Paki bastards that are out there raping our children right now? *Right now. Right now.* Why don't you do something useful? Why do you let those Paki bastards get away with murder?'

'Stop,' Barry Wilder said, very quietly, and she stopped immediately, shaking her head.

'I'll walk you out,' I said.

'Don't bother,' said Jean Wilder. 'We can find the door ourselves. Go and catch some villains. Make yourself useful.'

When Edie and I went up to MIR-1, Tara was already running the voice biometrics on Wilder's interview.

'He's telling the truth,' I said.

A slim figure was standing by the window, looking down on Savile Row. She turned to face us and it took a long moment for me to recognise her.

'I want to show you something,' DCI Pat Whitestone said.

CHAPTER 19

Pat Whitestone sat at her workstation in MIR-1 and searched online until she found a ninety-second film of pure horror.

'Look,' she told us.

The footage was grainy, jerky, filmed by someone who was at the end of a long night. It opened on a club, the dance floor as crowded as a tube train at rush hour, the music a wall of booming noise. Boom, boom, boom. Girls in heels and miniskirts. Shirtless boys holding bottles. Dancing in a space where there was no room to dance. Boom, boom, boom. And then the first screams. High-pitched, disbelieving, the revellers all turning their heads, straining to see.

The crowd parted.

A boy with blood covering his face staggered across the dance floor.

Staggering on legs that were on the verge of giving out. His hands held out before him, groping for help.

Blinded.

The club began to glow with the white lights of phone cameras as more of them began to film the broken boy.

'Look what they did to my son,' Whitestone said.

'Online?' I said. 'How the hell can it be online?'

'Because fifty people got out their phones and filmed him. They *filmed* him, Max. Nobody helped him. But they all filmed him.'

On the film, the white lights followed fifteen-year-old Justin Whitestone as he sank to his knees in the middle of the empty dance floor and screamed. A terrible sound, filled more with fear than pain, and the pain must have been unbearable. Somebody laughed. The film stopped.

'Who have we arrested?' Edie said.

'Nobody,' Whitestone said. 'It happened in the toilets. Somebody put a bottle across his eyes in the toilets. The place was full of people but nobody saw a thing. My Just will need someone to take care of him for the rest of his life – and nobody saw a thing.'

'There must be CCTV cameras,' Edie said.

'Not in toilets,' Whitestone said. She was still staring at the frozen image on her computer screen. Her son on his knees, blood streaming from his torn eyes, the long-legged high-heeled girls and shirtless gym-fit boys standing behind him with their phones in their hands. 'No CCTV cameras in toilets, Edie. Invasion of privacy.'

'Pat?'

'Yes, Max?'

She was hypnotised by the image on the screen and still would not look at me.

'They must know who did it,' I said.

'Oh, they know all right. It's a gang from one of the estates behind King's Cross. The Dog Town Boys. Have you heard of them? I even know their names and where they live. But nobody saw anything, nobody is willing to come forward, and there are no cameras to prove a thing.'

I reached forward and hit the command and Q buttons on her keyboard. *Quit*. The image disappeared. She looked at me. But there was nothing I could tell her to stop the pain. And if it had been my child in the hospital, my Scout with her sight gone and her attackers still walking the streets, there would have been nothing that she could have done for me.

'They're getting away with it, Max,' Whitestone told me. 'But then they usually do.'

I was back at home before I managed to get anyone on the phone who had been involved in investigating the blinding of Justin Whitestone.

'Terrible thing,' said an old DI from New Scotland Yard. 'Well-educated kid like that, never in any bother, and some little herbert takes his eyes out for looking at him the wrong way or spilling his drink or whatever it was. They don't need an excuse, do they? Yeah, I remember the case.'

'Back up a minute,' I said. 'This is not an ongoing investigation?'

The DI sighed down the line.

'What can we do? Everyone's scared of the Dog Town Boys – and when I say everyone, I mean everyone in about a square mile of the council estates behinds King's Cross.'

'But this is one of our own,' I said. 'The boy is the son of my DCI at West End Central.'

'I know whose son he is,' said the DI from New Scotland Yard, the first frost coming into his voice. 'But the boy didn't see who glassed him – or so he says. And nobody in the club knows who did it – or so they say. There's not a lot we can do.' Now there was even more frost. 'And if it was West End Central running the investigation – there's bugger all you'd be able to do.'

I stared out the window. The dome of St Paul's bone-white in the moonlight, the party people rolling down Charterhouse Street, the lights of the meat market coming on for the long night shift.

'I know you did your best,' I said. 'It's just hard to believe that nobody gets lifted for such a serious assault.'

The DI softened.

'It's rotten, I know. But even if we lifted one of these little gangsters from the Dog Town Boys, it's not going to make the kid see again, is it? What can you do, eh? Sometimes the guilty just walk away.'

'And there was never a lead?'

I heard him hesitate. 'There was a girl. A young woman. From Hungary. Worked in one of those big Islington squares looking after kiddies of people who work in the City. A nanny. A nice Islington nanny called – let's see – Margit Mester. Twenty-two.

Lovely girl. When we went in that first night, stopped them all leaving and tried to have a word, I spoke to Margit Mester and she pointed out a local lad called Trey N'Dou.'

He spelled it for me.

'You know this Trey?' I said.

'Yeah, Trey N'Dou is the leader of the Dog Town Boys.'

I let that sink in. 'So what happened to your Hungarian witness, Margit Mester?'

I could already guess the answer.

'We brought her in for a line-up that included Trey and she didn't recognise him. Couldn't place him at the scene. It was noisy, confusing, upsetting. The usual bullshit when a witness gets cold feet.'

'Can I talk to Margit Mester?'

'If you go to Budapest.'

'She went home?'

'Couldn't get there fast enough when she twigged who she was pointing a finger at.'

Jackson came out of his room and crossed the loft. At the door, he raised his hand in salute and gave me his gap-toothed grin and pointed at the market. He was off to work. I lifted my hand – goodbye – and he slipped out.

'The big problem for us was that we didn't have CCTV,' said the DI, warming to his theme of the guilty going unpunished. 'You know the Met solves nearly one hundred murders every year with CCTV images? There are six million CCTV cameras in this country – one for every ten people – but not enough to stop every villain.'

Below me I could see Jackson walking towards Smithfield. But he did not go inside. He turned right and began walking towards Holborn Circus.

'And there's no CCTV cameras in toilets,' I said. 'Although they have them everywhere else, don't they?'

'I'm not allowed to disclose an image of a patient without their written consent,' said the security officer at the Whittington Hospital.

'I'm not looking for an image of a patient,' I said. 'I want to know who visited him.'

We were in the hospital's security bunker. It was a darkened room with no natural light where four large screens each showed a grid revealing nine CCTV images, everything from the car park to the maternity ward, the A&E department to the main foyer.

'How far can you go back?' I said.

'I can go back a month,' the security officer said. 'That's how long we store the images.' The grid of images was constantly changing on the large screens. 'We've got one hundred and fifty cameras – pretty standard for a hospital like the Whittington – and when bad things happen, like a sexual assault on a mixed ward, or a baby abduction on the maternity ward, or the assaults on our staff that happen every drunken weekend of the year – they usually get reported immediately. What we looking for?'

'Do you have images from the Critical Care Unit?'

He hit some buttons.

'Waiting room, nurses' station, entrance to the CCU – you need a card to get beyond the door. Nobody just wanders in.'

'Let's have a look at the nurses' station.' I thought about it. 'Let's start with weekend nights.'

The security officer went back to a Saturday night at the start of the month and found what I was looking for almost immediately.

'Stop it there,' I said.

Jackson Rose was on the CCTV.

He was holding a bouquet of flowers and smiling at a pretty Filipina nurse as if the flowers might possibly be for her as he walked past the nurses' station on his way to visit an old soldier in a coma.

You see London's homeless at night.

In the day they are invisible, or at least hard to tell from the people with homes. But at night they are revealed and there are places – pathetically few in a wealthy city of ten million souls – where they go to be fed.

One of those places is Waterloo. Under the arches where trains roar above your head, arches that are black with the fumes of today and the fog of long ago.

On this warm summer evening Jackson Rose stood at the back of a white van with a few other volunteers and spooned heaps of Phad Thai noodles on paper plates for men and women of all ages, all races, although many of them wore the rags of what had once been military uniforms.

I waited by the side of the white van, declining a nice old posh lady's offer of a cup of tea and 'some of Jackson's wonderful noodles'. He was trying to serve everyone, but new people kept arriving so in the end he handed over to the nice old posh lady and we walked beyond the arches until the noise of the trains receded and conversation was possible.

'You quit your job at Smithfield,' I said. It wasn't a question.

'This is more fulfilling,' he said. 'You still get your rent money, don't you?'

'You think I give a toss about rent money?'

He nodded at the men and women waiting in line for his noodles.

'A lot of them served. Iraq. Afghanistan. And Northern Ireland and the Falklands, some of the older ones.'

'Why didn't you tell me that you visited Bert Page?'

'Why would I?'

'Because you know exactly what I'm investigating. You know Darren Donovan put Bert in that coma. You know I'm out there looking for whoever topped Darren Donovan.'

Jackson glanced back at the van where the queue for noodles was growing.

'Ah, the late Darren Donovan. You seem more

concerned about this dead junkie than you do about the old man he ruined.'

'Look – I can understand why you'd be moved by Bert Page.'

He shook his head. 'Moved? Is that what you think I am, Max? Moved?'

'Call it what you want. I understand why you would care, OK? What I don't understand is why you wouldn't think to tell me.'

'Why should I? You already look at me sideways.'

'I don't mean to look at you sideways, Jackson.'

He laughed. 'Do you think I'm involved in any of this, Max? These vigilantes – the Hanging Club – you think I'm mixed up in it in some way?'

I remembered the *Show History* list on my laptop. And I remembered how he single-handedly demolished the men who attacked us on Charterhouse Street. And I remembered what he said.

One in the head and one in the heart.

'No,' I said. 'I don't think you're involved. But I think you're on their side.'

'Yeah, me and sixty million other people!'

I remembered the wild kid he had been. And I knew that wildness was in him still and that it would be there forever.

'I don't want you to get into trouble,' I said. 'I care about you, all right? I just don't know you, Jackson.'

He showed me his famous smile.

'You know me better than anyone,' he said. 'You

want some Phad Thai noodles? Best this side of Bangkok.'

I stared at him for a moment and then smiled back at him.

'Some Phad Thai would be great,' I said.

But I never got the chance to try Jackson's Phad Thai noodles. We were under the black arches of Waterloo when my phone began to vibrate.

EDIE WREN CALLING.

'They've got another one,' she said.

And I did not need to turn my head to know that Jackson was watching me, his face impassive, not smiling now.

CHAPTER 20

I came into MIR-1 thirty minutes later and saw the big HD TV screen was filled with a head-and-shoulders shot of a bearded man.

The beard was the frizzy kind that is missing a moustache. The man who wore it was light-skinned, pushing forty, with a small pillbox hat perched on his head and hooded eyes behind wire-rimmed spectacles. He wore plain grey robes.

'The victim of the latest abduction is Abu Din,' Pat Whitestone was saying. Edie Wren, Billy Greene and Tara Jones watched her from their workstations. They must have renewed Tara's contract, I thought, with a stab of elation.

'Abu Din was born in Egypt and granted asylum in the UK,' Whitestone continued. 'He is wanted for inciting acts of terror in the United States but currently resisting extradition from the UK. His appeal is pending at the European Court of Human Rights.' She nodded. 'Pretty much your basic hate-preaching scumbag.'

'You back?' I said.

'I'm back.'

'Good,' I said. 'I can't find the Abu Din hanging online.'

'They haven't hanged him yet,' Edie Wren said. 'Or at least they haven't put anything online.'

Billy Greene brought me a triple espresso and I smiled at him gratefully. It wasn't from the Bar Italia, but it would do for now. I bolted it down in one.

'What have they posted about him?' I said.

'Nothing that we can find on any of the usual platforms,' Edie told me. 'We've got an open line to Colin Cho at the Police Central e-crime Unit. The abduction is generating a lot of traffic. PCeU are on it. But Albert Pierrepoint himself is unusually silent.'

'How do we know it's them?' I said. 'They could be copycats. They could be self-radicalised. There are enough people out there who feel like they are on their side. How do we know it's the Hanging Club?'

'Educated guess,' said Whitestone. 'We've got CCTV of Abu Din being lifted. They're far too slick to be fan boys. Have a look at this, Max. Can you run it, Billy?'

Greene's fingers flew over his keyboard and the mugshot of Abu Din was replaced by black-and-white footage from a CCTV camera. The camera revealed a crowd of men kneeling in the road of a suburban street. A figure in grey robes stood before them. Abu Din. High above the street I could see the curved arch of Wembley Stadium, glinting in the sunshine at the end of another beautiful day.

'Abu Din was at the Wembley Central mosque, but they kicked him out after he went on *Newsnight* and praised the murder of six British soldiers in Afghanistan. So now he preaches in the street.'

I wanted another triple espresso.

'Abu Din,' I said. 'Why does his name seem familiar?'

'He's the one they call the Mental Mullah,' Billy said. 'I'll just fast-forward over the prayers, shall I?' The CCTV footage began speeding up. 'The papers tagged him the Mental Mullah after he said the killing of British soldiers was "a glorious thing".'

'He gets fifty grand a year in benefits for his wife and six kids,' Edie said. 'I reckon we must be the mental ones.'

'The papers had to stop calling him the Mental Mullah because it was considered offensive by mental health charities,' Billy said. 'Ah, this is the money shot.'

The CCTV footage slowed down to real time. There were perhaps one hundred men kneeling in the Wembley street. Abu Din himself faced them in his plain grey robes, flanked by what looked like a couple of bodyguards. Both of Abu Din's index fingers were pointing to the heavens. At the back of the crowd I could see a solitary uniformed policeman, a black officer with the height and bulk of a heavyweight boxer. I guessed he could handle himself. Watching this street wasn't an easy posting. The uniformed cop was standing directly in front of a young man in a wheelchair. There was a woman behind the wheelchair. Their dark good looks were so similar they could have been twins. The young man was holding up a placard. I could just about make out the words.

My Country – Love It or Leave It.

'Coming up now,' Billy said.

The policeman suddenly started to run. The woman gripped the handlebars of the young man in the wheelchair and seemed to hunch, as if expecting a blow. And then the crowd were all getting to their feet, pointing at something out of camera.

They began to scatter.

Running for their lives.

A black transit van was being driven at speed. It appeared to be heading straight for the crowd but suddenly it mounted the pavement to avoid the young man in the wheelchair. I automatically looked for anything that would make the transit van unique. Dents, scratches, words that had been sprayed over. But there was nothing. There was brown duct tape plastered over the registration plate. Simple but effective.

The crowd had done a runner. Apart from Abu Din, who was wagging an admonishing finger at the black van.

He was still wagging it when Albert Pierrepoint got out of the van. And then another Albert Pierrepoint. The faces of the two kindly uncles scanned the street. At the top of the screen I could see the young uniformed copper on his belly, radioing for assistance. Another kindly uncle sat at the wheel of the transit van, gunning the engine.

'Albert Pierrepoint masks,' I said. 'Nice touch.'

'And the duct tape over the registration plates is an even nicer touch,' Whitestone said. 'Whoever they are, they know exactly what they're doing.'

Abu Din's bodyguards were nowhere to be seen as the preacher was bundled into the back of the black van without ceremony. It began to reverse at speed down the suburban street and then it was gone, the street gradually filling with worshippers watching it leave, the uniformed copper slowly getting to his feet.

Billy hit a few buttons and the big screen became the standard CCTV grid of nine, all of them views of fast-flowing evening traffic.

'The CCTV followed them on the North Circular heading in an anti-clockwise direction and then we lost them. And then we picked them up again.'

The grid was replaced by a single still image of the transit van burning on what looked like the surface of an abandoned planet. In the background I could see the faded sign of a giant oil company.

'They switched vehicles,' I said.

'Disabled the cameras in this abandoned petrol station and torched their old ride,' Edie said. 'So we've got one CCTV camera for every person in London but it does us no good at all because we don't know what we're looking for.'

Telephones suddenly began to ring, chime and vibrate. Edie scanned a text on her mobile.

'Getting the first pictures from what we believe to be the execution of Abu Din,' she said. 'Let me put it on the big screen.'

She pounded her keyboard and a hangman's noose appeared on the TV. The camera zoomed in and then out again, as if getting focused. It settled on the noose, hanging stark against the familiar cell-like space, mildewed with the ages, beyond all light. Then the camera slowly pulled back and you could see the four black-coated figures.

'Production values definitely improving,' Edie muttered.

But this time was different. Because there was no condemned man wild-eyed with terror at the centre of it all. Instead the camera focused on a series of photographs on the wall.

Servicemen. Six of them. Smiling, happy, proud.

Edie looked up from her laptop.

'Getting reports – unconfirmed – that those are the Sangin Six.'

'I remember the Sangin Six,' I said. 'Sangin is a district in the east of Helmand Province, Afghanistan. Six of our servicemen – and women – were in a patrol vehicle in Sangin that got hit by an IED. They all survived the blast but then they were torn to bits by a mob. They didn't show it on the mainstream media because it was too gruesome. Body parts hanging from bridges while the locals danced in the street.'

The camera tracked slowly across the faces of the six dead soldiers. I looked across at Tara Jones who was running voice biometrics on the film.

She saw me watching her.

'Are you picking up any dialogue, Tara?' I said.

'Just ambient sounds,' she said. 'It's not traffic. Sounds like some kind of major building work going on nearby.'

'Abu Din was vocal in his praise of the killers of the Sangin Six,' Whitestone said. 'He insisted on calling them the Six Crusaders. The elderly grandmother of one of the Sangin Six said that he should be hanged.'

'Then why didn't they?' Edie said.

The camera zoomed in for another close-up on the empty noose. And then the image froze.

'Maybe it's a trailer,' Edie said. 'Stay tuned for the main event.'

'Maybe they think hanging's too good for him,' I said.

The early morning crowds filled the Imperial War Museum. But it was very quiet in the basement room where I sat with the young woman in a wheelchair. I had met Carol through my first SIO in Homicide and Serious Crime Command, DCI Victor Mallory. It was because of him that I could come to her for help at any time.

'I was in Camp Bastion when the Sangin Six died,' she said. 'It felt like a turning point in the war on terror.' A short laugh. 'That's when it started to feel like terror had declared war on us.'

She moved her wheelchair closer to the desk and scrolled through some images of hell. Jubilant crowds. Scraps of human remains. The pitiless sun of Afghanistan.

'I don't know how much you want to see of this stuff, Max,' Carol said. 'There's plenty that they couldn't show on the evening news, but I'm not sure you can learn anything from it.'

I checked my phone again for a message from Edie Wren. We kept expecting the execution to go live. But the morning after the abduction of Abu Din, it still hadn't happened.

'I really wanted to sound you out about Abu Din,' I said.

'The Mental Mullah,' she grinned. 'They took him, didn't they?'

I nodded. 'Who would want to string him up, Carol?'

'Are you kidding? Anyone who served. Anyone who loved someone who served.' She slapped the sides of her wheelchair without anger or self-pity. 'Anyone who came home in one of these.'

I thought of the two protestors held back by one uniformed cop in Wembley.

'But that's not the same as doing it,' Carol continued. 'And besides – the style's all wrong.'

'You mean abduction and the mock trial and the hanging?'

'All of it. The masks. The drama. The little

186

hashtags. Why hang him? There are far easier ways to kill someone.'

One in the head and one in the heart.

Jackson Rose, I thought. Who the hell are you? My phone began to vibrate.

'We've got Abu Din,' Edie said. 'And he's alive.'

CHAPTER 21

'Inshallah, there was a mighty fire,' said Abu Din. 'And it was revealed to me that this country is Dar al-Harb – the land of war.'

Edie looked at her notes.

'So this was when they burned the van just down the road from Brent Cross, right?' she said. 'This is when you had your revelation about the land of war? At Brent Cross?'

He turned his face away from her, the pink tip of his tongue flecking his lips. He smoothed down his grey robes and stared out of the window of his home. It was as if Edie had never spoken. I followed his gaze. On the street where they had taken him, his followers were already gathering, excited at the news of his miraculous return. Some of them were praying. Others were taking pictures with their selfie sticks.

Abu Din had been found alive at London Gateway service station, on the very edge of the city. He had spent the night locked up in the back of an abandoned container lorry until he eventually kicked his way out and raised the alarm. Perhaps his followers were right. It seemed a miracle that his execution was not being watched on YouTube.

'Please tell me everything you remember, Mr Din,' I said.

He nodded, his eyes behind the wire-rimmed spectacles flicking on me and then away.

'Allahu akbar,' he murmured, not for the first time. 'They took me. The men in their masks. And then they burned the first vehicle and put me in another vehicle. Then we drove to the car park with many lorries. The big lorries.'

'Container lorries,' I said.

'And all of them gathered around me as they locked me in the metal box.' His eyes swivelled to the heavens. 'But the metal was weak, Allahu akbar, and it was not my time to die.'

I looked down at his sandalled feet, both of them bandaged, both of them weeping blood where he had spent the night kicking out the rusted side of a container lorry.

'Did they say anything?' I asked.

'Before they locked me away, one of them – the big one – asked me if I knew why I was being punished. This made another very angry and he slapped the side of the lorry, calling for silence. They were trying not to talk. And then they locked me in and left me and all three of them returned to their vehicle. I heard it drive away.'

'Wait a minute,' I said. '*Three* of them locked you up? So there was another one that remained in the cab?'

'No. They all came to lock me away.'

'So you're saying there were only three of them?' I said.

Abu Din nodded. 'The two who took me and the one who was driving.'

Edie and I exchanged a look.

'Then where was the fourth man?' I said.

'Maybe he was driving the change vehicle,' Edie said. 'It was the smart move to switch vehicles and burn the kidnap van.'

'But he would still need a ride, wouldn't he? After the first vehicle was torched.' I turned back to Abu Din.

'Did you see their faces?' I asked him. 'Did they remove their masks? Did you hear voices? Did they say any names?'

'You asked me this already. I saw their white hands. I smelled their lack of faith. They were *kuffars* – unbelievers. Like you.'

'Any tattoos or distinguishing features on their hands? Did they say anything at all?'

He did not answer me.

'You're very lucky to be alive,' Edie said. 'You know that, don't you?'

He knew.

Abu Din gripped his right hand with the left, but still he could not stop it shaking. But he was playing the big man for the followers who were out in the street and who had crammed into the large council house in Wembley. We could hear them stomping around upstairs while we conducted our interview. And it crossed my mind that perhaps he truly believed that it was some god who had saved him today.

'It was not my time for *jannah*,' he said.

'*Jannah* is paradise, right?' I said.

He said nothing, unimpressed by my sketchy knowledge of Arabic. 'London cops know fifty words in fifty languages,' I said, smiling at him.

No response.

'Mr Din, we are going to give you an Osman Warning,' I said. 'It's an official warning that we believe your life is in mortal danger and we are offering you police protection.'

His thin-lipped mouth twisted into a smile.

'Do you think I need the protection of unbelievers?'

'Yes,' I said. 'And we'll talk again.'

We closed our notebooks.

Abu Din went off to address the followers who were gathering in the street. Edie and I went to the window and watched. It was the kind of shabby suburban street that looks grey and tired even in the middle of a blazing summer. But there was no mistaking the buzz of excitement that ran through it when Abu Din began to speak in Urdu.

'Why didn't they just do him straight away?' I said.

'Maybe their kill site was being used for a yoga class,' Edie said. 'Do you believe he didn't see or hear anything, Max?'

I nodded. 'If they knew enough to cover their

191

registration plates, and if they knew enough to burn all forensics in the van, then they knew enough not to make all the usual dumb mistakes – like calling each other by their names or showing their faces in the presence of their victim.'

We walked out into the street.

Beyond the heads of the crowd of men listening to Abu Din – and they were all men – I could see the uniformed black cop who had been minding the street when the transit van bowled up. Beyond him, the young man in the wheelchair was back with the young woman who accompanied him. They still had their placard and the young man in the wheelchair held it up as Abu Din slipped from Urdu into English.

'In the mighty fire much was revealed to me,' he declared. 'It was revealed that the black flag of Islam will fly above Buckingham Palace and it will also fly above Downing Street.'

'Don't hold your fucking breath,' Edie said.

Skirting the crowd, we walked to the end of the street and introduced ourselves to the uniformed cop. Our people were still here, but not in great numbers and holding back. The SIO – DCI Whitestone, back where she belonged – the CSIs and the search teams had all been and gone on this grey street and now they were up at the London Gateway services on the M1, rummaging around the derelict container where Abu Din had been imprisoned.

We showed our warrant cards to the uniform.

Up close he was far bigger than he had looked on CCTV and much younger. He couldn't have been long out of Hendon. *Rocastle*, it said on his name tag. He was embarrassed he hadn't done better when the transit van came barrelling down the road.

'You did the right thing,' I said. 'You got out of the way. They wouldn't have stopped for you or anyone else.'

'Did you see their faces?' Edie said. 'Hear anything when they got out of the van?'

'They had those masks on when I clocked them,' he said. 'The Albert Pierrepoint masks. There was a lot of screaming and hollering when they were getting Abu Din into the van, but I couldn't tell who was shouting.'

'If you catch them,' said a woman's voice, 'give them a medal.'

She was standing behind the young man in a wheelchair. For the first time I saw that he was wearing what looked like the remains of a uniform. Green army-issue T-shirt, DPM desert camouflage trousers that hung loosely on prosthetic legs fitted into Asics trainers so unused they could have just come out of the box. As they looked at my warrant card I saw they shared the same brown-eyed, black-haired good looks and the kind of skin that tans easily.

'DC Wolfe,' I said. 'But who are you?'

The woman laughed. At first I had thought they could be twins, but now she seemed to be a few years older than the young man in the wheelchair.

'You people are unbelievable,' she said, her mouth tight with bitterness. 'Mr Din down there is talking about flying his flag over Downing Street and you really want to see *our* ID?'

Quite a few reporters and photographers were hanging around, most of them at Abu Din's end of the street. But a couple of them stirred at the sound of the woman's voice raised in amused disbelief. I gave Edie the nod and she headed them off before they could come our way.

'This was a crime scene, ma'am,' I told the woman. And then I waited. She gave me a driving licence.

Piper Maldini, twenty-nine years old.

'I haven't got anything,' the man in the wheelchair said, panic in his voice. Piper Maldini soothed him with a touch of his shoulder. She fished an NHS card out of his rucksack. Philip Maldini, twenty-six.

'She's my sister,' he said.

I gave them back the driving licence and the NHS card. Piper's hand was still lightly resting on her brother's shoulder.

'You're here every day?' I said, as gently as I could.

Piper Maldini still took offence. 'Is that a crime, too?'

I shook my head.

'Was it the Hanging Club?' Philip Maldini said,

194

excitedly. He had none of the thin-skinned aggression of his sister. 'Is that who took him?'

I could give them a bunch of flannel or I could tell them the truth.

'We're working on that assumption, although we haven't ruled out that it could be a group of self-starters.'

'And he got away?'

'Yes.'

'Better luck next time,' Piper said.

'Why do you come down here?' I asked them.

'To confront the people who would dance on our graves,' Piper Maldini said. 'Why do *you* come down here, Detective? To protect the likes of Abu Din?'

'I'm just doing my job.'

'Isn't that what the guards said at the Nazi concentration camps?'

I stared at her. 'I don't think of myself as a concentration camp guard,' I said. 'Ma'am.'

'What would happen to me if I spewed the kind of filth that comes out of *his* mouth?' she said, gesturing to the man in robes droning away at the end of the street. 'If I preached hatred, and if I mocked boys who died for their country, and if I saw gays and women and Jews as less than human – what would you do to *me*, Detective?'

I leaned forward to look at the young man in the wheelchair.

'Thank you for your service,' I said.

I began to walk away. I didn't want to argue with her and I didn't want to arrest them. And I was afraid if I stuck around much longer I would have to do both.

Piper Maldini shouted at my back. 'Detective!'

I turned to look at her. She was gripping the side of her brother's wheelchair with one hand and with the other she was pulling up the sleeve of her T-shirt to show me the tattoo on her bicep. I had seen the tattoo before. It was a British Army tattoo. Five red and black poppies under six words.

ALL GAVE SOME – SOME GAVE ALL

'My brother wasn't the only one who served,' she said.

CHAPTER 22

I awoke near the end of the night, at that moment when deep, restorative sleep enters the dreaming shallows.

The first rays of sunrise were filling the big windows of the loft with a milky light. I heard Stan sigh and settle by my side and I reached out to stroke him, reassuring him it wasn't time to get up yet.

But my phone was vibrating. It was DCI Whitestone.

**Press conference –
West End Central –
0800 sharp.**

I looked at the clock by the side of the bed. 04.45. I lay back with a sigh, my hand on fur that was smoother than silk. Stan's huge round eyes were watching me in the half-light.

'Nobody sleeps any more, Stan,' I said.

Scout was spending a couple of nights at Mia's, an extended sleepover that was only possible during her long summer break, so after I had walked and fed the dog I waited for Mrs Murphy to arrive and then headed off for work hours before I really needed to. There was no sound from Jackson's room.

MIR-1 was empty when I arrived at West End Central carrying a triple espresso from the Bar Italia on Frith Street, Soho. As sometimes happened when I had not slept well, I could feel my old injuries coming back, reminders of ancient pain that my grandmother would have called 'playing up'.

There was a three-inch scar on my stomach where a man who was now dead had stuck his knife.

There was the lower part of my ribcage on the right-hand side where I had torn my internal intercostal muscles – the muscles that let you breathe – when I had fallen through a table. And there were assorted knocks that I had picked up in the gym, trying to be a tough guy.

They all hurt today.

So I took off the jacket of the suit that I had got married in and got down on the floor of MIR-1 to do some stretching. It was the only thing that made all that old bone-deep pain go away. I had learned the moves watching Stan. He did them every time he got up.

I settled in a neutral position on my hands and knees and then curved my spine, raising my head as I pushed back my shoulders. Just like Stan. And then the other way round, arching my back and trying to make my chin touch my navel. Just like Stan. I breathed out, feeling better already, and settled for a moment on my hands and knees before straightening my arms and legs and pushing my butt into the air. And that is the position I was in when I saw Tara Jones watching me from the doorway of MIR-1.

'You do yoga?' she said. 'I'm impressed.'

I got to my feet, my face burning. 'What? Yoga? No! These are just some moves that Stan taught me.'

'Stan's your yoga teacher? He's good.'

'Stan's my dog.'

She came into the room and went to her workstation.

'Why are you in so early?' I said, and when she turned to look at me we both realised that she had not heard me.

'Sorry,' I said. 'Sometimes I forget.'

She was plugging her laptop into the workstation's computer.

She looked at my face. 'You forget I'm deaf?'

'Yes.'

'There's no reason to remember. My condition doesn't define me. It's a difficulty not a disability. My parents were told, "Your baby girl can have a disability or a difficulty. It's up to you." They treated it as a difficulty rather than a disability. And so do I.'

'I don't mean to offend you.'

'It's fine that you forget. You don't offend me.'

She waited for me to speak.

'I just wondered why you are here so early.'

The hint of a smile. She pushed the hair out of her face.

'I didn't mean to disturb your yoga session, Detective.'

I laughed uneasily. 'I don't do yoga.'

'Oh yes, you do,' she insisted. 'And so does your dog. Stan? Even if you don't know it.' She powered up her machine. 'Two things. I've been running biometrics on the most recent film. The background sound is building work. I know, I know – all of London is a building site. But this is not the sound of someone having a loft conversion or a new conservatory put in. This is heavy machinery, a hundred and fifty feet below ground. That's a major skyscraper going up. That narrows it down, doesn't it?'

I nodded. 'What's the other thing?'

'I did a review of your interviews with Mr Wilder and Mr Warboys. The interview with Mr Warboys has no biometrical anomalies. But I don't think that Mr Wilder was telling you the whole truth.'

I remembered Barry Wilder in the interview room and my total conviction that he had been telling the truth. He had nothing to do with the lynching of Mahmud Irani.

'I thought you said that voice biometrics was infallible?'

'I never said infallible. I said that it was light years ahead of twentieth-century tech like the lie

200

detector.' She hit the keyboard and called up the interview tape. 'Just watch, will you?'

I heard my voice.

'Did you have contact with Mahmud Irani after he was released from prison?'

I heard Barry Wilder reply and saw a yellow line jump across Tara Jones' screen like summer lightning.

'Yes . . . I got a knife . . . I was planning to stick it in his heart.'

'He's telling the truth,' I said.

'Yes, but even when he's telling the truth, his results show evidence of heart palpitations, raised blood pressure, shallow breathing. Initially I didn't run tests on statements that we believed to be true. And I should have done.'

'But he's nervous,' I said. 'He's in a police station. He's admitting that he considered killing one of the men who abused his daughter.'

She shook her head. 'It's more than that. Far more. His blood pressure was a reading of systolic 190 over a diastolic 110 – that's what doctors call a hypertensive crisis. Even when he was telling you the truth, his blood pressure was off the chart.'

'Are you saying he lied to me?'

'No,' she said. 'I'm saying that you didn't ask him the right questions.'

Whitestone froze.

She was staring out at the massed reporters, photographers and camera crews stuffed into the

201

first-floor media room at West End Central and they were all staring back at her, waiting for something to happen.

But nothing did.

This small, bespectacled woman, the most experienced homicide detective at 27 Savile Row, looked as if she did not understand what she was doing here, or what was expected of her. There was a statement in her right hand. I saw her fingers tighten into a fist, crumpling the statement.

I was on one side of her and the Chief Super was on the other. I saw the Chief Super gently touch Whitestone's back, encouraging her, urging her on. And still she did not move.

From the time Whitestone had arrived at MIR-1 today she had seemed distracted, tired, as though her mind was still with her son in the hospital. But I brought her some serious coffee from the Bar Italia and by the time our MIT had assembled, she was more like her old self. Now she had suddenly blanked.

'I've got it,' I whispered, and took the microphone. 'Good morning, ladies and gentlemen. I'm DC Max Wolfe of West End Central and I'm going to make a brief statement about our ongoing investigations and then take a few questions.'

Scarlet Bush stood up.

'I wanted to ask you about the victims of the Hanging Club,' she said.

I prised Whitestone's statement from her hand. She glanced at me for a moment and then quickly fled the room.

I looked down at the words she had written:
I'm going to make a brief statement.

Scarlet Bush was still talking. 'A child molester. A hit-and-run driver. A drug addict who put an old war hero in a coma. And now a hate preacher, popularly – and some would say deservedly – known as the Mental Mullah.'

I held my temper.

'What's your question?'

'How does it feel to be hunting men who millions consider to be heroes?

'Vigilantes are not heroes,' I said. 'Murderers are not heroes. Not in the eyes of the law.'

They were shouting questions at me now.

'The law is there to protect *everyone*,' I said.

'Even pedlars of hate like Abu Din?'

'Everyone. We will pursue the individuals who attempted to abduct Mr Din as vigorously as we would anyone else. That's the way it works, folks. Sorry to disappoint you, but that's the only way it can ever work.'

They were all shouting their questions at me now and I could feel a nervous Media Liaison Officer urging me to wind it up. But I maintained eye contact with Scarlet Bush.

'Murderers are not heroes,' I said.

'Depends who they murder,' she said, and they all laughed.

Whitestone was waiting for me in MIR-1.

'Max,' she said. 'I'm sorry. I couldn't do it.'

'It doesn't matter. I'm happy to do it. I don't care if they love me or not. I don't care what they write. I'm beyond all that now.'

'It's not that,' she said. 'I saw him.'

I stared at her.

'Who?'

'Trey N'Dou. The Dog Town Boy who blinded my son. He lives a mile from us. Can you believe that? I saw him in the street. I will always see him. When my son comes home – *he will be there.*'

She started for the door.

'Come,' she said. 'I'll show you.'

It was the other Islington.

Not the Islington where politicians eat their organic chicken and plot world domination, not the Islington where you can't even think about buying a house for less than two million, and not the Islington that is handy for a job in the City.

This was the other Islington, where the council estates stretch on forever, rolling all the way down from Angel to King's Cross, where the people with nothing live next door to the people with everything, and they don't enjoy it very much.

I parked up across the street from a kebab shop on the Holloway Road. A purple VW Golf was parked outside.

'They live in these streets,' Whitestone said. 'The Dog Town Boys. They're walking around. I will see them. And they will see me, Max. They will see me with my beautiful boy. The one whose eyes they stole. Trey N'Dou and his friends will see him and they will laugh at us, Max. *I know it. I know it. I know it.* I'll do something. If they laugh at us, I'll do something, Max, I swear to God I will.'

'Listen to me, will you? If you're inside, you're no good to your boy, are you? So you're not doing *anything*, all right? Stop talking like that, Pat.'

She jabbed a finger at the shabby street.

'That's him. That's the Dog Town Boy who did it. That's Trey N'Dou.'

A man-sized youth swaggered out of the kebab shop, eating with his mouth open.

'He's the one who did it? You're sure? You're absolutely sure?'

Hot tears were streaming down her face.

'How are we to live, Max?' she said.

I stood at the windows of our loft and watched Jackson coming home from Fred's gym. He was clutching a pair of my old worn fourteen-ounce Lonsdale gloves to his chest.

It was late in the evening, still very light, and the good weather meant the pubs all had crowds outside them. Directly below me, down on Charterhouse Street, there was a group of lads, maybe about a dozen strong, larking about right in front of the entrance to our loft. Jackson was heading straight towards them. Four storeys down, I heard the sound of breaking glass and laughter.

I watched Jackson.

I watched the lads.

I steeled myself to go down and help him.

But he didn't need my help.

They parted to let him through. They didn't look at him and he didn't look at them. But there was something about him that made them step out of his way. At the sound of his key in the door Stan got up and padded off to greet him.

The dog was all over him.

'Hello, little buddy,' he said, scratching Stan behind his extravagant ears. Jackson looked at me and saw my face and waited for me to speak.

'I need your help,' I said.

He nodded.

'Fine. Have I got time for a shower?'

Not – *Is it dangerous?*

Not – *What's all this about, Max?*

He just wanted to know if he had time for a shower. Just a calm acceptance that I needed him by my side tonight. I smiled to myself. He had never felt more like the closest thing I ever had to a brother. And I had never loved him more.

I looked out of the loft's huge windows, the last of the summer day's sunshine streaming in.

We wouldn't have to make a move until after dark.

'You've time for a shower,' I told him.

CHAPTER 23

It was knocking on for midnight when we drove north.

The traffic was light but there were still plenty of people on the streets, squeezing the last juice out of the hot summer night, rolling home from pubs and bars dressed for the beach. But on the Farringdon Road the postal workers were filing into Mount Pleasant, the Royal Mail sorting centre, for the graveyard shift and the sight of them going to work made it feel as if summer was nearly over. Jackson stared out at them as I told him the story.

'A boy was blinded,' I said. 'Sixteen years old. Somebody put a broken bottle across his eyes. Over nothing. No reason. No witnesses. Nobody arrested. Nobody punished. His name is Justin Whitestone and he's the son of my boss.' I swallowed down something hard and bitter. 'And the doctors have told his mother that he is never going to see again.'

Jackson nodded. 'Who did it?' he said quietly.

'There's a little mob called the Dog Town Boys,' I said. 'They're on the estates between King's Cross and Upper Street. The closest thing they've got to a leader is this Trey N'Dou. A reliable witness pointed a finger at him before she was frightened off.'

Jackson looked at me.

'And you want to even the score?'

I shook my head.

'I just want this Trey gone. I want him out of town. He's never going to go down – all the people who saw him blind that boy are too scared to talk. So what I want is to make him go away so that my friend never has to look at his ugly grinning face when she is out with her son.'

'And what do I do?'

'You watch my back.'

We were driving past King's Cross station. I turned onto the Pentonville Road. Ahead and above us we could see night lights of the Angel.

'I can do that,' Jackson said.

We were in a car park off the Liverpool Road.

It served a supermarket that stayed open twenty-four hours a day, but now it was almost empty. I parked a discreet distance from the purple Ford Escort. On the far side of the street was a bar called Dabs, the only sign of life and light in a bleak row of shuttered shops. It was impossible to tell if the shops were closed for the night or until hell froze over. A distant bass line rumbled from somewhere deep inside Dabs. There were youth on the street, most of them black, chatting with a bouncer. I wondered if the bouncer might be a problem.

'That's Trey's ride,' I said, indicating the purple Ford Escort.

'Are we going in or waiting outside?'

'We're waiting.'

'All right,' he said, and closed his eyes. He had the soldier's ability to sleep when he was presented with the opportunity. But we didn't have to wait long. Trey N'Dou came out of the club in the company of a skinny girl in a short skirt. I lightly touched Jackson's arm and he was immediately awake. We watched Trey and the girl walking towards the car park.

'What happens if he's not alone?' Jackson said.

'Then we leave it,' I said.

But Trey and the girl veered off towards a dark corner of the car park. They found a patch of scrubby grass and she sank to her knees. Trey stood above her, checking his phone.

No, he was not checking it.

He was taking her picture.

When she had finished, she got up and Trey zipped up and they walked back towards Dabs. As the girl disappeared inside, Trey turned and started towards the purple Ford Escort, its light flashing twice as he unlocked it. We waited for him to get close enough that he had missed the chance to run away.

Then I nodded to Jackson and we got out of the car.

'Hey,' I said, and as Trey N'Dou turned towards me I shoved him backwards into his car. He hit it hard and as he bounced off it, I turned him around, throwing his hands on the roof and kicking his legs apart. I began to pat him down.

Trey chuckled to himself.

'I smell bacon,' he said. 'Delicious bacon. Yum yum – smell that pig.'

'That's right,' I said. 'That's exactly what you smell. You in a gang, tough guy? Me too. I'm in the biggest gang in town.'

I patted him down, struggling to get my breathing under control, feeling myself trembling. I looked back at Jackson but he was calmly staring across the street, watching the entrance to Dabs.

I began pulling things from Trey's baggy trousers. First a small cellophane wrap of white powder. 'What's this, coke? That's up to seven years in prison for possession.' Next a lightweight pair of knuckle-dusters. 'Possession of an offensive weapon in a public place? That's another four years. I don't even have to plant anything on you, do I, tough guy?' Then a lottery ticket. I laughed. 'Your luck just ran out, Trey.'

And then his phone.

I pressed the photos icon. Then there were a number of options. *All photos. Videos. Bursts. Recently Deleted.* I pressed *Recently Deleted.* And I saw a crowded club. Laughter. Screams. And then Justin Whitestone staggering towards the camera, the blood streaming from his ruined eyes.

'You piece of shit,' I said, and banged the back of his head with his phone. His legs buckled but he didn't go down.

'I know my rights,' he laughed, and I saw something that I had not expected.

He wasn't scared of me.

And I needed him to be scared of me.

This was never going to work unless he was scared of me.

'Max,' Jackson said. 'We've got company.'

A car tooled slowly into the car park, music coming from inside, four faces, three black and one white, staring out as it circled us in a wide arc. The car stopped, its engine still running. Four doors came open. Jackson was already walking toward them as they got out.

'Nothing to see here,' he said to the first one, the driver, and hit him in the centre of his face with the palm of his hand, propelling him backwards, blood all over the hands clawing at the flattened nose. Jackson's right hand, the same hand that had executed the palm strike, was raised in what looked like a peace sign until he carefully drove the fingertips of his index and middle finger into the driver's eyes.

Then the other three were on him.

And Jackson took them out.

He slammed the side of his right foot against a knee and then his left foot into somebody else's knee.

A few wild blows rained down on him but not for long. He waded into them with his low, hard kicks to the knees and his hands and his elbows in their eyes. I was starting to understand his fighting technique. Knees and eyes. That's what he went for and

211

it is difficult to do much of anything, let alone fight back, when your knees or your eyes are gone.

All you can do is crawl away.

And that is what they did.

The four of them crawled away.

Somehow they got into the car and took off.

But Trey N'Dou still wasn't scared of me. He saw some weakness, or some reticence in me. Some line that he knew I would never cross. He looked at me and smiled. He knew I wasn't going to take out his eye or destroy his knees.

'I want you away from here,' I said, and he laughed in my face.

'And I want you to suck my cock until you love me,' he told me.

'Let me have him for a minute,' Jackson said, pushing me aside.

He grabbed the Dog Town Boy, swung a leg behind him and pushed his chest with both hands.

Trey N'Dou went down like a Greek bank.

And then I saw the gun in Jackson's hand.

It seemed to come from out of nowhere, but I knew I had watched him reach his right hand round to the back of his spine and produce it from under the Original Penguin polo shirt I had lent him.

Trey N'Dou saw it at the same time. I heard him whimper and then a hissing sound as he wet his baggy jeans. I could not breathe as Jackson straddled the Dog Town Boy and put the barrel of the gun in the kid's mouth.

'I can't hear you,' Jackson said, the boy gagging

on the gun. 'Louder. Come on. What is it you want? *We can't understand you.*'

Trey N'Dou was begging for mercy with a gun in his mouth.

Jackson took it out.

'*Please. Please. Please.*'

Jackson fired between his legs.

Twice.

I had heard guns fired with serious intent before. The sound always shocked me – the way it seemed to last for longer than it should, the way it seemed to rend the air, to tear it apart, to go on and on. Somehow this was different. The sound was more like two bombs going off.

I stood there paralysed, my ears ringing, my breath ragged.

I watched Jackson carefully pick up the spent brass from the gunshots.

He slipped them in his pocket.

'Am I dead?' Trey N'Dou said.

Jackson laughed.

'If you were dead you would have one in your head and one in your heart. Listen to my friend. Get out of the Angel. We don't give a toss if you go to Kingston-on-Thames or Kingston, Jamaica. Up to you. But you really don't want to see my face again. No more warning shots.'

Lights were coming on all over the Liverpool Road.

There was a group of people outside the club across the street, cowering behind cars and looking across at us. The bouncer was nowhere to be seen. But in the distance I could hear sirens and I wondered if they were coming for us.

'Let's get out of here,' I said.

We did not speak for quite a while.

I drove to the canals of Little Venice and parked up next to a line of houseboats showing no lights. I turned off the engine.

'Give me the gun, Jackson.'

He half-twisted, reached under his polo shirt and pulled it out. Then he gave it to me. I hefted it in my hand, feeling the weight of the thing, a bit less than a kilo, noting the way just the feel of it made my heart hammer in my chest.

'It's a Glock 17,' Jackson said, as if I might be wondering. 'Sometimes called a Glock Safe Action Pistol. It's a nine-millimetre, polymer-framed, short recoil semi-automatic.'

'I don't understand.'

'Polymer is what its frame is made of instead of steel – that hard plastic-type material makes it much lighter. Easier to carry, easier to conceal. Semi-automatic just means that when you fire a round, the spent brass is ejected and the chamber is reloaded.'

'I mean – I don't understand why you have it.'

He shrugged.

'The Glock 17 is standard issue these days, although the British Army's pistol of choice was the Browning for seventy years.' He nodded at the gun in my hand. 'I prefer this one,' he said. 'The Glock holds seventeen bullets – that's why it's a Glock 17 – the Browning only thirteen. And the Glock 17 is lighter, safer, more effective at close quarters when the fuzzy-wuzzies have got their hands around your throat.'

'And you just decided to steal one, did you?'

He looked offended.

'It's not stealing. The British Army has got twenty-five thousand of these things. I need it more than they do.'

'You fucking idiot.'

He watched me slip the handgun in the gap in my jeans where the bottom of my spine met the top of my butt. Then he smiled at me. The gap-toothed smile of Jackson Rose.

I felt like punching him in the face.

'You're not going to shoot yourself in the arse, are you, Max?' he said.

'No,' I said. 'I'm not going to shoot myself in the arse.'

He chuckled. 'Good.'

My mouth was totally dry.

'We did enough tonight to be put away,' I said.

'Only if they catch us. And they're not going to catch us.'

'Do you know who CO19 are, Jackson? They're the Specialist Firearms Command of the Met. If they had seen you in that car park tonight, they would have killed you.'

He stared straight ahead.

He was getting tired of being told off.

He sighed.

'So you want me to contain that little creep but you don't want me to – what, Max? – violate his human rights?'

'I can't be put away, Jackson. I've got Scout. I've got a daughter to bring up. I've got a life. A home. A family. I can't be around this stuff. I'm not like you,' I said, starting the engine. 'I've got something to lose.'

I saw the flash of pain in his eyes and I was glad to see it there.

We drove back to Smithfield in silence, the summer-night city empty now, and the BMW X5 always two or three mph below the speed limit.

There was a rage in him and it had always been there.

When we were two boys who didn't have one parent between us, I always thought of it as his wildness. But it was more than that – beyond the gap-toothed grin was a deep and abiding anger that Jackson Rose would carry to his grave.

Both of us were raised by someone who had to step in for our parents. My grandmother and his adoptive parents. But my parents died. And his left. Perhaps that was the difference between us. He had a father who didn't want his mother and a mother who didn't want him.

And it leaves a rage in you, being left like that.

I had always felt blessed. Lucky to have the mum and dad I had, although I would have liked them for longer. Lucky to have my grandmother, although I wished she hadn't enjoyed her smokes so much and had never got lung cancer. Lucky to have Scout, even though I would spend the rest of my days wishing she had known a family life without divorce. But I never felt sorry for myself, and I never felt that kind of rage.

I was, I guess, a glass-half-full kind of guy. My friend Jackson was a glass-half-empty, smash-it-on-the-bar-and-wave-it-in-your-face kind of guy.

I had seen his rage when we were young and trouble came calling. But it was different now, for now it was honed and polished.

Now someone had trained him for murder.

Stan came to greet us when we opened the door. The dog hated it when nobody was home and my eyes quickly scanned the loft for signs of the small puddles he sometimes deposited when he was anxious. But the floor seemed dry.

Jackson looked at the dog and not at me. He got down on his knees to fuss over the small red Cavalier.

'I was trying to help,' Jackson said quietly. 'That's all.'

'And you did help. In your own mad bastard way – you did.'

'But you can't be around this stuff.'

'No.'

'And that means you can't be around me.'

We were silent for a long moment.

He looked up at me and I nodded.

'That's right,' I said. I felt something fall away

inside me, something that I knew I would never get back. 'You're too dangerous,' I said.

He nodded, as if it was all settled.

'I'll pack my stuff and ship out. Say goodbye to Scout for me, will you?'

'Christ almighty, Jackson, you don't have to go *now*.'

He stood up and faced me.

'Ah, but I think I do, Max.'

We both looked down at Stan. The dog stared back at us, confusion in those perfectly round eyes, unable to read the mood. I wasn't sure I could read it myself.

'What are your plans?' I said, and the sudden formality between us broke my heart.

He shrugged.

'I don't know. I'll do what the army trained me to do,' he said.

'And what was that, Jackson?' I said.

He just gave me his gap-toothed smile.

Stan padded behind him to his room.

Jackson turned in the doorway.

'Max?'

I looked at him.

'You think that little gangster will bother your friend any more?'

'No.'

He nodded, satisfied.

'Me neither,' he said.

And then my oldest friend went into the guest room to pack his things.

CHAPTER 24

It felt wrong from the start.

I turned into Abu Din's street and the only police presence I could see was one unmarked 3-series BMW parked outside the large council house and the same young black policeman standing guard at the end of the road.

DCI Whitestone came out of the house with Edie and Billy Greene. Whitestone and Edie were in dark headscarves. I nodded to the two officers in the unmarked BMW as I went up to the front door.

'This is it?' I said. 'Feels a bit light. We just gave the guy an Osman Warning. We just told him his life was in mortal danger and offered him police protection.'

'The Chief Super considers it a proportionate response in this community,' Whitestone said. She indicated the street. Several groups of bearded young men hung around, quietly conferring as they watched the detectives. A solitary woman struggled home from the shops with stuffed Tesco bags, her face and body covered by a full black burka. 'That's an Armed Response Vehicle outside the house,' Whitestone continued. 'CO19 are going

219

to stick around until we've nicked these people. And there'll be two of our team in the house for the next forty-eight hours. It's not a bad idea to keep it semi-low-key around here, Max. We don't need lots of uniforms on the street.'

I nodded and watched her face beneath the headscarf, waiting for some sign that she knew what I had done last night with Jackson. Anger. Relief. Gratitude. Disbelief. I didn't know what to expect.

But DCI Whitestone just looked at her watch.

'So you're OK to take the first shift with Billy? Mr Din prefers having male officers in his house during the night.'

'Fine.'

'Then Edie and I will see you in the morning,' Whitestone said.

Edie took off her headscarf. 'Or by the end of the Dark Ages,' she said. 'Whatever comes first.'

After they drove off Billy went back into the house while I stood there watching the sun go down over the rooftops of Wembley, the last rays of the day glinting on the great white arch of the stadium that looms above everything in that part of town. It was only eight in the evening but already the day was done and there was a chill in the air that hadn't been there for months. Yes, summer was almost over now. I knew Scout felt as if it had gone on forever. But to me the season had passed in the blink of an eye.

I walked down to the young copper at the end of the street.

'PC Rocastle? I've got the graveyard shift. We're going to be in the house.'

'I'm on until midnight.'

I watched him hesitate.

'What's on your mind, officer?' I said.

'You really think they might come back, sir?' he said.

I pointed at the unmarked ARV parked outside the big council house.

'If they do,' I said, 'they better be ready to start shooting.'

The street was emptying as I walked back to the house. A middle-aged white woman and man were walking their German Shepherd. I nodded to them. They ignored me. I smiled at the dog's proud face and reached down to pet him.

And the woman spat as we passed each other.

A great glob of saliva glistened on the pavement between us. I stopped and stared at their backs. I saw tattoos on white flesh. And I saw their glances back – the man afraid, the woman more willing to show her contempt.

They don't get it, I thought. They have no clue what we do.

Without fear or favour, we protect everyone.

I had taken the watch in the living room at the front of the house and Billy was in the back garden. I stared beyond the net curtains as Abu Din reclined in his long grey robes and watched me.

'Who are those men parked outside my home?'
he said.

'They're police officers who are trained in the
use of firearms.'

He laughed. When I turned to look at him, Abu
Din gazed at me with great amusement.

'You don't seem very worried about the threat
to your life, Mr Din.'

'Because there is no threat to my life. It is not my
time for *shaheed*. Hasn't that been proved already?'

'*Shaheed* means martyr, right?'

'Literally *shaheed* means witness. But yes –
shaheed is the tribute we pay to believers who die
fulfilling their religious commitments. Their place
in paradise is assured.'

'Maybe you were just lucky.'

He stopped smiling.

'There's no luck needed, *alhamdulilah*. All praise
be to God. I have *tawakul* – reliance on God – so
I do not fear *shaytan*.'

'It must be nice to have such faith.'

He looked at me coldly. 'And it must be hell to
live without it.'

'One thing I don't understand . . .' I said.

'Oh, I think there are many things a *kuffar* such
as yourself doesn't understand.'

'I'm sure that's true. But there's one thing in
particular that I don't understand.'

'I'm waiting.'

'If you hate this country, sir – if you hate living
with the *kuffars* – then why don't you make *hijrah*?'

'*Hijrah*? Migration? Are you asking me why I don't leave this country?'

I nodded. 'Nobody's going to stop you, are they?'

He didn't even look offended.

'I don't need to leave, *alhamdulilah*,' he said.

'Why not?'

'Because everywhere belongs to God.'

And that was when they came.

A white transit roared into the cul-de-sac and slammed on the brakes, as if suddenly clocking the ARV.

'Billy!'

The white transit reversed at speed out of the street. The ARV was going after it. I saw the pure terror flash on Abu Din's face as I ran from the room. Billy Greene was right behind me.

I went out the front door in time to see the white transit van pulling away with the ARV on its tail. At the end of the street I could see the crumpled figure of PC Rocastle half on the pavement and half in the street. The taillights of the ARV disappeared.

'Call it in,' I told Billy, and began running towards the unmoving body of PC Rocastle.

And then another transit van – this one black – turned into the street and accelerated towards me.

'We've been suckered,' I said.

Billy was halfway up the garden path as the back doors of the transit van opened. I waved my hand at him to tell him to keep going.

'Get back in the house, Billy. Lock all the doors. And don't leave his side.'

I heard his footsteps on the garden path and then the front door slammed shut. I heard the door bolt and looked back to catch a glimpse of Abu Din's petrified face beyond the net curtains. And then I turned away because three dark figures were getting out of the back of the van. No Albert Pierrepoint masks tonight. No friendly uncles now. Their faces were covered with ski masks. No, not ski masks. Tactical Nomex face masks.

I clenched my fists as they came towards the house and swung a right at the first figure. And that was when my muscles went into involuntary spasm and I was suddenly down on my knees, a drool of saliva coming from the corner of my mouth. I vaguely understood that I had been shot with a taser or some other kind of electroshock CEW. My muscles were still twitching violently with shock and pain as strong hands lifted and loaded me into the back of the black transit van.

Inside there was a smell I knew from somewhere but it felt like it was long ago and far away.

Rank and sweet, like something good that had been left to rot.

The doors slammed shut.

My muscles flexed and trembled and now the pain began.

The transit van started to move.

And it was only then that I realised they had not come for Abu Din.

They had come for me.

CHAPTER 25

I sat on the bench of the transit van as docile as a lamb being led to slaughter, my mind feeling that it was separated from the rest of the world by thick soundproofed glass. I stared at the black Nomex face masks of the two figures sitting opposite me and they stared back, and for a while all I could think about was the way my muscles twitched and shuddered with a will of their own.

Then I took a breath and tried to think, sucking up the pain and pushing it to one side, telling myself that it would keep on getting better, moment by moment, and telling myself that I could take it.

Think.

There was a smell I knew in the back of the van.

Something foul that had once been sweet.

Rotting fruit.

Dead flowers.

Sugar and human waste.

Think.

I took a breath and looked again at the two figures on the bench opposite me. The big one – the one who had filled my nerve endings with electricity, the one who had picked me up as if I weighed nothing – was sitting by my side. And there had to be one more man driving.

Four of them. The full team. None of them were talking. None of them displayed any telltale tattoos or jewellery.

They were good.

But they were not cops.

If they had been cops – and there had always been the unspoken suspicion that the Hanging Club just might be rogue cops – they wouldn't simply have knocked the stuffing out of me with a cheap East European taser knock-off. *A formal arrest will always be accompanied by physically taking control*, was the first thing they taught you at Hendon. They hadn't done it.

They had merely flattened me with their pound-store taser and chucked me in the back of their van. Any cop would have done more. But I was not cuffed. I was not unconscious. And I would get stronger with every passing minute that I could stay alive.

I looked at the masked faces, realising they had still not said one word.

'So if you're all here, then who was driving the white van?' I asked.

'Friends,' murmured the large figure by my side.

'Friends?' I said. 'I bet you've got lots of friends, right?'

A fist pounded furiously on the back of the cab. The driver was sending a clear message.

No talking!

I glimpsed eyes wild with rage behind another black Nomex and I felt the three figures in the back of the van shift uncomfortably. So was that the leader behind the wheel?

I laughed and half-turned to look at the man by my side.

'You're the big man in town, right? Cleaning up the mean streets—'

I caught my breath as he placed the razor blade against the lid of my right eye.

Very gently, almost lovingly, he drew the sharp edge of the razor blade across the thin layer of skin that covered my eye, demonstrating how very easy it would be to slice it open, how little would be the effort required on his part, how pathetically fragile I was.

I thought of what had happened to Justin Whitestone and fought to control my breathing. My eyes, I thought, and my heart wanted to burst.

And I thought that was the end of all conversation. But the black figure holding the razor blade pressed against my eyelid leaned in close so that only I could hear what he had to say.

'And you protect the filth, little man, don't you? And that is why *you* have no friends any more. You stand guard at the door while the Pakistani child groomers rape our children and you tug your forelock while rich men murder the innocent and you devote yourself to cleaning the shoes of the scum of the earth. More than any of them, little man, you are the one who deserves to hang.'

And it was a voice I thought I knew from somewhere.

Once upon a time. Long ago and far away. My muscles twitched with pain and my mind was foggy with shock.

But I had heard that voice before.

He pressed the blade against my eyeball and, as stray muscles in random parts of my body still spasmed with shock, I tried very hard to not move.

Perhaps they're cops after all, I thought.

There was no change of vehicle. Perhaps they had learned their lesson with Abu Din. Perhaps the switch vehicle had been used to sucker the Armed Response Vehicle. And to sucker me, too. But there was no stopping this time.

We drove.

Fast but not that fast. There was little traffic around at this time of night, but the driver kept below the speed limit, like a good criminal should. Then we seemed to go slower and I thought we must be moving into town rather than driving out of it. There was no opening up on a motorway, only slowing down to an inner-city crawl.

Then we were on rough terrain, bumping over uneven surfaces, and going down.

The transit van stopped.

We had reached our destination.

The razor blade was drawn across my eyelid. I felt a sharp sting of pain and I cursed as a dribble of blood ran down my face like a teardrop.

'Be a good little pig and you can die with both of your eyes,' he said. 'You don't want to be on YouTube with your eyes hanging out, do you?' He laughed. 'Your daughter wouldn't want to watch that for the rest of her life, would she?'

The driver opened the back door. And then he didn't speak any more.

They helped me out into an abandoned underground car park. No, not abandoned. Unfinished. That was why there were no vehicles. This place was still being built.

There were junk-food cartons and empty cans littered around, the refuse of builders working underground in the summer heat. I thought of Tara Jones and her belief that major building work was happening near to the kill site.

Three masked faces stared at me for a moment and then turned away. The big one was behind me. A meaty hand shoved me in the back and I felt his breath as he walked behind me across the empty car park.

It was massive. Shopping mall? Office block? Luxury apartments? The three figures in front of me moved quickly and the big man behind gave me a casual crack across the back of my head whenever I seemed to slow my pace. He still held the razor blade between the thumb and index finger of his right hand and whenever he hit me,

I felt the blade randomly slash through hair and skin.

We came to a dimly lit staircase and started down. At the bottom – two storeys down? – we entered a broad, low-ceilinged tunnel. We were in total darkness now. But they knew where they were going. Then we were crossing uneven floor surfaces towards distant lights.

Machinery. Noise. I caught a glimpse of it.

It was a boiler room.

We walked past it and came to a door. The door was unlocked and we passed inside. We went down some more steps and came to a short, strange corridor that was like something from a dream.

We moved down it in slow single file.

And I could not believe what I was seeing.

The walls and ceiling came closer with every step.

I tried to clear my head. I thought my nerve endings were still rattled from the CEW.

But it was real.

The corridor really did become smaller. The ceiling really did get lower. By the time we reached the end we had to press our hands against our sides and lower our heads.

There was a room at the end of the corridor.

And my heart fell away. For I knew this room.

I saw the white tiles stained green and yellow by a century of weather and neglect. And choked down the sickness when I saw the kitchen step stool where they had stood Mahmud Irani, Hector Welles and Darren Donovan.

The room radiated pure evil.

The sharp red light of someone's smart phone was aiming at my face. From behind me the big man took my hands and I heard the jangle of the handcuffs. Finally they were taking full physical control. He was about to secure my hands behind my back so that I would hang quietly.

'Do you know why you have been brought to this place of execution?' he asked me.

And I fought for my life.

I dragged the heel of my right shoe from his kneecap to his ankle, feeling the skin peel away beneath his trousers, hearing him shriek with sudden agony, the handcuffs clattering to the ground.

Then the others were all on me, aiming wild, random punches that caught me on the ear and in the shoulder and did nothing, but one of them knew how to kick because I felt the air whoosh out of me as the toe of a shoe caught me just below the lowest rib and then in the soft spot low on my temple.

It was enough to put me on my knees.

The big man fell on me and grasped me in a headlock, cursing me, his breath sour against my face. The red light had fallen away. They were not filming me now.

'Fucking pig! Fucking bastard!'

It was a good headlock. I could not move my arms or my legs or my feet. So I pressed my mouth against his face and sank my teeth into his cheek, biting through the Nomex face mask and into his flesh.

He howled and tried to stand up as I held on like a dog with a dying rat. But I was weakened and breathless and sickened by those two kicks and the others pulled me off him.

I felt the noose drop over my head.

They lifted me up, not bothering with the handcuffs now, as they half-dragged and half-pushed me onto the stool, planning to do me as they had done Hector Welles, and I could see him before me now, his unsecured hands still tearing the flesh from his throat with his dying breath, clawing so hard that his fingernails were torn out and buried in his neck.

I screamed with rage and terror.

But I was exhausted.

Then I was standing on the kitchen step stool and my fingers were ripping at the rope around my neck. I looked up and saw that one of them had passed the rope over an ancient pipe that crossed the stained ceiling of that forgotten room. The masked faces were all looking at me, the big figure touching the torn Nomex face mask where it was stained with his blood.

Someone was trying to kick the stool away.

Two of them were shouting at each other.

'Do you know why—'

'Just do it!'

The stool flew away and suddenly there was nothing beneath my feet and the rope around my neck was strangling me. My eyes rolled into the back of my head and my fingers tore at the tightening rope for a second that seemed to last for a thousand years. In that never-ending moment I felt my head tip grotesquely to one side as the rope angled towards the knot and I could feel my body weight killing me.

The blood stopped flowing to my brain.

The air stopped flowing to my lungs.

I knew that I was dying.

I saw nothing.

I stared at the ceiling and I didn't see it.

I looked up at the rope and I didn't see it.

There was only the sensation of strangulation as my hands tore at the rope around my neck.

My hands fell away from my throat. My legs kicked and flayed, and I had nothing in me to stop them, and I felt myself on the very edge of the blackness that lasts forever, and it felt as sweet and welcome as home.

But then I reached behind me, my fingers scrambling under the back of my polo shirt, clawing at the base of my spine.

And I felt the plastic grip of the Glock 17.

Then it was in my right hand and I was pointing it at the ceiling, pulling the trigger, the crack of gunfire deafening in that confined place, then pulling the trigger again as fast as I could. I was aware of their screams and shouts but I kept pulling the trigger, trying to break the rope that was killing me, and then the sounds seemed to be coming from underwater and then I heard nothing, nothing at all, just an unbroken ringing in my ears as my heart surged with desperation when I realised that it had not worked.

I was still hanging.

The secret room turned red.

The blood flow to my brain had stopped and that blocked dam of blood seemed to be filling the room.

I closed my eyes.

My hand fell to my side. My fingers were opening, my friend's gun was slipping from my hand and the unbroken blackness was all I wanted now. I felt the full kilo of polymer and steel in my hand. Someone was trying to prise it from my grasp. I lashed out at them with my foot.

Then something happened in my ears.

I could hear them shouting again.

Scream. Shouts. Cursing.

They were on me, pulling on my legs, and I couldn't understand, then I saw they were trying to drag me down and get it done, finally get it done, get me over with forever.

And it revived me enough to kick out at their masked faces.

And I raised my right hand one last time.

Because I saw what I had been doing wrong. The range had to be point-blank. Nothing else would work. Everything else was useless. Point-blank or nothing. Point-blank or death.

I felt the barrel of Jackson's Glock 17 press

against the rope, press so hard that I could feel the impossible tightness around my neck become even tighter.

Then I pulled the trigger.

I was aware of the crack of gunfire, a sound that seemed to rip the air apart, and then I was falling, my feet and elbows connecting with human flesh and bone.

I hit the ground hard, the gun still in my hand.

My vision was blurred with what felt like blood and tears. But I could see they were running towards a broken gap in the wall. I pointed at the back of the big man as he squeezed through the gap and screamed a hoarse curse as I pulled the trigger, my eyes streaming.

I heard the metallic click of an empty magazine.

I pulled it again and again, even after the last of them had disappeared through the hole in the wall. White noise filled my head.

I got up, spitting out a bloody scrap of synthetic material that must have come from a Nomex tactical face mask.

I stuffed the Glock down the back of my jeans, hearing a mocking voice deep inside my head.

You're not going to shoot yourself in the arse, are you?

I took a painful breath.

And then I went after them.

I was sick to my stomach with pain and exhaustion but the rage inside was bigger than both of them. I went through the crack in the wall, stepping over scraps of rotted wood, and down the low-ceilinged tunnel until I found a stone staircase, going down even deeper into the ground. I went down the stairs slowly, moving in total blackness, afraid of falling, afraid they were waiting for me, smelling what seemed to be soot and sewers.

From somewhere I could hear the sound of heavy machinery but it became fainter as I went lower. Down and down until I reached an open space where a series of corridors met, the meeting point of a labyrinth of tunnels.

I stopped and thought I could hear voices in one of them. Then I went on, the ground always sinking beneath me. And just when I thought about turning back, when I thought I could sense the men waiting for me silently in the darkness, the stairs ended.

Ahead there were four identical tunnels, each with a rounded arch, wide but not high, built to process large numbers of people at once. They felt like they were all heading in the same direction. I carried on more carefully now, treading lightly, straining for sound.

But all I could hear was my own breathing.

And then I stepped into what looked like the train station at the end of the world.

There were two platforms facing each other across ancient tracks. It was a tube station, but nothing like one I had ever seen. The platforms were made of wood and I could see the remains of what had once been advertising posters on the black-and-white tiles of the walls. They had rotted away a lifetime ago. It reminded me of photographs I had seen of Londoners seeking safety underground during the Blitz. On a large red circle, the name of the station was written in black letters on a white background.

B L O O M S B U R Y

I shook my head in disbelief.

There is no tube station in London by that name.

I stared at the ghost station and knew I could wait for a hundred years and there would be no passengers and no trains passing through this place.

I felt a shudder of pure terror and wondered if I had died in the room with the tiles stained green by time.

Then I touched the livid weal that had been burned into the flesh around my neck and I flinched with the pain.

I was not dead yet.

I heard sounds coming from deep inside the tunnel.

I walked to the edge of the platform and stared into the blackness but I could see nothing. But the sound was real. It wasn't just in my head. I looked down at the tracks. There were four lines, two of them with insulators. I thought about that for a while.

The station was dead but that didn't mean that the lines were dead.

I was aware that in a working tube station the lines with insulators are live and will kill you instantly, and that the trains run on the other lines. But I also knew it was a myth that no electricity runs through the non-insulated train tracks – they carry enough voltage to power the signals. The fact is that making contact with any tube rail is likely to ruin your whole day.

I steadied myself on the edge of the platform, took a breath, and jumped down between the nearest two tracks.

And that was when I heard the train coming.

I quickly scrambled back up onto the platform, feeling the Glock scrape against my spine as it slipped from my jeans. I looked down at it, just about visible on the tracks, as a rat the size of a neutered tom cat skittered across it. Then the train was much closer. Lights blazed deep in the tunnel, twisting towards me and then away as the train snaked through the bowels of the city. I stood drenched in cold sweat on the platform as the train hurtled towards me like an avalanche.

It never reached the station.

At the last moment it veered into the darkness and away from me, a blur of speed and steel, a silver train with red doors and blue trim and a driver who caught a glimpse of me for a fraction of a section.

And stared as if I had been raised from the dead.

★   ★   ★

The driver must have called it in immediately.

I knew that any 999 call from the public about a possible armed or terrorist incident would be forwarded instantly to the Tactical Firearms Command desk where someone with the rank of inspector or above would assess the information to see if it fit the criteria for armed officers to respond. And I did.

By the time I climbed the tube station's long and winding staircase up to the street, they were waiting for me.

Armed officers from SC&O19.

They didn't think I was a ghost.

They thought I was a terrorist.

As I stepped out into the warm summer night, they started screaming at me. I could not tell where the voices were coming from but I could feel the adrenaline in the air. Then I saw their raised weapons. The Glock pistols. The Heckler and Koch submachine guns.

'Hands in the air and get down on your knees!'

'I am DC Wolfe of West End Central and I am complying with your command,' I said, as calm and clear as I could make it.

'Do it now! Do it now!'

I raised my hands and got down on my knees, the pavement surprisingly cold in the warm summer night.

Then I saw them.

Edging towards me, fingers on the triggers.

'There's a wallet in my right pocket which

contains my warrant card,' I said, still as calm and clear as I could make it, but finding it harder to sound like the voice of reason with my face pressed against the pavement.

Someone pushed a boot heel against the back of my neck. A pair of hands patted me down and another pair of hands went through my pockets. I lifted my lower body very slightly so they could remove my wallet.

'Don't move! Don't move!'

I felt the barrel of a Glock screw itself into my ear.

I held my breath. I did not move.

But even after they saw my warrant card they kept my face pressed to the pavement and my limbs spread wide. Even after they clocked my photo ID they kept me face down on the ground with a size-12 boot heel pressed firmly against the back of my neck.

And they kept me there for a long time.

It was as if nobody could be trusted any more, as if the world had gone insane, as if you never knew who might want to dance on your grave.

PART III

APPARATUS OF DEATH

CHAPTER 26

The view from the top of New Scotland Yard is spectacular.

When you are up there on the eighth floor you realise that the big modern office block located at 8–10 Broadway, Victoria, so self-consciously anonymous, sits at the heart of British power.

From the window of the room where I waited in my old Paul Smith wedding suit I checked my watch against two of Big Ben's faces as they struck noon and then looked across at the spires of Westminster Abbey and the Palace of Westminster and, stretching off to the north, the rooftops of Whitehall and Downing Street.

It took my breath away.

A portrait of the Queen smiled at me. Her Majesty was young in the picture, and the painting had those saturated Sixties colours where everything was slightly more vivid than real life. She looked like a nice lady who was happy that England had just won the World Cup. Apart from the portrait of the Queen, there was nothing on the walls of that waiting room but posters proclaiming the values of the Metropolitan Police. They all said the same thing.

THE MET VALUES:
PROFESSIONALISM - INTEGRITY -
COURAGE - COMPASSION

But on each wall the poster had a definition of a different value. PROFESSIONALISM was high-lighted on one wall, INTEGRITY on another, COURAGE on another and COMPASSION on the last, the one with the portrait of the Queen. I had no time to read about the different values because a civilian PA put her head around the door.

'They'll see you now,' she said.

I followed her inside where DCS Swire and DCI Whitestone were waiting for me in a top-floor corner room, the Chief Super at the head of a long boardroom table and Pat Whitestone at her right-hand side. Far below, the Thames shimmered like molten gold in the last of the summer sunshine.

'Max,' the Chief Super said. 'How are you?'

'Fine, ma'am, thank you. Nothing broken.'

The truth is my neck felt as though someone had tried to remove my head and I was so bone-tired that only a constant stream of triple espressos from the Bar Italia was keeping my eyes open. It had been a long night.

When the armed officers had allowed me to remove my face from the pavement I had been taken to West End Central where Edie Wren, roused from her bed in the early hours, had conducted what we call a hot debriefing – an interview conducted at the earliest opportunity to obtain as much information as possible in the aftermath of a serious incident. The Senior Investigating Officer almost always conducts a hot debriefing, but DCI Whitestone had been staying with her son at the hospital, and was unavailable. After the hot debrief I had gone home, slept for a few hours, parked Scout at Mrs Murphy's, then shaved, showered, got suited and booted and come straight to New Scotland Yard.

'I'm sorry I didn't have a chance to do the hot debrief myself,' Whitestone said. 'Just had some complications with one of his eyes and – well. I'm sorry.'

I shook my head. 'No problem, ma'am.' But I wondered how long Pat Whitestone could be the SIO of a major murder investigation when her personal life was taking up so much of her time.

'But DC Wren has done a thorough job,' the Chief Super said.

They both had a set of Edie's notes in front of them.

'So the assumption we're making is that they targeted you because you were effectively the public face of this investigation?' Swire continued.

I saw Pat Whitestone flush with embarrassment as she stared down at Edie's notes.

'Yes, ma'am,' I said.

'What do we know about them, Max?' the Chief Super said.

I wasn't surprised to be asked the same questions that Edie had asked me at the hot debriefing. That's the way we work. You ask a question again and again and again. Then you ask it again. And then you see if the answer is always the same.

'There were four of them,' I said. 'There seems to have been one missing when they attempted to abduct Abu Din. But last night – with me – they were at full strength. And they are highly organised, highly motivated and at least a couple of them appear to have received some kind of training. One of them does the heavy lifting. Another one had close combat experience.' I shrugged. 'They're tough, resourceful and barking mad.'

'Edie's notes say that one of them spoke to you,' said Whitestone.

I felt myself begin to tremble. I took a deep breath, held it and let it out slowly. I wasn't going to fall to pieces in this room.

'Yes, ma'am.' I nodded at the notes. 'He told me that the white transit van that distracted the ARV was driven by what he called *friends*.'

Whitestone turned to the Chief Super.

'We found it burned out in a car park in Notting Hill,' she said. 'We're looking for prints.'

The Chief Super laughed bitterly. 'Good luck with that.'

I didn't understand.

'Wait – our ARV *lost* the decoy van? How does an Armed Response Vehicle with two highly trained firearms officers lose a transit van on the North Circular?'

'The white van was driven by a wheelman,' Whitestone said. 'He wasn't some boy racer. He knew his stuff. He could drive and I mean, *really* drive. Like a pro. Like a professional wheelman. And he lost our ARV almost immediately because he entered the North Circular against the flow of the traffic.'

'He drove against the traffic?'

She nodded. 'And the ARV couldn't follow. Too dangerous. They're trained to shoot straight, not drive like Lewis Hamilton. They phoned ahead and by the time we found the white van – twenty minutes later – it was on fire.'

The Chief Super's mouth twisted with annoyance. 'They took you to the kill site, Max. Any thoughts on where it could be?'

I thought of the square room with the decaying tiles, turned green by a century of neglect, and the corridor they had led me down, where the walls and the ceiling were always closing in on me. Had I imagined that? In the bright light of the morning, I wasn't sure how much of the night had been real and how much the fevered imaginings of pure terror. There was a smell – wasn't there? It was sweet and rotten, like dead flowers, or sugar in a sewer. A rank sweetness that I knew from somewhere – or was that just in my head?

'We drove into the city,' I said. 'Somewhere very central. Underground. An abandoned building that was important a century or so ago. But I don't even know where you found me. Nobody's told me. I thought I saw a sign on the wall that said *Bloomsbury* . . . No, I mean, I definitely saw a sign on the wall that said *Bloomsbury* – but I never heard of a tube station with that name.'

'The tube station you found was closed in 1933,' Whitestone said. 'It was originally called British Museum. They were going to call it Bloomsbury but they changed the name before it ever opened. And in 1935 – a couple of years after it was closed – they shot a scene in a film called *Bulldog Jack* down there – a swordfight – and the producers put up signs saying *Bloomsbury*.'

'With Fay Wray,' Swire said. 'The *King Kong* girl.'

'I was looking at . . . a film set?'

'The tube station was real, Max,' Whitestone said. 'Only the sign was fake.'

'But if we know that I was in this tube station,' I said, 'then our search teams must be able to find the kill site.'

Whitestone shook her head.

'They're looking,' she said. 'But it's not that simple. London has hundreds of miles of disused tracks and literally dozens of abandoned underground stations. We know the one you came out of, but you don't know how far you walked and you don't know what direction you came from.'

'What about the Dog Support Unit? The sniffer dogs must be able to follow my trail from Bloomsbury back to the kill site?'

'Do you know the best way to distract a sniffer dog, Max?' Whitestone asked me.

'Introduce another animal, prey or food,' I said. 'Villains call it hiding the ball. You introduce a scent that's strong enough to distract the sniffer dogs from what they're meant to be hunting. Is that what they did?'

'Not them. It's the rats, Max. The millions of rats down there. The sniffer dogs don't have a chance picking up a trail in a world full of rats.'

'I want you to talk to Professor Hitchens later today,' the Chief Super said. 'There might be something you recall about the kill site that will ring some bells for him.'

'Yes, ma'am.'

'There's one thing I don't understand . . .' Whitestone said.

I waited.

'Why aren't you dead, Max?' she asked.

I had told Edie Wren everything that I could remember but I had not mentioned the Glock 17. Because I did not know where to begin with the Glock and I did not want my friend to go to jail.

But I knew that our people must have found the gun by now.

'The pipe they hanged me from broke and they took off,' I said in reply to Whitestone's question. 'Just lucky, I guess.'

Whitestone and Swire exchanged a look. I knew what was coming so I got there first.

'And they couldn't shoot straight,' I said. 'I

managed to get hold of their firearm after it was discharged. Presumably you've found it by now? Some kind of Glock. I'm no firearms expert.'

Whitestone glanced at her notes.

'Yes, a Glock,' she said. 'The search team found it down on the tracks of that old tube station.' She looked at me levelly, reading me the way I had seen her read so many faces in interview rooms. 'A Glock Safe Action Pistol,' she said. 'The British Army like them. Standard issue, apparently.'

'Forensics will find my prints all over it,' I said.

'You *shot* at them?' Swire said, her face darkening.

Every time a member of the Metropolitan Police discharges a firearm, he or she triggers an enquiry that treats him or her as a potential criminal. You are arrested. You are investigated. Unemployment and incarceration are both real possibilities just for pulling that trigger. Even if you shoot Osama bin Laden. And that's what they do to our highly trained Specialist Firearms officers, the Armed Response Vehicle officers and Tactical Support officers – the specialist police who are actually meant to be carrying a gun.

I had no idea what they would do to someone like me and I wasn't anxious to find out.

'The magazine was empty by the time I had the weapon in my hands,' I said. 'I pulled the trigger but it didn't go bang. I took it with me for evidence and dropped it when I got out of the way of a train.'

Silence.

They looked at each other and back at me. They were not sure if they wanted to buy it. I found I did not care.

'What about PC Rocastle?' I said.

'Who?' said the Chief Super.

'The uniformed officer who was on duty in Abu Din's street. I saw he had gone down when they took me away.'

'Oh – PC Rocastle got shot with whatever taser knock-off they used on you,' Whitestone said. 'He's shaken up. Nerve ends a bit scrambled. But he'll live.'

The Chief Super nodded once. The debriefing was over.

Her voice stopped me at the door.

'And one final matter, DC Wolfe,' she said. 'We've had an enquiry from the MoD about a misper.'

'A missing person?'

'Yes.' She stared down at her notes, although I felt she did not really need to. 'A Captain Jackson Rose,' she said. 'The MoD is anxious to contact him. We understand he's a friend of yours and wondered if you knew of his whereabouts?'

'Jackson was staying with me for a while. Then he left.' I stared at them. Their faces gave nothing away. 'Why does the MoD want to reach him?' I asked.

'That's MoD business not Met business,' the Chief Super said, a sudden frost in her voice. 'Do you have any idea where Captain Rose might be?'

I thought of a beach hut by the English seaside where the water was freezing cold even in the middle of a blazing summer, and I thought of two boys who believed that they would be friends forever.

'No,' I said.

CHAPTER 27

Tara Jones was standing outside New Scotland Yard.

There is an eternal flame in the lobby of New Scotland Yard, remembering the officers of the Metropolitan Police who died in the great wars of the twentieth century, and I paused by it to watch Tara Jones waiting out on the street.

Through the security fence I could see her standing by the revolving sign, a file in her hand, oblivious to the two young detectives who turned their heads to look back at her. She was one of those women who do not care very much about the effect they have on men. Or don't care at all. I came through the revolving metal gates that let you out of the New Scotland Yard and walked up to her.

And it was only then that I realised that she was waiting for me.

'They said you were dead,' she said.

'No.'

'On the Internet.'

I smiled. 'And it's usually so reliable.'

She smiled back at me. We still had not touched.

'Are you all right?' she said.

253

'Mustn't grumble,' I said. 'I'm fine. Really. It all could have been a lot worse.'

'I've got this for you.'

A double espresso from Starbucks. It's the thought that counts. I took a sip.

'Thank you.'

She shook her head. 'Oh God, oh God.'

'What?'

'Your *neck*.'

There was a thick red welt around my neck that was hidden under my shirt collar apart from where the rope had angled up to the knot, leaving a livid stripe of raw flesh slashed from my Adam's apple to left ear.

She touched my face with both her hands, her fingertips measuring the bones beneath my skin. I took her in my arms and lightly touched my mouth against her mouth. It wasn't quite a kiss. It was as if we were seeing if our mouths were a good fit. The preliminary exploration was a success. They seemed to fit perfectly. They seemed to fit better than any other mouth I had ever known. We tried again, deeper this time. Then we broke abruptly away, suddenly aware that we were standing under the revolving sign outside New Scotland Yard. But she took my hand and would not let it go. We walked toward my car.

She was not smiling.

'What just happened?' she said, running a hand through her hair, the gold wedding band glinting in all that shiny blackness.

'I don't know,' I said.

But it wasn't true.

I knew exactly what had happened.

It is when we are closest to death that we cling most strongly to life. It is when we can feel the chill of the grave on our skins that we crave the touch of warm human flesh. When we learn that we are all alone in the universe is exactly when we need another mouth. It is our most basic human impulse. The meaning of life is more life, I thought, pitching the empty Starbucks carton into a bin.

I squeezed her hand and smiled at her unsmiling face, and at that moment she was the only woman on earth that I wanted.

'Do you want to get a real coffee?' I asked her.

We drove to the Bar Italia.

I could have dropped the BMW X5 in the underground car park of West End Central and then we could have walked across Regent Street to Soho. That would have been the obvious thing to do. But I did not want to break the spell, I did not want her to change her mind about going for a proper cup of coffee, I didn't want her to change her mind about me.

Because as I steered the big BMW around St James's Park and Trafalgar Square and into the narrow streets of Soho, the spell between us felt like a fragile thing, as if it could dissolve at any moment.

Tara Jones stared straight out of the window and

twisted the gold band on the third finger of her left hand and wondered what the hell she was doing with me.

'Don't you have to go to work?' she said.

'They gave me the rest of the day off.'

'Because those men tried to kill you last night?'

I nodded. 'Some guys have all the luck.'

I found a parking spot on Old Compton Street and we walked to Frith Street while I told her a brief history of the Bar Italia.

'The Bar Italia has been in the same family for three generations now and they have their own secret blend of coffee that was invented by a man called Signor Angelucci who used to be next door and because their Gaggia coffee machine doesn't have a water filter no salts are run through it—'

She stopped me with a look.

'Max?'

'What?'

'You're babbling, just a little bit.'

'I'm nervous.'

She placed a kiss on my mouth. It felt good. Our mouths fit so well. Ridiculously, thrillingly well. I folded her in my arms and when she spoke her voice was muffled against the lapel of my old wedding suit.

'It's OK,' she said. 'You don't need to be nervous with me.'

We came apart and she slipped her arm through mine and we walked down Old Compton Street into Frith Street like a proper couple, a real couple, and it felt so natural and right and she smiled when she saw the green neon sign that announces the Bar Italia.

We sat holding hands under the large poster of Rocky Marciano that the champ's widow Barbara gave to the Bar Italia after he died because Marciano had always loved it here. But I didn't tell her about Marciano's relationship with the Bar Italia in case it led to some babbling. I kissed her mouth and drank a triple espresso and Tara had a cappuccino, and nobody took any notice of us because AC Milan was playing Inter Milan on the big screens and we were just another couple, lost in the backstreets of Soho.

'I don't know anything about you,' she said. 'And you don't know me.'

'You know me.'

'What were you like as a boy?' she said. 'Did you get bullied?'

I thought about it.

'No,' I said. 'I was a bit different because I lived with my grandmother. But I had a friend who was adopted. Jackson. My parents were gone and he never knew his mum and dad.' I smiled at the thought of Jackson Rose as a kid. 'We stuck together,' I said. 'For years.'

'I was bullied every day,' she said. 'I went to a normal school. Horribly normal. They – some boys, a little gang – they said I sounded like a seal when I talked. You know? That noise seals make? They said that's what I sounded like when I talked.'

She squeezed my hand, frowning at my face. 'What's wrong?'

'Nothing.'

I wanted to hunt them down.

I wanted to find them.

I wanted to be in a room alone with them for . . . oh, thirty minutes should do it.

'But it's all right now,' she said. 'So don't look like that. Smile again. Please?'

'OK.'

'It was only a few pathetic idiots. And it made me stronger. Children will pick on anyone who's a bit different. And you,' she said, gripping both my hands and shaking them. 'You live with your daughter. Just you and her. I heard at the office. I don't know who told me.'

'Scout. She's nearly six.' Tara waited for some kind of explanation. I shrugged. 'It happens.' I smiled to soften the words. 'I didn't plan it. Nobody plans to be a single parent. That's the way it turned out. We were left to get on with it. And we did. We do.'

'It must be hard.'

I shook my head.

'Scout makes it easy. And it's not really just the pair of us. There's Stan, our dog. And we've got a lot of support.' I thought of Mrs Murphy and her family. I thought of Scout's buddy, Mia, and her family. I thought of my colleagues up at West End Central, who always found a spare desk and some pens and paper for drawing whenever I had to bring Scout to work. I thought of Edie Wren.

'There's a lot of people around us who want us to make it,' I said.

'I don't know how you do it. Aaron – my husband – and I find it tough enough with a full-time nanny.'

I didn't want to hear about Aaron the husband. I didn't want to think about any of that. Not today. Not in here. So I touched her hair. Her shining, swinging, fabulous hair. I had wanted to do that for quite a while.

'It needs a wash,' she said.

'Yes, it's a disgrace,' I smiled. 'I don't know how you have the nerve to step out of the house.'

'Funny man. I've never seen you in a suit before,' she said, running her fingers under the lapels of my jacket.

'I got married in this suit,' I said, and when I looked down at her hands on my lapel I saw that the blue wool was shiny with time. I had never noticed that before. My wedding suit was old.

She brought her face close to mine.

'You should get a new one,' she whispered.

She gave me a coffee-flavoured kiss and slipped off the stool. 'Time to get back to the real world,' she said.

The traffic was unmoving on Shaftesbury Avenue when we started back to West End Central so I put on the blues-and-twos and everything that blocked our path quickly got out of the way.

'Oh *God!*'

Tara sank deep into her seat, laughing with some combination of embarrassment and delight as the two-tone siren howled and the grille lights blazed and London made way.

We laughed out loud all the way back to Savile Row.

And it was only hours later, after Scout had fallen asleep on the sofa reading a book called *I Like This Poem* and the bells of St Paul's were chiming the hour that I suddenly realised Tara Jones had never heard the sound of the blues-and-twos.

CHAPTER 28

I was jolted from sleep when my phone began vibrating on the small bedside table, moving in jerky little circles as if it had a life of its own. I swung my legs out of bed. Six a.m. and the sky was still almost black. The days were getting shorter.

A woman was crying at the other end of the line. It took me a moment to realise that she was Alice Goddard.

'They are going to let one of them out! They are going to let him off! Max, he's going to get away with killing my husband!'

'Slow down, Alice. What's happening?'

She got it out. One of the gang who had killed Steve Goddard was trying to get his verdict declared unsound.

'Which one?' I said, although I could already guess.

'The one who filmed it on his phone. Jed Blake. Do you remember him? He's saying – he's saying he didn't take part, that it was nothing to do with him . . .'

I remembered all three of them. The coward.

The weakling. And the bully. They had been cocky enough in Court Number One of the Old Bailey but far less impressive when I had first encountered them in Interview Room 2 at West End Central.

I had seen the bully blank-faced with callous indifference, too stupid to realise the enormity of what he had done. And I saw the weakling wet himself at the prospect of a prison sentence.

And I saw the coward – Jed Blake – crying for his mother, head in his hands as if he could not bear to look at the interview room, repeating over and over again that he had not laid a fist or a boot on Mr Goddard, that he had just pointed his phone and pressed *record*.

'Listen to me, Alice. It sounds like this Jed Blake creep is seeking permission to appeal. The judge at their trial decided that they were all in it together. But Blake's lawyer is probably going to argue that his conviction was unsound because they were not all in it together.' The words stuck in my mouth, but I had to spell it out to her. 'Because Blake was only filming what happened and not taking part in the beating.'

I heard her crying into the phone. Quietly now, knowing this was no nightmare. This was her life.

Her voice was very small. 'But what does it all mean? He's not really going to get out, is he?'

'Alice – if it goes to appeal, I can't tell you what way it's going to go. I'm not a criminal lawyer. And even if I was, I still couldn't call it. But if

Blake seeks permission to appeal, he has to file what they call a Form NG – Notice and Grounds of Appeal, setting out what his lawyer says was wrong with his conviction. If the Form NG is granted by the judge, then it goes to the Court of Appeal at the Royal Courts of Justice in the Strand. And if the judge there decides it's an unsafe conviction, he could walk. I'm really sorry.'

Sorry this world will not leave you alone. Sorry I can't do anything to make it better. Sorry your husband got kicked to death for defending his family.

'I'll be there with you,' I promised. 'You don't have to go through this alone. I'll be right by your side in the courtroom.'

But by then she had hung up.

I walked into the loft and stood by the large windows, watching the sun come up over the roof-tops of Smithfield and the Barbican, first light shimmering on the dome of St Paul's Cathedral and, even closer, the bronze statue on top of the Old Bailey, blindfolded Lady Justice, her out-stretched arms perfectly balanced between the scales in her left hand and the sword in her right.

And although the blindfold Lady Justice wears was meant to make all her judgements seem impartial and wise, today it just made her justice seem random and mindless and cruel.

Stan watched me carefully from his basket and when I went to the door and began putting my boots on, he padded over, his round eyes shining and his tail wagging with delight. We went downstairs and into the street, the Cavalier so relaxed by my side, his old leather lead so loose, that it felt as though we didn't need it at all. We were walking past Smiths of Smithfield when out of nowhere he tried to dash out into the traffic.

The lead snapped tight and a black cab flew past, inches from his head, its horn blaring.

I crouched down to look into my dog's face. Those great black marbles of eyes were wild and his tongue – as pink as Duchy of Cornwall organic ham – lolled out of his panting mouth. He sniffed the morning air, savouring some perfume that only he could detect.

'What's wrong with you, Stan? Christ almighty, you could have been killed!'

And then I saw the woman with her white miniature poodle on the other side of Charterhouse Street. I looked at Stan. He panted some more, and he wouldn't meet my eye. I shook my head with disbelief.

'That's why you would get yourself killed?' I said. 'Just for a sniff of some girl dog?' I pushed my face close to his and he licked my nose, trying to make amends. 'Listen to me. *Don't make me do it. I don't want to take you to the vet's, OK? I don't want to have you . . . done. But I will if you keep throwing yourself into traffic.'

I didn't speak to him for the rest of the walk. But as he did his morning business in West Smithfield and I read the inscriptions from *Oliver*

Twist that cover all the benches, the passage about Bill Sykes dragging Oliver through Smithfield meat market, Stan kept stealing glances at me.

As if I, of all people, should understand.

Scout was up when we got back.

She was still in her pyjamas and was on a step stool in the kitchen, standing on tiptoes to rifle through the cupboards.

'I'm making you breakfast,' she said. 'Jackson taught me to cook.'

'What you making, Scout?'

'Toasted jam sandwich.'

'Sounds good. Don't put your fingers in the toaster.'

She raised her eyebrows. 'Duh.'

'Need some help, angel?'

'No.'

'Looking forward to going back to school and seeing all your friends?'

'I really need to concentrate now.'

'Sorry.'

So Scout prepared our breakfast and Stan curled up in his dog basket and I got out plastic bags full of brand-new school clothes, and the iron, and long spools of name tags that ran on and on like all the days of my daughter's childhood. *Scout Wolfe*, they said. *Scout Wolfe, Scout Wolfe, Scout Wolfe.*

And my eyes suddenly blurred over as I stood there with the iron and the name tags and the new school clothes, watching Scout liberally slapping strawberry jam over a slice of thick brown bread. Stan got up and padded into the kitchen, smacking his lips and correctly guessing that there would soon be stray pieces of bread falling from the sky.

I wiped at my eyes with the back of my hand and I stared dumbly at the name tags in my hand. *Scout Wolfe*, they said. *Scout Wolfe*.

And with all my heart I ached for a real family for Scout and for me, a mended family, a restored family, a family that looked like all the other families in the world, a family with nobody missing and nobody gone and nobody wandered off, and I longed for that new family as only a man who has lost his old family ever can.

Then Mrs Murphy came into the loft wearing her green winter coat, wishing everyone good morning, Scout and me and Stan, and saying that this was the first day that she'd felt the chill of autumn in the air, and she gently took the iron and the *Scout Wolfe* name tags from my hand.

'Here,' said Mrs Murphy.

'I'm no good at it,' I said.

'Don't worry,' Mrs Murphy told me. 'Your daughter will love you for your heart, not your housework.'

CHAPTER 29

'Where's the kill room, Hitch?' I said.

It was still early enough for the last of the dawn mist to drift across the rooftops of Mayfair and we were all standing before the massive map of Greater London that covers one wall in MIR-1, West End Central, 27 Savile Row.

Whitestone. Edie. Billy Greene. Tara Jones. Dr Joe. And the history man, his great egghead frowning with concentration.

'It can't be far,' I said. 'I bet it's a ten-quid black cab ride from where we're standing. Where did they take me, Hitch?'

'You were somewhere in the darkness, Max,' Professor Hitchens said, his huge head nodding at the map. His nicotine-stained fingers reached out for that great urban sprawl of green and grey and ten million souls. 'Down in that other London that exists below the surface. Ackroyd is very good on that subterranean city in *London Under*: "Tread carefully over the pavements of London for you are treading on skin," Hitchens said, closing his eyes to recite from loving memory, "a skein of stone that covers rivers and labyrinths, tunnels and chambers, streams and caverns, pipes and cables, springs and passages, crypts and sewers, creeping things that will never see the light of day."'

'But it was *real*,' I insisted, touching the welt around my neck, feeling the way it ran up to just under my ear. 'It wasn't some mythic underworld. It wasn't a fantasy. It's *there*. And I can't believe it's impossible to find.'

'The search teams are still down there,' Whitestone said. 'The sniffer dogs are having a lovely time chasing rats. But they're drawing a blank and the Chief Super is going to wind it up at the end of play today.' My SIO was staring at me. 'And I still don't understand how you walked away.'

'Me neither,' I said.

'And another thing I don't understand . . .'

I waited.

'Why didn't they record it?' she said. 'Why aren't you up there on YouTube?'

'Maybe they thought that killing a cop would not play well with the #BringItBack brigade,' Edie suggested. 'They might have lost a few followers on Twitter if they had done our Max. A few people might have unfriended them on Facebook or started a petition on Change.org. Maybe they were afraid of the trolls.'

'I don't think they're that sensitive to public opinion,' I said. 'I saw a red light just before it all kicked off. They were planning to film it. I don't think they have any qualms about killing a cop.

They think we protect the people they hate.' I looked at Hitchens. 'You really don't have any idea where they took me?'

'Subterranean London is endless, Max,' he said. 'It's not another city – it's a thousand cities. Ten thousand cities. What exactly are those search teams looking for? A passage that hasn't been used for a hundred years? Do you know how many disused tube stations there are in London, Max? South Kentish Town – closed in 1924. Lords – closed in 1939. North End – abandoned in 1906. There are twenty-three abandoned tube stations and God knows how many miles of abandoned track.'

'Yes, but most of those derelict tube stations are much further out than the British Museum stop.' I tapped the map on Charterhouse Street. 'This is the heart of the city. Tara, didn't you say there was some serious building going on nearby?'

She keyed up the film the Hanging Club had uploaded the night that Abu Din did a runner. The figures were in black shadows. But as the camera slowly tracked across the photographs on the wall of the dead soldiers, the happy, proud and young faces of the Sangin Six, she cranked up the volume of the background noise.

'It's not traffic, is it?'

'No,' Tara said, studying a line that jolted and jarred across the graph on her laptop. 'Because the noise sometimes stops. And the traffic never stops. I still think it's some kind of major building work going on next to the kill site.'

'But the whole of London is a building site,' Edie said.

'Not buildings like this,' Tara insisted. 'This isn't a house in Hampstead or Chelsea being done up for a Russian oligarch. This sounds like a major development – maybe pile columns for a skyscraper foundation. That narrows it down, doesn't it?'

I smiled at her. 'It certainly does.'

She looked away, biting her lower lip as we listened in silence to the background noise and she studied her graph. I have no idea how Tara registered the sound but to me it sounded like the gods were doing a spot of DIY.

'Is that a thousand tons of concrete and steel being poured underground?' Whitestone said. 'It could be.'

When the film had ended I turned to Professor Hitchens.

'There's something I saw that never appeared on any of their films,' I said. 'To get to the kill site, they took me down a corridor that got smaller. It was tiled in the same way as the kill site. White tiles that had rotted with time. White tiles that were so old you could not really call them white any more. They were green as much as white. They were in the kill room and they were in this corridor that got smaller with every step that I took – the ceiling got closer to my head and the walls came in. It was like somewhere in a bad dream But it was real. Did you ever hear of somewhere like that?'

Hitchens shook his head.

'The big problem is that, after leaving the kill site, you can't tell us if you were walking in a circle or a straight line,' Hitchens said. 'So we don't know if the station where they found you is next door or several miles away.' He looked at Whitestone. 'I can't overemphasise how vast London is below ground. All those forgotten tunnels, all those uncharted hallways, all those derelict passages – there is a parallel London with layer upon layer of geologic time.'

'We appreciate all your help, Professor,' said Whitestone.

'Come on, Hitch,' I said, indicating the frozen image of the kill site. 'Look at that room! Those tiles have to be at least a century old. Doesn't it ring any bells?'

'I wish I could be of more help,' said Professor Hitchens, touching his mouth with those nicotine-stained fingers. I could feel the lopsided welt around my neck throbbing with my frustration. Then I rubbed his great bald egghead to comfort him.

'No problem, Hitch,' I said.

You're not the only history man in town, I thought.

The Black Museum is cold and dark.

The temperature is low in order to preserve the microscopic particles of human flesh that still attach themselves to certain exhibits – some of

271

them 140 years old – while the restrained lighting prevents the Museum's exhibits from fading. The subdued lighting does something else. It gives London's most secret room an aura of quiet menace.

When I arrived at Room 101, New Scotland Yard, Sergeant John Caine was just finishing a tour for a dozen uniformed police cadets from Hendon.

'Give me give a couple of minutes, Max.'

I stood at the back of the tour group.

The young men and women were in a sombre mood. The Met calls the Black Museum – or the Crime Museum, the official name that is increasingly used – a learning resource. And it will certainly tell you more than you really want to know about human nature.

The fledgling cops were staring up at a high shelf on which was displayed a collection of death masks, three-dimensional plaster casts of heads of executed men and women. They were all dark brown, the shade of a burned coffee bean, apart from the very oldest, which had turned jet black over time. The heads were all smooth and their eyes were all closed. But there the similarities ended – the death masks had been taken from faces young and old, fat and lean, male and female.

'Are they *real*?' said a young copper who looked as though he only shaved once a week.

'All of them are real but none of them will bite you,' said John Caine, standing behind the group.

'They were all taken from the deceased immediately after they had been executed for murder.'

John cleared his throat and the cadets tore their eyes away from the macabre masks to listen to his closing speech.

'I hope you have enjoyed your tour today.' His shrewd, bright eyes considered them. 'When you join the Metropolitan Police you will all be issued with a warrant number. It is a little-known fact that these numbers are consecutive and have always been consecutive since the force began. I hope you had a chance today to look at the exhibit dedicated to the brave men and women who have died in the service of the Metropolitan Police. Every one of them had a warrant number and you will, too.

'The very first warrant number was issued to Constable William Atkinson in 1829 – number one. On his first day in the job, and the very first day that the Met walked the streets of London – 29 September 1829 – Constable Atkinson was dismissed for public drunkenness.'

Laughter. Sergeant Caine allowed himself an ironic twist of the mouth.

'But I know that you will be a credit to the Met, and to the generations who served before you. Take care of yourself and each other. Thank you and goodbye.'

They gave him a round of applause.

After he had escorted them to the first-floor lift, he came back and peered at my neck.

'Max, you're the only person I've ever seen whose looks have been improved by hanging.' Then, for the first time in my life, he briefly hugged me. 'Welcome home. I'll put the kettle on, shall I? Your mob still babysitting Mustapha Pee?'

'Abu Din? No, somebody from in here is watching over him. SO15 – Counter Terrorism Command.'

'So an apologist for terrorists is being looked after by the policemen who protect us from terrorists? Somebody's had an irony bypass.'

He placed two mugs of tea on his desk. As always, his mug proclaimed BEST DAD IN THE WORLD. My one said NOT ALL WHO WANDER ARE LOST.

I took a sip. Strong and sweet. John Caine always gave me three sugars without asking.

'I need to know where I was, John. We need to find the place they hanged Mahmud Irani – and Hector Welles – and Darren Donovan . . .'

'And you.'

'And me. Same kill site. Same location. And nobody at West End Central has got a clue. We've rented an academic, a historian from King's College, and even he is drawing a blank.'

John sipped his tea.

'Talk me through it,' he said.

And so I did. All of it. From the moment the white van drew away to the armed guard outside Abu Din's council house to the appearance of the black van. From the unimaginable muscle spasms of being shot by a conducted electrical weapon to the mystery ride to the kill site. I told him how I had fought for my life.

And I even told him the one thing that I had held back from everyone else. I felt the need to tell someone.

I told John Caine how I had aborted my hanging.

'Hold on. You had a gun?'

'A Glock 17. Belonged to an ex-serviceman friend of mine. I'll not tell you his name, if that's OK.'

'I don't need to know his name, Max. But you were armed?'

'I took it from my friend because I was afraid of what he might do with it. And I took it with me to Abu Din's house because I thought the Hanging Club would not hesitate to kill me to get to Abu Din. I was going to get rid of it after that, chuck it in the Thames from the middle of a bridge.' I thought of young Steve Goddard Junior and his knife. 'Or drop it down a drain,' I said.

I was covered in a cold sweat at the memory of having the gun in my hand and wanting to kill them with it. It felt like I had broken enough fire-arms regulations to get slung out on my ear, or slung in a room with bars on the window. I silently thanked the heavens that it was our people who had found the gun.

'Have you still got the Glock?' John asked.

'No.'

'Good boy.'

He wasn't interested in the gun any more. There

are a lot of firearms in the Black Museum. Guns held no special fear or fascination for Sergeant John Caine.

'Then you went after them,' he said.

'This is where it gets blurry. We were underground. And they went deeper underground. It was totally black – stairs that led to a tunnel that led to a passageway – big arched columns that were meant to process large numbers of people. It looked like a football stadium at first – it had that kind of epic quality to it, as though thousands of people were going to pass this spot.'

'And it turned out to be an abandoned tube station.'

'British Museum. You ever heard of it?'

He shook his head. 'But London is full of disused underground stations. They've been closing them down since 1900. They were very busy during the Blitz. Since then, not so much. And they found you outside British Museum, right? It's pretty central, Max.'

'I know,' I said, and we sipped our tea in silence. I could feel the sugar kicking in.

'One other thing,' I said. 'When they were taking me to the kill site, they took me down a corridor, and it was like something from a nightmare, something from a fairy story. Because it kept getting smaller. It was *Alice in Wonderland* stuff. The roof came down, the walls came in, and by the time we got to the end of it I had my arms pressed against my side and my head hunched down.'

His face was suddenly white with shock.

'That's Dead Man's Walk,' he said. 'There's a reason the ceiling gets lower and the walls come in, Max. It's because when a man – or a woman – knew that they were about to hang, they went fighting mad. They went berserk. The corridor getting smaller was a way to physically control the condemned.'

I could feel the welt around my neck throbbing with blood.

'Where's Dead Man's Walk?' I said.

'You mean – where was it?' he said. 'Dead Man's Walk was in Newgate Prison. But, Max – Newgate was razed to the ground more than one hundred years ago.'

CHAPTER 30

'Dead Man's Walk was in Newgate Prison,' I told Whitestone as I walked back to my car. 'Don't let Professor Hitchens leave. I'll be there in five minutes.'

I put on the blues-and-twos for the short drive to 27 Savile Row, fully expecting to find MIR-1 feverish with excitement when I arrived. But they all looked up at me as if it was just the end of another long day. Whitestone. Edie. Billy Greene. Tara. And Professor Hitchens, who had an ancient map of London, coloured gold and black, spread out across four workstations.

Whitestone gave me a sad smile.

'Looks like chump bait, Max,' she said. 'Sorry.'

'What's chump bait?' Tara said.

'Chump bait is a false lead,' I said. 'Chump bait is deliberately sending an investigation in completely the wrong direction. But—'

'Newgate Prison no longer exists,' Hitchens said. 'You have to get that into your head, Max. I have no idea where you were taken, but it couldn't have been Newgate. This is Charles Booth's map of London in 1899. It's what they call a "poverty

278

map" – it was originally drawn to show areas of chronic want in the city. Black indicates poverty, gold indicates wealth.' His index finger tapped the centre of the map. 'What does that say?'

I stared at the map. And there it was, between Smithfield meat market and St Paul's Cathedral, right at the very heart of the city.

'*Newgate Gaol,*' I read.

'That's right. As you can see, Newgate Prison is clearly visible at the end of the nineteenth century. And now look at Booth's poverty map of 1903, just four years later.'

He unfolded what looked like an identical black and gold map of London and spread it on top of the first.

'No Newgate,' I said.

Hitchens nodded.

'Because Newgate was razed to the ground in 1902,' he said. 'The prison stood for nearly a thousand years, but it was completely demolished at the start of the twentieth century. The Central Criminal Court – the Old Bailey – was built on the site. It was a deeply symbolic gesture. One kind of British justice – medieval, brutal, retributive – was replaced at the start of the new century with another kind of British justice – modern, fair and just.'

'So *nothing* of Newgate remains?' Whitestone asked. 'Nothing at all?'

Hitchens began folding up his maps.

'There's a very nice pub opposite the Old Bailey – the Viaduct Tavern – with what's left of Newgate's cells down in the beer cellar,' he said. 'Debtors' cells that held up to twenty people. They say the smell was so bad that it could have choked a horse. But I've seen them and they don't match Detective Wolfe's description. In fact, they're nothing like them. Your colleague at New Scotland Yard is quite correct, Max – your description perfectly matches the corridor in Newgate Gaol called Dead Man's Walk. It progressively narrowed so that the condemned man – or woman – could not turn around to fight or flee. But it hasn't existed for over one hundred years.'

They were all looking at me with something approaching pity.

'But it was real,' I said. 'I saw it. I walked down it.'

'The internal architecture of Newgate is well documented,' Hitchens said. 'The prison appears on the very first map of London drawn in 1575 by Georg Braun and Franz Hogenberg. More than anywhere that ever existed, Newgate represented traditional British justice, red in tooth and claw. So whoever abducted you knew exactly what they were doing. They knew exactly what that corridor resembles.' He slipped his maps into his man bag and wiped his hand across his sweating forehead. 'But trust me – it couldn't have been Newgate.'

'I want to check out the pub,' Whitestone said. 'The Viaduct Tavern.'

'There's not much there,' Hitchens said. 'Certainly nothing that—'

Whitestone raised one hand, silencing him, and I saw the thread of steel inside this unassuming woman. Her world had been torn apart this summer but she was still running this murder investigation and she wanted to see the cellars of the Viaduct Tavern.

It wasn't a suggestion.

Thirty minutes later we were all down in the beer cellar of the Viaduct Tavern on Newgate Street. Hacked into the walls were cells that could have been built to contain large animals. They were cold, dark and reeked of ancient terrors. The pub above was a place of warmth and cheer and it was light years away from this ancient place of horrors. The cells seemed designed to muffle human screams. I felt my skin crawl.

Whitestone and Edie were looking at me.

'Anything look familiar?' Whitestone said.

'This is not where they took me,' I said. 'Nothing like it.' My spirits sank. 'Chump bait, as you say.'

'Fair enough,' Whitestone said, patting me lightly on the back. 'Every investigation has its share of false leads, Max, and this was one of them.'

We went up to the pub. The Viaduct Tavern is a beautiful Victorian pub with a wrought-copper ceiling that gives the place a warm and rosy glow. After the fetid air of the cells, being up here felt like breathing out. I sank into the nearest chair. Suddenly I was very tired.

'I think we deserve a round,' Whitestone said. 'I'll get them in.'

Hitchens was excited. 'Their selection of real ales is first class,' he said.

I saw Tara Jones slip outside. I placed an order for a sparkling mineral water and a triple espresso and followed her. She was staring up at the sky. I looked up at the white wash of moonlight on the dome of the cathedral.

'It's beautiful, isn't it?' I said.

'I wasn't looking at St Paul's,' she said.

And I saw what she had been looking at.

The giant black silhouettes of the cranes standing out against the night sky, those huge constructions that dwarfed even the highest shining towers, the cranes that would build tomorrow's skyscrapers.

I drove her home. It was surprisingly easy to arrange. Nobody looked at us twice when I offered to give her a lift back to Canonbury. But she was distant in the car and when I touched her arm she just shook her head.

'You don't want to be that guy, Max,' she said.

'What guy?'

'The cynical romantic. The man who gets his heart broken early on and spends the rest of his life moving from one married woman to the next. Taking no chances, risking nothing, leaving all these wrecked marriages in his wake that, most times, never even know that they're wrecked.' She shot me a brief look. I smiled at her beautiful face. She didn't smile back. 'Women will come to you,' she told me. 'All kinds of women. Don't make the mistake of only wanting what you can't have. Don't become that man, Max. I mean it. You're better than that.'

I laughed.

'I have no idea what you are talking about,' I said.

But I did and she could see it in my face.

We had reached Canonbury Square and she told me I could let her out at the corner. I said that I would drive her to her front door and she didn't argue with me. But of course I understood that I could not kiss her goodnight in front of her home.

The door opened as she went up the path and I could have looked away but I forced myself to watch. Her husband appeared in the light of the doorway, shirttails outside his trousers and a glass of red wine in his hand, the successful money man at the end of his busy day, and I saw them briefly kiss. More of a quick peck between two sets of lips than a proper kiss. There was affection in the gesture, and familiarity, and even love – the kind of quiet, understated love that comes with the years.

But there was no hunger.

There was nothing like our coffee-flavoured kisses in the Bar Italia.

What she had with her husband was very different.

Their front door closed and I went home and read about Newgate Prison until the sky began to lighten.

I read of how a gaol had been built on the fringe of a Roman fort, a place of punishment born at a moment in history so unremarkable that no man ever thought to record it or remember it.

And as the meat market buzzed with its night-time life beyond the windows of our loft, I read of Newgate becoming a crucible of misery and disease and corruption across the centuries, constantly destroyed and rebuilt, destroyed and rebuilt, burned to the ground in the Great Fire of 1666 and rising yet again, like a disease that could never be killed.

I read of the virulent strain of typhus that fermented in Newgate's filthy black depths. I read of Rob Roy and Casanova rotting there, and of Robin Hood and Captain Kidd dying there, and the London crowds who queued to peek at its horrors and flocked to see its public executions and the appalled visitors like Charles Dickens who saw Newgate as London's mark of eternal shame.

And as the total blackness of the night began to bleed away into the milky dawn, I read how, at the start of the twentieth century, Newgate was torn down brick by brick by brick, as if the city was seeking to hack out the tumour that had grown in its heart for almost a thousand years.

And when real morning came, one of those cold bright mornings that make summer suddenly seem like the stuff of dreams, I shaved and showered and I walked Stan and I made Scout breakfast and saw her settled with Mrs Murphy.

Then I walked to the Old Bailey to wait for justice.

CHAPTER 31

As I waited for Alice Goddard inside the Central Criminal Court I stared up at a large shard of broken glass embedded in the wall at the base of the main staircase.

The jagged chunk of glass was as big as a dinner plate. It glinted with the golden light of an early autumn morning as the traffic of the Old Bailey bustled beneath it. The QCs in their wigs and gowns, the lawyers in black carrying cardboard boxes of evidence, judges, jurors, witnesses and – mostly younger, poorer and blacker than everyone else – the defendants in their best suits or newly laundered sportswear.

At least, I *thought* it was a chunk of glass. It *looked* like a chunk of broken glass. But I couldn't understand how it got up there. Perhaps I was seeing things. Security at the Central Criminal Court is tighter than any public building in the country. No mobile phones, no bags and no food and drinks are allowed. So how did a random hunk of broken glass get stuck in the wall?

'It's from the IRA car bomb in 1973,' said a voice beside me.

I looked at him. He was a large man with the beginnings of a beard. There was a name card on his dark suit.

ANDREJ WOZNIAK, it said. BAILIFF.

And now I knew him.

He was the court bailiff who had stood in front of me and blocked my path when Steve Goddard's killers had got away with murder.

He was the big man who had prevented me from doing something stupid.

I held out my hand and he shook it.

'Before my time,' he said. 'But I understand the IRA made a bit of a mess. One dead and two hundred injured that day.' He nodded at the broken glass embedded in the wall, almost smiling now. 'We keep it as a souvenir.'

'Let's hope it doesn't fall on some judge's wig,' I said.

Wozniak laughed.

'It's buried quite deep,' he said. 'I think we're safe.'

Wozniak had a reassuring presence. Although the Central Criminal Court is the venue for some of the highest profile cases in the land, a large part of its daily life is devoted to cases concerning gangs. Far more than the average policeman, the bailiffs of the Old Bailey have to be physically capable men with skill sets somewhere between diplomats and bouncers.

Over Wozniak's shoulder I could see Alice Goddard coming through the main doors. Her children,

Stephen and Kitty, followed her. Now I saw the entire family looked much older than the night I met them. The children on the edge of maturity, and Mrs Goddard worn down by stress, growing old before her time. She waved to me. The big bailiff was still looking up at the chunk of broken glass buried deep into the wall of the Old Bailey.

'All this time,' he said. 'Just think.'

The gang of three had been reduced to one.

Jed Blake, in his best suit. Looking nervous. Sitting in the dock and scanning the public gallery for familiar faces. They had been a gang the night that Steve Goddard died. When they had been arrested, and when they were questioned, and when they were charged, they had been a gang.

Different kinds of creeps, certainly. The coward. The weakling. And the bully. But undoubtedly a gang. They had felt like a gang when we brought them in and separated them in different interview rooms. They had felt like a gang when we charged them. And when they had gone down for involuntary manslaughter, they had felt like a gang. But now Jed Blake sat in the dock alone, anxious to abdicate from the gang, as his wigged and robed lawyer argued in an expensively educated accent that there had been a terrible miscarriage of justice.

Because they were never really a gang, he insisted.

'My Lord, there was *no* joint enterprise,' the lawyer said. 'My client was under the impression that he was joining his friends for a game of *soccer* in the local park. He took *no part* in the involuntary manslaughter of the deceased. He is a young man of *impeccable character*, My Lord. The suggestion that there was *joint enterprise* was predicated on the fact that my client filmed the assault.'

The judge frowned over his reading glasses at the trembling youth in the dock. There was a kiss tattoo on Jed Blake's neck. I had never seen one of those before. I don't think they will catch on. It's going to look silly when he's sixty.

'Do you understand the premise being suggested by your legal representative?' the judge said.

Jed Blake snapped from his reverie. 'Sorry, sir? What, sir?'

Irritation flickered across the claret-faced features of the judge.

'Young man, all judges sitting at the Central Criminal Court are referred to as "My Lord" or "My Lady" regardless as to whether they are High Court judges, Circuit judges or recorders – do you understand?'

'Yes . . . My Lord.'

'Good. Your Mr Gilkes here argues that you had no intention of causing any physical harm to the late Mr Goddard. In common law legal doctrine there is something called *common purpose* – also known as joint criminal enterprise or common design. It imputes criminal liability for all participants in a criminal enterprise from all that results of that enterprise. Under the doctrine of common

288

purpose, if a gang murders a man then all members of that gang are responsible for his death, regardless of who dealt the fatal blow.'

Jed Blake's mouth lolled open. He was trying to keep up.

The judge continued.

'You are here today to request leave to appeal against the verdict of involuntary manslaughter on the premise that you were never part of the gang that committed involuntary manslaughter. What do you have to say for yourself?'

'Please, My Lord,' the boy said, and burst into a fit of snotty sobbing. For a minute the only sound in the court was his weeping.

The judge cleared his throat.

'Do you need a glass of water?' he asked.

'No, My Lord.'

'Do you need a fifteen-minute break?'

'No, My Lord. Thank you very much for asking, My Lord. It's very kind of you, My Lord.'

Blake wiped his nose with the back of his hand. He smiled bravely. The judge frowned at him over his reading glasses.

'What were you *doing* outside Mr Goddard's property?'

'I thought we were, like, going to play football, My Lord.' Blake's rat-like features pinched with cunning. 'The only reason I filmed it was because I was messing about with my phone when he – the man – came out of his house. I was scared of him, My Lord. I could see he had lost his rag – that he was angry, My Lord. My mates – they had the bundle, My Lord. We were just mucking about, My Lord. It was just a laugh! A bit of a laugh, My Lord! I don't know how it happened. The altercation, My Lord. I just froze. I didn't touch him. It wasn't me. It was my mates, My Lord. It's completely wrong that I got done.'

The judge thought about it for a moment.

'Leave to appeal . . . granted,' he said.

I looked up at the public gallery. Heavy-set women with tattoos were celebrating as though they were at a football match. Blake's mother, sisters, perhaps a girlfriend.

The lawyer was puffed up with pride.

'It's not fair, is it, Max?' Mrs Goddard said quietly.

I looked at the stony face of her son, Steve Junior, and the quiet tears of her daughter, Kitty. And then I looked at Alice.

It clawed at my heart that she felt the need, even now, to keep her voice down.

'No,' I said. 'It's not fair.'

I stood at the base of the main staircase and stared up at the broken shard of glass from an IRA car bomb buried deep in the wall.

All that time. Just think.

The crowds at the Old Bailey were thinning out now.

But I lingered, staring up at the detritus of an old war, troubled by a thought that I could not name.

290

Just think.

Then I began to move, walking up the main staircase of the Old Bailey, unsure what I was looking for.

I went through a door and into a long, lavish dining room. It was set for dinner. Perhaps fifty places. A signed portrait of the Prince of Wales smiled at me.

And then I saw it. A heavy black iron door-knocker attached to a square of hard wood, ancient but unmarked, the wood dark brown with time.

The doorknocker of Newgate Prison. It was as black as the grave. And I could see where the old saying comes from. *As black as Newgate's knocker.* And as I stared at it I could understand – really understand for the first time – that Newgate Prison had once stood on this same ground.

All that time.

Just think.

I went out of the door as some kind of manservant was coming in. 'Can I help you, sir?' he said, but I was already past him, going back down the main staircase and through the marble halls of the Old Bailey.

STAFF ONLY, said a door, and I went through it. It was a long corridor with offices on one side. I walked past the offices, looking in, seeing that they were quite small, glimpsing screen savers on computers and the remains of café-bought lunches eaten at the desk, seeing the faces of all those office workers weary with mid-afternoon torpor.

Everyone ignored me. There was an unmarked door at the end of the offices. It was unlocked so I went through that, too, and down a staircase, deep into the bowels of the building. I could hear machinery rumbling and wheezing, like the engine room of some old ocean liner. I came to an ancient boiler room.

This basement area was bathed in a weary green light. There was an unmarked door at the end of the corridor. It was locked.

'Are you all right?'

I turned to face Andrej Wozniak.

'I just want to check something out,' I told the bailiff. 'Do you have a key for this door?'

'I can find you one.'

'Thanks.'

He was back within minutes. I stood aside as he unlocked the door for me and I went through, descending another flight of stairs. There was no light now apart from what seeped down from the boiler room. It was colder down here, and getting darker by the second as I continued down the stairs, and I could feel the weight of the city was pressing down on me. Wozniak's footsteps were right behind me.

I stepped into a room that was abandoned years ago.

'What's down here?' I said.

'Storage rooms,' said Wozniak. 'But there's a lot of damp so we can't keep papers down here. They rot.'

I walked on. There was empty room after empty room, the damp showing through the cracked and peeling plaster.

And then I opened a rotten wooden door and finally there was a room that I recognised.

A room with white tiles that had turned green with time.

A room that was shaped like a cube.

You could smell the decay.

'You having any luck?' Wozniak said.

I thought he was talking about Mrs Goddard.

'They gave the boy leave to appeal his conviction,' I said. 'They said it wasn't joint enterprise.'

'I meant the other thing,' he said. 'Your murder investigation. Any luck with that?'

It was like a room that I had seen in a dream. Everything felt slightly changed from what it should be. There was no kitchen step stool. The stool where they had stood Mahmud Irani. And Hector Welles. And Darren Donovan. And me.

It was not dark. A green light ebbed into the room from the boiler room a floor above. My eyes scanned the floor.

There was no gun.

And there was no rope hanging from the ceiling.

And so I was wrong. This could not be the place.

I was overthinking it. I was trying too hard.

'The other thing,' Wozniak repeated. 'The Hanging Club.'

'We'll find them,' I said. 'You can't go around helping yourself to revenge.'

He chuckled. 'But it's not revenge, is it? It's a signal. It's saying, "This is still our country. You can't do what you like here. We're not going to let you."'

'That's one way of looking at it.'

And then I saw it. The dull gleam of a single casing.

I picked it up and looked at it.

Spent brass, I thought.

This was the place.

I held it in my hand, and I turned to smile at Wozniak.

And then I saw something that his beard could not quite hide.

The teeth marks that I had left on his face.

CHAPTER 32

There was a door on the far side of that square room with the rotting tiles and I already knew what was beyond it.

No, not a door – a black slit in the wall, just big enough for a man to pass through. Taking my time, not looking at the big man, I walked across to it and saw the corridor.

It had not been a dream.

It was the corridor where the walls came in and the ceiling came down.

'Dead Man's Walk,' Wozniak said. 'It narrows to stop a man – or woman – going insane at the sight of the scaffold. Can you imagine what it felt like? Hearing the crowd outside. Knowing the agonies that were waiting for you. Dead Man's Walk was behind the prison. Originally it connected the gaol to the sessions house next door. It became the most practical way of transporting some wretch to the scaffold. But it's just one of a labyrinth of tunnels. Hardly anyone knows that so much of Newgate is still down here.'

'I've seen enough,' I said.

'Maybe too much,' he said, and quietly closed the door.

A green light still seeped into the room and for the first time I noticed the air vent high up in one wall. But it was like breathing the air of dead men.

And now I looked at him.

'Newgate was a nice touch,' I said. 'A shame that nobody recognised it. But who knew that so much of it was still left down here.'

He did not move. I took a step towards him, staying just beyond arm's length.

Timing and distance, I thought. Remember your boxing at Smithfield ABC. Remember all those hard hours. Remember the lessons of Fred.

'Mind you,' I said, 'bringing back Newgate does make you and your friends look bat-shit crazy.'

He laughed bitterly.

'I think it makes us look like the last sane men alive,' he said. 'We executed an abuser of young girls. We executed a hit-and-run driver who killed an innocent boy. We executed a stinking scumbag drug addict who destroyed an old man who fought for our nation's freedom. And *we're* the crazy ones? You protect these scumbags. You hold their coats while they commit their crimes. You worry about their human rights while they're raping our children.'

'Shut up now,' I said. 'I'm arresting you—'

He kicked me across the room.

One kick, perfectly executed, that caught me high in the midriff with the side of his enormous right foot, whooshing the air out of me as it lifted me off my feet and threw me backwards.

It felt like the first time I had been kicked by someone who really knew what he was doing.

Wozniak crossed the room and pulled me up by the lapels of my wedding suit. I heard the material rip and felt him adjust his grip. I weigh eighty kilos. He tossed me into the centre of the room as if I weighed nothing. My trousers tore across the backside as I hit the ground. I watched him touch one lapel of his jacket.

He brought out an old-fashioned razor blade from behind the lapel. It's an old bouncer's trick. If anyone ever grabbed his lapel, they would soon wish they hadn't.

He started towards me.

I tried to roll away but he was fast for a man that big and then he was directly above me and I saw the razor blade in his right hand and I watched him set himself on the balls of his feet and I could hear someone screaming and it was me and then he came down on top of me like a bomb. As he came down I drove my right fist up into his heart with every scrap of my remaining strength. The air went out of him and he flinched with shock and pain.

But it didn't stop him.

Shit, I thought. That punch always used to work for me.

He settled his massive weight on top of me, but not exactly the way he'd planned. He had one knee pressed into my chest, the other pinning down my left shoulder, the razor blade still in his right paw, but his body was twisted from the one shot that I had landed.

I had hurt him. He was breathing hard. The sweat rolled off him and dropped onto my face. His free hand pinned down the top of my right arm but there was diminished strength in it.

That's the thing about big men. They wear themselves out.

'Little man,' he said, as I thrashed like something dying in a bigger animal's mouth, flailing at him with my legs. 'Don't you know that you should be on our side? Can't you see that we're doing the job you should be doing? Are you so stupid—'

I wrenched my right arm free and stuck my thumb in his left eye. Then I kept it there. He jerked away from me with a scream and then I was on my feet and trying to slam the sole of my right shoe into his knees, and I realised that I was trying to fight like Jackson Rose, going for his eyes and his knees, kicking him again and again, catching his shin and his calf muscle and his upper thigh, kicking him everywhere apart from his knee.

But he backed off with one hand over his eyes and I went after him, still kicking.

I took my breath and I took my aim.

And finally I caught him, my right foot striking him on the side of his knee, buckling the big man and making him roar like a wounded bear, swiping out at me with the blade in his right hand. I felt something sharp pass across my forehead and then

298

it was warm and wet but there was no pain yet, and I realised he had cut me with his blade.

But he was done.

And so was I.

I sank to my knees, the blood flowing freely now, my hands covered with it as I tried to keep it from my eyes and Wozniak crumpled against the wall, moaning as he measured the damage. I stared at my hands, weak with the loss of blood and the paralysing shock of being cut. And when I looked up I saw him hobble through the crack in the wall of that secret room.

I must have gone after him because I was aware of passing down Dead Man's Walk and into the broad, low-ceilinged tunnel that has waited beyond it for centuries.

I found the stone staircase that went deeper into the city and I took it, hearing Wozniak ahead of me, making the infuriated sounds of a wounded animal. We moved slowly. I looked at my phone once. But there was no signal down here. This was the past.

The stairs ended.

I called his name.

'Wozniak! Wozniak!'

But he kept on and so I went after him, deeper into that other city, the forgotten city, the underground city, to where the stairs finally ended and there were four identical tunnels, each with a rounded arch, wide but not high, built to process large numbers of people who had been dead for nearly a hundred years.

And I reached the train station where two wooden platforms faced each other across the ancient tracks and where, on a big red circle, the name of the station was written in black letters on a white background.

B L O O M S B U R Y

I watched Wozniak disappear off the end of the platform and hobble into the darkness. There was a light deeper down the tunnel. It was getting closer. It twisted and turned in the darkness. I watched him limp towards it, a giant of a man who could hardly walk now.

I stood on the edge of the platform but I went no further as I watched him disappear into the black. The light of the approaching tube train hurtled still closer and although I knew it would never reach this abandoned station, I understood that it would reach the man hobbling in the darkness.

'Wozniak!'

He was gone now but I heard the tube train twist and turn and speed away to light and life and some station where the commuters and tourists were waiting, and I heard the wheels of steel screaming with protest as the driver applied the emergency brakes as he saw, far too late, the man who shuffled towards him in the darkness.

But I did not see him die and if he made a sound, then I did not hear it.

CHAPTER 33

What remained of Newgate Prison was a crime scene now.

Deep in the bowels of the Old Bailey, our people waited at the perimeter that Whitestone had decided should begin at the boiler room. CSIs, photographers, forensic scientists, geo-forensic specialists were all struggling into their white Tyvek suits, overshoes and masks, waiting for the go-ahead from the Senior Investigating Officer. TDC Billy Greene was helping a young uniformed officer put up the barrier tape, a major incident scene log form in his hand, ready to sign them in and out.

Inside the square room with the rotting tiles, Whitestone and I stood on forensic stepping plates. Above her face mask, the eyes behind her glasses roamed the room.

'So this was the holding cell,' she said. 'Where they kept the condemned before they took them outside to hang them.' She took off her glasses and polished them. She was thinking about the perimeter of our crime scene. 'I know where it begins,' she said. 'But I don't know where it should end.'

A figure in a white Tyvek suit squeezed through the gap in the wall that led into Dead Man's Walk. A stray strand of red hair fell across Edie Wren's forehead. She pushed it away.

'The tunnel at the end leads from here – Newgate – to St Sepulchre's church across the way. It dates from 1807. Hangings were massive crowd-pullers – twenty-eight people died when a pie stall overturned – so they built the tunnel to allow the priest to minister to the condemned man without having to force his way through the crush.'

'There's at least one staircase leading off the tunnel,' I said. 'But I've been down there. It goes on forever.'

Whitestone thought about it for a moment.

'Establish the other side of our perimeter at the far end of the tunnel,' she told Edie.

'Ma'am,' Edie said, and disappeared back inside Dead Man's Walk.

'Shall I tell the Crime Scene Manager to send them in?' I said.

'Give me a minute,' Whitestone said.

I knew that every SIO valued this first look. For all our stepping plates and bunny suits and blue gloves, once we started work, this place would never look the same again.

'So nobody knows this place is down here?' she said. 'That's hard to believe.'

'It's not preserved,' I said. 'It's just here – the holding cell, Dead Man's Walk. Like the cells in the pub across the street. There's no conservation order on it. There's no blue plaque outside. It has just survived, by some fluke of history. It's not open to tourists. It's not open to anyone. I doubt if more than 1 per cent of the staff of the Central Criminal Court have ever been down here, or even know it exists. One day they'll replace that boiler room outside and it will all be swept away with no fuss and no ceremony. And nobody will be sorry to see it go because nobody was ever proud of Newgate. Not now. Not ever. Just the opposite. From the time Charles Dickens came to Newgate in 1836, it was a source of national shame.'

'It's the perfect kill site. You can smell death in the air. How many hanged at Newgate?'

'One thousand, one hundred and sixty-nine – not including Mahmud Irani, Hector Welles and Darren Donovan.'

'Do we know how Wozniak accessed this place from the street?'

'I've asked the search teams to work their way through all the underground car parks of the surrounding office blocks. It might take a while, but they'll find it.'

'You've carried this investigation, Max,' she said.

She was staring down at a smear of blood on the floor. It was next to a scrap of torn wedding suit.

'You've had a lot on your plate,' I said. 'How's he doing? How's Just?'

'He's coming out of hospital soon,' she said. 'He's coming home.'

'I'll drive you,' I said, wanting to do something for the pair of them, wanting to make it right, and knowing that I never could. I felt my face burning because it seemed like a pathetically inadequate thing to offer, to drive Whitestone and her son from one end of the Holloway Road to the other.

But she shot me a grateful smile.

'That would be a big help, Max,' she said. Then she nodded at the door, and the perimeter beyond, suddenly all business. 'Let them in,' DCI Whitestone said.

We went deeper into the city.

Lit by the torches of our phones, Whitestone and I passed through Dead Man's Walk and into the underground tunnel that links Newgate to St Sepulchre's church, descending the stone staircase and carefully picking our way through the blackness until we reached the four identical tunnels with the rounded arch, and passed through them to the two wooden platforms of the abandoned British Museum tube station.

Deep inside the tunnel we could see the lights of the emergency services, retrieving the remains of Andrej Wozniak.

'Who was he?' I said. 'What do they say up at the Central Criminal Court?'

'Apparently he was very good at his job,' Whitestone said. 'A master of decorum who you wouldn't want to mess with.'

'Yes,' I said. 'He stopped me once. After the

304

verdict at the Goddard trial. When I might have done something stupid. Something that I would have lived to regret.'

'From what they tell me, he was a typical Old Bailey sheriff. You know what they're like. They are actually a great bunch of guys. Staying calm and collected in the face of every scumbag that passes through their doors.'

'He told me we were on the same side. Just before he tried to cut out my eyeball.'

'He was single, never married, no children, thirty-nine years old. Third-generation Anglo-Polish. His grandfather came over here to fly Hurricanes for the RAF in 1939.'

'The Polish Air Force. There were twenty-five thousand of them. They were the largest non-British contribution to the Battle of Britain.'

Deep in the tunnel we could see the lights of the emergency services, hear the calls of the men, see a silver glint of the tube train that had claimed Andrej Wozniak.

'What happened to him?' I said. 'How did he make the leap from Old Bailey bailiff to the Hanging Club? It has to be something more than staring at the daily parade of scumbags.'

'There was a girl,' Whitestone said. 'His fiancée. From a different faith. Wozniak was a Catholic and the girl's family violently objected. Kicked her out of the house. Disowned her. Called her a whore for falling in love. Priti – that was her name. Nobody ever went down for it, but she was the victim of an acid attack. A relative walked up to her as she was coming home from work and threw acid in her face.'

'Christ Almighty.'

'And apparently Priti couldn't live with it. None of it. Not the separation from her family, not what a family member did to ruin her face. Maybe she couldn't bear to see the look in Andrej Wozniak's eyes. The pity. The sadness. The rage. Maybe Dr Joe can explain it to you. I wouldn't know where to begin. You know what the biggest lie in the world is?'

'Tell me.'

'That everything happens for a reason. It's not true. Some things are totally without reason. Some things – the things that hurt the most – are totally meaningless. Some things make no sense and will never make sense.'

I felt like she was talking about herself and her son as much as Andrej Wozniak and his fiancée. I was silent, hearing her breathe in the darkness. Then she adjusted her glasses and went on with her story.

'Wozniak came home to their flat one night and Priti had hanged herself. He was on compassionate leave for six months. He came back to work at the start of the summer, just before they picked up and hanged Mahmud Irani. Did you know that Irani had a daughter?'

I didn't have to think about it.

'Wozniak's fiancée,' I said. 'Priti.'

Whitestone nodded. 'And nobody was ever punished for the acid attack on Priti. At least, not until Wozniak came back from compassionate leave. I suppose someone has been punished now. But where did he find the rest of them?'

I thought about it.

'He found them among the ranks of people who were just like him,' I said. 'Let down by the system. Humiliated by slick lawyers. Sickened by watching evil bastards get away with murder.'

The lights were coming closer.

They were white and blinding and you could feel their heat.

We saw the sweating, haunted faces of the men and women who carried their terrible cargo in a collection of body bags.

'He found them at the Old Bailey,' I said.

CHAPTER 34

I watched Tara Jones cross MIR-1. I watched her every step of the way. I couldn't take my eyes off her. I thought she might have said something about my new suit. I thought she might give me some secret smile. But she just placed a thick file on my desk.

'You might need this,' she said.

It was the original voice biometric analysis of the interviews with Paul Warboys and Barry Wilder. She returned to her desk with her shoulders slumped and her hair hanging in her face, as if something precious had already been lost. But I couldn't work out what.

'Check it out, Max,' Edie said.

She was running the kidnap of Abu Din for Dr Joe up on the big HD TV screen. The black-and-white CCTV footage showed scores of men kneeling in the drab Wembley street as Abu Din faced them in his long grey robes, flanked by a couple of heavies, his index fingers pointing to the heavens, as if predicting rain.

'Do you want me to fast-forward to the van, Dr Joe?' Edie said.

'Just let it run at normal speed, please,' said the forensic psychologist. We were all looking now. Edie and Billy Greene. DCI Whitestone and me. And Tara, her chin lifted as her eyes flitted from the screen to Dr Joe's lips.

'What exactly are we looking for, Dr Joe?' Whitestone said.

'We're looking for what they don't want us to see,' he said.

At the back of the crowd I could see PC Rocastle, his heavyweight's bulk standing directly in front of Philip Maldini in his wheelchair, his sister Piper behind him, her hands resting on her brother's shoulders as he held up his placard.

My Country – Love It or Leave It.

And then it all kicked off.

PC Rocastle began to run, desperately shouting into the radio attached to his shoulder. Philip Maldini's wheelchair lurched onto the pavement and his sister seemed to place herself between the young man and what was coming down the street. And then the crowd was getting off their knees.

Pointing. Shouting. Running for their lives.

The black transit van came into frame and seemed to aim itself at the crowd, suddenly mounting the pavement to avoid the Maldinis.

The transit van came to a halt.

The crowd was gone.

Abu Din was wagging a finger at the black van.

'You can't park that there, mate,' Edie said, and we all laughed.

And then we stopped laughing as Albert Pierrepoint got out of the van. And another Albert Pierrepoint. The masked faces scanned the street. At the top of the screen I could see PC Rocastle, flat on his belly, calling it in. When he turned his head to check the street, you could see a third Albert Pierrepoint at the wheel of the transit van, gunning the engine.

'Stop,' Dr Joe said.

Edie hit a button and froze the frame.

In total silence we stared at the three Albert Pierrepoint masks on the screen.

Then Dr Joe spoke.

'Those Albert Pierrepoint masks serve a dual purpose,' he said. 'They're more than symbolic. Yes, the Hanging Club see themselves as justice incarnate. Yes, they see themselves as meting out punishment to the wicked. Yes, they believe they are the heirs of Pierrepoint. All of that is true. But those masks also serve a practical purpose – *we focus on them*. We look at the masks. They distract our eye. They sidetrack our senses. They're a diversion.'

Professor Hitchens walked into MIR-1. He placed his motorbike helmet on his workstation and waddled off to the coffee machine. I walked to his workstation, picked up his motorbike helmet and threw it at him as hard as I could. It hit him high and hard and sent a fountain of cappuccino all over him.

310

'You fucking maniac, Max!'

Then I was in his face.

'You *knew*,' I said. 'You knew that it was Newgate, Professor. That little farce you played in here. *And you knew*. You knew from the start!'

He was backing away from me with sudden fear in his eyes.

'No,' Hitchens said. 'No!'

Edie Wren and Billy Greene were grabbing my arms. I shrugged them off.

'Come on, Hitch,' I said. 'Newgate! The human zoo. Chamber of horrors. Monument to the cruelty of this great city. "*Abominable sink of beastliness and corruption.*" Come on! You're one of this city's leading historians! You're telling me you didn't know that Newgate was still down there, buried alive under the Old Bailey? I don't believe you, Professor.'

'You knew?' Whitestone said to him, her voice hard and cold. 'Is this true?'

He ran his hands down his coffee-stained shirt.

'No,' he said. Then he hesitated. 'Not immediately . . .'

Whitestone exploded. 'Jesus Christ!'

'It seemed so unbelievable at first,' he said. 'That they could possibly be so bold. But – as a place of execution – Tyburn was followed by Newgate, and so it made perfect sense.'

'When did you know?' Whitestone said, white-faced with controlled fury.

'From the start,' I said. 'He knew from the start.'

'No!' he said. 'Not from the start!'

'You obstructed this investigation,' Whitestone told him. Her voice was not much more than a whisper but I had never seen her so angry. 'You nearly got one of my team killed. Do you know what that means, Professor? *You've obstructed a murder investigation. You've perverted the course of justice. You've concealed evidence.* Do you think you *could* do three years' hard time, Professor Hitchens? I'm not sure you would make it.'

There was true terror in his eyes now. Not the fear that I might give him a slap across the cakehole. The fear that he could end up in jail.

'I didn't know from the start, I swear it,' he insisted. 'It was only from the time they took Abu Din. When he got away and they showed pictures of the Sangin Six on those walls . . . the walls of . . .'

'Newgate,' I said for him. I shook my head. 'What's in it for you? Why keep it a secret? Who are you to let these creeps deal out death and judgement?'

I saw the anger flare in his eyes.

'And who are you to deny it? Look at the filth they hanged, Max. Mahmud Irani – a child groomer who disfigured his own daughter! Hector Welles – a rich banker who killed a child in his sports car! Darren Donovan – a junkie who ended the life of a war veteran!'

I grabbed him by the scruff of his neck.

He flinched away from me.

'I've done nothing wrong,' he whimpered. 'I

never lied to you! I never wanted anything bad to happen to you, Max!'

I was struggling to control my rage. I had him by the lapels and I would not let him go. He held up his hands to protect his face. I could see his fingers, stained dark yellow with nicotine. But I was not going to hit him. And he knew it.

The knowledge emboldened him.

'You think it stops here?' he said. 'After you catch them? It will go on. They've lit a fire that will never go out until we have burned this nation clean.'

And suddenly I realised that I could smell him. The lifetime of cigarettes, and the cheap cologne he used to cover it. And it reminded me of another smell, of unfiltered Camels and Jimmy Choo perfume and Juicy Fruit chewing gum. And I suddenly laughed out loud.

'There was a smell in the back of the van,' I said to Whitestone. 'It was a sickly-sweet smell. Like dead flowers. Like rotting fruit. Something foul that had been sugar-coated with something sweet.' I stared at her. 'And I know where it came from.'

'What are you saying?' Whitestone said.

I had let go of Professor Hitchens. I had forgotten all about him. But his smell – his stinking roll-ups and the buckets of cologne – had unlocked a door that had been closed to me. There was a rank smell of cigarettes, perfume and chewing gum behind that door.

I slapped my hand on the thick folder that Tara had given me.

'Bring them in,' I said. 'Paul Warboys. Barry Wilder. And Philip Maldini.'

Whitestone and Edie exchanged a look.

'The kid in the wheelchair?' Whitestone said.

'The three of them. And do it now. I'm not asking you to arrest them. I want them to come in voluntarily. But if they refuse, I want us to have the power to bring them in.'

'And how do I do that?' Whitestone said.

'I want you to designate the three of them as significant witnesses. Warboys. Wilder. And Maldini. That would work, wouldn't it?'

Whitestone shook her head, although it was doubt rather than denial. It was the responsibility of the SIO to identify significant witnesses, to record her decision in the investigations policy file and be prepared to justify why a witness was given SW status in court. If any or all of this blew up in someone's face, it would not be my face. It would be the Senior Investigating Officer's face.

'Pat,' I said. 'I need you to trust me on this one.'

DCI Whitestone stared at me for a moment and then she nodded. 'OK.'

Edie indicated Professor Hitchens. 'What do we do with him, ma'am?' she said.

'Get him out of my sight,' DCI Whitestone said.

An hour later the four members of our MIT were in the CCTV bunker of West End Central.

It was a darkened room where one large screen showed a grid revealing nine live CCTV images.

Together they surrounded the block around 27 Savile Row. One camera showed West End Central's underground car park. One camera looked north on Boyle Street. One camera looked south on Clifford Street. Three cameras looked out on Burlington Gardens. And three cameras surveyed Savile Row – looking north, looking south and looking directly down on the steps below the big blue lamp.

'Here they come,' Greene said.

We watched Barry and Jean Wilder arrive outside West End Central. They waited under the big blue lamp, Jean Wilder smoking furiously.

'What are we looking for?' Whitestone said.

'Watch,' I said.

A black cab pulled up. The driver helped Piper Maldini manoeuvre her brother's wheelchair out of the taxi. Philip Maldini settled in his wheelchair, nodding briefly to Barry Wilder.

'Do Barry Wilder and Philip Maldini seem like friends to you?'

'No.'

'That's because they have never met before,' I said. 'Now look at Jean Wilder and Piper Maldini.'

The two women were conferring like old friends.

Jean Wilder threw a cigarette in the gutter and immediately pulled out another. Piper Maldini held a match for her. Jean Wilder lightly touched the younger woman on her arm.

'Do they look like strangers to you?' I asked.

Whitestone was staring at me.

'What are you saying, Max?'

315

'The discrepancies on Tara's voice analysis were not because Barry Wilder and Paul Warboys were guilty,' I said. 'It was not even because they were lying. It was because neither Paul Warboys or Barry Wilder were telling us the whole truth.'

They were all looking at me now.

'That smell in the back of the van was cigarette smoke covered by perfume and chewing gum,' I said. 'Lots of unfiltered Camels masked with a good spray of Jimmy Choo perfume and plenty of Juicy Fruit. Dr Joe said we were being distracted by the masks and he was right. It made us miss the most obvious thing about the Hanging Club.'

On the CCTV outside 27 Savile Row, Piper Maldini and Jean Wilder suddenly stared up at the camera watching them.

'Three of them are women,' I said.

CHAPTER 35

The four of them were waiting outside the interview rooms.

Jean Wilder's jaws moved furiously as she watched us coming down the corridor. In the confined space outside the row of interview rooms, the smell of unfiltered Camels, Jimmy Choo and Juicy Fruit almost made me gag.

She looked me in the eye and she saw that I knew.

'One thing I don't understand,' I said.

Jean Wilder laughed bitterly. 'I think there are a lot of things you don't understand!'

I glanced at Piper Maldini. And I watched her mouth tighten as she saw that it was over now. Perhaps it had been over from the moment Andrej Wozniak disappeared under the steel wheels of a tube train. Or perhaps they would have kept going until there was not one of them left. We would never know.

'Why Darren Donovan?' I asked Jean Wilder. 'You had a good reason to hate Mahmud Irani and so did Andrej Wozniak. The Warboys had a good reason to hate Hector Welles for killing their grandson.' I nodded at the Maldinis and their dark good looks seemed to drain under the lights of West End Central. 'And I understand why you would hate a man like Abu Din,' I said quietly. Then I stared into Jean Wilder's furious face. 'I can even understand why you would hate me for getting in your way and for coming after you.'

Jean Wilder shook her head.

'You really don't understand. Believe me.'

'Jean,' her husband said. 'Don't say anything.'

'Shut up,' she told him. 'We don't hate you because you came after us. We hate you because you're always on the side of the filth. You protect the men who rape our daughters because you care more about their human rights than you do about our children. It's a fact. You don't care. You don't get it. You truly *don't* understand. And that's why we hate you.'

I looked at Piper Maldini.

'There were only three of you when Abu Din was abducted,' I said. 'At first I thought it was because you, Piper, were seen day after day on that street in Wembley and one of the faithful might recognise you – even behind an Albert Pierrepoint mask. But that wasn't it, was it?'

Piper Maldini still had not spoken. Her brother twisted in his wheelchair to look at her.

He didn't know, I thought.

He didn't know until now.

'You were driving the white van,' I said to her. 'You were not usually the driver. But driving was your role that night, wasn't it? And you did it well.'

She shook her head.

'I want a lawyer,' she said.

'You're going to need one,' Whitestone said.

Jean Wilder was laughing as she took out a pack of cigarettes.

'There's no smoking in here,' Edie said.

Jean Wilder ignored her.

She lit up, sucked hungrily on her cigarette and considered me, her eyes narrowing through the rising smoke.

'You actually have to ask why we did that stinking junkie,' she said, shaking her head with wonder. 'Because your little cop-like brain can't understand why anyone would want to remove someone like that – a drug addict who robbed and as good as killed an elderly war veteran for his pension money. You don't get it, do you? You don't understand that this country is better off without him, do you? Darren Donovan died because he *deserved* to die. Because your laws are too weak to deal with someone like that. Because your courts are too full, and the lawyers too slick, and the police too overworked – the poor little lambs.' She was enjoying her cigarette. 'Somebody had to do him,' she said. 'And it fell to us. He *deserved* to hang. Isn't that reason enough?'

'How did it work?' I said. I looked at Barry Wilder. 'Did Andrej Wozniak make contact with you when Mahmud Irani was on trial at the Old Bailey?'

'My husband had nothing to do with it,' Jean Wilder said. 'Leave him out of it, will you?'

'Leave him out of it?' I said. 'Nobody gets left out of it. Do you know the sentence for conspiracy to murder in this country? Life imprisonment.'

'It was the women,' Piper Maldini said quickly, one hand on her brother's wheelchair. 'It was only the women. Right from the start it was the women. Andrej contacted Jean. Jean approached me . . .'

'And Wozniak brought in Doll Warboys,' I said. 'Where is she?'

'Their lawyer just informed us that both Mr and Mrs Warboys respectfully decline to attend any further interviews voluntarily,' Edie Wren said. 'They're making us do it the hard way.'

'They're probably on their way to the airport,' I said. 'Billy, check out today's flights to Spain from all London airports. Don't let them board a plane.'

Billy ran off to do it.

Piper Maldini was standing in front of her brother, shielding him, desperately pleading with Whitestone.

'Do you understand me?' she said. 'It was always Andrej and the women. Always the women. Only the women.'

'Because our men were too weak,' Jean Wilder said, and her husband hung his head. 'The men were too afraid of what would happen to them if they got caught.' She stubbed out a cigarette on the floor and immediately lit another one.

Edie said, 'There's no—'

Jean Wilder raised a hand.

'I've got lung cancer, darling,' she said. 'Terminal. It's spread everywhere. Malignant tumours that are bigger than your breasts. I'm not scared of lung cancer. And I'm not scared of dying. So why the *fuck* should I be scared of you, you little ginger bitch?'

'Because I'm the little ginger bitch,' Edie said, stepping forward, 'who is arresting you for murder.'

Jean Wilder went for her, throwing one big wild right that failed to connect before her husband had a chance to grab her. Piper Maldini was screaming something at Jean Wilder as Whitestone attempted to pull her away.

Nobody paid much attention to the young man in the wheelchair.

One hour later Paul Warboys opened the front door of his Essex mansion.

Every time we had met, the last of London's celebrity gangsters had dressed for either Majorca, Spain – shorts, Hawaiian shirt, leather sandals – or Brentwood, Essex – polo shirt, chinos, Asics.

But today he was dressed for a wedding.

Paul Warboys wore a formal morning suit. A long-tailed black jacket, grey trousers and a pale lemon waistcoat. White shirt, blue tie, and a white carnation in the buttonhole. The flower was fresh but the suit, while high-end Savile Row, looked as though it was perhaps forty years old.

He smiled at me with what looked like genuine affection.

'Hello, Max.'

'Going to a wedding, Paul? I thought you might be on your way to the airport.'

'I don't run away. Never have. Never will.'

His eyes flickered on Billy Greene's face and then to the BMW X5 parked on his gravel drive.

'Is this it?' he said. 'Just you and this young man?'

'This is it,' I said.

'You could have come mob-handed,' Warboys said.

'No need, is there?'

He shook his head. 'No need. But I appreciate it anyway, Max.'

'Andrej Wozniak is dead,' I said. 'Jean Wilder and Piper Maldini have been arrested for the murder of Mahmud Irani, Hector Welles and Darren Donovan. That just leaves Doll Warboys. That just leaves your wife.'

He stood to one side to let us enter.

A white English bull terrier came padding down the hallway. He had tiny black eyes that gleamed with life and a forehead that sloped the entire length of his head.

He sniffed my hand with recognition.

'Hello, Bullseye,' I said. 'Hello, old buddy.'

'I didn't know until today,' Paul Warboys said.

When I didn't reply I felt his mood change, and saw his tanned face darken. The rage that had helped him stand his ground against the Krays and the Richardsons half a lifetime ago was never far from the surface.

'You can believe that or not, I don't give a toss,' he said. 'Doll's dad – my late father-in-law – was a black cab driver. He had her tooling up and down the Walworth Road when she was ten years old. Sitting in that black cab, hardly able to see over the steering wheel, the old man killing himself laughing in the back seat.' He smiled fondly at the image. 'Driving in London was in her blood. She knows these streets. She can drive. So she drove for them, Max. That's all she did. Christ, she was old enough to be the grandmother of the rest of them. But she was the driver. Because of what that bastard Welles did to Daniel. Two years for killing an innocent little kid!' He gripped my arm and, even at his advanced age, I felt the power of the man and I was glad to have Billy by my side. *Doll was the driver.* I told you – not my style. Not my style at all, Max. If I was going to slot the bastard, it wouldn't have been with a rope. Just the driving, Max, that's all she did.'

I patted his powerful arm.

'We can talk about all that later, Paul,' I said gently. 'But right now you have to take me to Doll.'

We stood there in silence for a moment. Then he ran a hand through his thinning blond hair and smiled with sadness. There was no point in fighting it.

'She's waiting,' he said.

We followed him upstairs to the master bedroom. He opened the door and we saw Doll Warboys lying on top of the covers.

Billy cried out beside me.

Doll Warboys was wearing her wedding dress, her eyes closed and her hands together as she clasped a bouquet of fresh flowers to her lifeless chest.

I moved quickly to the bed and touched her wrist and her skin had the texture of paper. It was very cold.

On the bedside table were a dozen pill bottles and a half-drunk glass of red wine. I read their labels as I felt her pulse. Zolpidem. Zaleplon. Zopiclone.

Enough sleeping pills to help you sleep forever.

Billy was calling for an ambulance. He was still young enough to believe that it was never too late to get help. But in the end we all run out of time.

I looked at Paul Warboys as he stared at the woman he had married a lifetime ago.

'All these years,' he said. 'And she still fits into her wedding dress.'

CHAPTER 36

It was not over.

The two surviving members of the Hanging Club were on remand in Her Majesty's Prison Holloway, sometimes known as Holloway Castle, where they would remain in single cells until brought to trial at the Central Criminal Court, almost always known as the Old Bailey.

Jean Wilder and Piper Maldini could avoid a trial by entering a plea of guilty on all counts of murder, but it was not going to happen – we had already been informed by the Crown Prosecution Service that both women would be entering pleas of not guilty. Jean Wilder and Piper Maldini wanted their day in court. They wanted, I guessed, to tell the world exactly why they had murdered Mahmud Irani, Hector Welles and Darren Donovan. Like all true believers faced with the end, they dreamed of armies rising behind them.

This final stage of the investigation meant that our Murder Investigation Team would be confined to our desks on the top floor of 27 Savile Row for the next couple of months. You hear a lot about the Golden Hour after a murder is committed. Well, these were the bread-and-butter weeks of arrest to trial – collating evidence and preparing statements, long days of snatched meals eaten at workstations and a waterfall of coffee.

The paperwork had just begun. Prosecutors from the CPS would come and go as they built their case. The police detect, investigate and arrest and the CPS make it stick in court. At least, that is the theory. So our investigation was not over but we were in the home straight.

And that's why when I entered MIR-1 on the morning after the arrests of the surviving members of the Hanging Club, I found Tara Jones clearing her desk.

There was nobody else around. I stood before her as she pushed the shining veil of hair from her face, her wedding ring gleaming like a sliver of gold on black velvet. She did not smile at me as she placed files in a cardboard box.

'Buy you a coffee?' I said. 'Bar Italia? Your favourite?'

'And then what happens, Max?'

'I don't know,' I said.

Your mouth, I thought. Coffee-flavoured kisses. Your eyes looking into my face. Your hands in mine. And then another triple espresso before I have to come back to work. That sounded good to me.

I reached out to touch her arm just above the elbow. With the temperatures suddenly dropping, she was wearing a sweater today, and my fingertips brushed cashmere. She did not pull away but TDC Billy Greene came in just then, calling a jaunty 'Morning all!' as he swung his backpack on his desk, got out the sandwiches that his mum had made him, and powered up his computer. I stood there staring at Tara and there was something in her eyes that I knew I would never get past.

'Shall I tell you what happens, Max?' she said, her voice little more than a whisper, although Billy was already leaning forward, lost in his screen, munching one of his mum's sandwiches. 'If we get what we want, it will not make us happy.'

'What do you mean?' I said, even though I knew exactly what she meant.

'There are no happy endings, Max. Whatever we do. Whatever lies we tell. Whoever we hurt. It's not meant to be for you and me. And you know it's true.'

'I just want a triple espresso,' I said. 'You wouldn't deny a man a triple espresso, would you?'

She shook her head. 'I wouldn't do that.'

'But first I have to do something. Pat Whitestone's son is coming home today. Will you wait for me?'

She touched my hand and smiled at last. 'Please, Max,' she said. 'Go.'

I waited outside the main doors of the Whittington Hospital, alone apart from a hollow-eyed man in his dressing gown sucking on a cigarette like it contained the only air on the planet.

327

I was expecting Pat and Justin to come out with some kind of farewell committee of doctors and nurses, but they came through the big glass doors alone, Justin in dark glasses, his mother lightly guiding his arm, the pair of them the same height now, Whitestone holding a small suitcase and a paper bag from the pharmacy. They seemed to move in careful slow motion, adjusting to this new reality. Neither of them said much and what they did say concerned the practicalities of getting into the big BMW X5 that I had parked in a doctor's bay, the diesel engine running in case I had to move it.

And then I drove them home. From the Whittington Hospital, at the north end of the Holloway Road, to their two-bedroom flat in Islington, at the other end of that road, the kebab shops slowly making way for cafés and the junk shops for antique emporiums as we got closer to the Angel.

I drove. That's all I did. It didn't feel like much. In fact, it felt like nothing. I wanted to do more. I wanted to say something to Pat Whitestone that she could hold when she went forward. But I drove in silence, watching the teenage boy in his dark glasses in the back seat with his small, fair-haired, bespectacled mother, the traffic sluggish on the Holloway Road, and all of their new lives before them.

Whitestone helped Justin to his bedroom and when she returned to the living room I told her the only thing that I had to offer.

'Tara Jones talked to me about being deaf,' I said. 'She told me that the way she had always dealt with it was by acting as if she had a difficulty and not a disability.' I shook my head. 'I know it's easier said than done, Pat.'

But Whitestone nodded. 'I know what she means. You don't have to be defined by the worst things that happen to you. No matter how hard it is, it doesn't have to be the whole story.' She smiled. 'I look at him, Max, and he's still my boy. It's still him. Still my Just. That doesn't change and it will never change. He's still my baby.' She laughed, took off her glasses and wiped her eyes with the back of her hand. 'That sounds corny.'

'It sounds true,' I said.

I indicated her laptop on the dining table. 'Can I show you something?'

'Go ahead.'

I went online.

'I've been thinking,' I said. 'Look.'

On the screen was a logo of two white figures – a human and, by his side, a dog.

'Someone goes blind in this country every hour,' I said. 'But the guide dog service help thousands of people – the blind and partially sighted – every year. They train the dog – a cross between a Lab and a Golden Retriever works best – and then the dog stays with you for six or seven years until they retire. Some people have eight dogs in a lifetime. And I think you and Justin . . .'

'It's something to think about, Max.'

I scrolled down the page. There were images of dogs who seemed to combine great beauty with intense seriousness.

'*We will not rest until people who are blind or partially sighted can enjoy the same freedom of movement as everyone else,*' I read.

'Max?'

I looked at her.

'You've done enough,' she said.

We stared at each other.

And I saw that she knew. Perhaps she did not know everything about the night that Jackson Rose and I came to the Angel to confront the leader of the Dog Town Boys. But she knew enough. Of course she knew. DCI Pat Whitestone is the best homicide detective in West End Central.

'We'll be all right,' she said, staring out of the window. 'The pair of us.'

I nodded to the window. It was one of those strange moments when the city seems totally empty.

'It's a good neighbourhood,' I said.

'It is now,' said Pat Whitestone.

I drove back to West End Central, just about resisting the urge to put on the blues-and-twos. I parked my BMW X5 under the big blue light outside 27 Savile Row and, too impatient for the lift, I ran all the way to the top floor.

But MIR-1 was empty.

I looked at my phone but there were no messages.

That was all right. I was happy to be spared a text message. It really wasn't necessary. Because I got it. The day grew cool, the shadows long, and soon the lights would be coming on in the big Georgian houses of Canonbury Square.

And Tara Jones was already home.

CHAPTER 37

Then summer was done with us.

There were new school shoes waiting in the hall. Scout's uniform was not as ridiculously big as it had been a year ago and she no longer needed my help to put it on. September had swung round again but it was different from all the other Septembers.

'I can do it myself,' Scout said, struggling gamely with the buttons of her yellow shirt. 'Even the socks.'

First thing in the morning and from the window of our loft I could see the dome of St Paul's surrounded by an untouched blue sky, but down on the street the breath of the Smithfield porters made misty clouds.

On that first day of term we had breakfast at Smiths of Smithfield as a special treat – porridge with honey for me and pancakes for Scout, grapefruit juice for both of us and the best triple espresso this side of Soho. Then we walked to school, kicking through the leaves and conkers underfoot, Scout with Stan's lead wrapped twice around her hand, the dog's tail erect and feathery, as flamboyant as a peacock's feathers, his round eyes gleaming with anticipation and his fur exactly the same shade of burnished chestnut as the autumn leaves.

You could feel the time passing, and you could even taste it in the crisp morning air, but it was a good feeling.

When Stan and I said goodbye to Scout at the school gates it was a shock to realise that she was no longer the youngest or the smallest. She fell into smiling step with her friend Mia, and Stan whimpered with grief to see her go. But of course she never looked back at us.

And as we were walking home Stan caught the scent of a Labradoodle bitch on the far side of the street and without warning hurled himself into the traffic.

I pulled him out from under the wheels of a florist's van and called the Well Animal Clinic as soon as I got home. He retreated to the sofa and watched me on the phone with mournful eyes, his head resting on his front paws in classic Cavalier style.

'I'm sorry, Stan,' I said, hanging up. 'But what else can I do?'

The world was turning and nothing could stop it.

'He's good off lead,' Scout told the vet on Friday night. 'And he's good *on* lead. It's just . . .'

She shook her head, her voice trailing off, and we three humans stared at Stan on the vet's table, the dog jumping up to lick my face, his paws against my chest, desperate to demonstrate his unconditional love, trying to ingratiate himself even at this late hour, still with total faith that I could save him from his fate.

The vet laughed and scratched Stan behind the ears and finished Scout's sentence for her.

'It's just that you're growing up, aren't you, Stan?'

The vet, Christian, had known Stan since he was a pup. Christian had given Stan his first vaccinations, microchipped him, nursed him to health when we were worried he had kennel cough. Despite a phobia for needles, and indeed an aversion to any kind of physical discomfort, Stan always looked forward to his trips to see Christian at the Well Animal Clinic. He liked the attention, he favoured the tasty treats they kept in reception, he enjoyed encountering other dogs and meeting exotic animals like cats and hamsters.

But now we were here to talk about castration and the thought of it made me sick to my stomach.

'Neutering is not as clear cut as people believe,' Christian said. 'Every dog is different. Some need it. Some don't. Do it too soon and you will alter the nature of your dog. Do it too late and it will make absolutely no difference to his nature.'

We all looked at Stan. He wouldn't leave me alone. *You can save me from this if you want to,* he seemed to say, climbing into my arms.

'Is your dog neutered, Christian?' Scout asked the vet.

The vet adjusted his glasses.

'No,' he said. 'But you have to decide what's right for Stan. Does he put himself in danger because he has reached sexual maturity?'

Scout and I looked at each other.

We both knew the answer to that one.

And so we made an appointment to bring him back in the morning.

We walked through the meat market's great arch to the strip of shops on the far side of the square. The shops were closed and silent but light and music drifted out from one of the flats above.

MURPHY & SON
Domestic and Commercial Plumbing
and Heating
'Trustworthy' and 'Reliable'

We went up a flight of stairs to the flats. Mrs Murphy opened the door with a couple of children and a dog underfoot. Scout and Stan flew inside as if this was their second home. The Murphys' flat was, as usual, full of family and I smiled as I heard the greetings called out to my daughter and my dog.

'You'll come in for a cup of tea,' Mrs Murphy predicted. 'The gang's all here. Big Mikey. Little Mikey, Siobhan and the kids. You should see Baby Mikey walking about like he owns the place.'

'I'd love to, but I have to run.'

She frowned with disapproval. 'Work?'

'Fred's.'

'Defend yourself at all times,' Mrs Murphy advised.

It was one of those nights when I desperately needed to train. Fred saw it and he was happy to push me hard.

'You're so lucky to be training,' he said, as he drove me through one of his favourite circuits. Ten three-minute rounds banging the pads with ten burpies and twenty press-ups instead of a minute's rest in between, Fred slapping me round the ear with a cracked leather pad whenever I dropped my guard, the rounds passing until I lost count, until I was so exhausted that I was on the very edge of sickness.

'You'll sleep well tonight,' Fred said.

And that would normally have been true. But when we were back at the loft and Scout was brushing her teeth as I turned down the lights, Stan watched me with his huge adoring eyes, certain that the coming weekend held nothing but fun for us, certain that I would never betray him, his love and trust so unquestioning that it filled me with shame.

I crawled into bed weak with exhaustion.

And I still couldn't sleep.

In the morning Stan was sick.

Elaborately sick at both ends. Extravagantly sick.

His cage was a mess of bodily fluid that had erupted from everywhere it could. Foul liquid stuck to his basket, his blanket and his magnificent fur. Stan laid stock still in a puddle of watery filth, staring with numb disbelief at Scout and I, unable to understand what had happened during the night.

We put him in the bath and cleaned him up. Then, when most of the mess had been washed away, and he was starting to get his natural biscuit-smell back, I called the vet's.

'Oh, poor old Stan,' said the kindly receptionist at the Well Animal Clinic. 'Probably something he ate. Best leave the surgery for another day.'

Scout was fussing over him in the bathtub. The projectile vomiting and volcanic diarrhoea had left him bewildered. He looked forlorn, and half his usual size, with his fur sopping wet. But he watched me grinning in the doorway of the bathroom and a familiar, fun-loving glint suddenly lit up those eyes like black marbles.

Hampstead Heath was waiting for us.

Even in September, they were still swimming in the mixed bathing pond.

We saw the distant bathing figures laughing at the cold as we cut across the great rolling expanse of Pryor's Field, Stan hanging back to hunt small flying creatures in the long grass, then sprinting to catch up when Scout called his name. Then we were in the thick forest that separates the bathing ponds from the highest point on Hampstead Heath, and Scout kept Stan closer now. A young fox stalked across our path, checked us out and in an instant was gone. We pushed on, the ground always rising, and suddenly we came out of the trees and onto Parliament Hill, blue sky all around and the city spread out below us, a sight to steal your breath away, and it was as if London belonged to us.

My phone began to vibrate.

EDIE WREN CALLING, it said.

'It's Abu Din,' Edie said. 'Guess what? Somebody just slotted the bastard.'

Saturday afternoon at the Imperial War Museum.

The museum was crowded but down in Carol's small basement office the sound of the crowds seemed far away, like an old soldier's memory of war. Carol expertly spun her wheelchair in a circle as she closed the door behind us. The BBC news was playing on her iMac.

'Do you have anything on Special Operations in Afghanistan?' I asked.

'Some,' she said, and hesitated. 'You know those servicemen – the ones who were killed, the Sangin Six – were regular army. They weren't Special Ops.'

'I know.'

'And there's restricted viewing on anything to do with Special Ops, Max.'

I nodded. We stared at each other for a bit. Then she sighed.

'You can't take anything away,' she said.

And so Carol placed a fat green file marked *UKSF* on the desk and then made us two mugs of builder's tea – they don't do triple espresso in the Imperial War Museum – deftly if noisily manoeuvring her wheelchair in the cramped office as she got the kettle on.

I waded through pictures of Special Operation Forces in Afghanistan. There were endless images of heavily armed fighting men on what looked like the surface of the moon, all of them with their faces obscured. There were pixelated faces, blacked-out faces and smudged faces, and the men wore civilian clothing, camouflage gear and fleeces on rocky terrain that looked as though it was either searing hot or freezing cold, with nothing in between.

It looked like the harshest place on the planet, but the men seemed as happy as larks, posing proudly with their assault rifles on land where it looked as though nothing good could ever grow.

Many of them had beards but a few were cleanly shaven and as I sipped my strong sweet tea I found him, posing in profile in a T-shirt and cargo trousers that were stuffed with kit, his weapon held at a 45-degree angle.

I read, '*The relevance of this photo is simply the weapon – an M249 SAW featuring the collapsible Para stock and a 200-round plastic assault pack. This operator wears civilian clothing.*'

The top half of the operator's head was blacked out but you could still see his smiling mouth.

339

The gap-toothed grin of my oldest friend was unmistakable.

'Have you seen this?' Carol said.

She was looking at the screen of her iMac. Blue lights swept a drab street in Wembley. The police tape was going up.

BBC BREAKING NEWS: HATE CLERIC FOUND MURDERED

Carol swivelled in her chair to look at me.

'Is it true?' she said. 'Somebody just killed this bastard?'

'Apparently,' I said.

'Did they hang him?'

I closed the thin green file.

'Shot him,' I said, sipping my tea. 'One in the head and one in the heart.'

AUTHOR'S NOTE

Strangely enough, Newgate Prison is still down there. It is true that not much remains of the country's most notorious prison, but all that Max Wolfe discovers – the condemned man's holding cell and Dead Man's Walk, where the ceiling and the walls contract like a corridor in a nightmare – is, rather incredibly, still buried deep beneath the Old Bailey.

What remains of Newgate is not preserved or conserved, for nobody was ever proud of the London's most notorious prison – chamber of horrors for eight hundred years, the human zoo, 'the grimy axle around which British society slowly twisted'. As Max suggests, no doubt one day it will all be swept away in a mad fit of rebuilding, but for now, it is still down there. You just go down to the basement of the Old Bailey. And then you keep going.

As for Albert Pierrepoint, whose name and image is appropriated by the Hanging Club, he was of course the nation's executioner in the middle of the twentieth century, hanging 435 people, including 202 Nazis found guilty of war crimes.

Pierrepoint, by this time sickened of capital punishment, retired to work as a publican. He wrote in his autobiography, 'Capital punishment, in my view, achieved nothing except revenge.'

No doubt this is true. But as Sergeant John Caine asks Max Wolfe up in the Black Museum – 'What's wrong with a bit of revenge?'

Tony Parsons,
London, 2016.

Books are to be returned on or before
the last date below.

-3. MAR 1997

10. APR. 1997

-5. DEC. 1997

30. APR. 1998

20. MAY 1998

2 1 MAY 1998

16. JUN. 1998

24. JUN. 1998

14. SEP. 2005

3 0 MAY 2012

2 2 MAY 2013

1 1 MAR 2014

LIBREX—

Other titles in the series
INSIDE THE ANCIENT WORLD
General Editor: M. R. F. Gunningham

Robin Barrow: *Athenian Democracy*
Meg Parker: *Socrates and Athens*
David Taylor: *Cicero and Rome*
Martin Thorpe: *Homer*
John Sharwood Smith: *The Bride from the Sea*
Robin Barrow: *Greek and Roman Education*
Kenneth McLeish: *Roman Comedy*
Diana Topham-Meekings: *The Hollow Ships*
John Richardson: *Roman Provincial Administration*
Alexander McKay: *Vitruvius, Architect and Engineer*
Massey and Moreland: *Slavery in Ancient Rome*
David Taylor: *Roman Society*

INSIDE THE ANCIENT WORLD

AENEAS AND THE ROMAN HERO

R. D. WILLIAMS

Nelson

Thomas Nelson and Sons Ltd
Nelson House Mayfield Road
Walton-on-Thames Surrey
KT12 5PL UK

Nelson Blackie
Wester Cleddens Road
Bishopbriggs
Glasgow
G64 2NZ UK

Thomas Nelson Australia
102 Dodds Street
South Melbourne
Victoria 3205 Australia

Nelson Canada
1120 Birchmount Road
Scarborough Ontario
M1K 5G4 Canada

© R.D. Williams 1973

First published by Macmillan Education Ltd 1973
ISBN 0-333-14745-6

This edition published by Thomas Nelson and Sons Ltd 1992

I(T)P Thomas Nelson is an International
      Thomson Publishing Company

I(T)P is used under licence

ISBN 0-17-438505-6
NPN 9 8 7 6 5

Printed in Singapore

Contents

	List of illustrations and map	6
	Preface	7
1	Virgil's life and times	11
2	Rome's destiny: The Golden Age	17
3	Aeneas – the new hero	28
4	Virgil's private voice: Dido, Turnus, Juno	61
	INDEX	72

List of Illustrations

Virgil and the Muses
(*Mosaic from Sousse*)   10

Statue of Augustus
(*Prima Porta*)   15

Venus Erycina
(*Coin of Considianus*)   18

Temple of Jupiter, Juno and
Minerva on the Capitol
(*Coin of Vespasian*)   27

Aeneas offering sacrifices
(*Ara Pacis*)   29

Ara Pacis
(*South-east corner*)   30

The goddess Pietas (*obverse*) and Aeneas carrying Anchises
    (*reverse*)   37
(*Coin of Herennius*)

Octavian (*obverse*) and Aeneas carrying Anchises (*reverse*)
(*Coin of Octavian*)   37

Aeneas, Anchises and the Palladium
(*Coin of Caesar*)   40

Temple of Vesta in the Roman Forum – traditional home of the
    sacred objects brought by Aeneas from Troy   40

Aeneas and the Sibyl
(*Vatican MS of Virgil: fourth century*)   45

The Roman Forum   70–71

Map of Aeneas' journey   38–39

General Editor's Preface

To get *inside* the Ancient World is no easy task. What is easy is to idealise the Greeks and Romans, or else to endow them unconsciously with our own conventional beliefs and prejudices. The aim of this series is to illuminate selected aspects of Antiquity in such a way as to encourage the reader to form his own judgement, from the inside, on the ways of life, culture and attitudes that characterised the Greco-Roman world. Where suitable, the books draw widely on the writings (freshly translated) of ancient authors in order to convey information and to illustrate contemporary views.

The topics in the series have been chosen both for their intrinsic interest and because of their central importance for the student who wishes to see the civilisations of Greece and Rome in perspective. The close interaction of literature, art, thought and institutions reveals the Ancient World in its totality. The opportunity should thus arise for making comparisons not only within that world, between Athens and Sparta, or Athens and Rome, but also between the world of Antiquity and our own.

The title 'Classical Studies' (or 'Classical Civilisation') is featuring more and more frequently in school timetables and in the prospectuses of universities. In schools, the subject is now taught at Advanced Level as well as at Key Stages 3 and 4. It is particularly for the latter courses that this new series has been designed; also as a helpful ancillary to the study of Latin and Greek in the sixth form and below. (Professor Williams gives the passages he quotes from Virgil both in the original and in translation.) It is hoped that some of the books in the series will interest students of English and History at these levels as well as the non-specialist reader.

The authors, who are teachers in schools or universities, have each taken an aspect of the Ancient World. They have tried not to give a romanticised picture but to portray, as vividly as possible, the Greeks and the Romans as they really were.

The author's object in *Aeneas and the Roman Hero* has been to explain and illustrate the ideals of the newly-founded Roman Empire as they are reflected in Virgil's *Aeneid*. The poem was written at a time when national and patriotic hopes were high, when it seemed that Rome had left behind the sufferings and bloodshed of a series of civil wars, and was poised to enter a period of peace and prosperity, and to spread to the rest of the world the benefits of her civilisation.

7

In the *Aeneid* Virgil explores the advantages and the problems which this world-destiny involves by symbolising them in an epic narrative – the story of Rome's first founder, the Trojan prince Aeneas. We see in him a person devoted to the high ideals of his mission, ready to sacrifice his personal life for the benefit of future generations: to the best of his ability he follows what he sees as his divine duty. Yet in the course of doing so he is involved in dilemma after dilemma: he must give up his love for Dido (and so destroy her happiness and finally her life itself); he must fight against violent opposition, though he wishes to be a man of peace. He must decide at each and every point how to deal with the human problems which constantly beset him. He must be a new type of hero appropriate for the new Roman world as Virgil saw it – not aggressive or self-seeking, yet brave and firm.

Virgil's portrayal of Aeneas' efforts to achieve this kind of leadership is so sensitively done as to show that the problems of a Trojan prince who lived 3000 years ago shed light on the perpetual problems of the human race. This perhaps is what great poems are about – they illuminate what is universal by their treatment of the particular: and this is why, in Professor Williams's view, Virgil's *Aeneid* continues to be one of the important poems of our civilisation.

January 1973   MICHAEL GUNNINGHAM

Acknowledgements

The publishers wish to acknowledge the following sources of photographs:

Ashmolean Museum pp. 18, 37, 40

Trustees of the British Museum pp. 27, 37

Fototeca Unione & American Academy, Rome pp. 29, 30

Giraudon, Paris p. 10

The Mansell Collection p. 15

The Vatican Museum, Rome p. 45

Illustrations on pages 40 and 71 were taken by the author.

Virgil and the Muses (Mosaic from Sousse)

I

Virgil's life and times

PUBLIUS VERGILIUS MARO (his name in English is generally spelt 'Virgil') was regarded by the Romans as their greatest poet, and most lovers of poetry ever since have agreed. His influence on the Romans themselves, from the time of his younger contemporary Ovid onwards, was profound and his works immediately became school and university text books as well as sources of inspiration for poets, critics, and thinkers; they have remained so for more than two thousand years.

The reasons for admiration have been diverse – always his diction and the music of his hexameter, often his perfection of structure and form, sometimes his ethical and religious message, sometimes the drama of his narrative, sometimes the pathos of the 'tears in things', sometimes his reflection of the Roman character, sometimes his love for the traditions and customs of remote Roman antiquity. All of these things are present in the *Aeneid*, and different generations have admired some more than others according to their own viewpoints; no other poet of the ancient world has had such influence over such a wide area of different literary interests.

Virgil was born in 70 BC near Mantua, in North Italy; his father was a peasant with a small farm, and throughout Virgil's poetry can be seen his love of the Italian land and the simple virtues of the people who cultivated it. He received the best possible education of the time, first at Cremona, then Milan, then Rome. He would have received a thorough training in the Greek and Roman poets, and in rhetorical method and philosophy; his knowledge of Greek and of the Greek way of life was detailed and profound. His whole life was that of a poet and a scholar; he played no part personally in military or political life, and is said to have been somewhat delicate in health and shy and retiring in personality. But as we shall see he took a great interest in Roman national affairs, and was closely in touch with current events through his friendship with men who were directing the movement of affairs, such as Pollio, Gallus, Maecenas, and the Emperor Augustus himself.

His earliest certain work (there are some minor poems ascribed to him, few of which are genuine) was the collection of ten pastoral poems known as the *Eclogues* ('Selections'). These were composed between 42 and 37 BC, and they brought him immediate recognition; he became an important member of the literary court circle under the patronage of Maecenas, to whom he dedicated the *Georgics*, his next work (composed between 37 and 30 BC). This is a treatise in four books about agriculture, designed not so much to provide systematic instruction as to inspire his readers with a love of the land and portray the rewards of the farmer's hard work.

After the publication of the *Georgics* in 30 BC Virgil dedicated himself to the epic poem for which he had been preparing himself all through his life. We know he had thought of and rejected certain themes, such as a poem on the Alban kings or on the exploits of Augustus; the subject he finally chose was the legendary origin of Rome through the foundation in Italy by Aeneas of Lavinium, which founded Alba Longa, which founded Rome. Aeneas was an exile from Troy after it was sacked by the Greeks (in the twelfth century BC) because of the capture of Helen by Paris, and it was laid upon him as a divine mission to take his companions to a western land to found a city which would, as the centuries rolled by, achieve world dominion and civilise all mankind. The choice of the subject satisfied Virgil for many reasons – in the first place the legend, though very well known, was fluid and could be adapted and re-arranged for poetic purposes (for example Dido did not figure at all in the prose version of the legend); secondly it was national and Roman but not too close to history; thirdly it was set in the distant past and could contain elements of adventure and other-worldly imagination like Homer's *Odyssey*; fourthly it could combine past and present over a span of more than a thousand years: its setting is the distant past, but by means of dreams and prophecies, and descriptions of the first celebrations of well-known contemporary customs (foreshadowing Roman values in the character of her first founder Aeneas), it could also be contemporary.

Virgil spent eleven years on the composition of his poem, and in 19 BC, when he planned to spend another three years working on it, he undertook a journey to Greece to get local colour for the revision of the Greek parts of the poem. He fell ill on the journey and returned to Italy but died soon after landing at Brundisium. His dying wish was that the poem should be burnt, but the Emperor Augustus forbade this and the poem was published posthumously.

Essentially the *Aeneid* is a national poem, a picture of Roman character and ideals written at a time when optimism was in the air and the Romans felt that a new and glorious chapter was on the point of opening. Virgil shared in the hope and excitement of the time, and wrote his poem to explore what the Romans were like, what they should be like, and what they could teach the world. To understand the climate of public opinion which the poem reflects (and leads) we should look briefly at the historical circumstances of the time.

Virgil began to compose the *Aeneid* immediately after the inauguration of the Roman Empire following the battle of Actium in 31 BC. At this battle Augustus (Octavian as he was then called) defeated his fellow countryman Antony who was aided by Cleopatra, and the long period of civil war came to an end. The whole of Virgil's life had been lived in a period of impending or actual civil war; when he was born the civil war between Marius and Sulla had not long been ended, and the sparring for position between Julius Caesar and Pompey culminated in 49 BC, when Caesar crossed the Rubicon and a year later defeated Pompey's forces at Pharsalus. Julius Caesar's period of supremacy was short-lived; the daggers of the conspirators struck home on the Ides of March, 44 BC, and there followed what must have been the worst period of all, with constant fighting between rival groups in Italy. The defeat of Brutus and Cassius at Philippi in 42 BC did not end the internal struggle; Sextus Pompeius and his rebels were not finally defeated until 36 BC, and the Roman world then awaited the final showdown between the victors of Philippi, Octavian (Augustus) and Mark Antony. This came eventually at Actium in 31 BC, and Augustus became undisputed master of the Roman world.

Not surprisingly the Romans had felt guilt as well as fear during this long period of civil war: these feelings are well reflected in two of Horace's *Epodes* (written in the last and worst ten years before Actium). Here is a paraphrase of the beginning of *Epode* 16:

> Another generation is now being worn away by civil wars, and Rome rushes to destruction by her own strength. Rome survived Porsena and the Germans and Hannibal, and we ourselves are destroying her, we a wicked generation of guilt-laden stock, and the land on which Rome stands will be possessed again by wild beasts.

Virgil had had personal experience of the miseries of the civil wars when farms around Mantua (perhaps including his own) were confiscated for the resettlement of demobilised soldiers after Philippi, and the first and ninth of his *Eclogues* are about the wretched plight of the dispossessed. In *Eclogue* 1 (64 f.) the shepherd Meliboeus laments that he must leave his farm and go far away, and never again see his little cottage and his corn-crop growing in the fields. 'Shall some accursed soldier possess my beautiful fields, some barbarian my crops? See to what misery civil war has brought us!'

At the end of *Georgics* 1 (written just before Actium) Virgil appeals to the gods to permit Octavian to save the Romans from their sad plight:

> Oh permit this young man to save our ruined generation! Long enough now have we with our blood atoned for the perjury of Laomedon's Troy . . . right and wrong are turned topsy-turvy, there

are wars everywhere in the world, every shape of sin, no proper honour paid to the plough, the fields go to rack and ruin in the absence of the farmers, and the ploughshares are beaten into swords.

And the passage ends with a comparison of the state of affairs in the Roman world with a runaway chariot where the charioteer cannot control the horses.

After Actium Rome got a charioteer who could exercise control in the person of her first Emperor. What wonder that the Roman people, and not least the poets, felt that the long nightmare was over, and that their world had returned at last to sanity? The feeling of relief gave way to one of positive optimism; Rome could now be true to her real self, and achieve what never had been achieved before. These were the hopes prevalent during the first dozen years of Augustus' rule, when the *Aeneid* was being written.

The policy of Augustus, now that he was master of the world (whatever his policies may have been earlier, and there is evidence that he was often ruthless) was aimed essentially at moderation and stability. He had to avoid the mistakes of Julius Caesar, and cloak his absolute authority behind the appearance of constitutional rule and the restoration of the Republic. Apart from the political necessity he seems to have been a genuine lover of the old Roman tradition, and in his social and religious policy as well as in his constitutional settlements he aimed to restore the old way of life, to seek to encourage the qualities which in the past had made Rome great, and could again make her greater still. He sought to bring back the *mos maiorum*, the 'custom of our ancestors', and in this he had the strong support of very many Romans, certainly including Virgil.

But first and foremost Augustus proclaimed that he had brought peace: he twice closed the gates of the temple of Janus which were open in times of war (and had been open through almost all Rome's tempestuous history), and the fighting which took place in his reign was always on the frontiers or in remote parts of the Empire. The citizens of Rome could indeed feel that peace had at last been restored.

We need not here dwell on Augustus' constitutional settlements in which he 'handed back the state to the people', and 'held more prestige but no more power than his colleagues' (these are quotations from his auto-biography, the *Res Gestae*). He avoided in fact all appearance of power-seeking or megalomania. But his social and religious ideas are very relevant to a study of the *Aeneid* because they were shared by Virgil, as indeed by very many of the Romans.

We can read in the preface to Livy's history, written at the beginning of Augustus' reign, a lament for the ancient virtues of the Romans and a complaint that the general standard of conduct had greatly declined in his

Statue of Augustus (*Prima Porta*)

own days. Augustus set out to remedy this, as far as possible, by legislation, and eventually in 18 BC a series of *Leges Iuliae* set limits to expenditure, encouraged family life, penalised sexual laxity. This represented the feeling of many Romans in these years; how far such moral aims can be achieved by legislation is always doubtful (as Horace said: 'What is the use of laws without moral standards to back them?'), but what is plain is that Augustus was expressing the attitude and wishes of many of his subjects when he attempted this legislation (Horace in *Odes* 4.15 praises Augustus for having put bounds to licence, removed sin, and brought back the old way of life by which Rome had grown great).

Similarly in the area of religion Augustus tried to encourage a return to the old standards. He restored the temples that had fallen into disuse (eighty-two of them, according to the *Res Gestae*); he revived ancient cults and ceremonies wherever he could. Here again he was in tune with many contemporaries: in a severe poem (*Odes* 3.6) Horace tells the Romans that they will have to pay for the sins of their ancestors until they restore the temples and crumbling shrines of their ancient gods. Augustus regarded himself as especially under the patronage of Apollo, and built a splendid new temple to Apollo on the Palatine: always and in every way he showed himself the champion of the traditional religion.

What was the relationship of the *Aeneid* to these governmental policies? Quite simply Virgil (like many others) thought along broadly the same lines. No one could have loved the ancient traditions of Rome more than Virgil did, and the qualities by which Rome in the past had grown great – religion, devotion to duty, loyalty, family affection – were those which, by upbringing and personal inclination, he most admired. He was a quite close friend of Augustus, and he must often have discussed with the Emperor the prospects and hopes for a new positive way of life, based upon the old values. The emperor and the poet had the same ideas – not without very good reason. The *Aeneid* reflects the governmental policy of Augustus in moral, social and religious ideas, not because they were Augustus' ideas but because they were Virgil's. When the question is asked, as it often is, 'Did Augustus exert pressure on Virgil to write the *Aeneid*?' (or 'Is the *Aeneid* a piece of governmental propaganda?'), the answer should be that Augustus was just as responsible for the *Aeneid* (and no more so) as Virgil was responsible for the social and religious reforms which Augustus inaugurated. Both men saw things the same way; one acted by political power, the other by poetry.

2

Rome's destiny: The Golden Age

THERE can be no doubt that it was Virgil's primary intention in the *Aeneid* to portray the hopes and aspirations which have been outlined in the previous chapter. The feeling abroad in the first years of Augustus' rule was one of excited optimism – it seemed that after the horrors of civil war Rome had at last found again her true self, and Virgil (like Horace in his Roman Odes, Book 3.1–6) was inspired by this feeling, and set out to portray it in epic form. As the poem took shape, however, it became more apparent to Virgil that the Roman destiny could not in fact be achieved without great sacrifices, suffering and devotion on the part of the Romans themselves, and also disaster to those who stood in the way (like Dido, Turnus, and countless Latin and Rutulian warriors). So powerful was Virgil's sympathy for the defeated that it often seems to conflict with the triumph of Rome's achievement – especially when Dido is brushed aside and trampled upon by its requirements; but the Roman vision is never quite lost sight of, and indeed often is powerfully predominant. The pathos and suffering which it involved will be discussed in another chapter – here we may concentrate first on defining and appreciating the optimistic side of Rome's destiny.

We may best illustrate this from four great patriotic passages in the poem, interlinking them with a brief account of the intervening narrative and of the shorter indications of Roman greatness which occur throughout. The four major passages are: (i) Jupiter's prophecy in Book 1; (ii) the pageant of Roman heroes in Book 6; (iii) the pictures on Aeneas' shield in Book 8; (iv) the reconciliation between Juno, great opponent of Rome, and Jupiter in Book 12.

(i) Jupiter's prophecy (*Aen.* 1.257–96)

The poem begins with a firm statement of how Aeneas was destined by fate (line 2, *fato profugus*) to leave Troy and found a new city in Latĭum (i.e. Lavinium) which would be transferred first to Alba Longa and then to Rome. The queen of heaven, Juno, is opposed to this destiny because

B

of her hatred for the Trojans and love of Carthage (fated to be overcome by Rome); she arouses a storm, causing the Trojans to be shipwrecked on the coast of Carthage. Venus, mother of Aeneas and protecting deity of the Roman people, goes to Jupiter and indignantly asks why the promised glory of Aeneas and his Trojan-Roman descendants is· thus being frustrated. Jupiter replies in a serene survey of what Rome is destined to achieve, and promises that it will indeed come to pass. He tells her (1.261 ff.) that Aeneas will wage a great war in Italy, crush their proud peoples, and establish for his nation a way of life and a new city.

Venus Erycina (Coin of Considianus)

Ascanius, his son, also called Iulus, will succeed to his kingdom and found Alba Longa, and three hundred years later Romulus and Remus will be born of the priestess Ilia (Rhea Silvia) and the god Mars; Romulus will found Rome and call the people Roman after his name. 'To these' (promises Jupiter, 1.278 ff.) 'I set no bounds in space or time – I have given them rule without end.' Imagine the impact of this tremendous promise on Virgil's contemporaries – a world empire, unending, under divine providence. Jupiter goes on to promise that Juno will be reconciled (as she is in Book 12) and will join with him in cherishing the Romans, 'rulers of the world, the race wearing the toga' (282). One day Greece will be conquered – we remember how the Greeks have just destroyed Troy, from which Aeneas is a homeless fugitive. There will be born from the stock of Aeneas' son Iulus a Caesar of Julian race (notice how Virgil uses the etymology of Iulus–Julius) who will extend his empire to the Ocean (i.e. the boundaries of Europe) and his fame to the stars. This is Augustus Caesar, adopted son of Julius Caesar, and thus of Julian race. One day, continues Jupiter to Venus, you will receive him in heaven; he too will become a god. And his speech ends with an inspiring promise of peace throughout the world, concord among all people, conquest of violence and hatred. Here it is in Virgil's Latin:

> aspera tum positis mitescent saecula bellis;
> cana Fides et Vesta, Remo cum fratre Quirinus
> iura dabunt; dirae ferro et compagibus artis
> claudentur Belli portae; Furor impius intus
> saeva sedens super arma et centum vinctus aënis
> post tergum nodis fremet horridus ore cruento.

(1.291–6)

And here in Dryden's spirited and vigorous translation (1697):

> Then dire debate and impious war shall cease,
> And the stern age be softened into peace:
> Then banished faith shall once again return,
> And vestal fires in hallowed temples burn.
> And Remus with Quirinus shall sustain
> The righteous laws, and fraud and force restrain.
> Janus himself before his fane shall wait,
> And keep the dreadful issues of his gate,
> With bolts and iron bars; within remains
> Imprisoned Fury, bound in brazen chains;
> High on a trophy raised, of useless arms,
> He sits, and threats the world with vain alarms.

This is indeed a prospect for which men then, as now, might well strive: this is the hope in which the *Aeneid* was conceived. It did not wholly come true – yet the achievement of the Romans, as civilisers and law-givers in the Mediterranean world for more than four centuries after Virgil's times, was such as not to be entirely unworthy of these majestic and splendid prophecies.

(ii) The pageant of Roman heroes (*Aen.* 6.756–853)

The progress of Aeneas towards the fulfilment of his mission through the first six books of the poem will be described in the next chapter; here, however, we may notice a number of passages, especially prophecies and visions which define the nature of Rome's mission, before discussing the great pageant which ends Book 6.

After the landing of the Trojans on the shores of Africa Virgil tells of the kindly reception which are given by Dido, queen of Carthage, and of how Dido falls in love with Aeneas and asks to hear the story of his wanderings. The second book describes the fall of Troy, the events of the last night of the city once sovereign in all Asia. It is a book of tragedy, brightened only by occasional glimpses of the greatness of Rome, destined to be born from Troy's ashes. When the wooden horse is taken within the walls, the ghost of Hector appears to Aeneas, telling him to flee from Troy, which is doomed, taking with him Troy's gods in order to found a new city, a mighty one, across the seas (2.293–5). Aeneas is slow to obey this vision, feeling himself bound to join in the last resistance with his comrades, and he has to be reminded by Venus of the need to escape with his family (594–600) because of the absolute inevitability of Troy's downfall. In the escape he loses his wife Creusa, and her ghost reiterates Hector's message – he must escape and found a new city by the river Tiber.

In the third book Aeneas describes the long wanderings of seven years' duration while he tried to discover the destined site of his city. The weariness of the seemingly unending journey is relieved with prophecies of greatness to come (far off in the future as it must have seemed to the storm-tossed exiles): at Delos Apollo prophesies that the house of Aeneas will rule the whole world, and his son's sons, and those who come after (3.97–8); in Crete the Penates (the gods of Troy) appear to Aeneas in a vision and promise him that they will raise his descendants to the stars and give empire to his city (158–9): at Buthrotum the seer Helenus gives a long prophecy of the rest of the voyage, ending with the exhortation that Aeneas should press on and make Troy mighty by his deeds (462). These notes of hope brighten the weary quest for what seem to Aeneas to be 'the ever-receding shores of Italy'.

In the fourth book the vision of Rome fades as Aeneas stays on and on with Dido in Carthage, forgetful of his fate. Finally Jupiter intervenes by sending Mercury to remind him of his destiny. Here are Virgil's words:

> non illum nobis genetrix pulcherrima talem
> promisit Graiumque ideo bis vindicat armis;
> sed fore qui gravidam imperiis belloque frementem
> Italiam regeret, genus alto a sanguine Teucri
> proderet, ac totum sub leges mitteret orbem.
>
> (4.227–31)

This is Jackson Knight's translation (Penguin Classics, 1956):

> It was never for this that the most beautiful goddess, his mother, twice rescued him from his Greek foes. This is not the man she led us to think that he would prove to be. No, he was to guide an Italy which is to be a breeding-ground of leadership and clamorous with noise of war, transmit a lineage from proud Teucer's blood, and subject the whole earth to the rule of law.

The passage is of great importance as defining Rome's two-fold mission – first to rule over warlike Italy, and secondly to bring the whole world beneath the sway of laws. First conquest – then civilisation: this, as we shall see, is the message of Anchises' ghost in Book 6.

Aeneas leaves Dido, not of his own free will but under the compulsion of duty (4.361), and after celebrating funeral games for his father Anchises in the fifth book, arrives in Italy and descends to the underworld to learn from Anchises' ghost in Elysium more about the nature of his future destiny. His experiences in the first two-thirds of the sixth book are gloomy and sad, but when he reaches Elysium and is welcomed by his father the mood changes, and Anchises describes to his son at length the multitude of ghosts of the great Roman heroes waiting by the stream of Lethe to be born into the upper world – as they will be if Aeneas can succeed in his mission of founding Rome.

As Anchises describes the ghosts (756–846) they pass in a pageant before the eyes of the reader's imagination: first the kings of Alba Longa (establishing a mood of tradition and antiquity), and then the first king of Rome, Romulus himself, son of Mars, destined to found a city which will bound its empire by earth's limits and its spirit by those of heaven itself, great mother of men, like Cybele, great mother of gods. So far the pageant has been chronological: now the chronology is broken by more than 700 years as Romulus is followed by Augustus, second founder of Rome. All Virgil's art is employed in the description of Rome's first emperor:

> hic vir, hic est, tibi quem promitti saepius audis,
> Augustus Caesar, divi genus, aurea condet
> saecula qui rursus Latio regnata per arva
> Saturno quondam, super et Garamantas et Indos
> proferet imperium; iacet extra sidera tellus,
> extra anni solisque vias, ubi caelifer Atlas
> axem umero torquet stellis ardentibus aptum.

> (6.791–7)

This is Copley's version (Bobbs-Merrill, Indianapolis, 1965):

> Here is the man you've heard so often promised:
> Augustus, son of godhead. He'll rebuild
> a golden age in Latium, land where once
> Saturn was king. Past India, past the Moor
> he'll spread his rule to zones beyond the stars,
> beyond the ecliptic, where Atlas carries heaven,
> and bears on his back the spinning, star-tricked wheel.

The description of Augustus continues with a list of the places he will conquer (the Caspian realms, the Maeotian land, the Nile – this last a reference to his victory over Antony and the Egyptian Cleopatra at Actium in 31 BC), and compares him with Hercules and Bacchus. The point of the comparison is threefold – first in the vast tracts of land all three covered in their various activities, second in the civilising influence they brought, and thirdly in that Hercules and Bacchus were in legend mortal men who for their great services to civilisation were deified; the reader is invited to infer that Augustus too deserves, or will deserve, this distinction.

The pageant continues with the kings of Rome; Virgil pauses on Numa, the second king, because he symbolised for the Romans the non-military aspect of their mission. Romulus, the first king, was a figure of bravery and military strength; Numa is the embodiment of religion and civilisation. Virgil speaks of him as 'conspicuous with his olive branch, carrying the sacred emblems' and as the man who 'will found the little city securely on the basis of law'. The idea of the Romans first as world-conquerors by divine providence, and then as world-civilisers is vividly symbolised in the description of the second king.

After the kings come various heroes of the republic: first Brutus, the founder of the republic, who expelled Tarquin the Proud; then the Decii, the Drusi, Torquatus, Camillus, who saved Rome from the Gauls; then Caesar and Pompey, presented in sad tones because of the civil war which they fought against each other – now, in Augustus' time, hopefully a thing of the past; then the conquerors of Greece and of Carthage, and finally Fabius Maximus, who 'by delaying saved the Roman state'. This is a reference to the most critical period of Roman history, when after his victories at Lake Trasimene and Cannae in 217–16 BC the Carthaginian leader Hannibal appeared to have Rome at his mercy. Fabius, however, by refusing pitched battle and harrying Hannibal wherever he went enabled the Romans to recover their strength and finally prevail. Fabius comes last in the pageant because he symbolises survival, because he exorcises Dido's curse in 4.625 ff. (where she had called for an unknown avenger to arise from her bones), and because he was described by Ennius in a famous line which Virgil quotes, thus adding to the long list of heroes of history a tribute to his great predecessor in literature.

When the pageant is over Anchises summarises the mission of Rome in these lines:

> excudent alii spirantia mollius aera
> (credo equidem), vivos ducent de marmore vultus,
> orabunt causas melius, caelique meatus
> describent radio et surgentia sidera dicent:
> tu regere imperio populos, Romane, memento
> (hae tibi erunt artes), pacique imponere morem,
> parcere subiectis et debellare superbos.
>
> (6.847–53)

Others will beat out the breathing bronze in softer lines (I believe it myself), they will bring forth living faces from the marble, they will plead cases better, and describe the wanderings of the heavens with their measuring-rods, and tell of the rising stars. But, Romans, you must remember to rule the peoples with your government (such shall be your arts), and to add civilisation to peace, to spare the conquered and cast down the proud.

It is clear that the first four lines refer to the Greeks. Virgil concedes to them supremacy in sculpture, oratory and astronomy (in all of which the Romans achieved no mean success) in order to emphasise the more strongly the aspects of Roman supremacy. The Roman 'arts' to balance the Greek achievement are in the province of government (*regere imperio*), and government is defined as first achieving peace and then superimposing civilisation (*morem*): finally peace is a matter of sparing the conquered and overthrowing the aggressor. These sonorous lines convey an optimistic picture of Rome's destiny – one which they did not perhaps wholly achieve in the four centuries of Roman imperial power after Augustus, but in which their advances towards a conception of world peace, wise administration, humane tolerance, have left a deep influence upon modern man in the western world. This is in essence what Virgil in the *Aeneid* felt that the Romans could achieve – and they went in fact a long way towards it.

(iii) The shield of Aeneas (*Aen.* 8.626–731)

After the vision of the Roman heroes in the underworld Aeneas returns to his men at Cumae, and they sail north to the Tiber; their arrival at the famous and historic river is described in a passage of idyllic and serene beauty (7.25–36). They are hospitably received by King Latinus, who recognises in their arrival the fulfilment of an oracle that his daughter was to marry a foreigner and from the union of the peoples would arise a race that would raise the Latin name to the stars (7.98–101 and 270–2). But this happy situation is changed by the intervention of Juno, who persuades Turnus the Rutulian, already betrothed to Latinus' daughter Lavinia, to take up arms against the newcomers. War breaks out, and Virgil gives a catalogue of the Italian forces opposing the Trojans, a vivid portrayal of the peoples and places of his beloved Italy. The *Aeneid* presents the paradox of how the defeated (the Italians) in fact contributed much more to the future Roman people than the victorious Trojans (this is discussed more fully in the next section).

Aeneas leaves to get help from Evander, an Arcadian king whose city Pallanteum is built on the site of the seven hills where centuries later Rome was to arise. In the description of Aeneas' visit to the site of Rome which occupies Book 8 Virgil gives a peaceful picture shot through with future destiny. Aeneas visits the famous places of Rome: the Carmental gate, the Lupercal, Argiletum, the Capitol – 'golden now,' says Virgil, 'but then rough ground of thickets and brambles' (8.348). Evander's son Pallas is sent with a contingent of warriors to help Aeneas, and Venus arranges with Vulcan for a new shield to be made for Aeneas.

The idea of describing pictures on a shield is taken from Homer, where Achilles, because Patroclus had borrowed his armour and Hector had despoiled him of it, is provided with a new shield by his goddess mother; the pictures on it are described at length. Aeneas in Virgil has not lost his shield, but what Virgil achieves by giving him a new one is the opportunity of another review of Roman history and achievement comparable with the pageant in Book 6. And he gives it at this very last moment before the full-scale fighting begins in Book 9 so that the reader may once again be reminded of how much depends on the success of Aeneas' mission.

The scenes from Roman history which are depicted on the shield are chosen partly because they lend themselves to pictorial description, and partly as examples of the qualities which the Romans most admired in the heroes of their race, qualities which they hoped they could show again in the future in the revival and expansion of their greatness under Augustus. The first picture shows the twins Romulus and Remus being suckled by the she-wolf: this was the most famous Roman emblem of all, frequently depicted in visual art, especially on coins, and it symbolises the simple origins and powers of survival of the Roman people. There follows a picture of the rape of the Sabine women and the subsequent reconciliation between the Romans and the Sabines, as a result of which the Sabine king, Numa Pompilius, eventually succeeded Romulus – here again is the note of religion and civilisation which Numa symbolised in the pageant. Next is Mettus, suffering a horrible punishment for breaking his promise – the Romans always thought of themselves as people who kept their word, and regarded their enemies, such as the Carthaginians, as perfidious. Next is depicted the attempt by Lars Porsena of Clusium to restore the exiled Tarquin, who had been the last king in Rome; included is a description of Horatius Cocles holding the bridge, and the maiden Cloelia swimming the Tiber.

At the top of the shield there is a picture of how the sacred geese gave the alarm as the Gauls attacked the Capitol; religious ceremonies are depicted in the same scene, and the powerful impression given that the gods had saved Rome from extinction because the Romans were a religious people, chosen for world empire because of their right relationship with the gods. At about the same time as Virgil was composing the *Aeneid* Horace wrote an Ode (*Odes* 3.6) in which he urged the Romans to return to their traditional worship, summarising (line 5) the Roman destiny in the words *dis te minorem quod geris imperas*: 'because you are servants of the gods, you are masters on earth.'

All the pictures described so far have been round the edge of the shield: in the centre are pictures of the battle of Actium, the last battle of Rome's civil war at which in 31 BC Augustus defeated the forces of

Antony and Cleopatra. We see Augustus going into battle, leading the Italians, along with the senate and the people and the gods of Rome (678–9); opposing him with barbarian forces from the East are Antony and Cleopatra, the latter with snakes behind her head (symbolising her suicide through an asp's bite after the battle). The gods of Rome (Neptune, Venus, Minerva, Apollo) are drawn up in battle against the eerie and gruesome deities of the Egyptians, such as the dog-headed Anubis. Next Cleopatra is shown in flight, seeking safety between the banks of the Nile; and finally we see Augustus celebrating his triumph in Rome, with appropriate sacrifices to the gods who have given Rome the victory, and reviewing the conquered peoples who come from the farthest confines of the known earth.

Here is the passage in Virgil:

> at Caesar, triplici invectus Romana triumpho
> moenia, dis Italis votum immortale sacrabat,
> maxima ter centum totam delubra per urbem.
> laetitia ludisque viae plausuque fremebant;
> omnibus in templis matrum chorus, omnibus arae;
> ante aras terram caesi stravere iuvenci.
> ipse sedens niveo candentis limine Phoebi
> dona recognoscit populorum aptatque superbis
> postibus; incedunt victae longo ordine gentes,
> quam variae linguis, habitu tam vestis et armis.

(8.714–23)

and this is Dryden's translation:

> The victor to the gods his thanks expressed,
> And Rome, triumphant, with his presence blessed.
> Three hundred temples in the town he placed,
> With spoils and altars every temple graced.
> Three shining nights and three succeeding days
> The fields resound with shouts, the streets with praise,
> The domes with songs, the theatres with plays.
> All altars flame: before each altar lies,
> Drenched in his gore, the destined sacrifice.
> Great Caesar sits sublime upon his throne,
> Before Apollo's porch of Parian stone:
> Accepts the presents vowed for victory,
> And hangs the monumental crowns on high.
> Vast crowds of vanquished nations march along,
> Various in arms, in habit, and in tongue.

These are the pictures on the shield: Aeneas marvels at them (729–31) not knowing what they are, and 'raises on to his shoulder the fame and destiny of his descendants.' In picking up the shield he literally shoulders Rome's history; throughout the poem he metaphorically shoulders the task of inaugurating that history.

(iv) The reconciliation of Jupiter and Juno (*Aen.* 12.791–842)

In order to fulfil the destiny laid upon them the Trojans are forced to fight the opposing forces under Turnus, and the battle scenes of the last four books are fierce and costly to both sides. Venus intervenes again (10.18 ff.) to appeal for her Trojans, and Juno opposes her pleas; the battles continue until finally single combat between Aeneas and Turnus is arranged. Aeneas swears an oath to abide by the result of the single combat (12.176 ff.) in which he promises in the event of victory not to make the Italians subservient to the Trojans, but to join the two peoples under equal conditions. But the Rutulians break the truce, and Juno continues to intervene to help Turnus (as Venus does to help Aeneas) until Jupiter tells Juno that she must now give in. He says that she knows Aeneas is destined for glory, and that her opposition must cease.

Juno yields, asking for one condition. This is that (823 ff.) the Latins shall not have to alter their name and be called Trojans, or change their language or their way of dress. She asks that the Roman stock shall be strong through Italian valour, and that Troy shall vanish. Jupiter accepts her condition.

> do quod vis, et me victusque volensque remitto.
> sermonem Ausonii patrium moresque tenebunt,
> utque est nomen erit; commixti corpore tantum
> subsident Teucri. morem ritusque sacrorum
> adiciam faciamque omnis uno ore Latinos.
> hinc genus Ausonio mixtum quod sanguine surget,
> supra homines, supra ire deos pietate videbis,
> nec gens ulla tuos aeque celebrabit honores.
>
> (12.833–40)

Here is Day Lewis's translation (Hogarth Press and Oxford Paperbacks, 1952):

> Willingly I grant what you ask: you have won me over.
> The Italians shall keep their native tongue and their old traditions;
> Their name shall not be altered. The Trojans will but sink down in
> The mass and be made one with them. I'll add the rites and usage
> Of Trojan worship to theirs. All will be Latins, speaking
> One tongue. From this blend of Italian and Trojan blood shall
> arise

A people surpassing all men, nay even the gods, in godliness.
No other nation on earth will pay such reverence to Juno.

Temple of Jupiter, Juno and Minerva on the Capitol (Coin of Vespasian)

We notice in these final decrees of Jupiter not merely the acceptance of Italian rather than Trojan supremacy in the mixture of their races which will produce the Roman people, but also the great insistence on the religious qualities of this people that will rule the world. The Roman mission is first to conquer the proud (because the gods wish it so, for the benefit of the human race), and then to establish for all peoples a civilised way of life based on religious worship of the powers greater than themselves.

After this reconciliation in heaven the poem ends quickly on the human plane, as Aeneas wounds and then kills Turnus. The proud have been conquered, Turnus by Aeneas in Virgil's poem, and Antony by Augustus in the real history of Virgil's time – a thousand years later. The road is open for what Pliny called 'the boundless majesty of the Roman peace' (*immensa Romanae pacis maiestas*).

3
Aeneas – the new hero

IN order to present the destiny of Rome as outlined in the previous chapter, Virgil had to create in his hero a prototype of the Roman character, a person who showed by his behaviour the kind of qualities which had made Rome great and would make her greater still. He had to be an ideal Roman with qualities of leadership, a sort of model for Augustus and his successors. (It is a great mistake to think that Aeneas was modelled on Augustus; it is rather the case that Virgil is trying to depict a character upon whom Romans of his day could model themselves.)

In drawing the character of his hero Virgil had chosen a legend which gave him a fairly free hand. Aeneas in Homer is an important Trojan prince, but one whose character is fairly vague: he is brave and religious, but he has no special traits which would have to be reproduced by Virgil (as for example Odysseus or Achilles had). The details of the Aeneas legend in Greek and Latin literature had been very varied, and Virgil could adapt and recast it for his own purposes. To a large extent he could create the character of his hero exactly as he wanted it.

But how did he want it? The very word hero was associated with the heroic age, the days of Mycenae and Troy of which Homer had written, and the qualities of a hero of those times were entirely different from those needed in Virgil's day, when the complex organisation of Rome called for abilities and characteristics of another sort altogether. This was Virgil's problem – to present a character appropriate to be called a hero in a time which (like our own) was no longer 'heroic'. In one sense of course Aeneas does live in the heroic world – he is a contemporary of Achilles and Odysseus, and his dramatic date is twelfth century BC. But in another sense he is the first Roman – he has to foreshadow the qualities of a different civilisation altogether. He has to step out of one world (the world of Troy, finally destroyed by Greek fire) into another, into a western land which will ultimately rule the world. What will be the qualities appropriate for this new civilisation? Obviously not the same as those of the old – but how far different and in what ways?

The character and the ideals of Homer's heroes are fairly easy to define.

Aeneas offering sacrifices (Ara Pacis)

Achilles lived in a world of a simple sort, and knew precisely what was expected of him. He does not have deep intellectual or emotional problems; his is a direct straightforward way of life, in which the honour of the individual is the main and basic standard of behaviour. He has to be true to himself and his reputation, and so act that he preserves his honour and does not fall below what is required of him. He must be brave, and never drop short of the expected standard of bravery which his position as the greatest Greek warrior calls for. His behaviour is always direct, impetuous, spontaneous, not concerned with others except in so far as his behaviour towards them modifies his own individual glory and prowess. Such a figure in Roman society would be hopelessly out of place, and Aeneas had to be drawn differently.

Again, let us make a comparison with Homer's Odysseus. Odysseus, man of many resources, had the task of surmounting endless difficulties in order to return home to his native land of Ithaca where his wife Penelope was loyally awaiting him, in order to resume the old life he had left. Aeneas on the other hand had no home to return to – his home in Troy had been destroyed and he had to find a new home and indeed a new way of life in a far distant country. Odysseus by his superior skill and endurance finally reached home when all his companions, lesser men, had fallen by the wayside; but Aeneas had to reach his new promised land with all his companions safe – otherwise the new settlement could never be founded. In brief the Homeric heroes are great individualists, but

29

Ara Pacis (South-east corner)

Aeneas has to be the social man, the man who through his care for others succeeds in leading his group or his society, not aiming to achieve personal satisfaction by surpassing others in excellence, but to use his qualities in order to achieve *their* success.

This basic feeling of social responsibility in Aeneas is especially defined by Virgil in the standing epithet he gives to his hero – *pius*. The Latin word is difficult to define briefly in English – essentially it means 'aware of one's responsibility', 'dutiful', 'devoted to others'. It means that such a person puts other considerations before his own interests. This quality of being *pius* (*pietas* is the noun) may be shown by subordinating one's own desire to various other loyalties: (i) to the gods and their requirements, hence our English derivative 'piety'; (ii) to one's country – here the idea of patriotism comes in; (iii) to one's family, a form of devotion to others which the Romans specially esteemed; (iv) to one's friends; and (v) to one's subordinates. Often these different categories may overlap, and it is not always essential to define which one of them is specially relevant at any one time as long as we recognise that this is the essence of the man – he tries to shoulder his responsibilities, to face his obligations. He must not yield to personal ambition or the desire for self-aggrandisement; he must be first and foremost a valuable member of society, commanding respect because it is known that he is not self-seeking.

Now such a person in literature does not always satisfy the desires we may have for the grandiose, the sublime, the superhuman. Aeneas does not cut the figure of an Achilles – he does not stride magnificently through life brushing off all opposition in superior self-confidence of his own ability; and for this failing he has often been censured by the critics. But it is not that Virgil has tried to create another Achilles and failed to do so; it is that he has tried to create an entirely different kind of hero. We may all decide personally whether he has been successful in his new creation – and may well decide that he has not; but we must not judge Aeneas adversely because we think he ought to be like Achilles.

It is time now to look at the way in which Virgil has presented Aeneas in his poem, asking ourselves not 'Has Virgil succeeded in making Aeneas like Achilles?' but 'Has Virgil succeeded in making Aeneas unlike Achilles?' There are three particular aspects of Aeneas' character which can focus our thoughts as we follow him through the poem: (i) has he a free will of his own, or is he too often a puppet? In other words, what is the relationship of a man of destiny to the powers to which he has devoted himself; is there freedom in service to an ideal? (ii) What are the limits of his human strength – is he weak when he should be strong? (iii) Does he always live up to the ideals (which Dryden admired in him) of 'piety to the gods, care of his people, justice in general towards mankind'? We shall find that Virgil has provided a series of situations in which all these problems can be sympathetically examined, in which there is no exaggerated simplification, no suggestion that because Aeneas is strong and good he can easily do what is to be done, but rather an investigation of what is meant by 'strong' and 'good' and how one particular person tried to solve the ever-recurrent problems which fortune sends upon the best of us as well as the worst of us. Above all it is the human experience and problems of Aeneas as a human person (not a super-human person) which are emphasised in the *Aeneid*.

Book 1

Before the narrative begins Virgil tells us in his introduction and invocation the nature of Aeneas' mission, and of his divine calling. In the second line of the poem we learn that Aeneas came to Italy from Troy because he was 'an exile by fate' (*fato profugus*). Fate is all the time behind the human action. This is a main way in which Virgil's poem differs from Homer: in Homer fate indeed governs men's actions, but it is a short-term fate, something which determines the problems of the moment, or at the most of a man's lifetime – but in Virgil fate has its plan for hundreds and thousands of years ahead. In a paradoxical way it requires the co-operation of man for its fulfilment, and this co-operation Aeneas for his part is resolved to give to the utmost of his human ability.

Next we learn of the hostility to Aeneas of Juno. This is explained on several levels – on the mythological level it is because Juno was angry with the Trojans on account of the judgement of Paris, when she was passed over in favour of Aphrodite in a contest of beauty; on the historical level it is because she favours the city of Carthage, the great rival of Rome for Mediterranean supremacy; on the symbolic level she personifies the 'slings and arrows of outrageous fortune', the apparently senseless mishaps and disasters which come upon men as they strive for worthy ends. Throughout the poem, as we shall see, she opposes Aeneas although she knows she is inferior in power to Jupiter who supports him; and though she cannot ultimately change the fates, she can and does cause such suffering and setbacks as to make it constantly uncertain when and how the fated destiny can come true.

Virgil asks (lines 8–11) what is the cause of this suffering inflicted on the good: 'tantaene animis caelestibus irae?' ('can there be such great anger in heavenly hearts?'). To define the 'good' he uses the noun especially used of Aeneas – *pietas*: if a man shows this quality of self-sacrifice, why must he suffer? The question runs through the poem, and it is not satisfactorily answered; but it is in the exploration of this question and its implications that much of the deepest insight and human sympathy of the *Aeneid* is shown.

The narrative of Book 1 begins when the Trojans, after seven years of wandering, are just leaving Sicily for Italy, on the very last stage of their journey. Juno intervenes and causes a storm, and our first meeting with the hero of the poem is in the midst of this storm. We might expect him to show courage and resolution in the face of this dangerous situation – but in fact he acts otherwise: he is terrified.

> extemplo Aeneae solvuntur frigore membra;
> ingemit et duplicis tendens ad sidera palmas
> talia voce refert: 'o terque quaterque beati,
> quis ante ora patrum Troiae sub moenibus altis
> contigit oppetere! o Danaum fortissime gentis
> Tydide! mene Iliacis occumbere campis
> non potuisse tuaque animam hanc effundere dextra.

$$(1.92–8)$$

Straightaway Aeneas' limbs were loosened by cold fear; he groaned and holding out his two hands to the stars thus he spoke: 'O three times and four times fortunate those whose lot it was to fall in death before their parents' eyes beneath the lofty walls of Troy! O son of Tydeus, bravest of the race of the Greeks – could I not have fallen on the plains of Ilium and breathed forth my life, killed by your hand. . . .'

Virgil has most deliberately shown us Aeneas on his first appearance as a frail mortal, put under pressures which are almost too great for him to bear, and under this latest disaster of his seven year wanderings almost ready to give up, and wishing that he were dead. We realise at the outset that the hero of the poem is not someone of superhuman strength who can retain his confidence in all adversity, but rather a brave man near the end of his tether. We wonder here, as we often shall again, whether Aeneas will manage to keep going.

Finally the storm is calmed by Neptune, and in the first simile of the poem Neptune in calming the storm is compared with a statesman calming a violent mob, rioting and hurling stones and torches. Two things are very striking about this simile: first that it is presented as it were the wrong way round, with the world of nature compared with the human world instead of vice versa. Thus it compels our attention for its other aspect: this is that it uses the key words of the poem – *furor* for the violent quality of the mob, and *pietas* for the responsible attitude of the statesman. The task of Aeneas throughout the poem is to try to calm the force of *furor* ('violence', 'madness', 'frenzy') in others and in himself by means of *pietas* ('thought for others'). He does not find it as easy to calm the storms of the human heart as Neptune found it to calm the waves.

Aeneas with some of his ships lands safely in Africa (the remainder, except one, is also safe in another part) and he goes out to forage and organise food and shelter for his men. As the Trojans prepare to restore their strength by feeding on the stags Aeneas has shot, their leader makes a heartening speech:

> o socii (neque enim ignari sumus ante malorum),
> o passi graviora, dabit deus his quoque finem.
> vos et Scyllaeam rabiem penitusque sonantis
> accestis scopulos, vos et Cyclopia saxa
> experti: revocate animos maestumque timorem
> mittite; forsan et haec olim meminisse iuvabit.

(1.198–203)

Friends, we have experienced suffering before, we had suffered worse than this, and the gods will bring this too to an end. You have endured the fury of Scylla and approached those deep-roaring cliffs, you have known the rocks of the Cyclops: rally your courage and

C

33

banish sad fear; perhaps one day the memory of this too will be a cause of joy. . . .

A heartening speech – but Virgil immediately tells us that Aeneas' confidence was pretended – he was putting a bold face on it: 'Thus he spoke, and sick at heart with great anxiety he pretended hope in his expression and hid his anguish deep in his heart' (1.208–9).

Thus in the opening scene Virgil has especially shown us that Aeneas is a mortal man of limited strength, and has come near to the end of it. Now the narrative switches to heaven, where Venus complains to Jupiter of the sufferings her son is undergoing, ending with the phrase *hic pietatis honos*? – 'Is this the reward for duty well done?' The reader echoes the feeling of indignation against whatever powers there be. Jupiter's reply tells in serene and majestic phrases of the glory that awaits Aeneas. This passage has already been discussed (pp. 18f.) and all that need be added here is to emphasise the closing image of the speech, the picture of *Furor impius* in chains, conquered by peace and justice. Here then is the hope that Aeneas by founding the city destined to become Rome will begin a process of taming the wickedness and frenzy in human hearts by means of *pietas*, devotion to others.

Aeneas sets out to explore the land where he and his men have been shipwrecked, and he meets his mother, the goddess Venus, disguised as a huntress. She tells him that he has come to Carthage, where Dido is queen, and asks who he and his men are. In reply he says that they are Trojans and that he is Aeneas, man of destiny ('sum pius Aeneas'). This key word *pius* has already been used of him twice in the narrative (220, 305), and now his own use of it emphasises his knowledge that he is a man with a calling, a man whose actions must be determined not primarily by his own wishes and desires but by the requirements of the mission to which he has dedicated himself. In addition to this his use of the word here has about it an implied indignation, just like Venus' question to Jupiter ('is this the reward for duty well done?'). I am trying, says Aeneas, to fulfil a mission which has been placed upon me, and yet nothing will go right for me. Here I am, shipwrecked on the coast of Africa, after having been driven out of Asia and Europe. We see here a man who has willingly given himself to the fulfilment of a mission, but has by no means yet acquired the strength and the certainty which will enable him to press on against all setbacks and over all obstacles. He is frail and human; his resolution has its limits, and he has nearly reached them. The task he has undertaken, that of setting going the Roman way of life in a hostile and alien world, is almost too great for his strength. But he does not give up – this is the essence of the new kind of heroism.

As Venus leaves him he recognises his goddess mother and rebukes her

– not without reason – for her cruelty to him. 'Why do you so often mock your son with false disguises? You too are cruel' (407–8). He is a solitary and lonely figure, beset by cruel difficulties of all sorts, with his father dead, his son still young, no strong companions to help him. His seconds-in-command are shadowy figures, none more so than his faithful companion Achates, who plays an altogether passive and colourless role in the poem. What a contrast with the Greek heroes in Homer's *Iliad*, strong men supporting each other even without their strongest of all, Achilles: Agamemnon, Menelaus, Odysseus, Diomedes, Ajax, Idomeneus, and countless more. Aeneas has no such powerful support in his mission.

As Aeneas goes with Achates to the city of Carthage he marvels at the activity and achievement of Dido's people, and he gazes on a city rising up out of nothing – his own city, he reflects, is not yet founded: 'O fortunati quorum iam moenia surgunt' (437) – 'Lucky those people whose city walls are already rising.' He looks at the pictures on Juno's temple wall, scenes depicting the war against the Greeks in which he had just fought and lost, and he speaks what are perhaps the most famous phrases of the poem: 'sunt hic etiam sua praemia laudi, sunt lacrimae rerum et mentem mortalia tangunt' (461–2) – 'here too glorious deeds have their reward, here too there are tears for the things that happen, and mortal suffering touches the heart.' Aeneas gains confidence from the knowledge that the Carthaginians too are people who are sympathetic towards suffering and appreciative of bravery, and this confidence is wholly justified in the reception which the Trojans get from Dido, Queen of Carthage. She welcomes them with a serene grace and dignity which is immensely impressive, and Aeneas responds with words of deep gratitude. Gifts are exchanged, a royal banquet prepared – but beneath the idyllic appearance lurk the seeds of tragedy and doom. Through the intervention of Cupid and Venus Dido is made to fall in love with Aeneas, and Virgil insets into his narrative phrases which look forward to the inevitably unhappy outcome – for Aeneas is not free to stay with Dido; he must sacrifice himself and her for the demands of his mission.

Books 2 and 3

At the end of Book 1 Dido asks Aeneas to tell his story, and he does so in the next two books. They are therefore a flashback, earlier in time than the narrative of Book 1, and so they give us our earliest glimpse of the character of Aeneas, and are specially significant because his character emerges from his own words – it is his own version of himself which we read. The second Book tells dramatically and tragically the events of just one night, the night of Troy's downfall; the third Book tells the long and weary story of seven years' wandering and searching for the place of the destined city.

The first part of Book 2 describes how the Trojans were persuaded by Sinon to take the wooden horse filled with Greek warriors into the city. Aeneas himself does not enter the story till after this, when he tells of how, on that night, the ghost of Hector appeared to him in his sleep and told him that Troy was doomed, could no longer be saved – 'if it could have been, it would have been saved by my right hand' (291–2) – and that Aeneas must escape, taking with him the gods of Troy, and found a new city far off over the sea. This is the first indication which Aeneas has had that he is a man with a mission; and his reaction is by no means one of immediate acceptance. Finding the Greeks within the walls he rushes madly out to sell his life dearly:

> arma amens capio; nec sat rationis in armis,
> sed glomerare manum bello et concurrere in arcem
> cum sociis ardent animi; furor iraque mentem
> praecipitat, pulchrumque mori succurrit in armis.
>
> (2.314–17)

> Madly I seized my weapons; nor did I think about it once I had done so but my heart was aflame to gather a force for fighting and rush to the citadel with my companions; frenzy and anger drove on my thoughts, and I decided that death in battle would be a glorious end.

Here we see the Homeric warrior of the heroic age, impetuous, courageous, ready to sell his life dearly, ready with the splendid gesture, the heroic impulse; Aeneas has not yet begun to learn that his mission must preclude the glorious death. His life is not his own to give away; it is owed to those who depend on him. Not for him the grand gesture – he must learn the long hard way of ever struggling on towards his dimly seen goal. He must step out of Homer's world and become the first Roman.

But he is slow to realise this; Hector's message is ignored as he fights madly to try to save those of his friends he can, and to rally them to the defence of the doomed city. 'Let us die,' he cries (353), 'hurling ourselves into the midst of the fighting.' He and his followers are compared with wolves in their frenzy for slaughter (355 ff.); he continues to fight wildly, to try to sell his life dearly; he calls on the ashes of Troy to testify that he did not try to avoid the heat of the battle, and that he had sought death (431 ff.). He feels the heroic warrior's guilt at having escaped when so many brave men died; he cannot yet accept that he must willingly shoulder a different task.

Next he is forced to witness the horrible sight of the death of Priam's son, Polites, and then of the old king himself at the hands of the violent Pyrrhus. Only now for the first time does he think of any of his obligations other than that as a warrior of Troy; now he recalls his own old father, Anchises, perhaps exposed to the same fate as Priam, and his wife Creusa and his little son, Iulus. On his way to his home he meets Helen, the cause of the war, sheltering from the fighting at the temple of Vesta; anger and rage overcome him (575) and he is on the point of killing her when Venus intervenes and stops him. This passage is not in the major manuscripts of Virgil, and though he certainly wrote it there is reason to believe that he may have intended to change it; but what is important is that Virgil's concept of the character of Aeneas while he was still in Troy is such that he could have thought of killing a woman. He is still impetuous, violent, a victim of that angry passion (*furor*) which throughout the poem he attempts – with very incomplete success – to conquer.

The goddess Pietas (obverse) and Aeneas carrying Anchises (reverse) (Coin of Herennius)

Venus urges him to think of his family's safety and to concentrate his thoughts on escape, not vengeance; she shows him the supernatural vision of hostile deities destroying Troy, and convinces him (as Hector had not been able to) that armed resistance is useless. Aeneas cannot at first persuade Anchises to leave, but a supernatural omen convinces him that the gods wish it; and carrying his father on his shoulders, leading his little son by the hand, and with Creusa his wife following behind he sets out to escape. In the confusion Creusa is lost; Aeneas rushes back to find her, but is confronted by her ghost, telling him that she is not destined to

Octavian (obverse) and Aeneas carrying Anchises (reverse) (Coin of Octavian)

come with him. He must travel far over the seas (780 ff.) and find a western land where the river Tiber flows though the fertile fields. All this, she insists, is destined by fate (777–8).

Aeneas now gathers his followers together, and as the dawn rises leads them off into the hills to prepare for their escape over the seas. The long night of Troy's agony is over, and the new dawn portends the new city that will arise from Troy's ashes, the golden city of Rome.

Map of Aeneas' journey

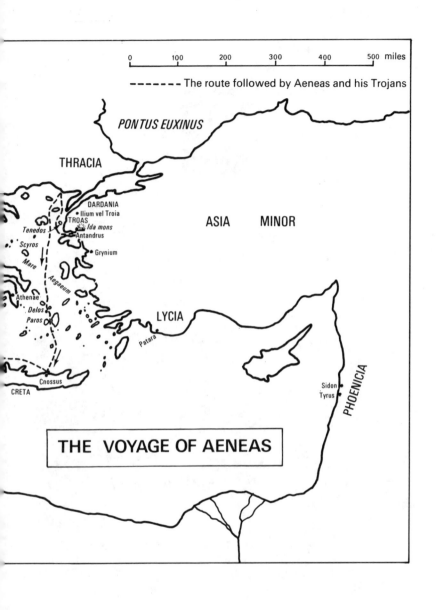

THE VOYAGE OF AENEAS

In the second book then we have seen how Aeneas to begin with was no different from any Homeric hero. He was brave, reckless, inclined to

Aeneas, Anchises and the Palladium (Coin of Caesar)

the heroic gesture. He has to learn a new way of life, and in the long years of the voyage, described in the third book, we see him beginning to learn.

Temple of Vesta in the Roman Forum—traditional home of the sacred objects brought by Aeneas from Troy

As Aeneas had had to endure the sorrow of the loss of his wife and many of his friends in Book 2, so now he must endure the dangers and tedium of the search for his city. It is a story of many false trails, and of oracular assistance given chiefly by Apollo which gradually brings the

Trojans nearer and nearer to their western land. First they land in Thrace where a terrifying omen drives them away; they come to the island of Delos where Apollo tells them to seek out their ancient mother. Mistakenly they think this is Crete, but are turned from that island by a plague. Then the Penates appear to Aeneas telling him that Italy is the aim of their quest. They pass the island of the Harpies and the site of Actium and at Buthrotum receive a long prophecy from Helenus. They land in Italy, but on the wrong side; from here they go to Sicily and round the island, and from there – Aeneas tells Dido – the storm drove him off his course to Italy and on to the coast of Carthage.

Throughout this third book Aeneas learns more about the intentions of the gods for the exiled Trojans, and of how success depends on endurance and especially on a right relation with the gods. Prayers and sacrifices form a recurrent theme in the book, and in this as in all else Aeneas is very greatly helped and encouraged by the guidance of his father Anchises. Anchises gives to Aeneas the encouragement and advice which Aeneas learns it is his duty to give to his son Iulus and to all those dependent on him. At the very end of the voyage, at Drepanum in Sicily, Anchises dies and Aeneas is left to complete his mission on his own.

Book 4

This is the book in which Aeneas comes nearest to abandoning his mission; here, as our attention is concentrated on the pathos of Dido's love for Aeneas, we are furthest of all from thoughts of Rome and Roman destiny. Dido has fallen in love with Aeneas, and he, forgetful for a time of his mission, as he well might be after all he has been through, stays with her during the winter months, not thinking any more of his destiny and the divine task he has undertaken. Dido for her part has no thoughts other than her love for Aeneas and her desire to keep him with her; she is persuaded by her sister Anna to break the vow she had made to the ashes of her dead husband Sychaeus, and she no longer cares for the well-being of Carthage; her city's activities grind to a halt (4.86–9). The goddesses Venus and Juno conspire together to arrange a 'marriage' between Dido and Aeneas as they shelter together in a cave; the supernatural powers of nature convince Dido that it is a real marriage; as the lightning flash seems to her to be the wedding torch, the Nymphs sing a bridal song, and Juno herself witnesses the 'marriage'. Following this rumour spreads abroad stories of their 'wedding', and causes Iarbas, one of Dido's suitors, to pray to Jupiter that this Trojan interloper be not permitted to win Dido's favour.

This causes Jupiter to intervene; he instructs his messenger Mercury to go to Aeneas and tell him that he is failing in his divine duty, in his mission to found a city which will bring the whole world under the sway of its laws. Mercury delivers the message and for the first time in the book our attention is concentrated not on Dido but Aeneas. Aeneas is aghast at this message from heaven – as well he might be, for it brings him to a realisation of his forgetfulness. His human weakness is here apparent: he had yielded to the temptation to stay when he should not have done so, and his failure here not only jeopardises his position as a willing servant of providence, but also leads directly to the death of Dido, who had been led to believe that Aeneas would stay.

Aeneas in this conflict between love and duty decides immediately for duty – 'he longs to get away and to leave the land he loves' (281); but where Virgil puts the emphasis is not on the triumph of the right, the victory of Rome over a dangerous obstacle, but on the suffering and death of Dido. She appeals to Aeneas to stay; he replies that he must against his will follow his divine mission. His speech is cold, deliberately so because he is afraid of being shaken in his resolve: 'because of the orders of Jupiter he kept his eyes unmoving and with a great struggle concealed the love in his heart' (331–2). He argues that he had not entered a marriage compact (which is true), and that he is forced by heaven's decrees to go to Italy; he tells her that Mercury has just appeared to tell him so. His arguments have no effect on Dido; realising that he intends to go she curses him and prays for vengeance. She collapses and is escorted away, and Aeneas is left alone. Virgil summarises his plight in four moving lines:

> at pius Aeneas, quamquam lenire dolentem
> solando cupit et dictis avertere curas,
> multa gemens magnoque animum labefactus amore
> iussa tamen divum exsequitur classemque revisit.
>
> (4.393–6)

But Aeneas listened to the call of duty, and although he longed to lighten her sorrow with consolation and to turn away her anguish with his words, groaning deeply and shaken to the heart by his deep love, nevertheless followed out the orders of the gods and went back to his fleet.

Nothing could more clearly reveal the conflict in the unhappy Aeneas: his devotion to his mission has prevailed over his personal wishes, his intellectual and moral decision has prevailed over his emotional agonies. The sacrifice is very great; Rome could only grow by the great sacrifices of her servants. Not every reader of *Aeneid* 4 perceives this, because Dido, whose sufferings end in tragedy, commands far more attention than Aeneas, who overcomes his sufferings; the extent and significance of our sympathy for Dido will be discussed in the next chapter, but what we must notice here is that Aeneas sacrifices his personal life for what divine voices tell him he must do for the good of his people and of the world.

Once the decision has been taken and he is no longer with Dido, Aeneas is able to resist all further pleas; 'the fates stand in the way, and the god blocks his mortal ears which would have listened' (440). In a memorable simile Virgil compares Aeneas with an oak tree, buffeted by the winds but holding firm in spite of all: 'his resolution remains unchanged, the tears fall in vain' (449).

The same night Mercury appears again to Aeneas and tells him to leave immediately, before Dido takes some action to stop him. The Trojan fleet sails, and Dido, calling curses upon Aeneas and all the Romans, kills herself.

Book 5

The Trojans are driven by a storm to the western shores of Sicily, where they land and pay religious ceremonies at the tomb of Anchises, the anniversary of whose death it is. They celebrate funeral games in his honour, and the majority of the book is taken up with a description of these. The emotional tension is greatly diminished, but tragedy strikes again when the Trojan women are persuaded by Juno to set fire to the ships to prevent further voyaging over unknown seas. This new blow reduces Aeneas to a state bordering on despair, and he prays to Jupiter either to quench the flames or to send his thunderbolt upon them to end everything. Aeneas is given his epithet *pius*, and he appeals to Jupiter's own *pietas* towards men.

> tum pius Aeneas umeris abscindere vestem
> auxilioque vocare deos et tendere palmas:
> 'Iuppiter omnipotens, si nondum exosus ad unum
> Troianos, si quid pietas antiqua labores
> respicit humanos, da flammam evadere classi
> nunc, pater, et tenuis Teucrum res eripe leto.
> vel tu, quod superest, infesto fulmine morti,
> si mereor, demitte tuaque hic obrue dextra.
>
> (5.685–92)

Then Aeneas, man of god, tore his robe from his shoulders and called on the gods for help, holding out his upturned hands: 'Almighty Jupiter, if you do not yet hate the Trojans to a man, if your loving-kindness of old looks on mortal sufferings, grant the fleet to escape the fire, now, father Jupiter, and save the frail fortunes of the Trojans from destruction. Otherwise, the one thing left, cast me down to death with your deadly thunderbolt and overwhelm me with your right hand'.

Aeneas' prayer is answered, and the fire quenched, and all the ships saved except four. But the disaster has made him despondent and uncertain, and he reaches here his lowest ebb, actually wondering whether to 'forget the fates'.

> at pater Aeneas casu concussus acerbo
> nunc huc ingentis, nunc illuc pectore curas
> mutabat versans, Siculisne resideret arvis
> oblitus fatorum, Italasne capesseret oras.

$$(5.700-3)$$

> But father Aeneas, deeply shaken at this bitter blow, pondered over his deep anxieties turning his thoughts in his heart one way and another: should he settle in the Sicilian fields, forgetting the fates, or keep on for the shores of Italy?

He listens to a consoling speech, full of Stoic phrases about endurance, from the old priest Nautes, but he is far from heartened; he continues to be racked by his worries and uncertainty. It is not until Jupiter sends him a vision of the ghost of his father Anchises confirming the suggestions of Nautes (to leave behind the weak and press onwards himself with the strong) that he is able to recover something of his strength and confidence. Anchises tells him to continue onwards to Italy and there to enter the underworld (by way of Lake Avernus near Cumae) and to meet with him in Elysium: there he promises that he will reveal to Aeneas the future destiny of his race. The ghost disappears and Aeneas first humbly performs worship to the gods; then he arranges to leave behind some of his people in Sicily, and himself departs with the rest for Italy. The significance of this episode is tremendous – here is a man sorely tried, buffeted by adverse fortune, scarcely able to continue, yet receiving, at the hour of imminent defeat, supernatural aid and strength. This is the point at which the mission is most nearly abandoned, and had Aeneas not been a man who could hear the divine voice and respond to it, the mission would indeed have been abandoned. Rome was founded by the heroic endeavours of its men with the assistance of divine aid given to those willing and worthy to receive it; and it was in this way that it could achieve and maintain its greatness.

Book 6

This is the crucial book in the development of Aeneas' character and resolution. Everything that has gone before is summarised in it, and from it all the events of the rest of the poem take their starting point. At the beginning of his experiences in the underworld, and during the first two-thirds of the book Aeneas is still backward-looking, regretful, uncertain; but after his meeting with Anchises and the revelation of the future destiny of Rome he is strengthened and resolved to be successful in his mission.

Aeneas and the Sibyl (Vatican MS of Virgil: fourth century)

The first section of the book (1–263) describes the preliminaries to the descent. An atmosphere of supernatural awe is built up by the description of the Sibyl's prophetic frenzy, the search for the golden bough, the death of Misenus and the funeral ceremonies for him, the sacrifices preliminary

45

to the descent. The formidable task awaiting Aeneas is grimly outlined by the Sibyl:

o tandem magnis pelagi defuncte periclis
(sed terrae graviora manent), in regna Lavini
Dardanidae venient (mitte hanc de pectore curam),
sed non et venisse volent. bella, horrida bella,
et Thybrim multo spumantem sanguine cerno.

(6.83–7)

O you who have at last finished with the great perils of the sea (but worse await you on land), the Trojans shall come to their kingdom of Lavinium (so cast that anxiety from your heart), but they will wish that they had not come. I see wars, grim wars, and the Tiber foaming with torrents of blood.

She goes on to outline the opposition which Aeneas will meet, at the hands of mortal enemies and also through the continued opposition of Juno, and finally exhorts him: 'Do not yield to these troubles, but go the more boldly forward against them by whatever way your fortune permits it' (6.95–6). The reader wonders whether Aeneas will be able to muster the strength to do so.

Aeneas' reply, however, indicates his Stoic endurance, as he tells the Sibyl: 'No form of toil that presents itself to me is anything new or unexpected; I have thought it all over before, and gone through it all in my thoughts already.' He asks to be permitted to visit his father in the underworld; the Sibyl replies that to descend and return is granted to very few, but that if he finds and picks the golden bough he will be permitted to enter the realms of Pluto. Aided by his goddess mother Venus, Aeneas does so, and after the funeral celebrations for his friend Misenus he fulfils the appropriate sacrifices to the shades, and enters the underworld through the cave at Lake Avernus over which no birds fly.

The middle section of the book is presented in the form of a journey through the various parts of Pluto's realm as the Sibyl and Aeneas make their way towards Elysium where Anchises waits. Virgil uses the traditional geography of the underworld (the rivers with the ferryman, the dog Cerberus guarding the approach) as a setting for Aeneas' meeting with three of the ghosts of his past – Palinurus, Dido, Deiphobus. Aeneas had been closely involved with the death of each, and to each he speaks in tones of regret and personal remorse, still looking sorrowfully back upon the past rather than hopefully forward toward the future.

The first ghost Aeneas meets is that of his faithful helmsman Palinurus, swept overboard on the last stages of the journey from Sicily to Italy, and therefore unburied and forbidden to cross the Styx in Charon's boat.

Aeneas had been overcome with sorrow at the sight of all the unburied dead, thick as leaves falling in winter or birds migrating to warmer lands, and when he recognises Palinurus among them he blames Apollo for having broken his promise that Palinurus would safely reach Italy. Palinurus assures him that Apollo did not deceive him, for he swam to Italy but was killed on landing – he beseeches Aeneas for help, but Aeneas is powerless to give it.

The note of sorrow is even more dominant when Aeneas reaches the Fields of Mourning, the abode of those who died of unhappy love. Here he meets the ghost of Dido whose suicide when Aeneas left her is still fresh in the memory. We must pause on this passage, for it strongly emphasises what suffering Aeneas' mission had caused to both himself and Dido, and how he still cannot free himself from feelings of guilt and remorse about the past.

When Aeneas recognised Dido's ghost he wept and spoke to her in the sweet tones of love:

> infelix Dido, verus mihi nuntius ergo
> venerat exstinctam ferroque extrema secutam?
> funeris heu tibi causa fui? per sidera iuro,
> per superos et si qua fides tellure sub ima est,
> invitus, regina, tuo de litore cessi.
> sed me iussa deum, quae nunc has ire per umbras,
> per loca senta situ cogunt noctemque profundam,
> imperiis egere suis; nec credere quivi
> hunc tantum tibi me discessu ferre dolorem.
> siste gradum teque aspectu ne subtrahe nostro.
> quem fugis? extremum fato quod te adloquor hoc est.
>
> (6.456–66)

Unhappy Dido, then it was a true report that came to me, saying you were dead and had ended all with the sword? Alas, was I the cause of your death? By the stars I swear, by the gods above and any trust there is deep below the earth, unwillingly, O queen, I left your shores. But it was the orders of the gods, which now force me to travel through this land of shades, through ragged and forlorn places and deepest night, that drove me on with their commands – nor could I have believed that I was bringing you such great grief by my departure. Halt your steps and do not run away from my sight. Who are you running from? This is the last word, fate decrees it, which I may speak to you.

But Dido makes no response, standing motionless as if she were flint or marble; and finally she tears herself away and joins the ghost of her former husband Sychaeus. Aeneas, 'shaken by her unhappy fate, followed her far with tears in his eyes, pitying her as she went' (475–6).

In this passage, one of the most moving in the whole poem, we see the repetition by Aeneas of the reasons he had given to Dido in life to explain why he could not stay: he did not himself want to go, he insists, his personal decision would have been to stay with her, but he had to sacrifice all thoughts of self to the orders of the gods. Duty had to prevail over love, and at what a cost.

The other point of enormous significance here is that Aeneas is filled with guilt and remorse and sorrow over the disasters of the past. Though he knows intellectually that he has done the right thing, it gives him no satisfaction; he weeps and pities Dido, his thoughts are still in the sorrowful past. But what he has to learn, and what she teaches him now, is that the past is dead: nothing can alter it, there is no point in brooding over it. By her total rejection of him she makes it easier for him to learn this hard lesson. He will not ever forget her – how could he? – but he must accept that he must live for the future, not for the silent past.

The third ghost Aeneas meets is that of his comrade-in-arms, Deiphobus, and the effect upon him is similar to that of Dido. He feels guilt for having failed to help Deiphobus when he was killed on Troy's last night, for having himself escaped alive when Deiphobus and so many others died. But Deiphobus tells him not to blame himself, and as they part says to him

i decus, i, nostrum; melioribus utere fatis.

Forward, glory of our race, forward; enjoy happier fate in the future.

This is the essence of what Aeneas has learned: his thoughts must turn forwards and not backwards, and by means of the reliving of three crucial episodes of his past life, he is finally freed from them, and ready to go forward.

In the last part of the book Aeneas reaches Elysium, meets his father Anchises and learns more of the glorious future awaiting him. He has learned that he must leave the past behind; now he is given the resolution and confidence to face the future with joy and hope. Anchises greets him by saying:

venisti tandem, tuaque exspectata parenti
vicit iter durum pietas?   (687–8)

Have you come at last, and has your devotion to duty, awaited by your father, prevailed on your hard road?

This sums up the story of the first half of the poem: it is devotion to duty that has prevailed – by a narrow margin – and the road had indeed been hard. 'How much I feared', Anchises adds, 'that the realm of Libya [Dido's realm] might cause you harm.' Yes, indeed.

Now Anchises reveals to Aeneas the pageant of Roman heroes waiting to be born if Aeneas succeeds in his mission in founding his city (this passage has been analysed on pp. 17f.); and after the high point of the pageant, the description of the future emperor Augustus, he breaks off to ask his son this significant question:

> et dubitamus adhuc virtutem extendere factis,
> aut metus Ausonia prohibet consistere terra?   (806–7)

> And do we still hesitate to enlarge our prowess by deeds, or does fear prevent us from settling in Italian land?

Aeneas did not reply, but we can reply for him – there will be no more hesitation now. And when the pageant is concluded Anchises has 'fired Aeneas' heart with love for the glory to come' (889). He has passed from passive, almost reluctant, acceptance of a mission that seemed often too heavy for him and whose real nature he did not understand to a positive active love for his task.

Books 7–12

Virgil's presentation of Aeneas' character in the first half of the *Aeneid* has revealed the psychological conflicts, the inner battles which had to be fought and won before the foundation of Rome could be achieved. The second half shows a different kind of character study of the new hero. We know now that he will have the strength to prevail – the problem now is, how will he do it? How will he overcome the physical obstacles of opposition and warfare? How does the hero behave when he knows that what he must do is for the good of the world, but he comes up against people who do not accept it? Does he prevail by clemency? By negotiation? By violence? This is the question which Virgil explores throughout the last six books, finding no easy answer, but seeking to define, in one situation after another, what kind of behaviour seems appropriate for the prototype of a ruler of the Roman Empire.

Book 7

Near the beginning of the second half of his poem Virgil invokes the Muse again to tell him of the battles to be fought (*horrida bella*), and says that a greater succession of events rises up before him, and he undertakes

D

a greater work (*maius opus moveo*). Most readers find the first half of the poem more interesting than the second, and it is worth pausing for a moment to consider why Virgil says that the second half is more important (for this I think is what his phrase implies). The question can be answered on several levels; simply that from the preparations Virgil turns now to the achievement; or that from foreign countries he now turns to describe events in his own Italy; or that Homer's *Iliad* was regarded generally as greater than his *Odyssey* (*Aeneid* 7–12 resemble the *Iliad*, while *Aeneid* 1–6 are like the *Odyssey*). But any or all of these seem insufficient; it is perhaps rather that Virgil now comes to the consideration of how a worthy object (civilisation for the world) is to be achieved when it runs up against opposition. Virgil, like any Roman of his time, was enough of a realist to know that opposition would exist; historically it had existed throughout the whole period of Rome's rise to power, and had often involved violence. In the story of Rome's first founder this realistic state of affairs had to be presented; we see early in Book 7 that there were some who wanted to accept Aeneas peacefully, but others who did not. Virgil's problem was to try to define the best method of countering violence (the word *violentia* is used of Turnus and of no one else in the poem). He sets out to show Aeneas fighting only because he must, aiming to end it as mercifully as possible and establish a lasting peace. As will be seen, Aeneas does not succeed always in satisfying us that he can do this; he is sometimes, under provocation, ruthless and savage. But what is important is that Virgil has explored in situation after situation the pressures and ambitions and aspirations of men seeking victory, and enlarged the vision of the Romans and succeeding generations about the nature of conflict.

The seventh book begins serenely and optimistically, and it seems at first as though Aeneas will succeed in his dearest wish, to achieve his destiny without bloodshed. King Latinus welcomes the Trojans hospitably, and when he hears from Ilioneus that the fates have brought the Trojans to the river Tiber by the instructions of heaven, he recognises the fulfilment of an oracle that the princess Lavinia is to marry a stranger, and he sends gifts to Aeneas as a token that he will receive the Trojans in peace. But this happy situation is immediately destroyed by Juno, who summons up the fiend Allecto from the underworld to enrage Queen Amata and Turnus, the Rutulian leader who is already betrothed to Lavinia. Allecto symbolises the fury in human beings which causes them to profane peace (line 467), and she can only act upon Amata and Turnus because they are the kind of people liable to feelings of fury. Yet – and here is the focus of our interest in Virgil's treatment of the story – both have much to be said on their side, both have reason for fury. Amata wishes Turnus to be her son-in-law, and Turnus wishes to marry Lavinia and sees no reason to be pushed aside by a foreign invader (oracle or no oracle). Many have seen in the brave, forthright, impetuous Turnus the true hero of the poem; but this is a wholly mistaken view. Whatever may be said for Turnus, he is portrayed as too ready to leap to arms, too fond of fighting; this, as we shall see, is a major point of difference between him and Aeneas.

As a result of Allecto's intervention war begins, and the book ends with a catalogue of the brave Italian forces who went to war against Aeneas. Virgil makes no attempt to blacken the Italians because they are the enemy; rather they are treated with sympathy and admiration, and the prospect of war between them and the Trojans is shown to be senseless and pathetic (in a way almost an anticipation of Rome's civil wars), yet now (because of Allecto) unavoidable.

Book 8

How then is Aeneas to deal with the armed opposition? He does not rush straight in to combat; the first that we hear of him, now that war has begun, is his anxiety.

> magno curarum fluctuat aestu,
> atque animum nunc huc celerem nunc dividit illuc
> in partisque rapit varias perque omnia versat,
> sicut aquae tremulum labris ubi lumen aenis
> sole repercussum aut radiantis imagine lunae
> omnia pervolitat late loca, iamque sub auras
> erigitur summique ferit laquearia tecti.
>
> (8.19–25)

He tosses on a great sea of anxieties, and shoots his swift thoughts one way and another, rapidly directing them towards all kinds of aspects, turning them through all possibilities. Like flickering light reflected off the water in bronze vessels from the sun or the form of the shining moon, when it flits all around everywhere, rising up now to the heights and catching the gilt panels in the high ceiling.

Night falls, and all other creatures were enjoying deep slumber before Aeneas at last lay down to rest, 'disturbed in his heart by the grim war' (29). We see a picture of the rational hero, disturbed at the situation and pondering his best course of action – very much the opposite of the impetuous Turnus. As he sleeps the river-god Tiber appears to him, taking away his worries (35) with a heartening speech, telling him that he has indeed arrived at the site of his new city and that he must go for help to the Arcadian king Evander, at his city Pallanteum, a little way up the Tiber on the site where one day Rome will be built.

The rest of the eighth book is a peaceful account of Aeneas' visit to the site of the future Rome and of the making of new armour for him by Vulcan at Venus' instigation. There is no warfare in this book, and we see Aeneas in a context of friendship. He marvels at the beauty of Evander's little city, and he is told of the reasons for the sacrifices to Hercules then taking place. This is a prototype of the famous Roman festival in Hercules' honour at the *Ara Maxima*, and Virgil dwells on it at length, thus establishing a strong religious basis for Aeneas' conversation with Evander (both men are seen to be deeply religious) and also linking with Roman Stoicism. Hercules was a patron deity of the Stoic philosophy, being a type of strength against adversity and furthering the advance of civilisation by the removal from the world of various monsters. The story told in Book 8 about his defeat of the fire-breathing monster Cacus exemplifies this, and so do various references through the poem to Hercules and his deeds (e.g. 6.285 ff., the monsters at the portal of Hell, 6.801 ff..). In a sense Aeneas has to be a new Hercules, a man who for his deeds to improve man's civilisation was destined for deification; and the same is true in a sense of Augustus too, who is compared with Hercules in 6.801 ff.

It is perhaps in Book 8 that Aeneas is most truly himself.

Book 9

Aeneas plays no part in the events of the ninth book, which take place at the Trojan camp during his absence with King Evander. But the nature of his responsibility is made very clear, as during his absence disaster after disaster comes upon his men, and Turnus is able actually to breach the defence walls. The military bravery and leadership of Aeneas is very sadly missed.

Book 10

The return of Aeneas with his allies, by sea, is presented by Virgil in very vivid colours. As he comes in sight of his camp he raises his great shield aloft, and the light shines from his armour like a comet or like the star Sirius (270 f.), boding ill for his enemies. This is reminiscent of the picture of Augustus at Actium (8.678 f.); each of them is majestic, frightening, righteous as he moves to confront his enemies.

The battle develops; the opposing leaders, Turnus and Aeneas, each achieve great deeds. The narrative shifts to the young Pallas, sent by

Evander to help Aeneas. He faces Lausus, son of Mezentius, but Turnus sees him and calls on his allies to leave Pallas to him. The episode which follows is of crucial importance to the *Aeneid* and to Aeneas himself: Turnus ruthlessly and cruelly kills Pallas, thus providing the reason for his own death at the hands of Aeneas, who would have spared him after victory, had it not been for this. The crucial question we have to ask ourselves at the end of the *Aeneid* is whether Aeneas was justified in killing Turnus when he begged for mercy; the reason why he does not spare him is because he wants to take vengeance for Pallas. We must therefore examine this episode closely, asking ourselves whether Turnus' behaviour is such that we can approve Aeneas' later act of vengeance in killing him.

Turnus, when he sees Pallas, cries out:

> tempus desistere pugnae;
> solus ego in Pallanta feror, soli mihi Pallas
> debetur; cuperem ipse parens spectator adesset.
>
> (10.441-3)

It is time for you to rest from battle: I and I only am going to deal with Pallas, to me and me only is he due – I wish his father were here to see it.

Hard words, and cruel, and such as to turn sympathy away from Turnus, however much one accepts that it is his job to defeat the enemy, and that if he does not kill Pallas, Pallas will kill him. Pallas throws his spear first unavailingly; then Turnus hurls his, saying 'See whether my spear reaches its mark better', and Pallas is mortally wounded. Turnus standing over him speaks these words:

> Arcades, haec, inquit, memores mea dicta referte
> Euandro; qualem meruit, Pallanta remitto.
>
> (10.491-2)

'Arcadians, remember to take these words of mine to Evander: I send him Pallas back as he deserves to have him.'

Then he strips him of his sword-belt, rejoicing in the spoils. Now Virgil enters the narrative in his own person to comment:

> nescia mens hominum fati sortisque futurae
> et servare modum rebus sublata secundis!
> Turno tempus erit magno cum optaverit emptum
> intactum Pallanta, et cum spolia ista diemque
> oderit.
>
> (10.501-5)

How unaware are men's minds of fate and their future fortune, and of how to show moderation when uplifted by success! There will be a time for Turnus when he would give anything not to have touched Pallas, and when he will look back with loathing on this day and the spoils he took.

Here the ending of the poem is anticipated, when Aeneas was about to spare the wounded Turnus, but when he saw him wearing the sword-belt he had stripped from Pallas, he changed his mind and killed him.

The news reaches Aeneas, and for the first time since he left Troy we see him enraged, indeed berserk. His constant efforts to control the irrational elements in himself here break down: he yields to fury. Is he right to do so? Under this provocation one might perhaps think so; but Virgil disquiets us by presenting Aeneas' fury in the strongest possible terms. 'He hacks down with the sword everything in his path, in his hot anger cutting a broad path through the enemy line as he seeks you, Turnus, as you exult in your recent slaughter' (513 f.). Aeneas then takes eight captives alive to be sacrificed at the funeral of Pallas. This piece of barbarity is very startling indeed: to such a point can the most rational and considerate of military leaders descend under the pressure of battle frenzy and vengeance. The passage is based on one in Homer where Achilles, in his wild sorrow for the death of Patroclus, makes human sacrifice at his tomb; it is startling and horrible in Homer, but very much more so in the gentle Virgil. In Homer war is seen as part of the inevitable condition of man, yet atrocities such as this are nevertheless horrifying; but in Virgil war is seen as an evil which one day will pass away in the march of civilisation, and this kind of barbarity leads the reader to doubt whether human endeavour will ever rise superior to the evils of violence.

Aeneas' behaviour continues to be violent in the extreme: Magus begs for mercy and offers ransom, beseeching Aeneas by his father and young son, but Aeneas replies that all such possibilities have been removed by Turnus killing Pallas. This, he says bitterly, my father and my son would approve; and he kills the suppliant. Next he kills the priest Haemonides, and then Tarquitus, kicking his prostrate body, and telling him his body will be food for vultures or fishes. Many others he kills, 'raging victorious over the plain when once his sword had tasted blood' (569 f.). Next to meet him is Lucagus; he kills him and sarcastically boasts over him (591 ff.), and when his brother Liger begs for mercy Aeneas taunts him: 'die and do not be separated from your brother' (600). Virgil summarises this section thus: 'These were the men Aeneas killed on the battlefield, raging like a torrent or a black whirlwind' (602–4). The word *furens* ('raging') is the word constantly used in the poem of the irrational kind of human behaviour which man must strive to overcome.

The narrative now turns away from the battlefield to Olympus, and when we next hear of Aeneas he is attacking Mezentius (769); he wounds him and Mezentius' young son Lausus intervenes to save his father. He ignores Aeneas' warning and is killed. Then at last a revulsion of feeling sweeps over Aeneas – from hot joy in battle he turns in an instant to sorrow. 'He groaned deeply in pity, and held out his hand and there came into his mind the thought of his own love for his father.' He speaks to the dead man in tones of pity, does not strip him of his armour, and promises to return his body to his family. Obviously there is a comparison to be made here with Turnus' behaviour towards Pallas, and it is entirely in Aeneas' favour. This is the sort of man we have been led to believe that the hero of the poem will be, and for the most part this is indeed the kind of man he is. But he was not like it immediately after the death of Pallas, and we shall see that in the twelfth book he reverts again to wild fury. Two questions may be put: the first is 'Can Aeneas or his sons, or his sons' sons, gradually become better at controlling their wild fury?'; and the second is much deeper – 'Should men in the Roman world in every conceivable situation control their wild fury, or are there times when they should give it free rein?' If so, what are those times? Nothing could have been easier than for Virgil to avoid this dilemma, and to present Aeneas only in situations where he did and could show total self-control; but it was precisely this dilemma that Virgil insisted on confronting.

Book 11

The feelings of pity and sorrow which the death of Lausus induced in Aeneas are continued very powerfully indeed in the opening scenes of the eleventh book, as Virgil describes the funeral of Pallas. Here we see Aeneas showing his anguish at the suffering involved in war, organising the last rites for the dead boy in a passage where the echoes of the lyric poet Catullus emphasise the intensity of grief. He ends by saying:

> nos alias hinc ad lacrimas eadem horrida belli
> fata vocant: salve aeternum mihi, maxime Palla,
> aeternumque vale. (11.96–8)

The same grim fates of war call us away to other tears: hail for ever, mightiest Pallas, and for ever farewell.

Envoys come from the Latins asking for a truce to bury the dead, and Aeneas immediately grants it, saying:

> pacem me exanimis et Martis sorte peremptis
> oratis? equidem et vivis concedere vellem.   (110–11)

Do you ask me for peace for the dead, those taken off by the fortunes of war? I would indeed gladly have granted it to the living too.

These are expressions very far distant from those he had used to the warriors who begged him for mercy after the death of Pallas.

Aeneas goes on to emphasise that he does not wish to fight and has no personal desire for glory: 'I would not have come', he says, 'had not fate appointed this place for me to settle in; I do not wage war with the people. Turnus has persuaded King Latinus to reject the alliance he made with me; Turnus ought to settle the war by fighting me in single combat' (112–15).

The rest of the book is mainly taken up with an account of the fighting, especially of the death of Turnus' ally, the warrior maiden Camilla, and at the beginning of the last book Turnus sees that he must now himself face Aeneas.

Book 12

As we come to the decisive moment of the conflict between Turnus and Aeneas, it will be useful to pause for a moment to summarise the difference between their characters. Turnus is in every way a Homeric hero, possessing the outlook and character of an Achilles (with whom he was equated by the Sibyl, 6.89). He is impetuous, energetic, ruthless, violent; he represents personal prowess, irresponsible individuality in contrast with the public and social virtues which Aeneas shows, or seeks to show. He represents, to use Horace's phrases from *Odes* 3.4.65–6, *vis consili expers* (strength without wisdom) in contrast to the *vis temperata* (controlled strength) of Aeneas. He fights for his own glory and reputation; Aeneas fights because he must, in the bitter fulfilment of duty. He fights what the Romans would call a 'bellum iustum', a 'just war', and Turnus does not. These generalisations have already been illustrated from situations in the poem, and they can be reinforced by a study of the words used of each in the poem. Words used of Turnus and not of Aeneas are *violentia* ('violence'), *audax* ('bold'), *fiducia* ('self-confidence'), *insania* ('madness'), *turbidus* ('wild'), *superbus* ('proud'); words used more often of Turnus than Aeneas include *ardens* ('burning'), *furens* ('frenzied'), *ira* ('anger'). Words used of Aeneas and not of Turnus are – first and foremost of course *pius* and *pietas* ('devotion to duty'); *iustitia* ('justice'), *bonus* ('good'). The use of similes reinforces the picture: Aeneas is hardly ever compared with a wild animal (he and his followers are like wolves in Book 2 and Aeneas is like a bull in 12), while Turnus is compared three times with a lion, twice with a bull, twice with a wolf, and once with an eagle and a tiger. Finally the emblem on Turnus' helmet (7.785 f.) is a chimaera, an archaic monster, which belches forth fire which grows hotter as the battle becomes fiercer; this symbolises the archaic and barbaric energy of this survival of the heroic world which Aeneas seeks to leave behind.

Now as we have seen there are two qualifications to be made to the theme of the previous paragraph: one is that for all his violence there is something noble and splendid about Turnus, and the other is that for all his attempts to pursue the social virtues Aeneas sometimes falls into violence. But broadly and on the whole it is true that Turnus cares primarily for himself and Aeneas primarily for others.

We see the real Turnus at the beginning of Book 12: when he sees that everyone is looking to him, then like a wounded lion he rouses himself for defiance – he is on fire and violence possesses him (9). He proclaims that he accepts the single combat; when Latinus and Amata attempt to dissuade him at first he can hardly speak, and when the words tumble out they convey his impetuous passion to put himself to the ultimate test. He welcomes the opportunity to fight for his honour, he seizes the chance of the heroic gesture. He arms for battle – Virgil gives a long description of this (82 ff.) – and his eyes sparkle in anticipation (101 ff.). Battle is his business.

Arrangements are made between Latinus and Aeneas for the single combat, and Aeneas promises that if he loses he will withdraw; if he wins he will not subjugate the Italians and he seeks no empires for himself – the two peoples will be linked together for ever under equal laws. Aeneas' moderation and statesmanlike attitude is seen here at its clearest; he is always at his most admirable in formal situations where the clashing elements of personality can most easily be subdued.

The Rutulians are unhappy, as well they might be, that Turnus must fight for them all against so formidable an opponent, and they break the truce. Again we see Aeneas at his most admirable: he rushes out with head bare holding out his hands to restrain his men:

> quo ruitis? quaeve ista repens discordia surgit?
> o cohibete iras! ictum iam foedus et omnes
> compositae leges, mihi ius concurrere soli,
> me sinite atque auferte metus.

$$(12.313-6)$$

Where are you rushing to? What is this sudden tumult rising up? Oh control your anger! The treaty is already made and all its clauses agreed. It is right for me alone to meet him; leave it to me and away with your fears.

But as he speaks he is struck by an arrow, and has to withdraw from the battlefield; the wound is healed by Venus, and he returns to the fight. His deeds and those of Turnus are described side by side, and there is no difference between them. Under the anger caused by his wound Aeneas reverts to the violence of the battlefield, and fights like any Homeric hero.

The Trojans are successful in the fighting, and again Turnus prepares to meet Aeneas. Frequently in the events of the single combat we are reminded of the combat between Achilles and Hector told in *Iliad* 22, when Achilles chased Hector round the walls of Troy and caught and killed him: Jupiter weighs the fates of the opponents in the scales (*Aeneid* 12.725 ff., *Iliad* 22.209 ff.); Aeneas pursues Turnus as a hound pursues a stag (*Aeneid* 12.749 ff., *Iliad* 22.188 ff.); the onlookers are prevented from joining in (*Aeneid* 12.760 ff., *Iliad* 22.205 ff.); the chase continued round the walls, not for a prize in the games, but for the life of the loser (*Aeneid* 12.763 ff., *Iliad* 22.158 ff.); eventually the loser becomes like a man in a dream (*Aeneid* 12.908 ff., *Iliad* 22.199 ff.); finally the loser begs for mercy (*Aeneid* 12.930 ff., *Iliad* 22.338 ff.); he is not granted it, because (in the *Iliad*) he has killed Patroclus, because (in the *Aeneid*) he has killed Pallas. Turnus then is the Achilles figure who this time does not win; Aeneas is the Hector figure who this time wins.

We expect the new hero to act differently from the old in the moment of triumph; when Achilles had Hector in his power he refused all mercy and in a speech of arrogance and hatred alienated our sympathy from him. Aeneas surely, we feel, will behave differently; but we are wrong – he kills Turnus in a wave of anger and desire for vengeance. We must look at the passage in detail:

> ille humilis supplexque oculos dextramque precantem
> protendens 'equidem merui nec deprecor' inquit;
> 'utere sorte tua. miseri te si qua parentis
> tangere cura potest, oro (fuit et tibi talis
> Anchises genitor) Dauni miserere senectae
> et me, seu corpus spoliatum lumine mavis,
> redde meis. vicisti et victum tendere palmas
> Ausonii videre; tua est Lavinia coniunx,
> ulterius ne tende odiis.' stetit acer in armis
> Aeneas volvens oculos dextramque repressit;
> et iam iamque magis cunctantem flectere sermo
> coeperat, infelix umero cum apparuit alto

balteus et notis fulserunt cingula bullis
Pallantis pueri, victum quem vulnere Turnus
straverat atque umeris inimicum insigne gerebat.
ille, oculis postquam saevi monimenta doloris
exuviasque hausit, furiis accensus et ira
terribilis: 'tune hinc spoliis indute meorum
eripiare mihi? Pallas te hoc vulnere, Pallas
immolat et poenam scelerato ex sanguine sumit.'
hoc dicens ferrum adverso sub pectore condit
fervidus. ast illi solvuntur frigore membra
vitaque cum gemitu fugit indignata sub umbras.

$$(12.930-52)$$

Turnus, humbled, turned his eyes to Aeneas and held his right hand
out in prayer as a suppliant, and said: 'I have deserved it, and I
do not complain – use your good fortune. If any thought of my poor
father can touch you then I beg you (for you had such a father too,
Anchises) pity the old age of my father Daunus and send me – or if
you prefer my despoiled body – back to my people. You have won,
and the Italians have seen me defeated and stretching out my hands
to you; Lavinia is yours to wed; go no further in hatred.' Aeneas
fierce in his panoply stood still, shifting his gaze, and checked his
right hand; and Turnus' words began to move him more and more
as he hesitated, when the ill-starred sword-belt struck his eyes high
on Turnus' shoulder; the baldrick that had belonged to the young
Pallas with the studs he knew so well shone out, Pallas whom Turnus
had conquered with a fatal wound and laid low, and now was wearing
his foeman's emblem on his shoulder. Aeneas when he had gazed
long on the spoils that reminded him of his savage agony, set on
fire with frenzy and terrible in his anger said 'Are you going to be
saved from me here, wearing the spoils of my own people? It is
Pallas, Pallas I tell you, who sacrifices you with this blow, and
exacts punishment from your accursed blood.' As he said this he
buried his sword deep in his heart as he faced him, in hot anger;
but Turnus' limbs were loosened in the cold of death, and his life
with a groan fled complaining to the shades below.

The first thing that the reader feels here is sympathy for Turnus and regret
for Aeneas' action; notice that the very last line of the poem (this poem of
the destiny of Rome) is not about Aeneas or Rome at all, but about the
victim of Rome, the young Turnus whose life flies complaining to the
underworld. Small wonder in a sense that the pious readers of the Middle
Ages felt that Aeneas had not received the rewards due to him for his
success and that one Maphaeus Vegius in the fifteenth century wrote the
thirteenth book of the *Aeneid* in which the attention was focused on
Aeneas and his achievement, and the Trojan hero was duly received as a
god in heaven.

But that is not the way that Virgil has left it: Aeneas has failed to show the control and clemency which we expected of him. If it is argued that in this situation he cannot do otherwise, then it should be noticed that nothing could have been easier than for Virgil to avoid the situation. Turnus could have been killed, not wounded; then the question of clemency need not have arisen. It is quite plain that Virgil has deliberately ended with this dilemma – what does a man do under these stresses? And does he do what he should? Do we applaud or groan?

We must examine possible justifications. It could be said that Turnus represents a barbaric and antique way of life which can have no part in the new civilisation. It could be said that it is Rome's mission to 'cast down the proud' (*debellare superbos*), and Turnus is one of the *superbi*. There is clearly something in this, but Virgil has not emphasised this aspect: indeed the passage opens with Turnus described as 'humbled' (*humilis*).

The justification which Virgil has emphasised is the death of Pallas at Turnus' hands. We have already seen that the circumstances of this were such as to cause the reader to feel that Turnus deserved punishment, and this is in fact what Aeneas says – it is Pallas who inflicts the death wound. He kills him then in anger (*fervidus*), and out of vengeance. Are we to think that at the end after all his efforts to define a better way of life Aeneas has failed? Or are we to think that this is righteous anger, necessary to redress the wrongs of the past? Through the poem Aeneas has struggled to control frenzy and anger in himself and others; now he kills Turnus *furiis accensus et ira terribilis* ('set on fire with frenzy and terrible in his anger'). Through the centuries readers of Virgil have reacted in different ways to the ending of the poem; each reader must decide for himself whether Aeneas has acted rightly or not. What is certain is that Virgil's presentation of this dilemma sheds light on the eternal problems of the human condition.

Thus the character of Virgil's new type of hero is complex. For most of the time we admire him; but under the pressure of his own human nature he sometimes alienates, or partially alienates, our sympathy – as when he leaves Dido, when he goes berserk on the battlefield, when he kills Turnus. What is so fascinating about Aeneas in the poem is that he has his faults as well as his strengths, he has inner contradictions in his character which he attempts to resolve, sometimes successfully, sometimes not. He has a relationship with the gods but he remains human; in his journey through life he is sorely tested and sometimes fails, yet he keeps going; and in the end, against all the odds, and not always in the way he would have wished, he fulfils what he felt himself called on to do.

4

Virgil's private voice: Dido, Turnus, Juno

WE have in Chapter 2 listened to the public voice of Virgil extolling the hopes and ideals of Rome's mission for world civilisation; we have seen in Chapter 3 how Aeneas attempted to define in his own life the nature of this new civilisation, with only partial success; we come now to the elements in the poem which seem to modify or contradict the public optimism of Rome's Golden Age.

The *Aeneid* is no unthinking panegyric; if it had been, Dido and Turnus, the main opponents of the Roman mission, would have been portrayed as hateful characters. So far is this from being true that many have felt that the events of Book 4 'break the back of the poem' (in the sense that our sympathy for Dido is so profound that we tend to reject the Roman mission), and many too that Turnus wins our admiration at the end. These two are individuals who are in opposition to fate and the Roman order; they are minorities who are trampled over by the great Roman juggernaut. Dido is an individual who cares nothing for Rome or the world issues involved, but wishes simply to win the man she loves; and she is prevented from winning her happiness not by the man himself (who would have wished to stay with her) but by the large-scale cosmic destiny of Rome. As an individual she can do nothing; her happiness is unimportant in the world plan – yet every reader of Book 4 feels that it is unjust that it should be so. Again Turnus must be brushed aside by the march of events – he does not belong to destiny and he must pay for that. His cause is in his eyes wholly just – to resist the invader who wishes to steal his bride; but because the march of destiny is in a different direction, his happiness and his life must be sacrificed. And besides Dido and Turnus there are countless others on both sides who lose their lives because of Rome's destiny. There are Euryalus and Nisus, Pallas and Lausus; and there are many of lesser fame, such as Aeolus:

> hic tibi mortis erant metae, domus alta sub Ida,
> Lyrnesi domus alta, solo Laurente sepulcrum.

(12.546–7)

Here was your bourne of death – your lofty home was beneath Mt Ida, at Lyrnesus your lofty home, but your tomb on Laurentian soil.

And others too, not named or counted:

> cetera confusaeque ingentem caedis acervum
> nec numero nec honore cremant.
>
> (11.207–8)

The rest, a great pile of mingled dead bodies, they burn uncounted and unsung.

It is the tension between Virgil's public voice and his private voice which makes the *Aeneid* the great poem that it is. Few poets of any age have been able to sympathise with both sides to the same extent: Virgil was moved by the great vision of Rome's destiny, yet he saw some of the unhappy implications; he sympathised deeply with private sorrow, yet he still admired the Roman national programme. Our eighteenth century admired him for his national note, for his patriotic message, the Victorians admired him for his tears for the lonely individual. T. S. Eliot admired him for his positive moral and ethical message of Rome; Robert Graves has criticised him as being too much a spokesman of the Roman government; most twentieth-century critics have praised him for his sensitivity to sorrow. It is the many-sidedness of the poem that makes it great: lovers of the established order can see in it a plea for order; rebels against the establishment can see in it a case for the outsider. What both these groups should see is that Virgil sympathises with both and criticises both. Just as Socrates the rationalist had his mystical side, so Virgil, the spokesman of Rome, recognises that there are other important things in the world as well as Roman imperialism.

We may transfer this conflict between Virgil's public voice and his private voice into a literary context. We could say that the public voice of Virgil is that of Ennius, Rome's first great national poet, of Cicero, especially of Livy as revealed again and again in the praises of the old Roman character which he presents in his history. The private voice of Virgil is like the voice of Catullus, poet of the individual and his joys and sorrows, who cared little for politics or the achievements of Julius Caesar or the mouthings of statesmen, but only for the reality of his private life in the little group of his personal friends. For Catullus affairs of state were nothing; reality was in his own personal experience and his own joys and sorrows and those of his friends. Ennius is recalled and imitated far more often in the *Aeneid* than Catullus – but when Catullus is recalled it is almost always in the most moving passages of the poem. At the death of

Euryalus, Catullus is echoed with a flower simile; at the funeral of Pallas he is recalled several times; but above all he is recalled in the tragedy of Dido in Book 4.

Catullus' poem on the marriage of Peleus and Thetis (poem 64) contains a long description of the desertion of Ariadne by Theseus. She had helped him to kill the Minotaur, thus incurring the wrath of her parents, and she runs away with him: they stay on the island of Dia and in the morning Ariadne wakes to find Theseus gone. Catullus paints a most moving picture of the loneliness and helplessness of the deserted princess, and her soliloquy as she gazes over the empty waves is filled with the sorrow and pathos which Catullus so often expressed in his lyrics. Virgil's Dido, while very different in many ways, resembles Ariadne in the pathos of desertion, and when she pleads with Aeneas not to leave her (4.305 ff.) her speech recalls that of Ariadne as she reproaches him with broken faith, promised marriage, ingratitude. Later in the book, as Dido speaks her last words (657–8), she uses the phrases of Catullus' Ariadne as she says:

> felix, heu nimium felix, si litora tantum
> numquam Dardaniae tetigissent nostra carinae.

> Happy, oh all too happy I would have been if only the Trojan ships had never touched our shores.

The story of Dido's tragedy has always been the best known part of the whole *Aeneid*; this was true already in Ovid's time (*Trist.* 2.533 ff.) and has remained true ever since. In Chaucer's *House of Fame* Dido has twice as much space as all the rest of the *Aeneid*; tragedies on the theme were frequently written (for example Marlowe's *Dido Queen of Carthage*); of musical treatments Purcell's opera is well known; Walter Savage Landor represented the feelings of many Victorians when he said that there was nothing so sublime and impassioned in literature as the tragedy of Dido in *Aeneid* 4. It has been said that Dido is the only character created by a Roman poet to pass into world literature (unlike most other famous characters of classical poetry she does not figure in Greek literature).

Thus we have the paradox that the most un-Roman part of Virgil's epic of Rome is the best known part. The point does not need elaborating further: it would be difficult not to be moved to pity and sympathy for Dido. Why has Virgil done this, and so damaged our confidence in the validity of Rome's mission by making us sympathise so much with the person who tries to prevent it from coming true? Nothing could have been easier than so to portray Dido that when Aeneas got out of her clutches a feeling of relief and triumph could have been established. She could have been modelled on the witches in Homer's *Odyssey*, Circe and Calypso, or the

Sirens, who try to prevent the homecoming of Odysseus and whose failure to do so leaves us with a feeling not of sympathy for them but of admiration for Odysseus. There was too a special historical reason why Dido could have been presented like this; she was a Carthaginian, and in Rome's long history it was the state of Carthage which had come closest of all to destroying Rome and her mission, especially during the Second Punic War at the end of the third century BC when Hannibal crossed the Alps and seemed to have Rome in his power.

There were all these reasons then why Dido could have been presented unsympathetically, and we may hazard a guess (though it will only be a guess) that when Virgil first sketched out the plot of his poem he did not intend that Dido should win such sympathy. It was when he came to compose her story that he felt increasingly the pathos of the defeated, that he saw Dido's rejection not from Rome's point of view but from Dido's.

But when all has been said about our sympathy for Dido – and much more could be said, and indeed often has been said by those who have written about the *Aeneid* – it is right that we should finally look again at the other side. Intellectually we must approve of Aeneas' decision to leave. When Mercury comes to him to remind him of his destiny he recognises that he has been at fault and he immediately takes his decision for Rome. Against the pathos of Dido's pleas he stands firm with the resolution of duty, and as she turns from pleas to threats and curses he still stands firm. He has the will to prefer the future to the present.

Turnus in many essentials resembles Dido. In the structure of the poem he constitutes an obstacle to the divine will which must be overcome – yet when he is overcome there is powerful sympathy for him and a feeling of injustice. Many have seen in him the real hero of the poem (perhaps rather as William Blake suggested that in *Paradise Lost* Milton was 'of the Devil's party without knowing it'; it is very noticeable that in Milton some of Satan's traits and acts are based on Virgil's Turnus). Above all Turnus, like Dido, is shown not as an impersonal 'obstacle' but as a real human character. We have already discussed his youthful impetuosity, his energy, his bravery; we may now look at the way in which (in Book 12) Virgil shows his human qualities in the hour of his ultimate test. After the arrangements have been made for the single combat Turnus momentarily loses his impetuous self-confidence: the Rutulians feel that the conquest is unequal, and this feeling is heightened by Turnus' humble demeanour:

adiuvat incessu tacito progressus et aram
suppliciter venerans demisso lumine Turnus
pubentesque genae et iuvenali in corpore pallor.

(12.219–21)

Turnus increased this feeling as he came forward without speaking and worshipped at the altar humbly, with downcast gaze; his face was so youthful and all his young body so pale.

Again as the moment for facing Aeneas approaches Turnus realises, as Hector had done when facing Achilles (Homer, *Iliad* 22.300 ff.), that the gods are against him, and he now shows the same courage in facing death:

> terga dabo et Turnum fugientem haec terra videbit?
> usque adeone mori miserum est? vos o mihi, Manes,
> este boni, quoniam superis aversa voluntas.
> sancta ad vos anima atque istius inscia culpae
> descendam magnorum haud umquam indignus avorum.
>
> (12.645–9)

Shall I turn my back, shall this land see Turnus running away? Is it indeed so terrible to die? Shades of the underworld, be kind to me, for the will of the gods above is hostile. I shall come down to you an unsullied soul, free of such a sin as cowardice, never unworthy of my great ancestors.

We hear again, as Turnus says these words, the words of Hector (*Iliad* 22.304 f.): 'Let me not die without a struggle and ingloriously, but having done some great deed for future generations to hear', and more faintly but still unmistakably we hear again the words of Dido in her last moments of life (4.653 f.): 'I have lived, and the course Fortune allotted I have completed, and now my ghost in majesty will pass to the underworld.'

Jupiter decrees that divine assistance for Turnus (from Juno and Juturna) must cease, and he sends down a Fury in the shape of an owl, beating in Turnus' face. Our thoughts go back to the lonely and terrified Dido whose nightmare visions and torments of conscience were accompanied by the long-drawn hooting of an owl (4.462 ff.). There follows the lament of Juturna as the sister says farewell to her brother; there are echoes here of the lamentation of Anna for her sister Dido, as the wildness of grief is described, and both sisters lament their empty future and wish they had died too (12.869 ff., 4.672 ff.). The last scenes of the tragedy of Turnus are thus linked with the tragedy of Dido.

Aeneas challenges Turnus to battle, and magnificent in his hopeless defiance Turnus replies:

> non me tua fervida terrent
> dicta, ferox; di me terrent et Iuppiter hostis.
>
> (12.894–5)

Your hot words do not frighten me, fierce though you be; the gods frighten me, and Jupiter my enemy.

Yet he still fights on; he seizes a huge stone but is like a man in a dream, and cannot hurl it to its mark. Aeneas' spear-cast wounds him, and he begs for mercy as Hector had done (*Iliad* 22.338 ff.). But the opening words of Turnus' plea were not in Hector's speech:

> equidem merui nec deprecor, inquit;
> utere sorte tua.
>
> (12.931–2)

'I have deserved it,' he said, 'and I do not complain. Use your good fortune.'

This is not a recognition by Turnus that he was in the wrong: it is merely a statement that he has accepted a contest to the death and is prepared to abide by the consequences. It is a last splendid gesture of heroic defiance, and when Aeneas does kill him we feel pity and disquiet.

As with Dido, so with Turnus – Virgil has written partly from the point of view of the defeated. This is the price of Rome – with victory for one side goes defeat for the other. Aeneas' way of life was a better one than Turnus', and intellectually we applaud his victory, but we are not allowed to pretend that there is no more to be said.

Virgil's intention in his poem was to proclaim the message of Rome to mankind, to present her divine mission and extol its benefits; to set it against the sins and sorrows of the world and see whether it would solve them. He exemplifies the theme of suffering in the figure of Juno, hostile to the Roman purpose and therefore planning to bring all possible disaster upon Aeneas and his men. Virgil poses this problem in his invocation to the Muse:

> Musa, mihi causas memora, quo numine laeso
> quidve dolens regina deum tot volvere casus
> insignem pietate virum, tot adire labores
> impulerit. tantaene animis caelestibus irae?
>
> (1.8–11)

Muse, tell me the reasons – through what insult to her divinity or in anger for what cause did the queen of the gods cause a man outstanding for his devotion to duty to undergo such hardships, to experience such toils? Can there be such great anger in heavenly hearts?

This last phrase summarises the problem of human suffering and the difficulty mortals have in understanding why the good should suffer. Milton translated the phrase in *Paradise Lost* (6.788):

In heavenly spirits could such perverseness dwell?

and stated the purpose of his own poem in a way not dissimilar:

> That to the height of this great Argument
> I may assert Eternal Providence,
> And justify the ways of God to men.

(P.L. 1.24–6)

But Virgil has no positive position of faith like Milton from which he can 'assert Eternal Providence', and unlike Milton he finds only groping and uncertain answers as he explores the problem throughout the poem.

Much of the suffering which comes upon unhappy mortals has already been discussed in connexion with Aeneas in Chapter 3 and with Dido and Turnus in this chapter; it will be enough to give two additional illustrations. The first is the direct work of Juno right at the beginning of the poem; seeing the Trojans almost at their journey's end she persuades Aeolus, god of the winds, to cause a violent storm as a result of which one ship is lost and the rest split into two groups and shipwrecked on the coast of Carthage. This storm symbolises the hostile circumstances which can suddenly and senselessly (as it seems) strike men as they struggle towards a goal which they conceive it to be their duty to reach. Many of the subsequent sufferings which come upon the Trojans are the work of Juno, and in particular her hostility is reiterated at the beginning of the second half of the poem, when she invokes the very powers of the underworld to bring disaster and destruction. Her hostility is finally stopped by Jupiter (12.791 ff.), but not until she has involved her enemies in extreme peril and suffering.

The second illustration is from the end of Book 6. The pageant of Roman heroes waiting to be born has passed before Aeneas' astonished eyes, and his father has summarised for him the nature of Rome's destiny for world civilisation. We expect the book to end here, with the trumpet-notes of triumph for the now inevitable fulfilment of the mission. But it does not. Aeneas asks the identity of a young man shrouded in darkness, and is told of the great grief which his premature death will bring to the Romans. This is Marcellus, son of Octavia, Augustus' sister, who was marked out as Augustus' heir but died at the age of nineteen in 23 BC.

> o nate, ingentem luctum ne quaere tuorum;
> ostendent terris hunc tantum fata neque ultra
> esse sinent. nimium vobis Romana propago
> visa potens, superi, propria haec si dona fuissent.

(6.868–71)

My son, do not ask of the deep sorrow of your people. The fates will only give a glimpse of him to earth, and will not let him live beyond that. You gods, the Roman offspring would have seemed too powerful if these gifts had been hers to keep.

Here then is the balance of the *Aeneid*, triumph and disaster, joy and sorrow; it is part of Virgil's special art to have given us a sudden cloud of tragedy when the sky seemed clear.

Does Virgil then find no answer to the question of suffering? No complete answer certainly; yet there are two ways in which his deeply sensitive exploration of these things gropes towards an answer. The first is expressed immediately after the opening description of Juno's hostility:

tantae molis erat Romanam condere gentem.

(1.33)

So great a task it was to found the Roman race.

The implication of this theme, which runs all through the poem is that greatness is only achieved by great endeavour and so great suffering. It cannot be said that this idea is presented more than tentatively; certainly Aeneas does not feel it to such an extent as to derive certainty and joy from his dedication, and in this way he differs greatly from the early Christian heroes with whom he is often compared. But faint though the concept is it sheds its light in the dark places of the poem.

The second area in which an answer is sought is defined in the sixth book, where Virgil presents a view of the relationship between this life and the after-life which suggests that in some way not fully comprehensible to men virtue is rewarded in a richer life to come. Consider the inhabitants of Virgil's Elysium:

hic manus ob patriam pugnando vulnera passi,
quique sacerdotes casti, dum vita manebat,
quique pii vates et Phoebo digna locuti,
inventas aut qui vitam excoluere per artis,
quique sui memores aliquos fecere merendo.

(6.660–4)

Here is the band of those who suffered wounds fighting for their country; those who were pure priests in life, dutiful poets who spoke words worthy of Phoebus, or those who enriched life by discovering new ways of living it, or those who made some remember them by their service.

The last line opens the doors of Elysium to all, however humble, who have deserved to go to heaven.

Virgil expands his ideas (mainly Orphic and Stoic ideas) in the speech of Anchises (6.724 ff.). The world is made of two elements, matter and mind (or spirit); it is the task of everyone to live in such a way as to encourage the spiritual side. Our souls are imprisoned in our bodies as if in a prison, and will be tainted and stained by the things of the body, the more so in proportion to the attention given in life to the things of the body. After death purification takes place and those souls which can be sufficiently purified go to dwell in Elysium and then in the ultimate paradise; the rest drink of the river Lethe to forget their previous lives and are reborn in new bodies.

This is clearly a religion of hope, in very strong contrast with Homeric ideas about the afterlife. For the Homeric hero life on earth was all; it should be lived to the full, for the life after death was thought to be miserable and shadowy. The shade of Achilles told Odysseus (*Odyssey* 11.488 f.): 'I would sooner be the lowest serf on earth than king of all the dead.' The shift to an emphasis on the greater importance of the next life began with the Greek mystery religions, was especially prominent in Orphism and Pythagoreanism, and was assimilated and intellectualised by Plato; many of these Greek views were assimilated in Roman Stoicism. Virgil has presented an amalgam of these ideas, made rather more personal to the individual than was the case in Stoicism, and his poetical presentation has a real impact. Yet this must not be overstressed. The Middle Ages looked upon Virgil as a prophet of Christ, a pre-Christian, partly because of the prophecy of the birth of a child to inaugurate a new Golden Age (*Eclogue* 4) and partly because of the moral and spiritual values of the *Aeneid* which we have been discussing; but Virgil's beliefs were still uncertain, and when at the end of the sixth book Aeneas goes out by the gate of false dreams, we must surely think that Virgil means that the religion of the book is a poetic dream and not a revelation. The point can best perhaps be made by another comparison with Milton: where Milton proclaims the certainty of his doctrine, Virgil gropes towards his ideas in hope, not faith.

The nature of suffering is a cosmic problem to which Virgil's Roman theme had led him. Let us return finally to his Roman theme. In this chapter we have seen how the sensitive poet explored the deepest implications of the Roman world mission and found that there were many problems and uncertainties remaining. But – and this is vitally important – the vision never disappears, it is not eliminated by the passages of pathos. The poem is essentially optimistic in spite of its tears; the bright light of human achievement and human potential to achieve more shines though the dark places. Listen once again to the final phrases of Jupiter's promise:

> aspera tum positis mitescent saecula bellis;
> cana Fides et Vesta, Remo cum fratre Quirinus
> iura dabunt; dirae ferro et compagibus artis
> claudentur Belli portae; Furor impius intus
> saeva sedens super arma et centum vinctus aënis
> post tergum nodis fremet horridus ore cruento.

(1.291–6)

Then wars will be laid aside and the harsh generations become gentle; white-haired Trust and Vesta, goddess of the home, Romulus reconciled with his twin Remus, will administer justice. The gates of War, terrible with their tight iron fastenings, shall be shut: within, wicked Frenzy, sitting on a heap of weapons, his arms bound fast behind his back with a hundred knots of bronze, a ghastly figure with bloodstained lips, shall rage and rage in vain.

The Roman Forum

Index

Achilles, 28f., 56, 58
Actium, battle of, 13, 24f.
Alba Longa, 12, 17, 21
Allecto, 50f.
Amata, 50
Anchises, 20f., 37, 41, 44f., 48f.
Antony, 13, 25
Apollo, 16, 20, 40f.
Ascanius (Iulus), 18
Augustus (Octavian), 11, 13–16, 18, 21, 23

Bacchus, 21
Brutus, 22

Caesar, 13, 22
Carthage, 22, 32, 34f., 64
Catullus, 62f.
Cleopatra, 13, 25

Deiphobus, 48
Dido, 34f., 41f., 47, 61, 63f.

Eclogues, 12, 13, 69
Elysium, 68f.
Ennius, 22, 62
Evander, 23, 52

Fabius Maximus, 22
Fate, 31f.
furor, 33, 34, 37

Georgics, 12, 14

Hannibal, 22, 64
Hector, 19, 36, 58, 65
Helen, 37
Hercules, 21, 52

Homer, 24, 28, 50, 54, 58f., 69
Horace, 13, 16, 24

Iulus—*see* Ascanius

Juno, 17f., 26f., 32, 41, 43, 50, 66f.
Jupiter, 18, 26f., 43

Latinus, 23, 50
Lausus, 55
Lavinia, 23, 50
Lavinium, 12, 17
Livy, 15, 62

Maecenas, 12
Marcellus, 67f.

Numa, 22, 24

Octavian—*see* Augustus
Odysseus, 29
Orphism, 69

Palinurus, 46f.
Pallas, 23, 52, 55, 60
pietas, 30, 32, 33, 34, 43, 57
Priam, 36f.

Romulus, 18, 21, 24

Sibyl, 45f.
Stoicism, 44, 46, 52, 69

Turnus, 23, 50f., 52f., 56f., 61, 64f.

Venus, 18, 34f., 37, 41
violentia, 50, 56